The Essential

TÁIN BÓ CÚAILNGE

and Other Stories from the Ulster Cycle

The Essential

TÁIN BÓ CÚAILNGE

and Other Stories from the Ulster Cycle

edited and translated by Matthieu Boyd

a *Broadview Anthology of British Literature* edition

broadview press

BROADVIEW PRESS
Peterborough, Ontario, Canada

Founded in 1985, Broadview Press is a fully independent academic publishing house owned by approximately twenty-five shareholders—almost all of whom are either Broadview employees or Broadview authors. Broadview is supported by a collaboration with Trent University, a liberal arts university located in Peterborough, Ontario—the city where Broadview was founded and continues to operate. Broadview is committed to environmentally responsible publishing and fair business practices.

Canadian Cataloguing in Publication

Title: The essential Táin bó Cúailnge and other stories from the Ulster cycle / edited and translated by Matthieu Boyd ; general editors, The Broadview anthology of British literature: Joseph Black (University of Massachusetts), Kate Flint (University of Southern California), Isobel Grundy (University of Alberta), Wendy Lee (New York University), Don LePan (Broadview Press), Roy Liuzza (University of Tennessee), Jerome J. McGann (University of Virginia), Anne Lake Prescott (Barnard College), Jason R. Rudy (University of Maryland, College Park), Claire Waters (University of California, Davis) ; associate general editors, The Broadview anthology of British literature: Leonard Conolly (Trent University), Barry V. Qualls (Rutgers University).
Other titles: Container of (expression): Táin bó Cúailnge. English (Boyd)
Names: Boyd, Matthieu, editor | Black, Joseph, 1962- editor
Description: The Broadview anthology of British literature edition. | Includes bibliographical references.
Identifiers: Canadiana (print) 20250205335 | Canadiana (ebook) 20250205343 | ISBN 9781554815265 (softcover) | ISBN 9781460409152 (EPUB) | ISBN 9781037700026 (PDF)
Subjects: LCSH: Epic literature, Irish—Translations into English. | LCSH: Tales—Ireland. | LCSH: Legends—Ireland.
Classification: LCC PB1397.C7 E87 2025 | DDC 891.6/21—dc23

Broadview Press handles its own distribution in Canada and the United States:
PO Box 1243, Peterborough, Ontario K9J 7H5, Canada
555 Riverwalk Parkway, Tonawanda, NY 14150, USA
Tel: (705) 482-5915
email: customerservice@broadviewpress.com

Broadview Press books are imported and distributed in the United Kingdom and European Union by:
Gazelle Book Services Ltd.
White Cross Mills, Hightown, Lancaster, Lancashire, LA1 4XS
sales@gazellebookservices.co.uk

European Union – Responsible Person (for official use only):
eucomply OÜ
Pärnu mnt 139b14
11317 Tallinn, Estonia
hello@eucompliancepartner.com
+33757690241

Broadview Press acknowledges the financial support of the Government of Canada for our publishing activities.

Canada

Broadview Press® is the registered trademark of Broadview Press Inc.

PRINTED IN CANADA

1 2 3 4 5 6 7 8 9 10 25 26 27 28 29 30

Contents

A Note on the Maps

by Paul Gosling

The accompanying route maps are based on placenames mentioned in the oldest, twelfth-century versions of *Táin Bó Cúailnge*, supplemented by several instances of "route-lore" preserved in folk memory.

The *Táin* is replete with placenames; over four hundred are documented, although the totals and spellings vary across the different recensions of the story. In many respects, the whole story hinges on place, the toponyms providing a geographic frame for the episodic structure of the saga. In the text, placenames occur in lists and individually. For example, at least forty-seven placenames are mentioned in the "Muster of the Ulstermen" section, twenty-one in the "streams and rivers of Muirthemne," and seventy-eight in the tabulated list known as the "route of the *Táin*." The latter purportedly identifies all the places that Maeve's army passed through on the outward journey as they progressed from Rathcroghan, near Tulsk, County Roscommon, via Longford, Kells, and Slane, to the Cooley Peninsula in County Louth, the homeland of the famous Brown Bull of Cooley. When correlated with the placenames which feature individually in the narrative, these lists allow us to map many of the locations where the army fought, camped, or simply passed through on its outward journey. The placenames in the narrative also allow us to track the Ulster army led by Conchobar as he pursues Maeve (with the captive Brown Bull) back across the Irish midlands to Rathcroghan via Ardee, Mullingar, and Athlone. And, perhaps most poignantly, we can follow the Brown Bull at the end of the story as he retraces his footsteps back to his Ulster homeland from Connacht.

The key challenge in plotting the placenames on modern maps is to identify their locations—not an easy task given the age of the story and the fact that the landscape of Ireland has undergone dramatic changes in the intervening centuries. The earliest attempt to plot the route of the *Táin* is that by Standish Hayes O'Grady, published in 1899 as part of Eleanor Hull's *The Cuchullin Saga in Irish Literature*. Some seventy years later, Gene Haley, a postgraduate student at Harvard University, made major advances in identifying the placenames in his doctoral thesis. His research was incorporated into the maps which illustrate Thomas Kinsella's English translation of the story, published in 1970. However, as Haley's doctoral study was never published, in 2014 the present author reviewed the scholarship underpinning Haley's and Kinsella's maps, offering in the process some route revisions. Following on from this, a series of color brochures on the route of the *Táin* was published as "Heritages Guides" by the quarterly magazine *Archaeology Ireland* (2015, 2016, and 2019). During the compilation of the latter, some nineteen instances of "route-lore" about Maeve's epic raid were identified in oral and local history sources, details of which are published in "Ó Chrúachain go Cúailnge: the route of *Táin Bó Cúailnge* in local history and folklore sources," *Béaloideas* 91 (2023), 1–31.

All in all, some 240 placenames are mentioned in relation to the outward and homeward routes of Maeve's forces, of which around ninety-five can be identified with some certainty, although some are the names of rivers and regions rather than specific places. Allowing for the limitations of scale, seventy of these can be comfortably plotted on the maps, their original medieval orthography accompanied by the equivalent modern name.

Paul Gosling, Galway, June 2024

Maps

The route maps were specially prepared for this book by Paul Gosling, Adjunct Lecturer, Dept. of Heritage and Tourism, Atlantic Technological University, Galway City Campus, Ireland.

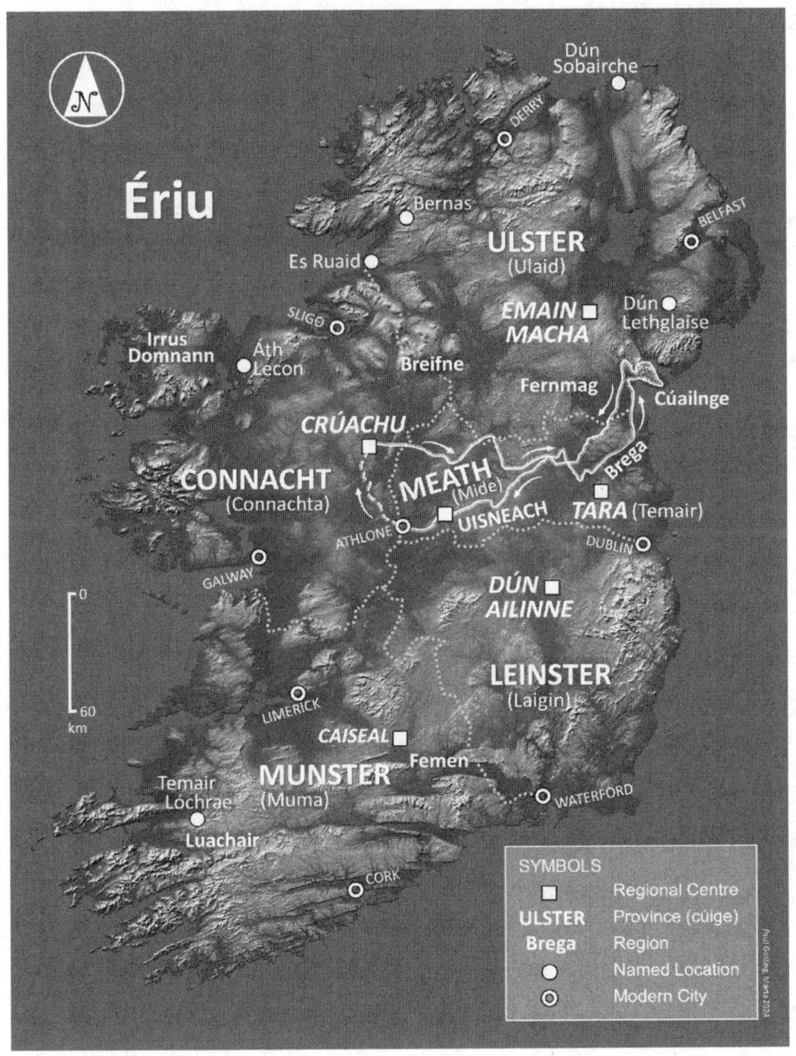

Map 1: Ireland and the Overall Route of *Táin Bó Cúailnge*

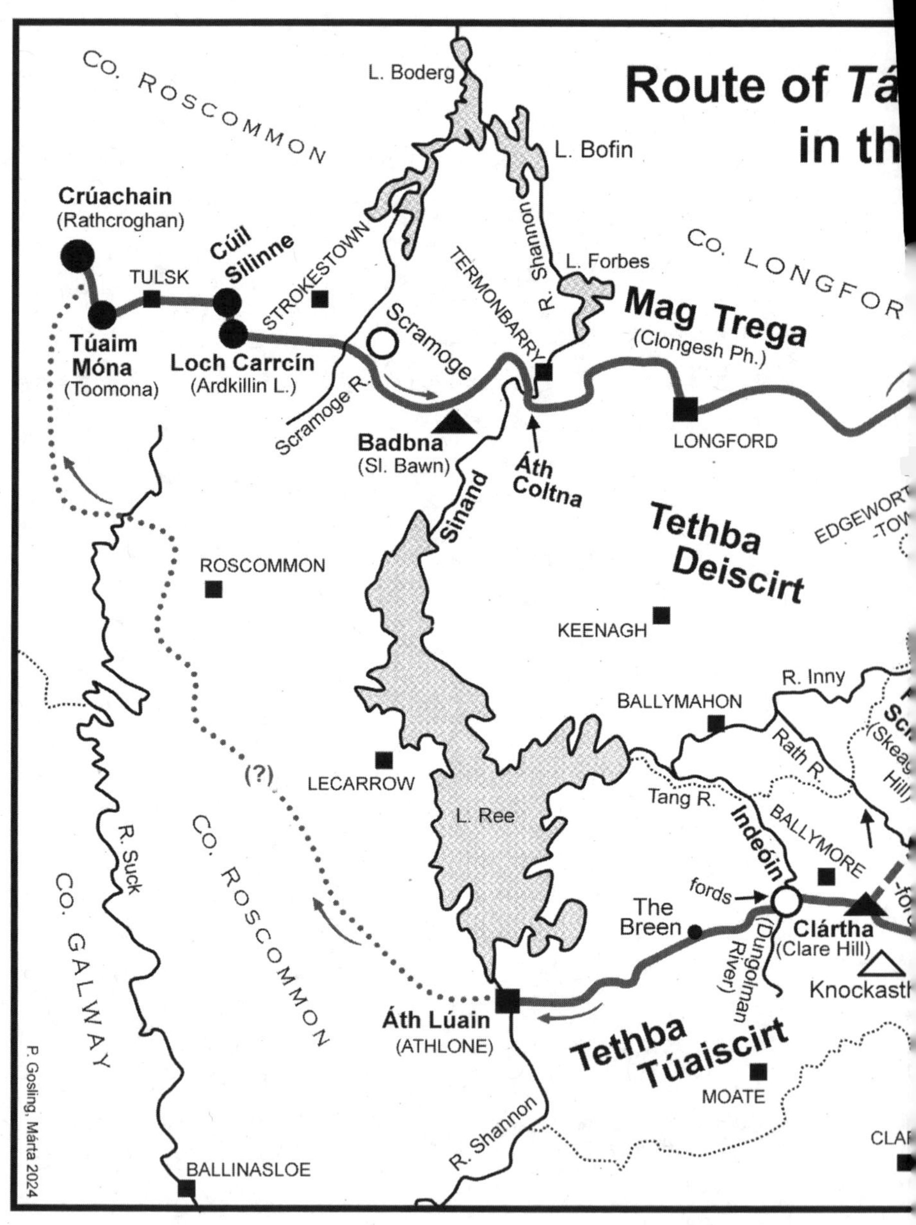

Map 2: Route of *Táin Bó Cúailnge* in the Midlands

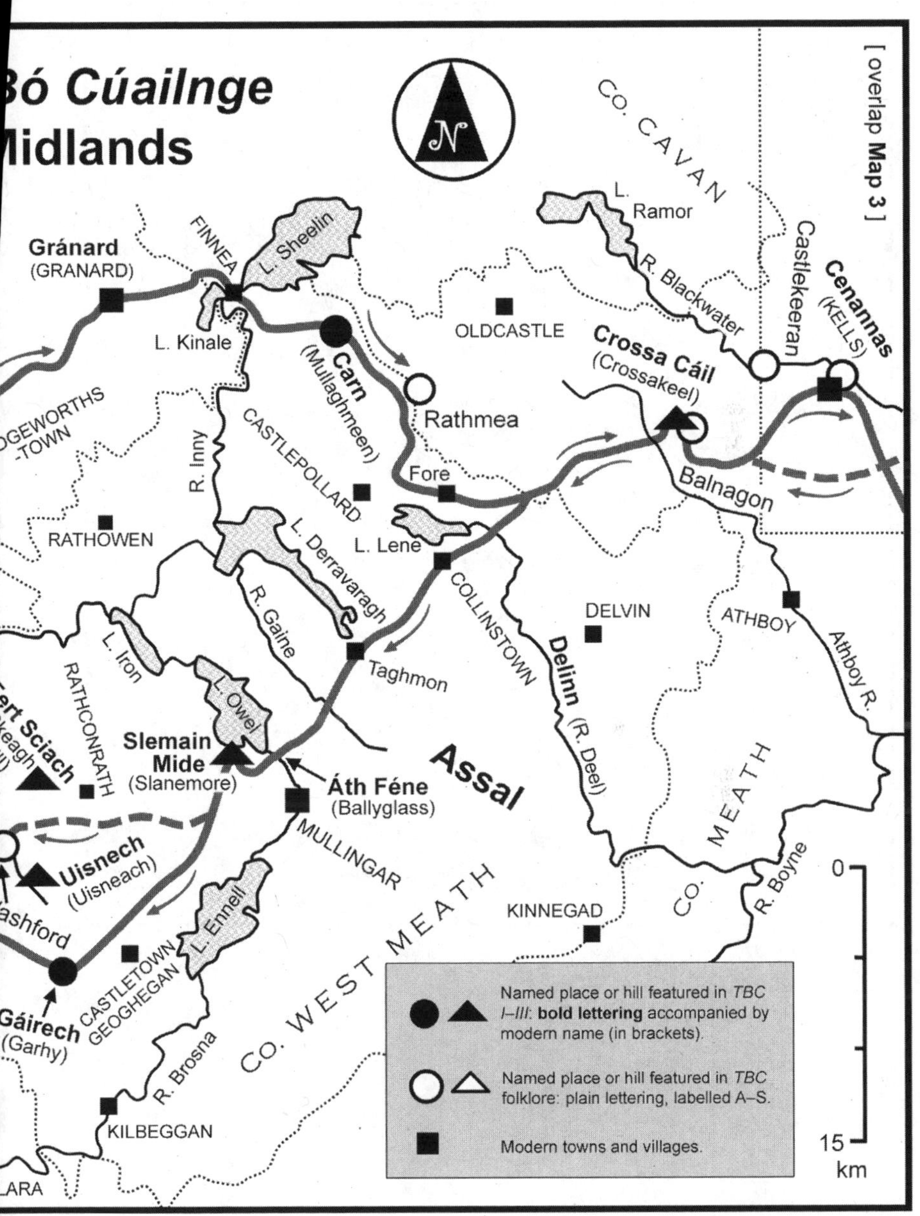

Bó Cúailnge
Midlands
[overlap Map 3]
CO. CAVAN
L. Ramor
Castlekeeran
Cenannas
(KELLS)
R. Blackwater
Gránard
(GRANARD)
FINNEA
L. Sheelin
L. Kinale
Carn
(Mullaghmeen)
Rathmea
OLDCASTLE
Crossa Cáil
(Crossakeel)
Balnagon
Fore
CASTLEPOLLARD
R. Inny
RATHOWEN
L. Lene
L. Derravaragh
COLLINSTOWN
R. Gaine
DELVIN
ATHBOY
Athboy R.
Delinn (R. Deel)
L. Iron
Taghmon
RATHCONRATH
L. Owel
Slemain Mide
(Slanemore)
Áth Féne
(Ballyglass)
Assal
MULLINGAR
MEATH
Uisnech
(Uisneach)
L. Ennell
CO. WEST MEATH
KINNEGAD
CO.
R. Boyne
Gáirech
(Garhy)
CASTLETOWN GEOGHEGAN
R. Brosna
KILBEGGAN
LARA
Named place or hill featured in TBC I–III: bold lettering accompanied by modern name (in brackets).
Named place or hill featured in TBC folklore: plain lettering, labelled A–S.
Modern towns and villages.
0
15
km

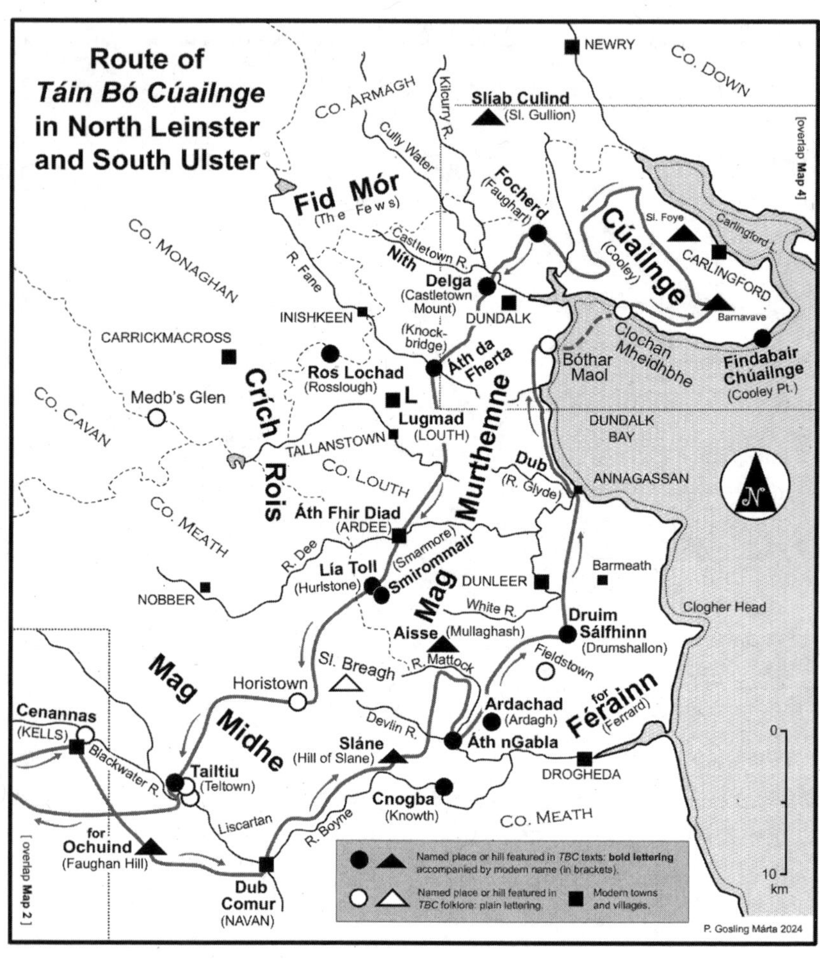

Map 3: Route of *Táin Bó Cúailnge* in North Leinster and South Ulster

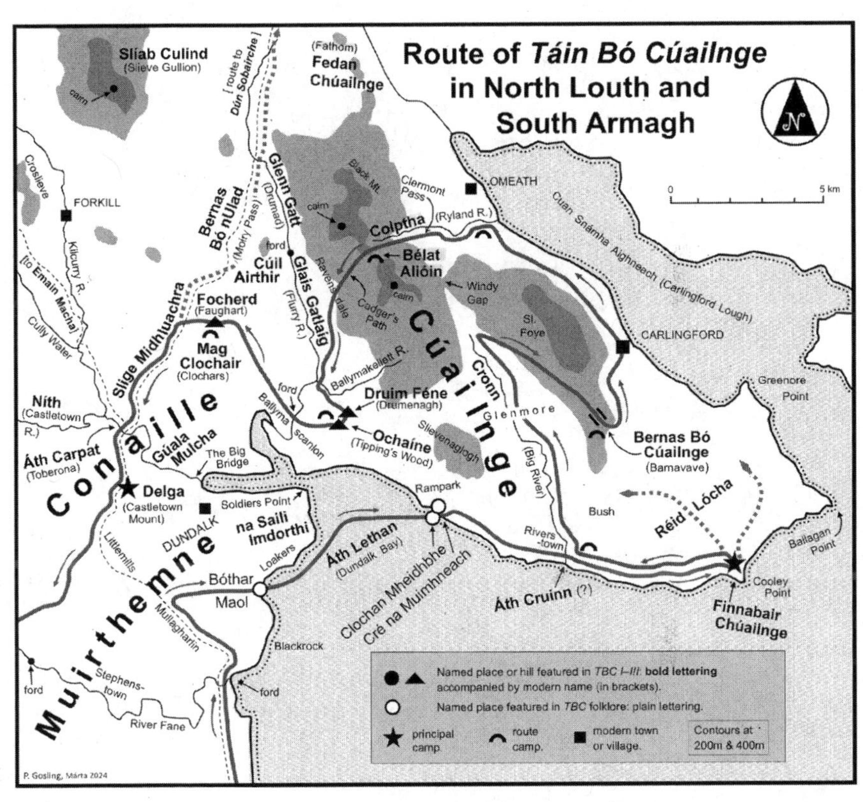

Map 4: Route of *Táin Bó Cúailnge* in North Louth and South Armagh

Character Trees

Factions in the Táin

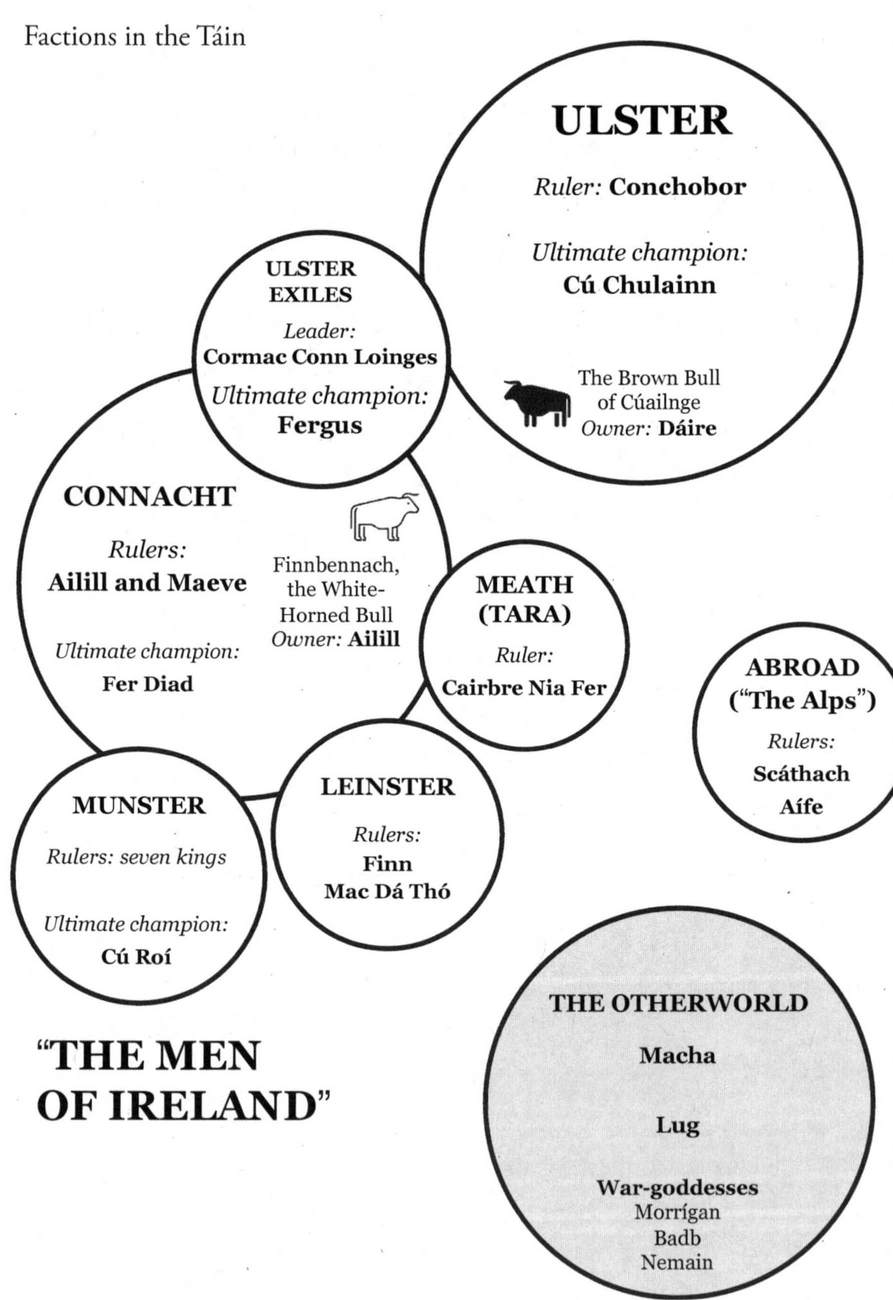

Legend

Men

Women

> name change

—— Descent (with arrow), or formal union

- - - - Informal, limited-time, coerced, or violent union; fosterage (with arrow)

.... Otherworld involvement

(C) Ruler of Connacht

(L) King of Leinster

(T) King of Tara

(U) King of Ulster

These trees are not exhaustive and represent a consensus or compromise among the texts in this book, which are not always in agreement. Individual texts may claim different relationships, add or subtract family members, and give different forms of names.

Tree 1: Conchobor, Cú Chulainn, and Ulster

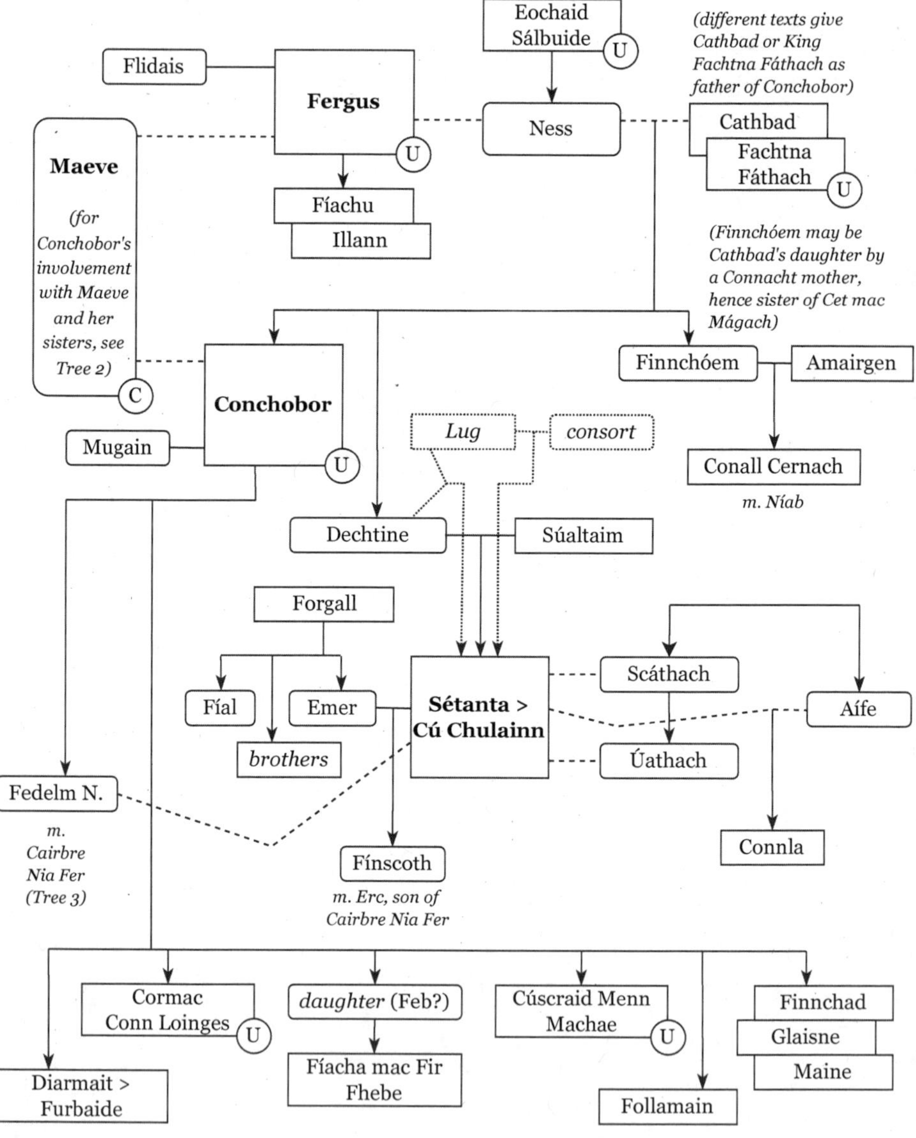

Tree 2: Maeve and Her Siblings

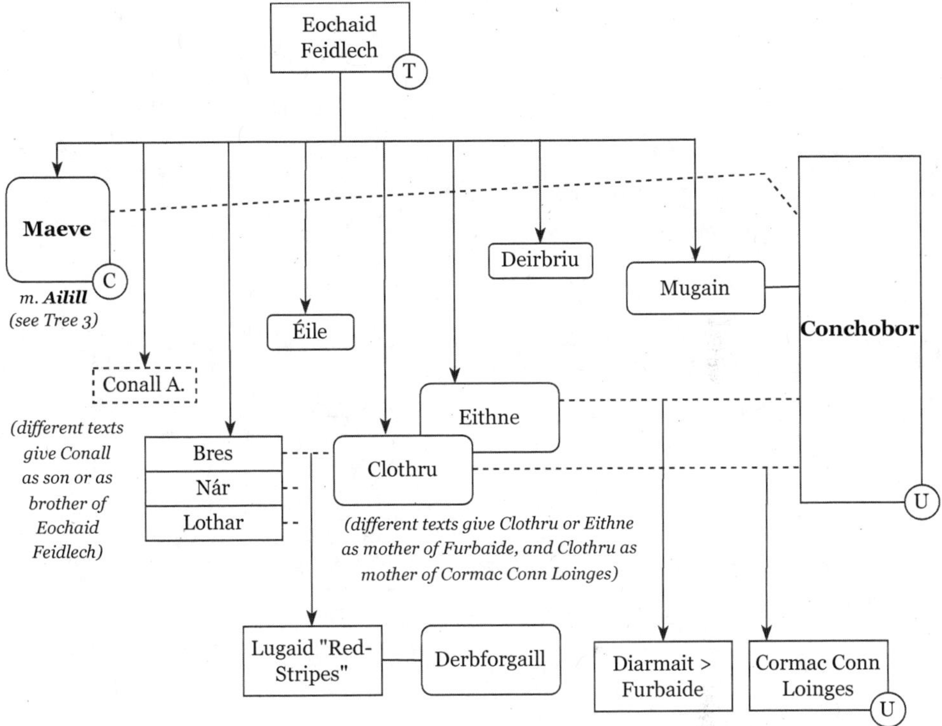

Tree 3: Ailill and His Brothers

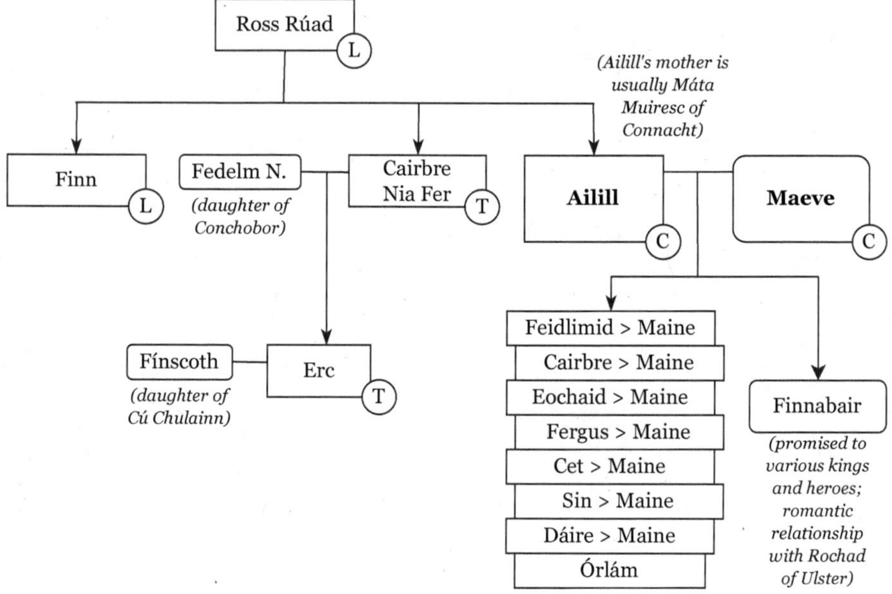

Tree 4: Cú Chulainn's Network

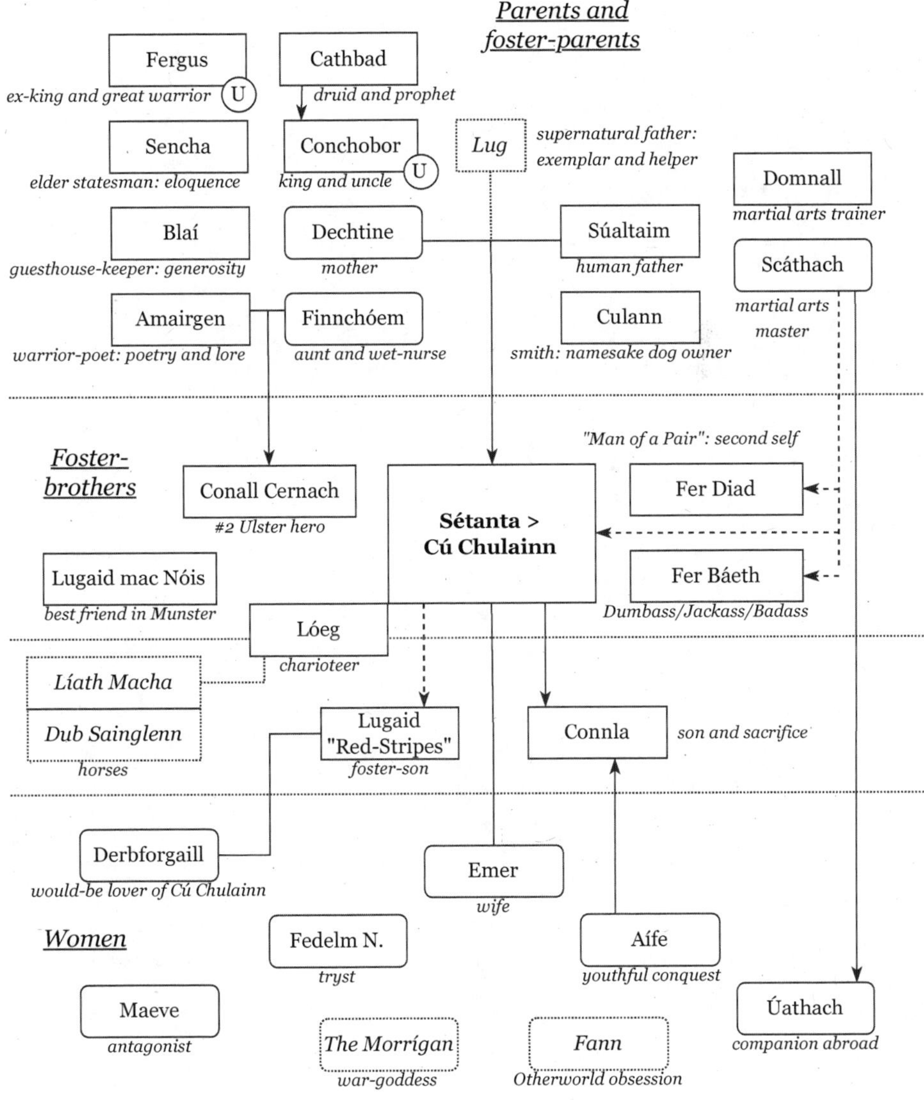

Introduction

Táin Bó Cúailnge,[1] "The Cattle-Raid of Cooley," otherwise known as "the *Táin*," is the centerpiece of the Ulster Cycle of heroic legend, one of the major bodies of saga literature in early Irish.[2] The *Táin* tells how Queen Maeve (*Medb*) of Connacht in the west of Ireland, with an army mustered from four of the five Irish provinces, invades the fifth province of Ulster, which closely approximates Northern Ireland today, to capture the extraordinary Brown Bull of Cúailnge, the Cooley Peninsula in modern County Louth.

The Ulstermen and their king Conchobor are, for supernatural reasons, temporarily helpless, but Maeve still has to deal with their champion, the demigod Cú Chulainn.[3] Nearly alone, Cú Chulainn stands against her armies all winter long, delaying her until the Ulstermen can rouse themselves for a climactic battle. Cú Chulainn's resistance takes the form of guerrilla tactics of intimidation, long-distance sniping with sling-stones, single combat with a series of opponents at river crossings, and massive pitched battles where the hero enters a mutant state of battle-frenzy, killing hundreds.

A complication: Maeve has with her a contingent of exiles from Ulster, including a former king of Ulster, Fergus mac Roích, who is also her lover. Fergus is one of Cú Chulainn's foster-fathers, and while he craves revenge against Conchobor for reasons of honor, he loves Cú Chulainn. Fosterage is one of the closest relationships in early Irish culture, and in pitting foster-father against foster-son, foster-brother against foster-brother, the text strains with tension and sorrow.

---

1 Pronounced "TOYN boh KOOL-nyuh/KOO-ling-yuh," or the "TOYN" for short.

2 The others are conventionally known as the Mythological Cycle, focusing on the Túatha Dé Danann or 'pagan gods' of Ireland; the Cycles of the Kings, focusing largely on the kingship of Tara; and the Finn or Fenian Cycle, focusing on Finn mac Cumaill (Fionn mac Cumhaill, Finn McCool) and his heroic warband. For an overview, I suggest Tomás Ó Cathasaigh, "Irish myths and legends," reprinted in *Coire Sois, The Cauldron of Knowledge: A Companion to Early Irish Saga*, ed. Matthieu Boyd (University of Notre Dame Press, 2014) 1–15, original version at https://journal.fi/scf/article/view/7403. On the term "cycles," see Erich Poppe, *Of Cycles and Other Critical Matters* (University of Cambridge: Department of Anglo-Saxon, Norse, and Celtic, 2008), https://www.asnc.cam.ac.uk/publications/Quiggin/ECQ%20Vol%209%202008%20Poppe.pdf.

3 Pronounced "KON-kuh-vur" and "KOO HULL-in" respectively. See the "List of important and recurring characters" and "Early Irish spelling and pronunciation" at the back of the book.

The *Táin* is best considered historical fiction.[1] It is notionally set in pagan Ireland around the time of Christ. One scholar famously called it "a window on the Iron Age,"[2] but although it is precisely rooted in the landscape, constantly testifying to how various places got their names (this kind of place-lore is generally called *dindshenchas*, pronounced "dinn-hen-uh-hus"), archeological research indicates a fair amount of anachronism in the descriptions.[3] The *Táin* is basically an epic. Some scholars hesitate to call it one because the text is not entirely in verse, and insist on calling it a "heroic tradition" or similar. Otherwise it meets a standard definition of the genre:

> a long narrative poem of heroic action: "narrative," in that it tells a story; "poem," in that it is written in verse rather than prose; "heroic action," [...] in that, broadly defined, it recounts deeds of great valor that bear consequence for the community to which the hero belongs. An epic plot is typically focused on the deeds of a single person or hero, mortal though exceptionally strong, intelligent, or brave, and often assisted or opposed by gods. Epic is set in a remote or legendary past represented as an age of greater heroism than the present. Its style is elevated and rhetorical.[4]

In form, the *Táin* is a prosimetrum, meaning prose interspersed with poetry. Although we have names for some of the scribes who worked on the manuscripts, the text itself is anonymous, and exhibits a kind of archaeological layering. The anonymity is standard for early Irish secular prose: to qualify as the top rank of *fili* or "poet," a role that extended to history, genealogy, and place-name lore, a candidate had to master 350 tales from what seems to have been a standard

1 Helen Fulton suggests "magic naturalism" (https://research-information.bris.ac.uk/ws/portalfiles/portal/303627860/Fulton_Magic_Naturalism_2011.pdf).

2 Kenneth Jackson, *The Oldest Irish Tradition: A Window on the Iron Age* (Cambridge University Press, 1964).

3 See J.P. Mallory, *In Search of the Irish Dreamtime: Archaeology and Early Irish Literature* (London: Thames & Hudson, 2016), which is full of relevant detail.

4 T.B. Gregory, "Epic: 1. History," in *The Princeton Encyclopedia of Poetry and Poetics* 4e, ed. Roland Greene and Stephen Cushman (Princeton University Press, 2012) 439–43, at 439.

repertoire. In the surviving lists,[1] these tales are grouped by subject matter: there are cattle-raids (*táin bó*, plural *tána bó*); tales of a hero's conception and birth (*compert*, "KOV-bert," plural *comperta*); tales of wooing (*tochmarc*, "TOCK-vark," plural *tochmarca*); accounts of someone's violent death (*aided*, "ATH-eth" with both *th* sounds voiced, plural *aideda*); and so on.

The *Táin* naturally invites comparison with the epics of Homer and Virgil, and many of its descriptive and rhetorical passages seem to be indebted to classical models.[2] Modern commentators have often called Cú Chulainn "the Irish Achilles."[3] Like Achilles, Cú Chulainn makes a deliberate choice to be famous at the cost of a short life, and according to one of the separate stories that functions as a prequel for the *Táin*, he sacrifices even his own son to his heroic calling. Only when he faces his beloved foster-brother Fer Diad does he seem to question whether it is worth it.

Meanwhile, Maeve seems to be after a bull, but what she is really after is respect—from her husband Ailill, from Fergus, from Conchobor with whom she has a painful history, from a world of men to whom most women, like Maeve's own daughter Finnabair, are mere trophies. But it seems that the story ultimately denies her that.

Does the *Táin* glorify war? Debatable.

Some commentators are measured: "The *Táin* is about war as a way of life and the strategies to cope with it. War is inevitable; it is neither good nor bad; it does not solve problems. It has its moments of elation and glory, but there is a price to pay."[4]

Some have seen the *Táin* as a wasteland of discarded values: social niceties, respect, honor, bonds of fosterage, ties of allegiance all fall

1 These lists are published in Proinsias Mac Cana, *The Learned Tales of Medieval Ireland* (Dublin: Dublin Institute for Advanced Studies, 1980).

2 See Brent Miles, *Heroic Saga and Classical Epic in Medieval Ireland* (Cambridge: D.S. Brewer, 2011), and for some broader context, *Classical Antiquity and Medieval Ireland: An Anthology of Medieval Irish Texts and Interpretations*, ed. Michael Clarke, Erich Poppe, and Isabelle Torrance (Bloomsbury, 2024), https://www.bloomsburycollections.com/monograph?docid=b-9781350333307.

3 But, so that the Ulstermen are all on the same side, the comparisons made in a 12th-century poem are of Cú Chulainn to Troilus, Fergus to Aeneas, Conchobor to Priam, and Conall Cernach to Hector: see *Classical Antiquity and Medieval Ireland*, 307–20.

4 Doris Edel, *Inside the Táin* (Berlin: Curach Bhán, 2015) 11.

by the wayside, eclipsed by greed, vengeance, and bloodlust.[1] The warriors of the *Táin* have rules, the early Irish equivalent of the Geneva Conventions: these are called *fír fer* (pronounced "feer ver"), which literally translates to "truth of men" but actually means the rules of fair play in combat. Maeve subverts or blithely disregards them when they inconvenience her. While this could be attributed to misogyny in how she is portrayed, Cú Chulainn himself has rules about not killing charioteers or women, and breaches them with regularity. Warriors are healed using chariot parts and become proto-cyborgs, killing machines. There may be nothing left in the end but, to quote the text, "rage [that] ruins the world." On this reading, what happens to the bulls at the end, the culmination of an immortal grudge, sums up the whole tale: "Like the armies they will fight, [...] and like the armies, neither will win. Such is the logic of war."[2]

(Of course, before it dies, the "winning" bull deposits body parts of the other bull around the countryside: this might preserve an ancient element of "creation by dismemberment" from pre-Christian cosmology, akin to how the world takes shape in the Norse Eddas with the dismemberment of the primordial giant Ymir. And even if it creates nothing else, violence can create a story ...)

Others see *condalbae* ("KON-dal-vuh"), love of kindred, as the *Táin*'s saving virtue.[3] Cú Chulainn's foster-brother turns against him, but his foster-father Fergus never does, and their agreement to yield to one another turns the course of the great battle. In this translation, *condalbae* is consistently rendered "kin-love" for ease of reference. It is at best an embattled virtue, since we do see family killing family, but it explains why Cú Chulainn's "Boyhood Deeds," told at length by the Ulster exiles to the Connacht invaders, are so integral to the *Táin*: they present the basis for Cú Chulainn's bond to the people of Ulster and to Ulster's otherwise problematic king. Marie-Louise Sjoestedt[4] associates Cú Chulainn with a paradigm of

1 A classic expression of this view is Joan Radner, "'Fury destroys the world': historical strategy in Ireland's Ulster epic," *Mankind Quarterly* 23 (1982) 41–60.

2 O.R. Melling, *The Druid's Tune* (Penguin 1984) 218. This is a Young Adult retelling of the *Táin* that I recommend highly.

3 See, for example, Tomás Ó Cathasaigh, *Coire Sois*, 9, 90, 194.

4 Marie-Louis Sjoestedt[-Jonval], *Gods and Heroes of the Celts*, trans. Myles Dillon (London: Methuen, 1949), *passim*.

the "hero within the tribe" (in contrast to the hero of the Finn Cycle, Finn mac Cumaill, who exemplifies "the hero outside the tribe"), and in the Boyhood Deeds the over-powered and undisciplined youngster learns to control his propensity for violence and to use it in the service of his people. One of these is the episode in which he gets his name, after he kills the smith Culann's guard dog and agrees to take its place until he can train a replacement. As a translation of *Cú Chulainn*, "The Hound of Culann" has a certain gravitas, and "Culann's Dog" less so: the boy balks at being called that, until it's explained to him that this will help him build his heroic reputation and make him the protector of all Muirthemne Plain. By the time Maeve invades, Cú Chulainn has built himself up into the designated protector of all Ulster, and has a history with the exiles in Maeve's army on which the story ultimately pivots.

Importantly, the *Táin* portrays a pre-Christian world. Early Irish manuscript literacy implies Christianity: it would have been monks who copied and preserved the source materials for the *Táin* and the *Táin* itself through at least the twelfth century.[1] They might have had complicated feelings about it, as suggested by the Latin endnote to the Book of Leinster version, translated below on p. 287, while "The Death of Cú Chulainn" suggests how eager some of the Irish were to save the hero's soul in a Christian context. The *Táin* seems to have been important religious and political propaganda. The ancient royal seat of Ulster at Emain Macha (pronounced "EV-win VACK-uh," the archaeological site now known as Navan Fort) is very close to the seat of "Saint Patrick's heir" the archbishop of Armagh, and the *Táin* might have been a way to boost the prestige of Armagh and the important Uí Néill dynasty aligned with it.[2]

1 In general, we owe the later manuscripts to families of hereditary poets and scribes rather than monks.

2 On the *Táin*'s associations with early Irish politics, a complex subject, see Thomas Charles-Edwards, "*Táin bó Cuailnge*, hagiography and history," in *Sacred Histories: A Festschrift for Máire Herbert*, ed. John Carey, Kevin Murray, and Caitríona Ó Dochartaigh (Dublin: Four Courts Press, 2015) 86–102. An older article on the *Táin*'s relevance to Armagh's interests is Alan Bruford, "Why an Ulster cycle?" in *Ulidia: Proceedings of the First International Conference on the Ulster Cycle of Tales*, 8–12 April 1994, ed. J.P. Mallory and Gearóid Stockman (Belfast: December Publications, 1994) 23–30.

Recensions

According to the prequel story "The Unveiling of the *Táin*," the text originated with Fergus mac Roích, who rose from his grave to recite it to poets from the entourage of the seventh-century poet Senchán Torpéist. But in actuality the *Táin* exists in multiple versions, known as recensions, in handwritten manuscripts. The oldest, Recension 1, is partially preserved in four different manuscripts including the famous *Lebor na hUidre* or "Book of the Dun Cow," which was written before 1106.[1] Recension 2 is the version found in the Book of Leinster, which was begun around 1160 and completed between 1201 and 1224.[2] Recensions 3 and 4 are late and fragmentary. The story is centuries older than the surviving manuscripts: the core of it dates back to the ninth century, and some of the relevant poetry is even older than that.[3]

---

1 The four manuscripts are: *Lebor na hUidre* (Royal Irish Academy ms. 23 E 25), the Yellow Book of Lecan (Trinity College Dublin ms. 1318, late 14th century), British Library ms. Egerton 1782 (early 16th century), and O'Curry ms. 1 (late 16th century). While the Old Irish period is c. 700–900 CE, Middle Irish is c. 900–1200, and Early Modern Irish is c. 1200–1650, the forms are datable in a way that makes it possible to recognize earlier language in later manuscripts. For what parts of Recension 1 are in which manuscripts, see the diagram in *Táin Bó Cúailnge: Recension I*, ed. and trans. Cecile O'Rahilly (Dublin: Dublin Institute for Advanced Studies, 1976), viii. To see images of *Lebor na hUidre* and the Yellow Book of Lecan, visit Irish Script on Screen, https://www.isos.dias.ie/, for the Royal Irish Academy and Trinity College Dublin: the *Táin* starts at https://www.isos.dias.ie/RIA/RIA_MS_23_E_25.html#57 in *Lebor na hUidre* and at https://www.isos.dias.ie/TCD/TCD_MS_1318.html#383 in the Yellow Book of Lecan (visibly begins mid-sentence; the beginning is missing). For more about these and other medieval Irish manuscripts and associated scribal practices, see Timothy O'Neill, *The Irish Hand* 2e (Cork University Press, 2014).

2 Trinity College Dublin ms. 1339. To see images, visit Irish Script on Screen for Trinity College Dublin. (The *Táin* starts from the colorful initial at https://www.isos.dias.ie/TCD/TCD_MS_1339.html#53.) There is a study of the manuscript by Dagmar Schlüter, *History or Fable? The Book of Leinster as a Document of Cultural Memory in Twelfth-Century Ireland* (Münster: Nodus, 2010).

3 Although it is not part of the *Táin* itself, the oldest surviving evidence of the story, the poem *Conailla Medb míchuru*, "Maeve made illicit/illegal contracts," dates from the early 7th century. For more on this, see Garrett S. Olmsted, "The earliest narrative version of the *Táin*: seventh-century poetic references to *Táin bó Cúailnge*," *Emania* 10 (1992) 5–17, and P.L. Henry, "*Conailla Medb míchuru* and the tradition of Fiacc son of Fergus," in *Miscellanea Celtica in memoriam Heinrich Wagner*, vol. 2, ed. Séamus Mac Mathúna and Ailbhe Ó Corráin (Uppsala: Uppsala Universitet, 1997) 53–70.

Scholars often quote Recension 1 over Recension 2, given its value as the earliest witness. Recension 2 is more polished and sometimes amplified, especially with dialogue (in O'Rahilly's edition it is 4925 numbered lines versus 4160 for Recension 1); it also paints a more idealized portrait of some of the characters. A characteristic situation is that Recension 1 will give alternatives for how something happened (for example, the way Cú Chulainn killed Culann's dog), while Recension 2 picks one and sticks with it. Recension 1 starts with Maeve gathering an army to invade Ulster, but doesn't say why. Recension 2 supplies the opening sequence of the "Pillow-Talk," which explains why she desperately wants the Brown Bull of Cúailnge, and also explains the curiously passive role of her husband Ailill: he might have nothing to prove, and (at least to start with) might just be along for the ride.

This translation is mostly of Recension 1. Some passages and details have been included from Recension 2 and are clearly marked as such.

The standard editions and translations of Recensions 1 and 2 for academic purposes are Cecile O'Rahilly's *Táin Bó Cúailnge: Recension I* (Dublin: Dublin Institute for Advanced Studies, 1976) and *Táin Bó Cúalnge* [sic] *from the Book of Leinster* (Dublin: Dublin Institute for Advanced Studies, 1967). Her translations can be read online at https://celt.ucc.ie/published/T301012.html and https://celt.ucc.ie/published/T301035.html respectively. Anything presented here in summary can be read there in full. Edel's book *Inside the Táin* is full of comparisons of the different recensions.

Prequels

Some of the circumstances in the *Táin*, such as where the bulls come from and what the exiled Ulstermen are doing in Connacht, make sense only with reference to separate stories known as "pre-tales" (*remscéla*, pronounced "REV-shkay-luh"). The story of "The Unveiling of the *Táin*" says there are 12 of these, and lists 10; other texts as well would seem to qualify. Like the *Táin*, and early Irish prose in general, all of this material is anonymous.

Ten prequels are translated here. Others are only summarized, for reasons of space. Fergus says how old Cú Chulainn is in the *Táin*, and on that basis we can suggest a timeline as follows. (See the graphic on p. 47.)

"The Unveiling of the *Táin*" is set around 600 years after the *Táin*, when the story has been lost and the poets are trying to recover it.

"The Ulstermen's Paralysis and the Twins of Macha" takes place either generations before the *Táin*, or during Conchobor's reign, at least 12 years before the *Táin*.

"The Birth of Conchobor" and "The Story of Conchobor mac Nessa" describe the birth of Conchobor, and his rise to the kingship seven years later. This might be 35 to 40 years before the *Táin*.

"Maeve's Series of Husbands, or The Battle of the Boyne" covers the early years of Conchobor's reign, Maeve's rise to power in Connacht, and her marriage to Ailill. "The Story of Mac Dá Thó's Pig" comes after that, maybe 15 to 20 years before the *Táin*.

"The Birth of Cú Chulainn" is 16 years before the *Táin*.

"The Wooing of Emer" is 5 years later, so 11 years before the *Táin*.

"The Death of Aífe's Only Son" is 7 years after "The Wooing of Emer," so 4 years before the *Táin*.

"The Exile of the Sons of Uisliu" is less than 4 years before the *Táin*.

"The Pig-Keepers' Feud" begins in the indefinite past, and ends as many years before the *Táin* as it takes a magical bull to reach its prime. (For a non-magical bull, this would be about 2 years. Add another year or so according to "Nera's Adventure," for the Brown Bull to sire a calf that Finnbennach can fight with.)

With a timeline like this, it can be tempting to treat these stories as chapters of a single narrative, as some books retelling "the Cú Chulainn saga" have actually done. One view is that "the public of early narrative did not seek to discover the unique world-view of a particular author, but rather, sought recognition of familiar codes and conventions shared from one work to another."[1] This is clearly true to some extent. Not only do the different stories cross-reference plot points, they also recycle standardized descriptions and draw on a common store of terms and concepts. But the texts also vary—not

1 Máire Herbert, "*Fled Dúin na nGéd*: a Reappraisal," *Cambridge Medieval Celtic Studies* 18 (1989) 75–87, at 75.

only in reporting facts, but also in the slant or focus they adopt. Variation is inherent and inevitable in oral and manuscript traditions unfolding over several centuries. But there are also signs of individual artistry (or clumsiness, although one idea about the terseness of the oldest Irish sagas is that they were notes to be fleshed out in performance, not necessarily to be performed as written). The texts might have been composed by accretion—a buildup and layering of voices over time—but, almost certainly, not by committee.

The prequels come with individual headnotes as an encouragement to think about them on their own terms as well as in relation to the *Táin* and to each other.

Early Irish texts are inventoried—with a list of the relevant manuscripts, editions, translations, and scholarly studies through approximately 2015—in Donnchadh Ó Corráin's three-volume *Clavis Litterarum Hibernensium ["A Key to the Writings of the Irish"]: Medieval Irish Books & Texts (c.400–c.1600)* (Turnhout: Brepols, 2017), which is an extraordinary resource if you can access it. (It's expensive and sells mostly to libraries.) Specifically, see the section on Medieval Vernacular Narrative Prose in Volume 3, 1259–1523. The dates in the headnotes for the texts translated in this book are mostly from Ó Corráin, and all the texts mentioned below are tagged with his item numbers. For everyone who can't consult Ó Corráin, the best option might be the CODECS database at https://codecs.vanhamel.nl/.

Here, whenever a text is mentioned, I try to list (i) the standard or most up-to-date edition of the Irish text; (ii) the best or most recent translation; (iii) the best translation you can read for free online (which might be an older one, with dated language), and (iv) any especially enlightening secondary sources. See also "Further Reading" below.

Aftermath

Early Irish heroes had memorable, if not always glorious, deaths. The *aideda* (sg. *aided*, pronounced "ATH-eth" with voiced *th*) or "death-tales" of Cú Chulainn, Fergus, Ailill and Conall Cernach, and Maeve wrap up various matters outstanding in the *Táin* and its pre-tales.

"The Death of Cú Chulainn" and "The Death of Conchobor" are transformative in how they present Cú Chulainn and Conchobor as men of Christian faith even before the coming of Saint Patrick and, in Cú Chulainn's case, even before the birth of Jesus, which he prophesies.

Other sequels to the *Táin* describe the ongoing warfare between the Ulstermen and their neighbors, and the challenges faced by Conchobor's successors. Those texts are presented here in summary.

The point about continuity among the prequels applies here too: the sequels' consistency with the *Táin* and with each other, and how much they can or should be thought of as developing a single continuous story, is a matter for discussion and debate, not something to be taken for granted. (Just one example: simply in terms of chronology, Conchobor's lifespan is sometimes said to match the lifespan of Jesus exactly, but this is hard to square with what we're told about Cú Chulainn's lifespan.)

Reception

In the Early Modern Irish period, Cú Chulainn largely took a backseat in literature and folklore to Finn mac Cumaill (Fionn mac Cumhaill, Finn McCool), although some of the bardic poetry and some dynastic propaganda preserved his reputation.[1] Never entirely forgotten, the *Táin* returned to popularity during the Irish Literary Revival, with Standish Hayes O'Grady's *History of Ireland* (1878–81),[2] Eleanor Hull's *The Cuchullin Saga in Irish Literature* (1898) and *The Boys' Cuchulain* (1904),[3] Lady Augusta Gregory's *Cuchulain of*

1 See Damian McManus, "Good-looking and irresistible: the hero from early Irish saga to classical poetry," *Ériu* 59 (2009) 57–109; Tomás Ó Cathasaigh, "Cú Chulainn, the poets, and Giolla Brighde Mac Con Midhe," in *Coire Sois*, 259–70; and Katharine Simms, "Propaganda use of the *Táin* in the later Middle Ages," *Celtica* 15 (1983) 142–49, and "The barefoot kings: literary image and reality in later medieval Ireland," *PHCC* 30 (2011, for calendar year 2010) 1–21. Meanwhile, for a sense of the huge amount of material associated with Fionn, see the Fionn Folklore Database at https://fionnfolklore.org.

2 See *Standish O'Grady's Cuculain: A Critical Edition*, ed. Gregory Castle and Patrick Bixby (Syracuse NY: Syracuse University Press, 2016), which compiles relevant material from the *History of Ireland*.

3 This book, illustrated by Stephen Reid, was also published as *The Story of Cuchulain* (1909) and *Cuchulain, the Hound of Ulster* (1911). As far as I can tell, they're all the same text.

Muirthemne (1902), and others, as well as scholarly translations by L. Winifred Faraday (1904), Ernst Windisch (1905, into German), H. d'Arbois de Jubainville (1907, into French), and Joseph Dunn (1914).[1]

William Butler Yeats and many authors of the Revival wrote poems and plays about Cú Chulainn and other heroes of the *Táin*. Breton nationalist writer Roparz Hemon did this during World War II.[2] Since then, famed poets Thomas Kinsella (1969) and Ciarán Carson (2007) have translated the *Táin* into acclaimed English versions. It has also been translated or adapted into Modern Irish, most recently by Darach Ó Scolaí in 2017,[3] while Nuala Ní Dhomhnaill, the best-known Irish-language poet alive today, deals with Maeve, Cú Chulainn, and the Morrígan in a suite of poems that give voice to the female characters.[4]

As an educator, Patrick Pearse, one of the leaders of the 1916 Easter Rising, took Cú Chulainn as a model for Irish boyhood; as a revolutionary, he took him as a model for political action.[5] Oliver Sheppard's 1911 statue of "The Dying Cuchulain," which shows the hero standing with a raven on his shoulder as in "The Death of Cú Chulainn" below, was placed in 1935 in the General Post Office in Dublin: it commemorates the Easter Rising and, in the words of

1 These titles are now in the public domain and can be found for free on Google Books and archive.org. The translation history of the *Táin* is the subject of Maria Tymoczko's *Translation in a Postcolonial Context* (New York: St. Jerome, 1999), and Declan Kiberd discusses "Augusta Gregory's Cu Chulainn: the rebirth of the hero" in *Irish Classics* (Harvard University Press, 2000) 399–419; see also Philip O'Leary, *The Prose Literature of the Gaelic Revival, 1881–1921* (University Park, PA: Pennsylvania State University Press, 1994) 223–79. There are many publications on Yeats and the Ulster Cycle. Martha J. Lee's "The Warped One: Nationalist Adaptations of the Cuchulain Myth" (Ph.D. thesis, University of South Carolina, 2019, https://scholarcommons.sc.edu/cgi/viewcontent.cgi?article=6308&context=etd) ranges as far as Carson's 2008 translation. Recent translators into other languages include Christian-J. Guyonvarc'h (1994) into French, and Matthias Egeler (2023) into German.

2 See Matthieu Boyd, "Roparz Hemon's Kouc'houlin," *Proceedings of the Harvard Celtic Colloquium* 32 (2012) 30–73.

3 For the translation history of the *Táin* into Modern Irish, see Darach Ó Scolaí, "The *Táin*: from Old Irish to Modern Irish," in *Táin Bó Cúalnge from the Book of Leinster: Reassessments*, ed. John Carey (Dublin: Irish Texts Society, 2020) 122–36.

4 See Nuala Ní Dhomhnaill, *Selected Poems/Rogha Dánta*, trans. Michael Hartnett (Dundrum: New Island/Raven Arts, 1993) 110–25.

5 See O'Leary, *The Prose Literature*, esp. 256–59 where he discusses Pearse's preference for Recension 2 over Recension 1 as source material for his school pageants.

statesman Éamon de Valera, symbolizes "the dauntless courage and abiding constancy of our people."

During "the Troubles" in Northern Ireland (1968–98), Cú Chulainn was pressed into service on both sides as a symbol of heroic sacrifice. He appears in both Catholic/Nationalist-Republican and Protestant/Unionist-Loyalist iconography, including the famous murals in Belfast.[1] As a hero associated with Gaelic Ireland and a "Celtic" past, he appealed to the IRA; given his role in the *Táin* as a defender of Ulster against the "men of Ireland," he was an easy fit for the goals of Loyalist paramilitary groups like the Ulster Volunteer Force and the Red Hand Commando.

The *Táin* has also been represented in public art in the Republic of Ireland, such as Desmond Kinney's 1976 mosaic mural in Dublin (the source of the cover image for this book); John Behan's 1989 sculptures in Dundalk; and Ann Meldon Hugh's 1998 sculpture of "Ferdia and Cuchulainn" in Ardee, County Louth, where the two of them fought.[2] It has inspired Irish composers, notably James Wilson and Aloys Fleischmann,[3] and musicians, notably the Horslips (*The Táin*, 1973) and Lorcán Mac Mathúna (*An Táin*, 2010).

Cú Chulainn now appears on Guinness Hurling Championship billboards ("The Stuff of Legend") and has given his name to the Cú Chulainn Coaster, the huge rollercoaster at Tayto (now Emerald) Park in Ashbourne, County Meath, built in 2015. Meanwhile, the *Táin* has had its share of modern retellings, by authors including Rosemary Sutcliff, Gregory Frost, O.R. Melling, Morgan Llywelyn, and Randy Lee Eickhoff. It has graphic novel versions by James Simmons and Martyn Turner, Colmán Ó Raghallaigh and Barry

---

1 See examples at https://cain.ulster.ac.uk/mccormick/photos/no205.htm, https://cain.ulster.ac.uk/mccormick/photos/no361.htm, and https://cain.ulster.ac.uk/mccormick/photos/no667.htm (the CAIN directory includes at least 16 murals that depict or mention Cú Chulainn).

2 See https://www.atlasobscura.com/places/tain-bo-cuailnge-mosaic (Kinney, now "permanently closed" or removed for renovation), https://createlouth.ie/john-behan/ (Behan), https://createlouth.ie/ann-meldon-hugh/ (Hugh).

3 See Angela Horgan Goff, "The Ulster Cycle: cultural significance for Irish composers," *Estudios Irlandeses* 12.2 (2017) 47–61, at https://www.estudiosirlandeses.org/2017/10/the-ulster-cycle-cultural-significance-for-irish-composers/, and "The significance of the *Táin* in the promotion of cultural nationalism with particular reference to two musical compositions inspired by Thomas Kinsella's 1969 translation," *Études Irlandaises* 46.2 (2021) 103–18, at https://journals.openedition.org/etudesirlandaises/11947.

Reynolds, Will Sliney, and Patrick Brown, and has spawned memes at https://incorrect-ulster-cycle.tumblr.com/. Cú Chulainn (as "Cuchulain, the Irish Wolfhound") has guest starred in Marvel's Guardians of the Galaxy comics, and (as "Lancer") in the anime Fate series, such as *Fate/Stay Night* and *Fate/Grand Order*. There is even a music video: "The Táin" by The Decemberists (2004).[1] However, the *Táin* has yet to be the subject of a feature film.

About This Translation

There are various translations of the *Táin* to choose from. This one tries to have an edge in these specific ways:

(i) a more approachable and even colloquial style, particularly aimed at university students and non-academic readers in North America, that maintains enough accuracy to support close reading;
(ii) in keeping with the richly intertexual nature of the early Irish sagas, more pre-tales and death-tales to accompany the *Táin* than ever before available in one package;
(iii) judicious abridgments (always signposted) to cut down on repetitive scenes of bloodshed and trivia, especially in the latter part of the *Táin* itself;[2]
(iv) corrections, insights, and background information drawing on the last 50+ years of specialist research.

Rather than attempt a seamless collage, this translation clearly distinguishes between material from Recension 1 and Recension 2 of the

1 See https://www.youtube.com/watch?v=_rVMgvojj5w or https://www.youtube.com/watch?v=UOYZuaLgoJo.

2 I can see this being controversial, since medieval authors wouldn't write, and medieval scribes wouldn't go to the effort of copying, things that they didn't think mattered. Ralph O'Connor, in *The Destruction of Da Derga's Hostel: Kingship and Narrative Artistry in a Mediaeval Irish Saga* (Oxford University Press, 2013), makes a strong case for taking seriously the long series of character portraits that seem to interfere with the plot of that saga. But students and the public have limited time; the abridgments were necessary to include more of the ancillary tales; I summarize explicitly everything that has been cut; and since O'Rahilly now exists as a free online resource, one can always "add to taste" on a second read-through.

Táin and details sourced from the different versions of other texts. It is also upfront about when it is making adjustments for clarity or leaving things out. The translations are sometimes freer when the meaning of the text seems clear, and more literalistic when meaning is uncertain and every word matters, such as in poetry.

The texts are full of difficult poetry, known as *rosc* or *retoiric*. This can be rendered impressionistically, at the risk of fudging what it actually says. A feature of university education in literature is that students are rightly encouraged to read closely and cite evidence from the texts to support their conclusions. This is challenging when not even experts can agree on the literal meaning, which occurs more often with Old and Middle Irish than with many other languages. I have tried to note whenever a reading is debatable, making some sections quite thick with notes. *eDIL*, often cited in the notes, is the electronic version of the Royal Irish Academy *Dictionary of the Irish Language based mainly on Old and Middle Irish materials* (1913–76), at https://dil.ie/. One aspect that can often survive translation is the runs of alliterating adjuncts that were a favorite ornament of the Irish: when the translation alliterates heavily, you can assume that the Irish does too. The texts are also fond of the Tironian note (named after Cicero's secretary, Marcus Tullius Tiro) *.i.*, the equivalent of our *i.e.*, (Latin *id est*, 'that is'), probably spoken in Irish as *ed ón*. While it might improve the narrative flow to prune back the *i.e.*s, or to reword them or replace them with appropriate punctuation, I have sometimes resisted this, in the spirit of encouraging a meeting with the text on its own terms. In several of the texts, the *i.e.*s introduce explanatory comments in the manuscripts that are known as glosses—adding a piece of backstory, identifying a more recent equivalent to an old placename, or giving a synonym for a difficult word.

I have benefited from existing translations of all the texts here, from the older work of Whitley Stokes and Kuno Meyer and their contemporaries, to the monumental achievements of Cecile O'Rahilly, to the books by Thomas Kinsella, Ciarán Carson, Jeffrey Gantz, and John Koch and John Carey that have so far been my best options for course texts, to unpublished Ph.D. theses from the last two decades, many of which are freely accessible in online repositories, giving everyone direct access to some of the latest research.

For some of the pre-tales and death-tales, there are engaging versions by Patrick Brown at https://paddybrown.co.uk and https://ulstercycle.wordpress.com/. Various poems within the sagas have been edited, translated, and annotated in specialist articles. I am grateful to everyone who made these contributions. While I haven't exhaustively documented previous translations in the notes to every tale, whenever my own version hinges on someone else's edition or interpretation, or when there is a particularly apposite discussion somewhere, I make sure to cite it. One goal of this, besides trying to get the translations right, is to invite my readers into the endlessly fascinating and dynamic world of Celtic Studies scholarship, where there is still a lot of work to do.

Key Terms and Concepts

From here on, words starred with asterisks the first time they occur on each page can be found in the glossary of terms and concepts at the back of the book. For example, kin-love,* the translation of *condalbae*, and fair play,* the translation of *fír fer*, are starred like this. The starred terms include archeological, legal, and supernatural elements.

The early Irish legal system was fairly complex and particular.[1] Modern democracies have a principle that everyone is equal before the law, but the early Irish legal system was proudly unequal. It assigned to everyone with legal rights a specific amount, known as honor-price,* that would be due to them for offenses against them that were deemed to involve their honor—anything from physical harm to giving them "a nickname that sticks."[2] Honor-price also determined the weight assigned to someone's evidence in court, the food they were entitled to be served when they visited someone, and

1 See the "Further Reading" section below, especially Fergus Kelly's *A Guide to Early Irish Law*. The payment of honor-price, the system of inheritance, and the importance of fosterage* are similar to medieval Wales: compare *The Four Branches of the Mabinogi*, trans. Matthieu Boyd with Stacie Lents (Broadview Press, 2017), 42 and 93–99 on honor-price; 36 and 117–18 on inheritance and fosterage. The traditional system of inheritance for Ireland and Wales was not primogeniture as in most of Europe, where the whole inheritance went to the firstborn son, but an equal split among the male heirs. (A woman could inherit if she had no brothers.) This could turn blood siblings into rivals.

2 See "The Story of Mac Dá Thó's Pig" for why nicknames could be a problem.

whom they could take under their legal protection.* Although there is a modern stereotype of "strong and independent Celtic women," this was a patriarchal society, and the sagas have their share of sexual violence and misogyny. Most women in early Ireland, regardless of social class, didn't have their own honor-price,* but came under the legal authority of their closest male relative, and had an honor-price that was calculated as a fraction of his. Some officers or employees (herald, charioteer, etc.) had their honor-price calculated in the same way, as a fraction of the king's they served. But poets* and Christian clergy had their own hierarchies that determined honor-price.

Fosterage* was historically important and has particular importance in the Ulster Cycle. It was a mark of high status for children to be fostered with other families, the more the better. The relationship was so close that the "mommy" and "daddy" words in Old Irish, *muimme* and *aite*, mean 'foster-mother' and 'foster-father,' as opposed to *máthair* and *athair*, "mother" and "father," for the biological parents. Fosterage created close emotional bonds that could lead to political alliances when the children grew up. In the sagas, conflicts between foster-relatives often seem transgressive and emotionally fraught, whereas blood relatives might attack each other without any documented hesitation or remorse.[1]

There was no police force, so the system relied heavily on contracts guaranteed or enforced by sureties.* There were practically no prisons (although kings were encouraged to make strategic use of a "foul dripping pit"[2]), so most crimes were punishable by having to pay compensation to the victim or their relatives, who could otherwise take justice into their own hands. (Offenses within a kin-group made this complicated, so the crime of *fingal*,* killing or injuring a relative, was uniquely serious.) Some situations could diminish a person's honor-price or make them lose it entirely: this was the historical threat posed by poetic satire,* which, in the sagas, could have magically destructive consequences.

---

1 Examples of blood relatives in conflict, and seemingly untroubled by it, include Monodar's killing of his brother Tinne in "Maeve's Series of Husbands," Scáthach's feud with her sister Aífe in "The Wooing of Emer," and Maeve's killing of her sister Clothru in "The Death of Maeve."

2 Kelly, *Guide*, 218–19.

An important supernatural concept relevant to the *Táin* and its associated tales is that of *geis** ("gesh"), translated elsewhere as "taboo" or "restriction." Many of the Ulster Cycle heroes have one: something they must do, must not do, or must not allow others to do, on pain of supernatural consequences including death.

More broadly, the events of the *Táin* and its associated tales are shadowed—and sometimes influenced or altered—by the Otherworld, the *síd* (pronounced like the English verb to *sheathe* a sword). The word *síd* means both "Otherworld" and "peace," and the two senses are related. There is an implicit or explicit contract whereby the conditions of peace and plenty that exist in the Otherworld* exist in the human world as well when the human ruler exemplifies truth and justice, especially in their public pronouncements and legal verdicts. This phrase for this royal righteousness is *fír flathemon* ("FEER VLATH-uh-vun"), literally "ruler's/prince's truth." Conversely, a royal injustice (*gáu flathemon*) could provoke backlash from the Otherworld and the supernaturally-facilitated destruction of the unjust king. This explains why Conchobor is said (in "The Story of Conchobor mac Nessa") to avoid giving judgments in public, to avoid the possibility of giving an unjust one.

The relationship between the king and the Otherworld could involve a drink given to the future king by a feminine personification of Sovereignty. Earlier scholars often read Maeve, whose name is widely understood as "Intoxicating One," as one of these "sovereignty goddess" figures, who underlie both the "Loathly Lady" motif in Middle English literature (as in Chaucer's "Wife of Bath's Tale"), and the *aisling* ("ASH-ling") genre of Early Modern Irish poetry, where the woman encountered represents Ireland.[1]

---

1 The two classic examples of the drink of sovereignty are in "The Adventure of the Sons of Eochaid Mugmedón" (*Echtra mac n-Echdach Muigmedóin*, Ó Corráin #1049), translated in *The Celtic Heroic Age*, 203–08, and "The Phantom's [Prophetic] Frenzy" (*Baile in Scáil*, ed. and trans. Kevin Murray, Dublin: Irish Texts Society, 2004). The classic presentation of the idea of the "sovereignty goddess" is by Proinsias Mac Cana, "Aspects of the theme of king and goddess in Irish literature," *Études Celtiques* 7.1 (1955) 76–114 (https://www.persee.fr/doc/ecelt_0373-1928_1955_num_7_1_1274), 7.2 (1956) 356–413 (https://www.persee.fr/doc/ecelt_0373-1928_1956_num_7_2_1292), and 8.1 (1958) 59–65 (https://www.persee.fr/doc/ecelt_0373-1928_1958_num_8_1_1303). A more recent treatment is Gregory Toner, *Manifestations of Sovereignty in Medieval Ireland* (University of Cambridge: Department of Anglo-Saxon, Norse and Celtic, 2018), https://www.asnc.cam.ac.uk/publications/Chadwick/HMC%20Vol%2029%202018%20Toner.pdf.

The inhabitants of the Otherworld* are the Túatha Dé Danann* or "Peoples of the Goddess Danu" (not to be confused with the ancient Greek "Danaans"), who were the pagan gods of Ireland, although we have very little indication of how they were worshipped. Over time they evolved into the fairies, the "Good People" of Irish folklore (so called not because they were always benevolent, but to avoid offending them). According to one Ulster Cycle saga,[1] when the human Irish, otherwise known as the Gaels or the "Sons of Míl," arrived in Ireland, they arranged to share the island equally, with the Gaels taking the half aboveground and the Túatha Dé Danann the half below. The Otherworld is more or less a parallel dimension, but it (or access to it) is localized in the "elf-mounds" or "fairy hills," for which the term *síd* is also used. These abodes can be natural features, but are often important prehistoric sites such as the hill-like passage tombs of Knowth, Dowth, and Newgrange on the river Boyne, known in the sagas as Bruig na Bóinne. The Otherworld often plays power-games with the human world: it might let loose creatures to lay waste the land (as in "The Birth of Cú Chulainn") or make other kinds of supernatural intrusions. These are more common at certain times of year, especially Samain* (corresponding to November 1) and Beltaine* (corresponding to May 1), when the Otherworld and the human world become more permeable to one another.

The Cast of Characters

The *Táin*, and the Ulster Cycle in general, have a sprawling cast of characters. Keeping track of all these people and their genealogies was a valued part of the poetic lore, and early Irish tradition explicitly valued obscurity and complication.[2] In this book, characters appearing in only one story or episode are introduced in footnotes as needed. Important recurring characters are listed in an appendix, along with their patronymics/matronymics, their heroic epithets, and pronunciation help. This is followed by a section on early Irish

1 "The Intoxication of the Ulstermen." See p. 131 below.

2 See Hugh Fogarty, "'Dubad nach innsci': cultivation of obscurity in medieval Irish literature," in *Ollam: Studies in Gaelic and Related Traditions in Honor of Tomás Ó Cathasaigh*, ed. Matthieu Boyd (Madison, NJ: Fairleigh Dickinson University Press, 2016) 211–24.

language and spelling and how names are constructed, for anyone who wants to understand why the pronunciations are what they are.

Here is an overview of the recurring characters. The family trees on pp. 14–19 should help to situate them.

The five provinces of Ireland are **Ulster** in the north, **Connacht** in the west, **Leinster** in the southeast, **Munster** in the southwest, and **Meath** in the notional center, around the preeminent royal seat of Ireland at **Tara** (*Temair*). The phrase "the men of Ireland" sometimes refers to all five provinces, but in the *Táin* it typically means the coalition of provinces that invades Ulster.

Ulster is ruled by **Conchobor**. His royal seat is at **Emain Macha**. His father is either Fachtna Fáthach, a previous king of Ulster, or the druid* **Cathbad**. His mother is **Ness**, daughter of Eochaid Sálbuide, another previous king of Ulster. His sisters include **Dechtine** and **Finnchóem**. His sons include **Cormac**, **Cúscraid**, **Follamain**, and **Furbaide**; his daughters include **Fedelm Noíchride** (or **Noíchrothach**).

Conchobor took over the kingship of Ulster from **Fergus**, one of the greatest Ulster heroes. Fergus is one of several foster-parents* of the #1 Ulster hero **Cú Chulainn** (named **Sétanta** at birth), who is the son of Conchobor's sister Dechtine. Cú Chulainn has a human father, **Súaltaim**, and a father from the Otherworld,* **Lug**.

Cú Chulainn's other foster-parents include Finnchóem and her husband, the poet* **Amairgen**; the elder statesman **Sencha**; and the guesthouse*-keeper **Blaí**.

The #2 Ulster hero is **Conall**, the son of Finnchóem and Amairgen and an elder foster-brother* of Cú Chulainn. The #3 Ulster hero is **Lóegaire**. Other important heroes are **Celtchar**, **Cethern**, **Dubthach**, **Menn**, **Muinremor**, **Óengus**, **Rochad**, and **Noísiu** and his two brothers. Other important Ulstermen are **Éogan**, king of Fernmag, who is a sub-king under Conchobor (and was once at war with him); **Dáire**, who owns the **Brown Bull of Cúailnge** (*Donn Cúailnge*) that is the object of the *Táin*; the smith **Culann**; and the troublemaker **Bricriu**.

Cú Chulainn's charioteer is **Lóeg**, and his horses are named **Líath Macha** (the Gray One of Macha) and **Dub Sainglenn** (the

Black One of Saingliu). Cú Chulainn studied abroad with the warrior-woman **Scáthach**, romanced her daughter **Úathach**, and impregnated Scáthach's sister **Aífe**, fathering a son named **Connla**. Some of Scáthach's students from elsewhere in Ireland became Cú Chulainn's foster-brothers,* notably **Lóch**, **Fer Báeth**, and **Fer Diad**. Cú Chulainn is now married to **Emer**.

As a result of Conchobor's actions toward Noísiu and his brothers after they run off with Conchobor's bride-to-be, **Deirdre**, an outraged Fergus, Dubthach, and Cormac (who receives the epithet *Conn Loinges*, "Leader of the Exiles") turn against Conchobor and go into exile in Connacht, taking with them other Ulstermen including Conall and **Fíacha mac Fir Fhebe**.

Connacht is ruled by **Ailill** and **Maeve**. Their royal seat is at **Crúachu**, sometimes called Crúachain.

Ailill is the son of Ross Rúad, a Leinster king, and a Connacht woman with Munster ancestry, Máta Muiresc. His brothers include **Finn**, king of the Gaileóin of Leinster, and **Cairbre Nia Fer**, king of Tara, who is married to Conchobor's daughter Fedelm Noíchride and has a son named **Erc**.

Maeve is the daughter of **Eochaid Feidlech**, a previous king of Tara. She has five sisters, including **Clothru**, **Eithne**, and **Mugain**. Mugain is Conchobor's wife and queen of Ulster. Clothru and Eithne are also involved with Conchobor and bear him children, including Furbaide, who is cut out of his mother's womb by Maeve. Maeve also has triplet brothers who are killed after conceiving **Lugaid Red-Stripes**, Cú Chulainn's foster-son,* with their sister Clothru.

Maeve has various lovers, including Fergus. Ailill is in possession of the **White-Horned Bull** (***Finnbennach***) that is the counterpart of Ulster's Brown Bull, and used to belong to Maeve, which is a source of contention.

Ailill and Maeve have seven sons named **Maine**; at least one other son (**Órlám**); and a daughter, **Finnabair**. Finnabair is used to entice various men to fight for Maeve. One of these is the hero **Fráech**.

Other important Connacht characters are the poet* **Fedelm**, the herald **Mac Roth**, Ailill's charioteers **Cuillius** and **Fer Loga**, and the seven warrior sons of Mágu, including **Cet**, **Ánlúan**, and **Dócha**.

There are seven Munster kings with Ailill and Maeve on their cattle-raid. These include **Lugaid mac Nóis**, a foster-brother* of Cú Chulainn. Munster is also represented by the great hero **Cú Roí**, who has a son **Lugaid mac Con Roí**.

The Otherworld* encroaches from time to time. Besides Cú Chulainn's supernatural father, the god Lug, there is the goddess **Macha**, the namesake of Emain Macha, who lays a curse on the Ulstermen, and three aspects of the war-goddess: **Morrígan** (also known as Bé Néit), **Badb**, and **Nemain**. Other figures mentioned are members of the Túatha Dé Danann* or the Fomoiri.*

Placenames

The events of the *Táin* are very precisely situated in the landscape,[1] and the narrative is intensely concerned with how the landscape and its placenames bear witness to what happened.

These are some of the important recurring placenames and their modern equivalents (see Map 1, the overall map of Ireland):

Áth Lúain ("awth LOO-in"), "Loin Ford": now Athlone, on the river Shannon on the border of Counties Roscommon and Westmeath, i.e., the border of Connacht

Bruig na Bóinne ("BRIG na BOY-nyuh"): the necropolis at Knowth, Dowth, and Newgrange on the river Boyne, featuring neolithic passage tombs associated with the Otherworld

Crích Rois ("kreek rosh"): the territory of the Fir Rois ("fir rosh"), now in County Louth and parts of Monaghan and Meath (see Map 3)

Crúachu ("KROO-uh-hoo"), the royal seat of Connacht: now Rathcroghan, County Roscommon (also called *Ráth Crúachain*, "ROTH KROO-uh-hin")

Cúailnge ("KOOL-nyuh / KOO-ling-yuh"): the Cooley Peninsula, County Louth

Dún Sobairche ("DOON SOV-ir-hyuh"): now Dunseverick, County Antrim

1 See the maps by Paul Gosling on pp. 9–13, and for more details, his article "The route of *Táin Bó Cúailnge* revisited," *Emania* 22 (2014) 145–67.

Emain Macha ("EV-win VACK-uh"), the royal seat of Ulster: now the archaeological site of Navan Fort, County Armagh

Fernmag, the "Plain of Alders," realm of Éogan mac Durthacht: now Farney, County Monaghan

Mag nAí ("mah nee"), Aí Plain: the plain around Crúachu, in Connacht

Mag mBreg ("mah mrey"), the Plain of Brega: the plain south of Ulster, to the north of Tara

Mag Muirthemne ("MWIR-thev-nuh"), Muirthemne Plain: around Dundalk, in County Louth

Sliab Fúait ("SHLEE-uv FOO-id"), Slieve Fúait: the highest point of the Fews mountains in County Armagh, marked as Fid Mór ("Great Wood") on Map 3. *Slieve* is the anglicization of *slíab* 'mountain.' This is used for convenience throughout the translation.

Temair ("TEV-wir"), Tara, seat of the kingship "of Ireland": Tara Hill, northwest of Dublin

The major rivers—the Boyne, the Liffey, the Shannon, etc.—are as they are today. But the river Cronn is now called the river Big in County Louth.

These are common elements of placenames, usually followed by a name in the possessive case (see "Early Irish Spelling and Pronunciation" for how this works):

Áth ("awth") = ford, river-crossing
Belach ("BEL-ock") = pass, gap
Bernas ("BUR-nas") = pass, gap
Brí ("bree") = hill
Clúain ("KLOO-eyn") = meadow
Druim (between "drim" and "drum") = ridge
Dún ("doon") = fort, stronghold, fortified residence
Fertae = grave, barrow
Fid ("FITH," with voiced *th*) = wood
Glen = glen, valley
Gort = field
Inbir ("IN-vur") = estuary

Lia = large flat stone, flagstone, gravestone
Loch = lake
Mag = plain
Ráth ("roth") = fort, stronghold, fortified residence
Sliab ("SHLEE-uv") = mountain (anglicized as *Slieve*)
Slige ("SHLI-yuh") = path, road
Tech (between "tycheck" and "tchyack") = house
Tír ("tyeer" or "tcheer") = land

Besides the maps in this book and the supporting research by Paul Gosling, there is a catalog and attempted identification of *Táin* placenames at https://iso.ucc.ie/Tain-cualnge/Tain-cualnge-names.html, with links to useful resources.

Further Reading

As a major work of world literature, the *Táin* alone has attracted a daunting amount of scholarly attention and popular comment. Various articles and books are mentioned in the notes, and will often be the best resources on particular topics, but the notes are far from exhaustive. Although there would be many other possibilities, I recommend the following as overall next steps.

A comprehensive resource on early Irish literature with several chapters focusing on the *Táin*: Tomás Ó Cathasaigh, *Coire Sois, The Cauldron of Knowledge: A Companion to Early Irish Saga*, ed. Matthieu Boyd (Notre Dame, IN: University of Notre Dame Press, 2014).

Literary close reading and analysis of the *Táin*: Ann Dooley, *Playing the Hero: Reading the Irish Saga* Táin Bó Cúailnge (University of Toronto Press, 2006), and Doris Edel, *Inside the* Táin*: Exploring Cú Chulainn, Fergus, Ailill, and Medb* (Berlin: Curach Bhán, 2015). And while parts of the book have been superseded, e.g., by Mallory's *Dreamtime* volume, Patricia Kelly's observations on "The *Táin* as literature" in *Aspects of The Táin*, ed. J.P. Mallory (Belfast: December Publications, 1992), 69–102, are still well worth a look.

On early Irish archeology and literature: J.P. Mallory, *In Search of the Irish Dreamtime: Archaeology & Early Irish Literature* (London: Thames & Hudson, 2016), and John Waddell, *Archaeology and Celtic Myth: An Exploration* (Dublin: Four Courts Press, 2015).

On the *Táin*'s affinities with the Greco-Roman Classical tradition: Brent Miles, *Heroic Saga and Classical Epic in Medieval Ireland* (Cambridge: D.S. Brewer, 2011); and *Classical Antiquity and Medieval Ireland: An Anthology of Medieval Irish Texts and Interpretations*, ed. Michael Clarke, Erich Poppe, and Isabelle Torrance (Bloomsbury, 2024), at https://www.bloomsburycollections.com/monograph?docid=b-9781350333307.

On the modern reception and translation history of the *Táin*: Maria Tymoczko, *Translation in a Postcolonial Context* (New York: St. Jerome, 1999), and Darach Ó Scolaí, "The *Táin*: from Old Irish to Modern Irish," in *Táin Bó Cúalnge from the Book of Leinster: Reassessments*, ed. John Carey (Dublin: Irish Texts Society, 2020) 122–36.

Background reading on early Irish law and society: Fergus Kelly, *A Guide to Early Irish Law* (Dublin: Dublin Institute for Advanced Studies, 1988), and *Early Irish Farming* (Dublin: Dublin Institute for Advanced Studies, 2000)—which, to buy, are best ordered from https://shop.dias.ie/. *Cáin Lánamna: An Old Irish Tract on Marriage and Divorce Law*, ed. and trans. Charlene Eska (Leiden: Brill, 2010), is a valuable primary text for discussions of gender; also important is Helen Oxenham, *Perceptions of Femininity in Early Irish Society* (Woodbridge: Boydell, 2016).

Background reading on early and medieval Irish history: Clare Downham, *Medieval Ireland* (Cambridge: Cambridge University Press, 2017). The Dictionary of Irish Biography, at https://www.dib.ie/, is an authoritative source on historical (and legendary) figures.

To learn more about Old Irish: Ranke de Vries, *A Student's Companion to Old Irish Grammar* 2e (Burlington, VT: Forgotten Scholar Press, 2020), and David Stifter, *Sengoídelc: Old Irish for Beginners* (Syracuse, NY: Syracuse University Press, 2006).

For research, https://codecs.vanhamel.nl/, https://bill.celt.dias.ie/, and the headnotes to the editions at https://celt.ucc.ie are dynamic resources that can be used to look up much of the latest scholarly work on the *Táin* and related tales. Through 2020, the Celtic Studies Association of North America (CSANA) also maintained a useful bibliography, free to download in its final version from https://celticstudies.org/wp-content/uploads/2021/10/CSANA_Bib_Database_Public-Final.pdf.

There is a recurring international conference on the Ulster Cycle that publishes its proceedings in edited collections with the title *Ulidia*. There have been six of these conferences since 1994, and four *Ulidia* volumes, the most recent being *Ulidia 4: Proceedings of the Fourth International Conference on the Ulster Cycle of Tales*, ed. Mícheál B. Ó Mainnín and Gregory Toner (Dublin: Four Courts Press, 2017). (*Ulidia* 5 is said to be forthcoming: see https://bsky.app/profile/davidstifter.bsky.social/post/3kvu4s575xt2f for the table of contents.) Journals like *Cambrian Medieval Celtic Studies* (*CMCS*), *Celtica*, *Éigse*, *Emania*, *Ériu*, the *North American Journal of Celtic Studies*, *Peritia*, and *Quaestio Insularis* are specialized but worth watching. Recent Ph.D. theses in online repositories can also be a treasure trove of information: for example, Mary Leenane, "The role of Cú Chulainn in Old and Middle Irish narrative literature with particular reference to tales belonging to the Ulster Cycle" (Ph.D. thesis, National University of Ireland, Maynooth, 2014, https://mural.may noothuniversity.ie/7731/). Finally, Anna Pagé's new blog at https://ulstercycle.hcommons.org/ is exciting and already full of information.

Abbreviations

These abbreviations are used in the notes:

The Celtic Heroic Age *The Celtic Heroic Age: Literary Sources for Ancient Celtic Europe & Early Ireland & Wales* 4e, ed. and trans. John T. Koch with John Carey (Aberystwyth: Celtic Studies Publications, 2003), online at https://archive.org/details/celticheroicage/page/n1/mode/2up

The Celtic Poets *The Celtic Poets: Songs and Tales from Early Ireland and Wales*, trans. Patrick Ford (Belmont, MA: Ford & Bailie, 1999)

CMCS *Cambridge/Cambrian Medieval Celtic Studies* (academic journal)

Coire Sois Tomás Ó Cathasaigh, *Coire Sois, The Cauldron of Knowledge: A Companion to Early Irish Saga*, ed. Matthieu Boyd (Notre Dame, IN: University of Notre Dame Press, 2014)

DIAS Dublin: Dublin Institute for Advanced Studies

eDIL The Royal Irish Academy *Dictionary of the Irish Language based mainly on Old and Middle Irish materials* (1913–76), now digitized and updated at https://dil.ie/

Four Courts Dublin: Four Courts Press

Gantz *Early Irish Myths and Sagas*, trans. Jeffrey Gantz (Penguin, 1981)

GEIL Fergus Kelly, *A Guide to Early Irish Law* (Dublin: Dublin Institute for Advanced Studies, 1988)

ITS London or Dublin: Irish Texts Society

Ó Corráin Donnchadh Ó Corráin, *Clavis Litterarum Hibernensium: Medieval Irish Books & Texts (c.400–c.1600)*, 3 volumes (Turnhout: Brepols, 2017), cited by item number

Ollam *Ollam: Studies in Gaelic and Related Traditions in Honor of Tomás Ó Cathasaigh*, ed. Matthieu Boyd (Madison, NJ: Fairleigh Dickinson University Press, 2016)

PHCC *Proceedings of the Harvard Celtic Colloquium* (academic journal)

ZCP *Zeitschrift für Celtische Philologie* (academic journal)

One Possible Timeline for the Stories in This Book

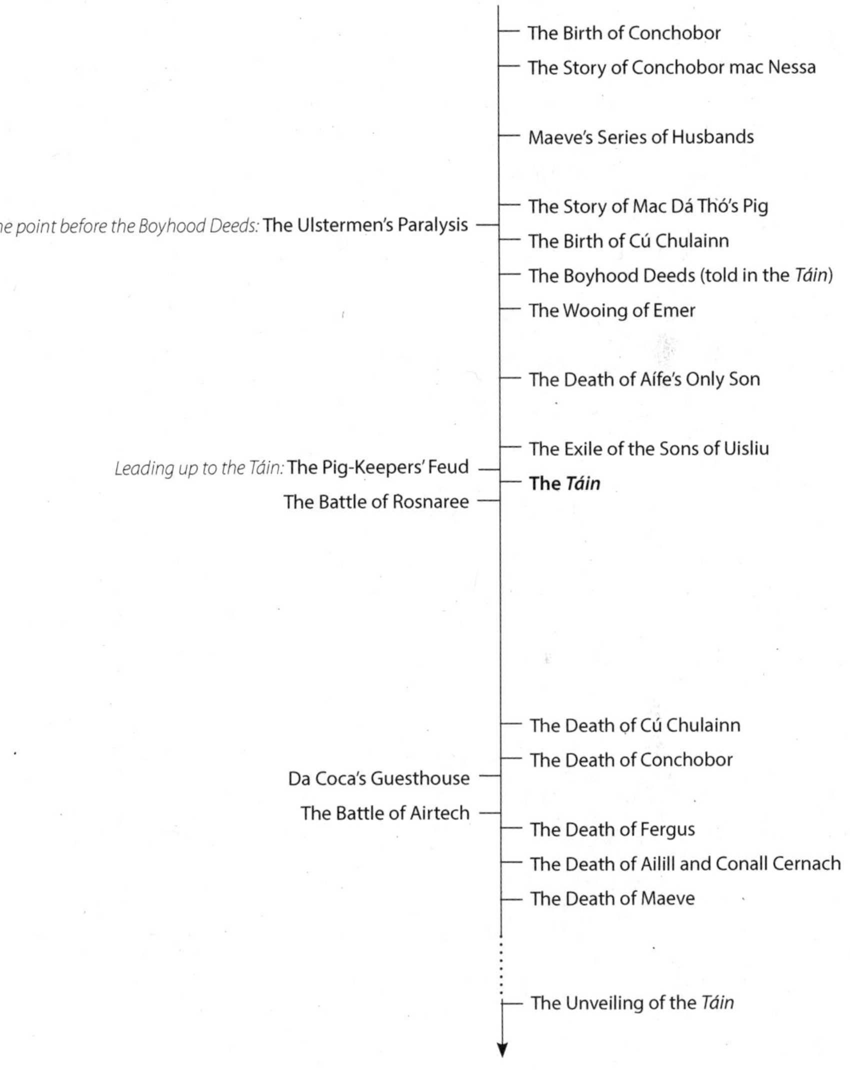

Prequels

The Unveiling of the *Táin*

*This ninth-century text (*Do f[h]aillsigud Tána bó Cúailnge, *Ó Corráin #1039) appears with Recension 1 of the* Táin *in British Library ms. Egerton 1782 and with Recension 2 of the* Táin *in the Book of Leinster.*[1] *It tells how Ireland's poets* recovered the* Táin *from the ghost of Fergus mac Roích after the story had been traded away for a compendium of Latin learning. The title is more commonly translated as "The Finding of the* Táin,*" but the* Táin *isn't "found" so much as "revealed" (see* eDIL, *s.v.* foillsigud*).*

The story involves the historical seventh-century poet Senchán Torpéist ("SHEN-hawn TOR-baysht"). The fourteenth-century tale Tromdám Guaire *(Ó Corráin #1122), translated as "Guaire's Greedy Guests" by Patrick Ford in* The Celtic Poets, *77–111, provides a more elaborate context for this.*[2] *The chief poet Senchán, with his retinue of poets, descends on the famously generous Connacht king Guaire Aidni (d. 663) and takes advantage of his hospitality, using the threat of satire* to make ridiculous demands. After going to extraordinary lengths to cater to them, Guaire and his hermit brother Marbán demand that the poets earn their keep by, among other things, reciting* Táin Bó Cúailnge. *When they turn out not to know it, they are formally banned from spending more than one night in the same place until they can discover it again.*

The translation uses the Irish edited by R.I. Best and Osborn Bergin in The Book of Leinster, *volume 5 (DIAS, 1967), 1119, at https://celt.ucc.ie/published/G800011E/text001.html, and by Kevin Murray, "The finding of the* Táin,*"* CMCS *41 (2001) 17–23.*

---

1 See https://www.isos.dias.ie/TCD/TCD_MS_1339.html#245, which is well past the end of the *Táin* itself on p. 104. The ordering of the texts in the relevant manuscripts is beyond the scope of this book, but is well worth looking into.

2 The title is literally "Guaire's heavy (i.e., burdensome) company." The Irish was edited by Maud Joynt, *Tromdámh Guaire* (DIAS, 1931), https://celt.ucc.ie/published/G301041/. The translation available online is by Owen Connellan from 1860, https://archive.org/details/transactionsofos05ossi/page/2/mode/2up?view=theater (the episode with Senchán and Guaire starts on 35). For discussion, see Feargal Ó Béarra, "*Tromdhámh Guaire*: a context for laughter and audience in Early Modern Ireland," *Laughter in the Middle Ages and Early Modern Times*, ed. Albrecht Classen (Berlin: De Gruyter, 2010) 413–28. Ó Corráin says the text is 11th-century "with some reworking," but I use Ó Béarra's dating of "no earlier than ca. 1300" for the form that survives. See Ó Béarra, 415n10, for the evidence "[t]hat certain elements of the narrative are older than the time the text was written."

The poets* of Ireland were summoned to Senchán Torpéist to find out if they remembered *Táin Bó Cúailnge* in full, and they said they didn't—only scraps of it. Then Senchán told his students to decide which of them would go, in return for his blessing, to the land of Letha[1] to learn the *Táin*, which the scholar had taken east in exchange for the *Etymologies* of Isidore of Seville.[2]

Emine, grandson of Ninene, and Muirgen, son of Senchán, traveled east: they came to the grave of Fergus mac Roích, and passed his tombstone at Bird Lake (*Énloch*) in Connacht. Muirgen sat by himself next to Fergus's tombstone, while everyone else went to find them a place to stay. So Muirgen started chanting as if he were talking to Fergus himself, telling him:

> "If this is your stone,
> shining one, bright lord,
> then I would know, son of Róech,
> with all its bold moves and butcheries
> about the drive that was driven
> on the day of battle
> for the Cúailnge cattle,
> in every detail,
> Fergus."[3]

Then a great mist formed around him, so his companions couldn't find him for three days and three nights, and Fergus himself came to him in resplendent attire, i.e., a green cloak, a hooded shirt with red embroidery, a gold-hilted sword, bronze sandals, and brown hair.

---

1 *Letha* Possibly *Letavia*, Brittany; mentioned again on p. 126.

2 *Etymologies of Isidore of Seville* The text actually says "the *Cuilmenn* ('Summit')," but the scholarly consensus is that this refers to Isidore's 7th-century treatise, seen as the apex of classical learning. The standard translation is *The Etymologies of Isidore of Seville*, trans. Stephen A. Barney, W.J. Lewis, J.A. Beach, and Oliver Berghof (Cambridge University Press, 2006). There is no record of who "the scholar" is supposed to have been who traded the *Táin* for it.

3 The translation of this difficult verse mostly follows Ann Dooley, *Playing the Hero*, 57 and notes, 232–33; compare John Carey, "Varia II: The Address to Fergus's Stone," *Ériu* 51 (2000) 183–87. It's possible that the second line is characterizing the stone as bright and princely rather than Fergus himself; that the fourth line refers to the testimony of wise men or to expeditions by champions; and so on.

Then Fergus told him the whole cattle-raid as it happened, beginning to end. (Others say it was told to Senchán after he fasted against[1] some saints who were descended from Fergus, and it wouldn't be surprising if that were the case.) They all went back to Senchán and told him about their experiences, and he was pleased with them.

These are the prequels of *Táin Bó Cúailnge*. There are twelve:[2]

- "The Taking of the Otherworld* Abode."
- "About the *Mac Óc*'s Dream."
- "The Pig-Keepers' Feud."
- "The Raid on Regamon's Cattle."
- "Nera's Adventure."
- "The Birth of Conchobor."
- "The Wooing of Ferb."
- "The Birth of Cú Chulainn."
- "The Raid on Flidais's Cattle."
- "The Wooing of Emer."

Some say that the stories about how Cú Chulainn went to the house of Culann the smith, about how he got his weapons and went for his first ride in a chariot, and about how he went to Emain Macha to meet the boys are part of the prequels. But actually, those stories are told in the body of the *Táin*.

Of the prequels listed here, "The Pig-Keepers' Feud," "The Birth of Conchobor," "The Birth of Cú Chulainn," and "The Wooing of Emer" are translated below as separate tales, and the stories about Cú Chulainn, collectively known as his "Boyhood Deeds" (macgnímrada), *are indeed part of the* Táin *itself: an extended series of flashbacks narrated by the Ulster exiles. The other titles from the list are summarized under "Other Prequels," pp. 153–56 below.*

1 *fasted against* To bring a lawsuit against someone of "exalted" status who was exempt from ordinary legal action, a plaintiff could initiate a formalized hunger strike (*troscud*), during which the respondent was also not allowed to eat before settling the claim. See *GEIL*, 182–83.

2 *twelve* Ten are listed. See the explanatory notes at the end of this story.

The Ulstermen's Paralysis and the Twins of Macha

This ninth-century tale (Ó Corráin #1022) appears with Recension 1 of the Táin *in the Yellow Book of Lecan and, in a somewhat different version, with Recension 2 of the* Táin *in the Book of Leinster. Since they're short, and each has different pieces of essential information, both versions are translated below as a case study in how "the same story" can vary in early Irish tradition and manuscript culture.*

The point of the story is to explain the condition that keeps most of the Ulstermen out of the Táin *until the final battle, and whose narrative function is to force Cú Chulainn to stand alone against the invading army all winter long. This condition, called the* ces noínden *or "nine-day affliction" (although it affects the Ulstermen in the* Táin *a lot longer than that), has been translated "debility" (O'Rahilly), "pangs" (Kinsella), and here "paralysis." While it has also been interpreted as a winter sleep, in this story it is a curse. After the king forces the goddess Macha to run a race against his horses when she is in labor, she curses the Ulstermen that whenever they come under attack, most of them will be incapacitated like women giving birth.*

This all seems to be happening well before the Táin, *since, according to the Book of Leinster version, it accounts for the name Emain Macha (supposedly "The Twins of Macha") for the Ulster royal seat, and takes place during the lifetime of a son of the Ulstermen's original namesake Curir Ulad. But elsewhere[1] the king in the story is identified as Conchobor. In that case, even if the story is supposed to be set in Ulster's recent past, it must be prior to Cú Chulainn's Boyhood Deeds since, according to the* Táin, *the Ulstermen are affected by it then.*

The curse exempts the women of Ulster (of any age), the boys, Cú Chulainn, and (in the Yellow Book version) anyone outside the bounds of Ulster, and it lasts for nine generations.

How can it be both an intergenerational punishment and one that doesn't affect the boys? If the events take place not long before the Táin, *it could be that anyone who is a boy at the time is not affected. Otherwise, the simplest explanation is that its effect on the Ulstermen increases as they reach adulthood: in the* Táin, *Cú Chulainn's childhood companions*

1 See *The Metrical Dindshenchas,** Part IV, ed. and trans. Edward Gwynn (Dublin: Hodges, Figgis, 1924) 124–31, at https://celt.ucc.ie/published/T106500D.html.

from the boy-troop, now about the same age as he is (16+), shake off their paralysis faster than the rest of Ulster, but still not immediately.

Why aren't Fergus and the Ulster exiles affected, not only when they're in Connacht but when they return to Ulster as invaders? The curse can't be so recent that they were outside the bounds of Ulster when it was laid, because of the Boyhood Deeds, so it would seem to track their allegiance: it's a magical curse, not a genetic one.

Why aren't Cú Chulainn and his human father Súaltaim affected? Because Súaltaim isn't an Ulsterman himself, and Cú Chulainn, besides spending his early childhood to the south, also has a supernatural father. Or there might be other reasons why Cú Chulainn isn't masculine or human enough to qualify.[1] *Why isn't Cú Chulainn's* charioteer *affected? Because he is an extension of the hero and, for narrative reasons, Cú Chulainn needs him. The Boyhood Deeds also give a reason why, in their quest for the Brown Bull, the invaders don't even try to massacre the helpless Ulstermen before they can recover, instead of waiting to fight them all in a climactic battle. Fergus explains that* "No one would dare shed the blood of anyone suffering from it because whoever does either contracts the same paralysis, or wastes away, or dies in short order."

*The translations use the Irish edited by (i) Vernam Hull, "*Nóinden Ulad: *The Debility of the Ulidians,"* Celtica *8 (1968) 1–42, and (ii) R.I. Best and Osborn Bergin in* The Book of Leinster, *volume 2 (DIAS, 1956) 467–68, reproduced with George Henderson's 1898 English translation at https://iso.ucc.ie/Noinden-ulad/Noinden-ulad-text.html. For discussion, see Gregory Toner, "Macha and the invention of myth,"* Ériu *60 (2010) 81–109.*

1 See most recently Finn Longman, "'What manner of man is this Hound?': gender, humanity and the transgressive figure of Cú Chulainn," *Proceedings of the Association of Celtic Students of Ireland and Britain* 8/9 (2023) 1–24, at 4, at https://finnlongman.com/wp-content/uploads/2023/03/Finn-Longman-What-Manner-of-Man-Is-This-Hound.pdf.

(i) Yellow Book of Lecan version (with Recension 1 of the *Táin*)

Where did the Ulstermen's paralysis come from? That's easy.* There was a prosperous tenant farmer in Ulster out among the mountain peaks in the hinterlands: his name was Crunnchu[1] mac Agnomain. He had accumulated great wealth out there in the hinterlands, and had a bunch of sons to keep him company.

The lady he lived with, the mother of his children, died. He went without a wife for ages. Then one day, when he was home in bed by himself, he saw a shapely woman coming towards him inside the main house. She was impeccable in the way she looked, what she wore, the way she presented herself.

The lady sat down in a chair by the fireplace and lit a fire. They spent the rest of the day like that, not talking. Then she brought in a kneading-trough and a sieve and got started making dinner. At the end of the day, she took some pails and milked the cows without being asked. When she came back inside, she turned sunwise* and went into the kitchen and gave the household[2] their marching orders, and then she sat down in a chair next to Crunnchu. Then everyone went to bed. She stayed up and banked down the fire, turned sunwise, then crawled under the covers with him and ran a hand over him.[3] They came together as one, and she ended up pregnant.

From then on, his wealth increased because he was with her. She was pleased to see him flourish, and pleased with the trappings that came with it.

The Ulstermen would often hold enormous fairs and gatherings. All the people of Ulster, men and women, used to go to the fair if they could.

---

1 *Crunnchu* Pronounced "KRUNN-hu"—nothing like "crunch" or "chew."

2 *the kitchen ... the household* Actually these have the possessive adjective: "her kitchen" (*ina cuile*, for which we would have expected *ina chuile* if it were "his kitchen") and "her (or his) household" (*a muintir*). The sense of this is clearer from the other version: she treats the household as her own and tells everyone what to do.

3 *ran a hand over him* Literally this would seem to mean "stroked his side." Hull's translation is "laid a hand on his privy parts." Kicki Ingridsdotter's Ph.D. thesis (https://www.diva-portal.org/smash/get/diva2:213892/FULLTEXT01.pdf) 24, discusses whether the semantic range of *táeb*, normally "side," will accommodate this.

"I'm going to the fair like everyone else," Crunnchu told his wife.

"You're not," said the woman. "That way you won't run the risk of talking about us, because our relationship will be over if you talk about me at the fair."

"I won't say a word there!" said Crunnchu.

The Ulstermen came to the fair and Crunnchu came along like everyone else. The fair was a glorious riot of people and horses and clothing. There were horse races, strength contests, target shooting,[1] marching, and parades at the fair.

In the afternoon, the king's chariot took the field. The king's horses triumphed at the fair.

Then the praisemongers[2] came, to praise the king and the queen, the poets[*] and the druids,[*] the royal household, the crowd, and the entire fair: "No horses like the king's horses have ever graced a fair. There isn't a swifter pair in Ireland."

"My wife is faster[3] than those horses," said Crunnchu.

"Arrest that man," said the king, "until the woman comes and competes."

They arrested him and the king sent messengers to the woman. She made them welcome and asked what brought them.

"We're here so you can come and get your husband off the hook. The king had him arrested because he said you were faster than the king's horses."

"Well this is just awful," she said, "because that wasn't an appropriate thing to say. But surely I can have a continuance,[4] because I'm pregnant and having contractions."

"Continuance or not," said the messengers, "he'll be killed unless you come."

---

1 *target shooting* For this word, *díbraicthi, eDIL* suggests "archery," but the bow and arrow are not part of the Ulster Cycle arsenal. This contest probably involved javelins or throwing spears.

2 *praisemongers* The expression here is *áes ind admolta*—the "folk of great praise," "eulogists," or "hype-men"—rather than *filid*, the word for the formal hierarchy of poets. Tomás Ó Cathasaigh, "Early Irish *bairdne* 'eulogy, panegyric,'" *Studia Celtic Fennica* 9 (2012) 54–61, discusses the extent to which these functions overlapped.

3 *My wife is faster* This race against horses has led to an identification of Macha as a horse-goddess, akin to Epona in classical antiquity. Similar reasoning was applied to Rhiannon in the Welsh *Mabinogi*: see Boyd, *The Four Branches of the Mabinogi*, 21–37.

4 *a continuance* This translates *turbaid*, a legal term for a postponement. The king's refusal to allow it is unjust in terms of early Irish law.

"I suppose I'll have to, then," she said.

She went with them to the fair, and everyone came to look at her.

"It's not right for everybody to be scrutinizing how I look," she said. "Why have I been brought here?"

"To race against the king's horses," said everyone.

"I get a continuance," she said, "because I'm having contractions."

"Then put the farmer to the sword," said the king.

"Wait for me for just a minute," she said, "until I give birth."

"No," said the king.

"Then shame on you for not granting me this small favor. And because you didn't, I'll bring even greater shame on you when this is over. Go ahead and let the horses loose alongside me."

And they did—and she was first across the finish line, ahead of the horses. Then she let out a scream of agony from her labor pains. Suddenly God made it all go smoothly, and she gave birth to a boy and a girl at the same time.[1]

As soon as the whole crowd heard the lady scream, it overwhelmed them, leaving them all as weak as the lady in labor.

"The humiliation you've inflicted on me will be a stigma to you from now on. When things are hardest for you, you'll have no more strength than a woman in labor to guard this province, and you'll be like that for as long as a woman spends in labor—that is, five days and four nights—and you will suffer from this unto the ninth generation—that is, for nine people's lifetimes."

That came true. It plagued them from Crunnchu's time until the time of Fergus mac Domnaill.[2] But this paralysis didn't use to affect women, or boys, or Cú Chulainn—because he wasn't one of the Ulstermen—or anyone staying outside their territory. That's how the Ulstermen caught the paralysis.

Finit. ("The end.")

---

1 *a boy … same time* Elsewhere their names are given as Fir and Fial, and Macha is said to have died afterwards: see Gwynn, *The Metrical Dindshenchas,** Part IV, 129. "God" here does seem to be to the Christian God: a Christian scribe or redactor of this story could have seen God's hand in things that in a pre-Christian context would be credited to nature, the pagan gods, etc. For the most thorough and extensive example of this tendency in the European Middle Ages, see *The Medieval French* Ovide moralisé*: An English Translation*, trans. and ed. K. Sarah-Jane Murray and Matthieu Boyd (Cambridge: D.S. Brewer, 2023).

2 *Fergus mac Domnaill* So far unidentified, according to Toner, "Macha and the invention of myth," 86.

(ii) Book of Leinster version (with Recension 2 of the *Táin*)

Where did the Ulstermen's paralysis come from? That's easy.* Crunniuc son of Agnoman was a prosperous landowner[1] in Ulster. He lived in the wilderness, up in the mountains, and had many sons. Then his wife died.

One day, when he was home by himself, he saw a woman walk into his house. He thought she looked stunning. She sat down and immediately started putting things in order, as if she'd always lived there. When it got dark, the household took orders from her without question.

She spent the night with Crunniuc. She was with him for a long time after that, and, thanks to her, they were never short on anything: food, clothes, or other supplies.

Not long after that, the Ulstermen held a fair. They all used to go to it—man and wife, son and daughter. And Crunniuc was heading there like everyone else. He had nice clothes on and looked handsome.

"You would do well," his wife told him, "not to say anything thoughtless."

"That's not going to happen," he said.

So the fair took place, and at the end of the day, the king's chariot came in first. His chariot and horses took the prize.

The crowd was saying, "There's nothing as fast as those horses."

Then Crunniuc spoke up: "My wife is faster," he said.

He was immediately seized by the king.

His wife was told about it.

"It's a real hardship for me," she said, "to go and free him when I'm this pregnant."

"Even if it is," said the messenger, "he'll be killed if you don't come."

Then she went to the fair, and started going into labor.

"Help me!" she said to the crowd. "All of you had mothers who gave birth to you. Wait for me to give birth!"

---

1 *prosperous landowner* In contrast to his position as a "tenant farmer" in the other version, this title, *briugu cétach*, would technically refer to a "hospitaller" or guesthouse*-keeper (*briugu*) with a hundred cows. The sense loosened over time, to farmer or landowner, and the normal expectation was for a *briugu*'s guesthouse to be in a well-traveled location, not out in the wilds the way Crunniuc's house is.

They wouldn't yield.

"All right then," she said, "this will bring a disaster down on you, one that will haunt the Ulstermen a long time."

"What's your name?" said the king.

"This fair," she said, "will carry my name and the name of my children forever. My name is Macha, daughter of Sainreth son of Imbath."

Then she raced the chariot, and as the chariot reached the finish line, she was there ahead of it, giving birth to twins, a boy and a girl. That was the basis of the placename *Emain Macha*, the Twins of Macha.[1]

As she gave birth, she screamed, and everyone who heard it was paralyzed for five days and four nights.

All the men of Ulster who had been there were stricken with the same condition for nine generations. Five days and four nights, or five nights and four days: that was how long the Ulstermen's paralysis lasted.

There were three groups of people not subject to the paralysis: the boys and the women of Ulster, and Cú Chulainn.

This was the period when the Ulstermen were subject to it: from the time of Crunniuc son of Agnoman son of Curir Ulad son of Fiatach son of Urmi, until the time of Forco son of Dallán son of Mainech son of Lugaid, etc. The Ulstermen (*Ulaid*) are named after Curir Ulad.

That's where the Ulstermen's paralysis came from.

A ninth-century anecdote about Cú Chulainn[2] *offers yet another explanation (which doesn't align very well with how the paralysis exists during his Boyhood Deeds): Cú Chulainn goes to the river Boyne in a way that reads as an intrusion on the Otherworld.*[*] *He is confronted by Fedelm Foltchaín (Fedelm "with Beautiful Hair") and her husband Elcmaire.*

---

1 *Twins of Macha* As a matter of fact rather than folk etymology, the translation should probably be "the Twin of Macha," singular: the hill of Emain Macha was considered a "twin" to the hill of Armagh (*Ard Macha*, "the Hill of Macha").

2 Ó Corráin #1032, edited and translated by Vernam Hull, "*Ces Ulad*: The Affliction of the Ulstermen," *ZCP* 29 (1962–64) 305–14, also translated by John Carey in *The Celtic Heroic Age*, 67–68. For discussion, see Toner, "Macha and the invention of myth."

He cuts off Elcmaire's thumbs and big toes, and then, either to appease Cú Chulainn or as revenge:

Fedelm promised to spend a year with Cú Chulainn and present herself naked to the Ulstermen beforehand. She exposed herself a year and a day after that, and that's what gave the Ulstermen a condition.

The Birth of Conchobor

This is the first recension of Compert Conchobair *(Ó Corráin #1026, eighth century), which appears with Recension 1 of the* Táin *in the Yellow Book of Lecan. It gives one version of the circumstances leading to the birth of Conchobor mac Nessa, Cú Chulainn's maternal uncle and the king of Ulster in the* Táin. *According to the different versions of his birth-tale, Conchobor's father was the druid* Cathbad; but other texts, like "Maeve's Series of Husbands" below, identify him as the son of Fachtna Fáthach (Fachtna "the Wise"), who seems to have preceded either him or Fergus as king of Ulster. This uncertainty about who Conchobor's father was might explain why he is more often known by the matronymic* mac Nessa, *"son of Ness." Besides that, in this story we see one of the functions of a druid, to pronounce on what activities are auspicious or inauspicious at a given time. Unusual circumstances of conception and an unusual (in this case, unusually long) form of pregnancy are hallmarks of the common narrative pattern for the lives of heroic figures, known as the International Heroic Biography, found in many cultural traditions throughout the world.*

The translation uses the Irish edited by Vernam Hull in "The conception of Conchobor," in Irish Texts, *Fasciculus IV, ed. J. Fraser, P. Grosjean and J.G. O'Keefe (London: Sheed and Ward, 1934) 4–12, at https://celt.ucc.ie//published/G301000/index.html. For discussion of Conchobor's birth-tales and parallels to their various elements, see Anna June Pagé, "Birth narratives in Indo-European mythology" (Ph.D. thesis, UCLA, 2014, https://escholarship.org/content/qt71m1f09s/qt71m1f09s.pdf), at 99–153.*

Ness, daughter of Eochaid Sálbuide (Eochaid "Yellow-Heel"), was sitting on her throne outside of Emain, surrounded by her royal maidens.

The druid walked past her, i.e., the druid Cathbad of the Tratraige of Mag Inis.

The girl said to him: "What's this hour lucky for, then?"

"It's lucky for getting a queen pregnant with a king," said the druid.

The girl asked him if that was true. The druid* swore by the gods that it was: a son conceived at that time would dominate Ireland.

The girl beckoned him over, not seeing any other men around.

She, Ness, was pregnant after that. The fetus was in her womb for three years and three months. At the feast of Othar she gave birth. Finit. ("The end.")

The Story of Conchobor mac Nessa

*This is a later version of Conchobor's birth-tale (*Scéla Conchobuir meic Nessa, *Ó Corráin #1093, first half of the twelfth century) that appears with Recension 2 of the* Táin *in the Book of Leinster. Ó Corráin calls it "an intertextual commentary on the classic sagas": "a wildly inflated account of Conchobor and his household, meant to ridicule heroics, and the appetites and violence of kings." Besides giving a different version of how Conchobor was conceived, this text tells how his mother arranged for him to take the kingship of Ulster away from Fergus, and describes some features of the Ulster court, including Conchobor's royal prerogatives and Fergus's superhuman proportions. The incredibly positive portrayal of Conchobor's reign is hard to square with the way he behaves in other texts, especially "Maeve's Series of Husbands" and "The Exile of the Sons of Uisliu."*

The translation uses the Irish edited by Whitley Stokes in "Scéla Conchobair maic Nessa: *The Tidings of Conchobar son of Ness,"* Ériu *4 (1910) 18–38, and another copy edited by Vernam Hull, "How Conchobar gained the kingship of Ulster,"* ZCP *25 (1956) 243–45. Inconsistencies in the portrayal of Conchobor's reign are tackled by Geraldine Parsons, "'Never the twain shall meet?' East and West in the characterization of Conchobar mac Nessa,"* Quaestio Insularis *4 (2003) 35–56.*

Conchobor mac Nessa was an illustrious, distinguished man: this tells how he rose to power over the Ulstermen. He was named after his mother, i.e., Conchobor's mother was Ness, daughter of Eochaid Sálbuide, king of Ulster.

This is why she was named Ness: she was put into fosterage* with twelve foster-fathers,* according to Eochaid's wishes. Assa ("Easy") was her original name, because she was extremely easy to raise.

There was a vicious *fían*-warrior* in Ireland at the time: his name was Cathbad mac Rossa. He was a druid* as well as a *fían*-warrior. He went on a rampage in the districts of Munster. He and his warband came to her (i.e., Eochaid's daughter's) foster-fathers' house. He killed all twelve of the girl's foster-fathers on the same night, and no one knew who had committed the slaughter.

After that, the girl took up the warband lifestyle, got herself some weapons, and roamed through Ireland in a band of 27, trying to find out who had killed her foster-fathers. And she laid waste the tribes: she laid waste to all of them equally, because she didn't know exactly who her enemies were.

"She should be called *Ní-hassa* ('Not-Easy') from now on," said everyone. That's how she came to be called Ness.

Then she went to raid in the province of Ulster. One day she went off by herself to bathe, when the same *fían*-warrior, i.e., Cathbad, came across her. He got between her and her spears, and grabbed her, and intimacy occurred,[1] so that she became his beloved wife and bore him a son. That was the boy we're talking about: Conchobor son of Cathbad.

In him—in Conchobor—a glorious dignity was born. That was only fitting, because he was born at the same time as Christ was born.[2] Seven prophets had been predicting him seven years before his birth: a wondrous birth would take place at the same time as Christ's birth, on the stone over there where Conchobor was born, and his name would be famous in Ireland.

Conchobor rose to great dignity seven years after his birth, when he took over the kingship of Ulster. It happened like this: his mother Ness, daughter of Eochaid, was single. And Fergus mac Roích was ruling Ulster at the time. He wanted the woman—Ness—to be his wife.

---

1 *intimacy occurred* The circumstances imply rape, but the Irish uses a neutral kind of euphemism, *commanarnaic dóib*, translated "they foregathered" by Stokes and glossed by *eDIL* as "used of sexual intercourse," with other examples that would seem consensual. For more on this episode, see Robbie Andrew MacLeod, "Female alterity in medieval Gaelic literature" (MRes thesis, University of Glasgow, 2018, https://theses.gla.ac.uk/9148/1/2018macleodmres.pdf), at 45–48.

2 *same time … was born* Compare "The Death of Conchobor," p. 323 below, which says that Conchobor shared Jesus' birthday, but not his birth year.

"No," she said, "not unless I get something in return: let my son be king for a year, so that in due course his son[1] can be called the son of a king."

"Agree," said everyone. "You'll still be our ruler, even if he's king in name."

After that the woman slept with Fergus, and the kingship of Ulster was nominally transferred to Conchobor.

Then the woman started giving instructions to her son, his foster-fathers,* and his household: to strip every second man of his wealth and give it to someone else.[2] And she forked over her own gold and silver to the Ulster champions as a further investment[3] in her son.

Conchobor's term ended exactly one year later. Then Fergus called in his pledges.

"Let's talk this over," said the Ulstermen. They came together in one big assembly. They found it deeply humiliating for Fergus to have used them as a bride-price. But they were thrilled with Conchobor for his generous patronage. This was the outcome of the discussion: "What Fergus sold should be taken away from him; what Conchobor bought, he can keep."

That's when Fergus was separated from the kingship of Ulster, and Conchobor son of Cathbad was appointed to the high kingship of a province of Ireland.

The Ulstermen had vast reverence for Conchobor. This was the extent of it: every time an Ulsterman took up with a marriageable girl, she would sleep with Conchobor the first night, so that he became her first husband.

There was never a wiser man born on this earth. He never delivered a judgment when he wasn't allowed to, to avoid giving a false judgment that would have blighted his crops.[4]

Also, there was never a mightier champion on this earth, and he

---

1 *his son* Stokes's edition has *frim mac*, "my son," which, Hull confirms, is the meaning in two of the three manuscripts of this episode. The third one has "his son," which, like Stokes, I find more logical.

2 *strip … someone else* Presumably the way this worked is that half the people would be grateful to Conchobor for making them rich, and the other half would hate Fergus for letting Conchobor rob them.

3 *further investment* Stokes reads it as "because of the result to her son," but in legalistic scenarios, the word here means an additional fine or penalty: *eDIL*, s.v. *iartaige*, and *GEIL*, 131. "Further investment" splits the difference.

4 *blighted his crops* See the discussion of *fír flathemon* in the Introduction, p. 37.

was never allowed to put himself in danger, i.e., to protect the king's son. Champions and war veterans and elite warriors used to form a screen in front of him in battles and skirmishes so he wouldn't be in any danger.

Every time an Ulsterman used to host him overnight, he'd spend the night sleeping with the man's wife.

There were 365 people in Conchobor's household, i.e., as many men as there are days in a year. They had an arrangement where one of the men was responsible for feeding them every night: the man in charge of the food on any given night would take his turn again in a year. The rations weren't small, i.e., every man got a pig, an ox, and a vat of ale. But there were men for whom that wasn't enough: for example, Fergus mac Roích, or so it's said. If this is true, he was a decent size, i.e., it wasn't too common for anyone else to have Fergus's "sevens." That is, it was seven feet from his ear to his mouth, and it was seven hands between his eyes, and his nose was seven hands long, and his mouth was seven hands wide. It took a bushel of water to wet his head so he could wash it. His penis was seven hands long. His scrotum was a bushel sack. It took seven women to satisfy him unless his wife[1] Flidais was there. He would consume seven pigs, seven vats of ale, and seven oxen, and he had the strength of 700 men. So he had to feed the household for a week longer than everyone else.

But Conchobor himself used to provide the food at Samain,* because of the enormous crowd. They had to be provided for because if any of the Ulstermen didn't come to Emain for Samain, they'd go mad, and their grave would be dug the next day, with slab and headstone.

The text continues with a description of Conchobor's three houses, the Cráebruad *(Red-Brown Branch),* Téite Brecc *(Speckled, i.e., Glittering, Hoard), and* Cráebderg *(Red Branch). Kings stay at the Red-Brown Branch; weapons and expensive serving-ware are stored in the Glittering Hoard; severed heads and plunder are kept in the Red Branch. The Ulstermen have to surrender their weapons because they are so quick to avenge insults and break out in brawls. There is a list of the names of the*

---

1 *his wife* Added for clarity.

heroes' shields: Conchobor's is the Óchaín, *Cú Chulainn's is* Fubán *(elsewhere* Dubán, *"Little Black One"), and so on. There are brief profiles of Fergus, Conall Cernach, and Cú Chulainn, citing Fergus's shearing of the hills of Meath at the end of the* Táin, *Conall's role as avenger of the Ulstermen and his deeds as reported in "The Story of Mac Dá Thó's Pig," and Cú Chulainn's mutation* and list of feats as reported in the* Táin. *There is a description of Conchobor's interior decoration, including a silver rod with three golden apples on it that he would shake to call for silence (and then you could hear a needle drop), and Conchobor's ale-vat (see p. 96). Lastly, there is a profile of Bricriu Nemthenga ("Poisontongue") mac Carbada, with the special detail that whenever he managed to keep a secret, he would develop a bulging boil on his forehead.*

Maeve's Series of Husbands, or The Battle of the Boyne

*This is a later text (*Ferchuitred Medba al. Cath Bóinde, *Ó Corráin #1055, twelfth or thirteenth century). Ó Corráin calls it a "late, derivative, and ill-ordered text on sagas and onomastics. Not a tale; rather a collection of scholar's notes," but what it says about Maeve and Conchobor is consequential. The story deals with Maeve and her brothers and sisters, the children of King Eochaid Feidlech of Tara, who had a large and dysfunctional family. Importantly, it describes Maeve's being given in marriage to Conchobor against her will (he was also married to her sisters Mugain, Eithne, and Clothru), her leaving him, and her later being raped by him. These are details never mentioned in the* Táin *itself, and so could be interpreted as retconning, given that not all the information here had necessarily been developed when either of the two main recensions of the* Táin *were composed. But some of the facts overlap with the earlier text "The Death of Maeve," pp. 335–37 below. Her painful history with Conchobor drives Maeve's subsequent actions, including her efforts to choose a husband who will stand up to Conchobor: she goes through at least three others before settling on Ailill. (Here Ailill is much younger than her, whereas elsewhere he is said to be the same age.) Read through the lens of this later text, Maeve's penetration of Ulster's territory in the* Táin *can be understood as a pointed reversal, writ large, of what Conchobor did to her.*[1]

The translation uses the Irish edited by Joseph O'Neill in "Cath Boinde," Ériu *2 (1905) 173–85. The various other stories related to Eochaid Feidlech's family are discussed by Edel Bhreathnach, "Tales of Connacht:* Cath Airtig, Táin bó Flidhais, Cath Leitreach Ruibhe, *and* Cath Cumair," CMCS *45 (2003) 21–42.*

1 See Matthieu Boyd, "Aspects of sexual violence in early Irish literature," *PHCC* 39 (2020, for calendar year 2019) 72–90, at 84–86, engaging with unpublished work by Abigail Burnyeat entitled "#MedbToo." Dooley, *Playing the Hero*, makes a complementary suggestion that in the *Táin*, "the really terrifying aspect of death for these heroes" is "the idea of the death of the hero [as] an enactment of a type of sexual assault that feminizes the defeated male" (168).

Ireland was once ruled by King Eochaid Feidlech,[1] of the seed of Rifad Scot from the tower of Nimrod, because every wave that invaded Ireland[2] was descended from Rifad except for Cesair's. He was called Eochaid Feidlech because[3] he was faithful (*feidil*) toward everyone, i.e., that king treated everyone justly.

He had four sons. Three of them were triplets[4] known as the Finn Emna ("Fair Undivided Ones"), i.e., *eamain* meaning "something that is not divided"—they were born at the same time. Their names were Bres, Nár, and Lothar, and they were the ones who conceived Lugaid of the Three Red Stripes with their own sister[5] the night before fighting the battle of Druim Críad[6] against their father. The three of them were killed there by Eochaid Feidlech, and Eochaid made the sacred prayer that no son should ever succeed his father in the kingship of Ireland, and that came true. His fourth son was Conall Anglonnach, the ancestor of the Conailli among the men of Brega.

---

1 *Ireland ... Eochaid Feidlech* Some steps of his genealogy—"son of Finn, son of Roigen Rúad, son of Easamain Eamna"—are omitted here for clarity. The title "king of Ireland" in early Irish literature corresponds to the kingship of Tara (a hill in County Meath, just northwest of Dublin), which was historically preeminent but never actually extended to control of the entire island.

2 *every wave that invaded Ireland* According to Ireland's "synthetic pseudohistory," represented primarily by *Lebor Gabála Érenn*, "The Book of the Taking of Ireland" (or "Book of Invasions"), which tries to reconcile Irish tradition with the Bible as a historical source, various waves of immigrants occupied Ireland before the coming of the Gaels and were almost entirely wiped out by floods, plagues, and war. See *The Celtic Heroic Age*, 223–71, for relevant translations.

3 *called Eochaid Feidlech because* *Cóir Anmann*, "Fitness of Names"—edited and translated by Sharon Arbuthnot as *Cóir Anmann: A Late Middle Irish Treatise on Personal Names* (2 vols., ITS, 2005–07)—gives different folk etymologies: *fedil-uch*, "long sigh," because of his grief at having to kill his sons when they rebelled against him; or because the ox-yoke was invented in his reign; or because he ruled for a long time (II, 104).

4 *triplets* Added for clarity.

5 *conceived Lugaid ... their own sister* Maeve's sister Clothru seduced her brothers so that they would be morally compromised and their rebellion against their father would fail. See "The Death of Maeve" for one version of the details. Clothru's son, referred to here as *Lugaid tri riab n-derg*, "Lugaid of the Three Red Stripes," is more commonly known as *Lugaid Riab nDerg*, "Lugaid of the Red Stripes" or "Lugaid Red-Stripes," and he became Cú Chulainn's foster-son* (see pp. 122, 336). The triplet brothers were all considered to be his fathers: he had horizontal red stripes dividing his body into three sections, each of which was supposedly contributed by one of his three fathers (see "Fitness of Names," II, 105). Lugaid has been studied in detail by Karen Burgess in "Disintegrating Lugaid Ríab nDerg: medieval Irish lore about a legendary king" (Ph.D. thesis, UCLA, 2004).

6 *Druim Críad* Now Drumcree, County Westmeath.

King Eochaid Feidlech had several daughters.[1]

There was Éile, wife of Fergal mac Magach. Bri Éili in Leinster is named after her. After Fergal, she was the wife of Sraibgend mac Niuil of the Erna, and she bore him a son, Máta mac Sraibgind, the father of Ailill mac Máta.

And there was Mugain "Prickly-Fuzz,"[2] wife of Conchobor son of Fachtna Fáthach,[3] the mother of Conchobor's son Glaisne.

And there was Eithne, another wife of that same Conchobor, and the mother of Conchobor's son Furbaide. He was called Furbaide because *furbad* means excision,[4] and he was excised or cut out from his mother's womb after she drowned in the river Bearramain, which is called the Eithne today—the river is named after her (i.e., Eithne). And Furbaide's real name was Diarmait.

And there was Clothru, the mother of Conchobor's son Cormac Conn Loinges. (Alternatively, Cormac's mother was Ness daughter of Eochaid Sálbuide.[5])

And there was Deirbriu, the namesake of the pigs of Deirbriu.[6]

And there was Maeve of Crúachu, another wife of Conchobor, the mother of Conchobor's son Amalgad.

---

1 *several daughters* Emended for clarity from "numerous offspring," since the sons have already been listed. Each of the daughters' first names is followed in the original by "daughter of Eochaid Feidlech," omitted in the translation.

2 *Mugain "Prickly-Fuzz"* Actually spelled *Mumain* here; but she is Mugain in the *Táin* and seemingly elsewhere else. Her epithet (here *Etanchaithrech*, elsewhere *Aitencaetrech*) is glossed in *eDIL* as "having furze-like body-hair."

3 *Conchobor son of Fachtna Fáthach* Conchobor mac Nessa: see the introduction to "The Birth of Conchobor," p. 62. In early Ireland, having multiple wives (polygyny) "was permitted, and probably widespread": see *GEIL*, 70–73.

4 *furbad means excision* Added for clarity: the text says only "because his *urbad* or cutting was done." When Furbaide's mother is said to be Eithne, her killer is Clothru's son Lugaid Red-Stripes, based on a druid's* prophecy that she would kill Clothru; Lugaid cuts Furbaide from the womb and ends up killing him seventeen years later. Burgess covers this in "Furbaide's tooth," *PHCC* 15 (1995) 42–55. "The Death of Maeve," below, has a different story of Furbaide's birth, according to which his mother was Clothru and Maeve killed her.

5 *Ness daughter of Eochaid Sálbuide* According to the different versions of Conchobor's birth-tale, this was Conchobor's mother, which would make Cormac's conception incestuous. (The tradition that has Fachtna Fáthach as Conchobor's father never says he had a different mother.)

6 *pigs of Deirbriu* These pigs have been investigated by Anna Pagé: see https://ulstercycle.hcommons.org/2024/10/28/derbriu-and-the-pigs-of-derblinne/. Pigs in general can have supernatural associations: see "The Pig-Keepers' Feud," p. 149 below.

Conchobor was Maeve's first husband, until she left him out of pride and went to stay at Tara with King Eochaid.[1]

The reason King Eochaid had given his daughters to Conchobor was that he, Eochaid Feidlech, had killed Conchobor's father[2] Fachtna Fáthach in the battle of Leitir Ruad[3] in the Corann, so he handed them over as compensation.[4] He also let Conchobor seize the kingship of Ulster, as opposed to Clann Rudraide.

So the first cause of the stirring-up of the Cattle-Raid of Cúailnge was Maeve's leaving Conchobor against his will.

Tinne son of Conra Cas, of the Fir Domnann, was king of Connacht at the time, and Eochaid Dála and Fidig mac Feicc, of the Gamanraid, were laying claim to the kingship.

Fidig went to Tara to rally the kings in his favor, and he asked Eochaid Feidlech for Maeve. Tinne got wind of this news and lay in ambush for Fidig. They met over the streams of the River Shannon, and Fidig was killed by the Children of Conra and Conra's son Monodar. That was the first cause of the war between the Children of Conra Cas and the Gamanraid.

Eochaid Feidlech committed a royal injustice against Tinne, driving him into the hinterlands of Connacht and installing Maeve in the royal seat of Crúachu. What actually happened, though, was that Maeve and Tinne kept up a relationship for a long time. And Maeve would host the fairs of Ireland at Crúachu, and the sons of the kings of Ireland used to be there with her, looking to trade blows in war against Conchobor's province. And Sraibgend mac Niuil of the Erna, and his son Máta mac Sraibgind,[5] came to Maeve looking to

---

1 *King Eochaid* Here and in the next sentence, the text calls him only "the king of Ireland."

2 *Conchobor's father* Added for clarity.

3 *Leitir Ruad* Otherwise known as Leitir Ruibhe, the setting for the 13th-century text *Cath Leitir Ruibhe* (Ó Corráin #1013), which has been translated by A.G. van Hamel, "The battle of Leitir Ruide," *Revue Celtique* 44 (1927) 59–67, at https://books.google.com/books?id=8qMZAQAAIAAJ&pg=PA59#v=onepage&q&f=false.

4 *as compensation* The word used is *eric* (*eDIL*, s.v. *éric, éraic*), which is normally translated "body-fine": under Irish law, this was the flat fee payable for a killing, on top of which one would also pay each member of the victim's kindred their respective honor-price.*

5 *his son Máta mac Sraibgind* Máta is normally identified as Ailill's mother (see the "Pillow-Talk" episode of the *Táin* and "The Death of Ailill and Conall Cernach," pp. 161 and 331 below), whereas Ailill's father is normally said to be King Ross Rúad of Leinster. The Erna are a population-group from Munster.

wage war against Conchobor over every grudge that existed between them.

Eochaid Feidlech held the Feast of Tara, inviting all the provinces of Ireland except Maeve and Tinne. The men of Ireland insisted that Eochaid bring Maeve to the gathering. Eochaid sent Searbluath ("Bitterspeed"), his woman messenger, to Crúachu to get her. The next day Maeve came to Tara and races were held at the fair for the next six weeks. After that the men of Ireland dispersed. Conchobor lingered behind the others at the gathering, watching Maeve, and when she happened to go and bathe in the Boyne, Conchobor came up on her there: he violated her and had sex with her against her will.

When people in Tara heard about this, the kings of Ireland rose up out of Tara, along with Tinne and Eochaid Dála. (Other versions say that Eochaid Dála had been killed by Tinne prior to that, fighting over the kingship of Connacht,[1] but that's not true.)

The banners of the king of Ireland were raised to attack the king of Ulster, and Tinne son of Conra challenged Conchobor to single combat. Conchobor accepted, and he happened to have Tinne's brother, Monodar Mór son of Conra, with him at the time, so he told Monodar to go smack down Tinne. Monodar said he would, and they had a bout of champions. Monodar killed Tinne: everyone said "What a feat (*écht*)!" and a druid* said "His name will be Mac Cécht[2] forever," and the name stuck.

Conchobor won the Battle of the Boyne against Eochaid Feidlech, and Sraibgend mac Niuil and his son died in the process. Eochaid Dála kept the fight going across Meath, over the green-streamed Shannon, and brought Maeve and the Connachtmen safely through thanks to his fighting prowess, so that no one challenged him from the Boyne to the Shannon.

The Fir Domnann, the Dal nDruithni, and the Firchraibi, from whom Eochaid Dála was descended, came to Crúachu after Tinne's

---

1 *of Connacht* Added for clarity.

2 *écht … Mac Cécht* An approximation of the wordplay here would be if everyone yelled (to borrow from the WWE's Legion of Doom) "What a rush!" and the druid* said "His name will be Mac Crush forever." But "Fitness of Names" (II, 120) interprets the *écht* element as 'murder' (cf. *eDIL* meaning I vs. meaning III): he was "a youth who committed the hardest murder to bear, i.e., he killed his own brother in combat."

death, because although they had broken up into three tribes, they had originally been one and the same, i.e., the descendants of Genann son of Dil son of Loch, and their background was Firbolg.[1] What they decided was that the kingship of Connacht should be conferred, with Maeve's consent, on Eochaid Dála. Maeve consented as long as he wasn't jealous, fearful, or stingy, because she had a *geis*[*] against marrying anyone with those three qualities.

Eochaid Dála became king via that process and spent a while in Crúachu as Maeve's husband.

That was when Ailill son of Máta, son of Sraibgend of the Erna, came to Crúachu. He was still a young child at the time, and had the rest of Sraibgend's children with him for Maeve to raise, because of her relationship to him, i.e., her sister Eile[2] was his grandmother.

After that, Ailill was raised at Crúachu until he was a heroic fighter in battles and skirmishes, and a tower of strength defending Maeve's province against Conchobor. He went on to become the head of her household: Maeve loved him for his good qualities, so he married her, and became her partner instead of Eochaid Dála.

This development made Eochaid jealous, and made all the Fir Domnann jealous out of sympathy for him. Their plan was to banish Ailill from Connacht, and all the Erna along with him, but Maeve wouldn't let that happen because she was fonder of Ailill than of Eochaid. When Eochaid realized she favored Ailill, he challenged him to single combat over the kingdom and the woman. Their fight was brutal, and Eochaid Dála was killed thanks to Maeve's trickery.

Ailill, with Maeve's consent, assumed the kingship of Connacht after that. He was king of Connacht when Conaire the Great was crowned king of Tara,[3] and at the start of the Táin against the Ulstermen.

---

1 *Firbolg* The Firbolg were people already living in Ireland when the supernatural Túatha Dé Danann[*] came there, and were defeated by them in the First Battle of Mag Tuired. The text about this battle (*Cath Maige Tuired I*, Ó Corráin #1018) has been edited and translated by John Fraser, "The first battle of Mag Tuired," *Ériu* 8 (1915) 1–63.

2 *her sister Eile* Paraphrased for clarity: the text says "Eile daughter of Eochaid Feidlech."

3 *of Tara* Added for clarity. The story of Conaire's reign is told in the saga "The Destruction of Da Derga's Hostel" (*Togail Bruidne Da Dergu*, Ó Corráin #1120), translated in Gantz, 60–106, and (abridged) in *The Celtic Heroic Age*, 166–84, and online in the older translation by Whitley Stokes at https://celt.ucc.ie/published/T301017A.html. The character Mac Cécht, first seen here as Monodar, appears in it as Conaire's champion.

Ailill was the father of Maeve's seven sons who were all named Maine.[1] And their original names weren't Maine, but as follows: Maine "Fatherlike" (*Athramail*) was Feidlimid, and Maine "Motherlike" (*Máthramail*) was Cairpre, and "Chatty" Maine (*Andoe*) was Eochaid, and Maine "Taciturn" (*Taí*) was Fergus, and Maine "Most Filial" (*Mórgor*) was Cet, and Maine "Honeyflower" (*Mílscothach*) was Sin, and Maine "Most Talkative" (*Mo-Epert*) was Dáire.

How come they were all named Maine? That's easy.* One day Maeve was at the gathering of Cluitheamnach and preparing to fight the battle of Finnchorad[2] against Conchobor, and she spoke to her druid:* "Which of my children will bring Conchobor down?" she asked.

"They're not born yet, unless they get rechristened," said the druid. "Anyway, Maine is the one who'll bring him down," he said.

So for that reason she slapped the name Maine on all of her sons, in case any one of them would be the one to bring down Conchobor, and those nicknames superseded their real names that they'd worn before.

Maeve thought the druid was referring to Conchobor son of Fachtna Fáthach, but it turned out to be a different Conchobor,[3] the son of the king of Scotland from across the sea. He was the one who fell there to Maine Andóe, son of Ailill and Maeve. The end.

---

1 *seven sons … Maine* The text says only "the Maines," which has been expanded for clarity, here and in the next paragraph. The name is pronounced "MAN-yuh." Their nicknames are glossed here according to "Fitness of Names" (II, 135), which says that *andoe* is equivalent to *antaí*, "non-taciturn," and *mó-epirt* should be understood as more talkative than the rest. But these two nicknames have been understood by others as "unslow, i.e., swift" and "beyond description," and *Mílscothach* has been glossed elsewhere as "honey-worded" (*eDIL*, s.v. *milis*, *-briathrach*). There is a slightly different list of their nicknames in the body of the *Táin*. The renaming of the Maines is discussed in general by Finn Longman, "Naming the seven Maines," *CMCS* 83 (2022) 1–18.

2 *the battle of Finnchorad* The saga focused on this battle (*Cath Findchorad*, Ó Corráin #1010) has been edited and translated by Margaret Dobbs, "The battle of Findchorad," *ZCP* 14 (1923) 395–420, at https://archive.org/details/zeitschriftfrc1314meyeuoft/page/394/mode/2up. This comparatively late and fragmentary text starts, instead of this business with the Maines, with the Connacht druids sacrificing "dogs, pigs, and cats" to "Mars, Osiris (?), J[upiter], and Apollo," and being told to bring the two great bulls which will be featured in the *Táin* to fight each other as a sign of which side will win the battle. The Brown Bull gores his opponent and sends him packing.

3 *a different Conchobor* Changed for clarity from "Conchobor, son of Arthur, son of Buide, son of Dungal."

The Story of Mac Dá Thó's Pig

*This text (*Scéla mucce meic Dathó, *Ó Corráin #1096, second half of the eighth century) appears with Recension 2 of the* Táin *in the Book of Leinster. It is often read as a parody: Ó Corráin, for example, says that "[o]ne of its purposes (and there are many) is to expose, with black humour, the dire violence, vulgarity, inhumanity, and sinfulness of the so-called heroic." Another thing it does is to present the state of the feud between Ulster and Connacht before Cú Chulainn rises to prominence (whether or not he is actually born yet). The primary Ulster hero at this time is Conall Cernach. The other Ulster heroes mentioned here—Lóegaire, Óengus, Éogan, Muinremor, Menn, Celtchar, and Cúscraid—all play a part in the* Táin *as well.*

*Here Conchobor of Ulster and Ailill and Maeve of Connacht are in competition for a dog named Ailbe ("AL-vuh"), belonging to the Leinster king Mac Dá Thó. The backstory on this dog is provided by "The Death of Celtchar mac Uthechair" (*Aided Cheltchair maic Uithechair, *Ó Corráin #959, ninth century),*[1] *according to which three puppies were found in the burial-mound of Conganchness ("Hornskin") mac Dedad, killed by Celtchar. The spotted one was this Ailbe; the brown one belonged to Culann the Smith (see Cú Chulainn's Boyhood Deeds in the* Táin*); and Celtchar took the black one and eventually had to kill it when it started ravaging Ulster.*

*While the rulers' focus is the dog, their warriors are more concerned with the giant pig that is served as the centerpiece of Mac Dá Thó's spread. The right to carve the pig is connected with the idea of the "Champion's Share" (*mír curad*), an honor awarded to the acknowledged top warrior at a feast. This appears to be related to a documented practice among the Continental Celts. For example,*

> [i]n the twenty-third book of his *Histories,* Posidonius [Greek historian and geographer, 150 BCE–c. 51 BCE] says that the Celts sometimes engage in single combat during their feasts. Arming themselves, they engage in mock-fights and sparring

1 This story has been translated by Kuno Meyer, *Death-Tales of the Ulster Heroes*, Royal Irish Academy Todd Lecture Series 14 (Dublin: Hodges, Figgis, 1906, at https://archive.org/details/deathtalesofulsteoomeye/page/n7/mode/2up) 24–31.

sessions with each other. Sometimes, however, wounds are inflicted and these mock-battles lead to real killing unless the bystanders restrain the combatants. Posidonius also says that in ancient times, the best warriors received the thigh portion during feasts. If another man were to challenge his right to the choicest portion, a duel was fought to the death.[1]

In this case the contest is supposed to be purely verbal, and until it degenerates into a brawl, it is not the role of the kings, including Fergus as a former king, to take part in it.

The translation uses the Irish edited by Rudolf Thurneysen in Scéla mucce Meic Dathó *(DIAS, 1934), at https://celt.ucc.ie/published/G301016/index.html.*

There was an illustrious Leinster king: his name was Mac Dá Thó. He had a dog. This dog defended the whole of Leinster. Its name was Ailbe, and it was famous throughout Ireland.

Ailill and Maeve sent messengers asking for the dog. And simultaneously, Conchobor mac Nessa sent messengers asking for the same dog. They were all made welcome and ushered into Mac Dá Thó's guesthouse.*

It was one of five guesthouses in Ireland at the time. The others were Da Derga's in the district of Cualu, and Forgall the Wily's, and Da Reo's in Breifne, and Da Coca's in western Meath.[2] It had seven doors, and seven gangways running through it, and seven hearths, and seven cauldrons. There was an ox and salted pork in every cauldron. Every man who came along was entitled to stick a fork in, and whatever he got on his first try was what he would eat. But if he didn't snag anything on the first try, he didn't get a second.[3]

---

1 Athenaeus, *Deipnosophistae* §4.40, trans. Philip Freeman in *The Celtic Heroic Age*, 10–11.

2 *Da Derga's … western Meath* Da Derga's is featured in "The Destruction of Da Derga's Hostel." Forgall the Wily appears in "The Wooing of Emer," below. Da Coca's is featured in "Da Coca's Guesthouse," summarized on p. 326 below. Da Reo's is in "Mac Da Reo's Guesthouse" (*Bruiden Meic Da Reo*, Ó Corráin #996), not covered in this book. For context, Cualu is the area south of Dublin that includes the Wicklow Mountains, and Breifne corresponds to modern Counties Leitrim and Cavan.

3 *Every man … a second* Kim McCone, *Pagan Past and Christian Present in Early Irish Literature* (Maynooth: An Sagart, 1990) 32, argues that this invites comparison with what happens in the Bible at 1 Samuel 2.12–17.

Mac Dá Thó had the messengers brought to his sleeping-compartment* to give them an audience before they got their food. They delivered their messages:

"We've come for the dog," said the Connacht messengers, "that is, to ask for the dog on behalf of Ailill and Maeve. And they'll give you a down payment of six thousand dairy cows, and a chariot, and the two best horses in Connacht, then give you the exact same thing again a year from now."

"And we've come to ask for it on behalf of Conchobor," said the Ulster messengers, "and Conchobor's no worse to have as a friend where treasure and cattle are concerned. The North will match their offer, and that will be the start of a beautiful friendship."

This sent Mac Dá Thó into a stupor: for three days he didn't drink, eat, or sleep, only tossed and turned from side to side.

Then his wife said: "You've been fasting a long time. You have food, but you're not eating it. What's wrong with you?"

He didn't answer her, so she said:

"Sleeplessness has come to stay with Mac Dá Thó.
He has something on his mind that he's not telling anyone.

He turns away from me, that fierce, brave warrior, and faces
the wall.
His clever wife is concerned that her husband can't sleep."

[He:] "Crimthann Nia Náir said:[1] Don't tell your secrets to
women.
They're bad at keeping secrets; we don't hand out treasures to
slaves."

---

1 *Crimthann Nia Náir said* Crimthann ("KRIV-thann") appears as a warrior killed by Cú Chulainn in "The Intoxication of the Ulstermen" (see p. 131), and is identified elsewhere as a king of Tara, the son of Cú Chulainn's foster-son* Lugaid "Red-Stripes"—which is hard to reconcile with the timeframe of the current story. For more misogynistic pronouncements from a legendary king, see *The Instructions of King Cormac mac Airt*, ed. and trans. Kuno Meyer (Dublin: Royal Irish Academy, Todd Lecture Series 15, 1909), 29–35, https://www.google.com/books/edition/The_instructions_of_King_Cormac_Mac_Airt/4-EOAAAAQAAJ.

[She:] "Even if it's a woman you're talking to, why not say it?
It doesn't cost you anything.
If there's something you don't understand, someone else might."

[He:] "Mac Dá Thó's dog:[1] it was a dark day when they came for it.
Many good men will die because of it. The fight over it will be beyond counting.

If I don't give it to Conchobor, that will be a dirty business:
his troops will leave nothing behind, cattle or land.
If I refuse it to Ailill, he'll decimate tribes across Ireland.
The son of Mágu[2] will carry us off, reduce us to bare ashes."

[She:] "I have advice for you about that: the results won't be awful.
Give it to both of them, no matter who dies because of it."

[He:] "The advice you're giving me gives me confidence.
Ailbe: god[3] sent him; no one knows who took him."

After that he got up and gave himself a shake. "Show us a good time," he said, "along with these guests who've come to us."

They stayed with him for three days and three nights. Then he pulled them aside, starting with the Connacht messengers.

"I've been very confused and worried about this," he said, "but it's all become clear to me now: I'm giving the dog to Ailill and Maeve.

---

1 *Mac Dá Thó's dog* Literally "the dog of Mes Roída Mac Dá Thó," giving the king a name or epithet that seems to mean "Fosterling of the Great Wood." The name *Mac Dá Thó* itself means "Son of Two Mutes."

2 *son of Mágu* There were seven sons of Mágu (see pp. 166 and 330), including the two in this text, Cet and Ánlúan. Especially since another one of the sons is named Ailill, their patronymic *mac Mágach* is often mixed up with the matronymic of Maeve's husband Ailill, normally *mac Mátach*, who seems to be the one Mac Dá Thó is referring to here. See Bart Jaski, "The strange case of Ailill mac Mágach and Cet mac Mátach," in *Clerics, Kings and Vikings: Essays on Medieval Ireland in Honour of Donnchadh Ó Corráin*, ed. Emer Purcell et al. (Four Courts, 2015) 440–51.

3 *god* Lower-case to reflect uncertainty about whether this is supposed to refer to the Christian God, since the timeframe here is definitely pre-Christian.

And they should come with pomp and circumstance to pick it up. They'll have food and drink and presents, and they can take the dog and welcome." They were thrilled.

After that he went to the Ulster messengers. "I've resolved my confusion," he said, "by giving the dog to Conchobor. And he should come in style to pick it up, that is, with all the Ulster nobles. They'll all get gifts and they'll be welcome."

He'd arranged for them to meet on the very same day, coming from the west and from the east, and they didn't neglect the appointment. Two provinces of Ireland showed up on the same day at the door of Mac Dá Thó's guesthouse.* He went out to meet them and bid them all welcome.

"We weren't expecting you, warriors," he said. "Still, you're welcome here. Come into the courtyard!"

Then they all trooped into the guesthouse, with the Connachtmen taking up one half of the house and the Ulstermen taking up the other half. The house wasn't so small: it had seven doors and fifty sleeping-compartments* between each two doors.

The faces at that feast were less than friendly. A huge number of them had feuded with others. The war between them was three hundred years before the birth of Christ.

Then Mac Dá Thó's pig was slaughtered for them. Sixty dairy cows had been devoted to feeding it for seven years. It must have been fed on poison, though, to bring about the slaughter of the men of Ireland over it.

The pig was served to them with forty oxen laid across it, not to mention all the side dishes. Mac Dá Thó himself presided over the feast.

"Welcome, everyone," he said. "All of this is less than you deserve. But the Leinstermen have plenty of oxen and pigs, and whatever you find lacking will be slaughtered for you tomorrow."

"That's a good-looking pig," said Conchobor.

"Agreed," said Ailill. "How's it going to be divided, Conchobor?"

"How else are you going to divide it," Bricriu mac Carbada called down from his sleeping-compartment,* "when you've got the elite warriors of the men of Ireland here, except by making it a competition? This won't be the first time you've all punched each other in the nose."

"So be it!" said Ailill.

"That's fine," said Conchobor. "We have lads in here who know their way around the border."

"You'll need them tonight, Conchobor," said Senláech Arad from Crúachain Con Alad in the west. "It's been plenty of times I've dropped them on their asses in the muck of Lúachair Dedad—plenty of times I've taken a fat ox off their hands."

"Not as fat as the ox I took off you," said Muinremor mac Gerrcinn. "I'm talking about your brother: Cruaichniu mac Rúadluim from Crúachain Con Alad."

"He wasn't any better," said Lugaid mac Con Roí, "than Inloth son of Fergus mac Léti, left dead by Echbél mac Dedad in Temair Lúachra."[1]

"What do you say," said Celtchar mac Uthechair, "to my killing Conganchness mac Dedad and cutting off his head?"

They went on arguing until in the end there was one man lording it over all the men of Ireland, i.e., Cet mac Mágach from Connacht. He hung up his weapons over everyone else's, and squatted next to the pig with a knife in his hand. "Now find me one man," he said, "out of all the men of Ireland, who can compete with me, or let me carve the pig!"

They couldn't find anyone willing to come forward. The Ulstermen were stunned into silence.

"Are you seeing this, Lóegaire?" said Conchobor.

"That's not right," said Lóegaire, "for Cet to carve the pig in front of us."

"Wait a minute, Lóegaire. Let's talk! You Ulstermen have a habit," said Cet, "whenever one of your boys first gets his weapons, he comes looking for us. So you came to the border. We met. You left behind your chariot, wheels and all, and your horses, and you only got away with a spear through you. You're not getting your hands on the pig like that."

Then Lóegaire sat down.

---

1 *Temair Lúachra* In west Munster: marked as Temair Lóchrae on Map 1. *Lúachair Dedad* is apparently in the same area. This was the territory of Lugaid's father. Why were the Ulstermen fighting down there? "The Intoxication of the Ulstermen," summarized on p. 131 below, gives one scenario.

"It's not right," said a tall blond warrior who climbed out of his sleeping-compartment,* "for Cet to carve the pig in front of us."

"Who's this?" said Cet.

"He's a better warrior than you are," said everyone. "That's Óengus mac Láime Gabuid ('Óengus son of Hand of Danger') from Ulster."

"Why's his dad called 'Hand of Danger'?" said Cet.

"Dunno—why?"

"I know," said Cet. "I came east one time. The alarm was raised. Everyone hurried up. So did 'Hand.' He threw a big spear at me. I threw the same spear back at him and took his hand off: it fell on the ground. What makes his son think he can take me?"

Óengus sat back down.[1]

"Bring on the next contestant," said Cet, "or I'll carve the pig."

"It's not right for you to carve it first," said a tall blond warrior from the Ulstermen.

"Who's this?" said Cet.

"That's Éogan mac Durthacht," said everyone, "king of Fernmag."

"I've seen him before," said Cet.

"Where did you see me?" said Éogan.

"Standing in your doorway while I drove off your cows. The alarm was raised across the whole country. You came when you heard it. You threw a spear at me and it stuck in my shield. I threw it right back at you and it went through your head and took out your eye. The men of Ireland can see you there with one eye:[2] I'm the one who took out the other."

---

1 *Óengus sat back down* Cet doesn't speak directly to the claim that Óengus is a better warrior: the father's shame, to which Óengus is linked by his patronymic glossed or reinterpreted by Cet, is apparently enough to discredit him. This happens again with Menn mac Sálchada below. While the dynamic here is specific to early Ireland (see next note), there is a timeless tradition in military lore of "badass" nicknames that are secretly anything but. This is well exemplified by pilot callsigns: see (informally) https://www.reddit.com/r/tumblr/comments/17vu1v9/nobody_is_ever_called_maverick_or_iceman_unless/ and https://www.f-16.net/callsigns.html, and (more formally) Ben "Lobo" Taggart, *What's Your Call Sign?: The Hilarious Stories Behind a Naval Aviation Tradition* (Atglen, PA: Schiffer, 2023).

2 *with one eye* A fascinating feature of this text is how physical impairments like Éogan's missing eye are mentioned not in the initial description, when a warrior stands up, but only after Cet has supplied the necessary detail to make them register as [continued ...]

Then Éogan sat down.

"Come on, Ulstermen, next contestant!" said Cet.

"You won't be carving it now," said Muinremor mac Gerrcinn.

"Is that Muinremor?" said Cet. "I just finished cleaning my spears, Muinremor. It hasn't been three days since I took three warriors' heads off your land, including your first-born son's."

Then Muinremor sat down.

"Next contestant!" said Cet.

"You got it," said Menn mac Sálchada ("Glory, son of War-Heel").

"Who's this?" said Cet.

"Menn," said everyone.

"What's this?" said Cet. "The sons of pissants with nicknames trying to compete with me? Because I was the priest who baptized his father with that name: I took off his heel with a sword, and he hobbled away with only one foot. What makes One-Foot, Junior, think he can take me?"

Then Menn sat down.

"Next contestant!" said Cet.

"You got it," said a big, graying, very ugly warrior from the Ulstermen.

"Who's this?" said Cet.

"Celtchar mac Uthechair," said everyone.

"Wait a second, Celtchar," said Cet, "unless you want to make this physical right now. I got to you, Celtchar, at your own front door. The alarm was raised. Everyone came. You came, too: you faced me in the doorway. You threw a spear at me. I threw one back at you, and it went through your thigh and the top of your balls. You've had bladder problems ever since, and you haven't fathered any sons or daughters since. What makes you think you can take me?"

Then Celtchar sat down.

---

shameful. For more on this, see Matthieu Boyd, "Modeling impairment and disability in early Irish literature," *PHCC* 41 (2024, for calendar year 2022), 35–82. Another recent contribution is Kim McCone, "Mocking the afflicted: morals and missing body-parts in *Scéla Muicce meic Da Thó* and *Waltharius*," *ZCP* 68.1 (2021) 197–248. The stories about the warriors' injuries here are echoed in "Fitness of Names" (II, 148–49).

"Next contestant!" said Cet.

"You got it," said Cúscraid Menn Machae (Cúscraid "the Stammerer of Macha"[1]), son of Conchobor.

"Who's this?" said Cet.

"Cúscraid," said everyone, "and he's the stuff of kings: just look at him!"

"No thanks to you," said the young man.

"All right," said Cet. "You came over to us the first time you got your weapons, boy. We met in the borderlands. You lost a third of your entourage, and here's how you got away: with a spear in your throat, so you can't get a proper word out, because the spear damaged your vocal cords. And you've been called Cúscraid the Stammerer ever since."

And that way Cet brought shame on the whole province.

As Cet was posing with the pig, knife in hand, they saw Conall Cernach come in. He leapt down into the middle of the house. The Ulstermen roared out a welcome to Conall. Conchobor took off his helmet and shook it triumphantly.

"I'm glad my dinner's ready," said Conall. "Who have you got doing the carving?"

"It's been conceded to the man there carving it," said Conchobor, "Cet mac Mágach."

---

1 *Cúscraid Menn Machae ... of Macha* The *Menn* element in Cúscraid's name is intertextually recognized as *2 menn* in *eDIL*, "stammering, inarticulate," but is homonymous with *1 menn*, "of persons, conspicuous, remarkable, notable," as in the name Menn mac Sálchada. (There is also *3 menn*, "a kid [baby goat]; a young animal in wide sense," and *4 menn*, in legal terms "a blemish, disfigurement, defect," which might derive from *1 menn* as "something conspicuous." Cet's reinterpretation of Menn mac Sálchada's name might extend to his first name as well, taking it from "Glory, son of War-Heel" to "Glaring Flaw, son of War Amputee." Actually, the English word "heel," with its possible meaning "ignoble person, villain [as in pro wrestling]," gives a sense of the linguistic flexibility involved.) When Cúscraid is first named here, he is said to be literally "the makings of a king (i.e., a royal heir) with respect to his appearance," so that his name might seem to mean "Cúscraid, the Glorious One of Macha." After the explanation of Cúscraid's impaired speech (which is *not* represented in writing as something like "You g-g-got it," so the audience doesn't immediately "hear" it when Cúscraid talks), Cet's statement translated here as "you've been called Cúscraid the Stammerer ever since" in fact presents the same name as before, Cúscraid Menn, in a context that disambiguates its meaning, possibly forcing some of the audience to reevaluate what they had thought it meant.

"Is that true, Cet?" said Conall. "You plan to carve the pig?"
Then Cet said:

"Welcome, Conall,
heart of stone,
savage frenzy of a lynx,
glitter of ice,
crimson force of fury
in the chest of a champion
battle-scarred and battle-winning.
Son of Finnchóem,
you rival me."

And Conall said:

"Welcome, Cet,
Cet mac Mágach,
home of a hero,
heart of ice,
a swan's plumage,
chariot-rider strong in battle,
raging ocean gale,
gorgeous burly bull,
Cet mac Mágach.

"It will be clear when we meet," said Conall, "and it will be clear when we part. Drovers will tell epic tales about us; leatherworkers[1] will bear witness. We two chariot-riders will stride forward into hardship, a furious fight with spear-shafts, trading deed for deed. One man will step over another in this house tonight. Now step away from the pig!" said Conall.

"What makes you think you're entitled to it?" said Cet.

---

1 *Drovers ... leatherworkers* Literally, "the man of goads ... the man of awls (or, with emendation, pegs)." Most people, following Thurneysen, take these as references to the lower classes as in my translation. William Sayers, "Conall's welcome to Cet in the Old Irish *Scéla Mucce mac Dathó*," *Florilegium* 4 (1980) 100–08, thinks that both terms refer to poets.* "It is inconsistent with the ethos of the aristocratic heroic society portrayed

"It's fair," said Conall, "for Cet to try to compete with me. I'll give you a one-on-one matchup, Cet. I swear* what my people swear, since I first had a spear in my hand, I haven't gone without killing a Connachtman every day and committing arson every night, and I've never gone to sleep without a Connachtman's head to prop my knee on."

"It's true," said Cet, "you're a better warrior than me. If my brother[1] Ánlúan were in the house, you'd have a whole other contest on your hands. It's too bad he's not here."

"He *is*, though," said Conall, pulling Ánlúan's head out from under his belt and flinging it at Cet so that it hit him in the chest and blood sprayed from its mouth.[2] Then Cet got up from the pig, and Conall sat next to it.

"Now let's get back to the contest!" said Conall.

The Connachtmen couldn't find anyone willing to come forward. But the Ulstermen put up a wall of bucklers[3] around Conall, because some bad men had adopted the bad habit of taking potshots across the house.

Then Conall went to carve the pig. And he took the end of the belly in his mouth, until he was done carving the pig. Then he slurped up the belly himself, i.e., as much as nine men could carry, leaving only scraps behind.

All he gave the Connachtmen was the two front legs of the pig, from under the throat. The Connachtmen found their serving small. They all stood up, then the Ulstermen stood up, and they went at each other. It started with a punch in the ear, and soon corpses were piled on the floor as high as the sidewall of the house, and rivers of gore came pouring out the doors. Then the mob broke open the doors and treated everyone to another round of drinks in the middle

---

in the Ulster cycle to suggest that a warrior like Conall would be concerned that his fame live on in other than his own noble class" (101), thus "'man of goads' may be a kenning for the poet, capable of both eulogy and satire" (101), and "the possibly satirical incitation symbolized by the goad is followed by the ambivalent check and challenge of the inscribed peg" (102). (Conall and Cet have a history: Cet is Conall's mother's brother. See "Fitness of Names," II, 141–42.)

1 *my brother* Added for clarity.

2 *from its mouth* Literally "his mouth." It's possible that this refers to Cet, because of how hard the head hits him in the chest. But most people read it as referring to Ánlúan: a sign that his head has been freshly severed.

3 *bucklers* Small round shields.

of the stockade, i.e., everyone was beating up everyone else. That was when Fergus grabbed a big oak tree that was standing in the middle of the courtyard, and tore it up by the roots.

Then they burst out of the stockade, and the battle raged on at the gate.

That was when Mac Dá Thó came out, leading the dog, to see which side it would pick, i.e., according to its doggy instincts.[1] It chose the Ulstermen and he let it loose to slaughter the Connachtmen, and they were defeated. They say it was on the Plain of Ailbe (*Mag n-Ailbi*) that the dog got hold of the suspension-beam* of Ailill and Maeve's chariot. Then Fer Loga, Ailill and Maeve's charioteer, struck it so that its body fell by the wayside and left its head embedded in the chariot-beam.[2] They say that's where the name "Plain of Ailbe" comes from—Ailbe was the name of the dog.

The rout continued northward.[3] At Dog's Head Ford (*Áth Cinn Con*) in Bile: that's where the dog's head fell off the chariot.

Heading west over the heathery moorland of Meath, Fer Loga, Ailill's charioteer, hopped down into the heather, and jumped into Conchobor's chariot behind his back, grabbing his head from behind.

"Watch out, Conchobor!" he said.

"Name your price!" said Conchobor.

"It's nothing much," said Fer Loga: "just for you to take me with you to Emain Macha, and for the single women of Ulster and the marriageable girls to sing songs about me every evening, saying 'Fer Loga's my loverboy.'" They had to do it, because they didn't dare go against Conchobor. And Fer Loga was allowed to go back west over

---

1 *its doggy instincts* *Rús con* is glossed by *eDIL* as "of a dog's instinct," but *rús* on its own is 'knowledge'; this is "an extraordinary dog," as a reviewer put it, "perhaps with a mantic power to foresee/choose winners and losers." The Irish doesn't distinguish "it" vs. "he."

2 "Fitness of Names" (II, 101), among other folk etymologies for the province of Connacht, derives it from "hound-slaughter" for this killing of the dog. The name Fer Loga seems to mean "Man of Lug": evidence of devotion to the pagan god who is Cú Chulainn's supernatural father?

3 *northward* This is followed by a list of placenames, moved here to minimize distraction: "over Belach Sen-Roírenn ('Old Roiriu Pass'), over Áth Midbine ('Half-Crime Ford') in Maistiu [the explanation of *Midbine* is given in Cú Chulainn's death-tale, p. 312 below], past Kildare, past Ráth Imgain in Fid n-Gaible ('the Fort of Imgan in the Wood of the Fork': now Rathnagan, County Kildare), to Áth Mac Lugnai ('Mac Lugnae's Ford'), past Druim-Dá-Maige ('the Ridge of Two Plains'), over Drochet Coirpri ('Cairpre's Bridge')."

Áth Lúain[1] a year later, taking two of Conchobor's horses with gold bridles on them.

That's the story of Mac Dá Thó's pig.

1 *Áth Lúain* See Map 2 for the location. The name is explained as "Loin Ford" in the *Táin*: see p. 282 below.

The Birth of Cú Chulainn

*This first recension of Cú Chulainn's birth-tale (*Compert Con Culainn, *Ó Corráin #1025, seventh century) appears with Recension 1 of the* Táin *in the manuscript* Lebor na hUidre. *As Ó Corráin notes, it comes from "the earliest surviving level of the Ulster tales, derived from the now-lost manuscript* Cín Dromma Snechta.*" The story covers how Cú Chulainn is conceived three times, and the arrangements that are made to foster* him.*

Like Conchobor, but even more so, Cú Chulainn has an unusual conception and gestation. He is conceived first by two Otherworld beings (call them "gods"), then by a god and a human, and finally by two humans. The first two iterations die, and we are to understand that each time, Cú Chulainn's spirit is recycled into the new fetus. This is consistent with what ancient Greek and Roman authors said about the Continental Celts and their druids,* which was that, like Pythagoras (compare Book 15 of Ovid's* Metamorphoses*), they believed in the transmigration of souls.*[1] *The god Lug is involved in the first and second conceptions, and the woman Dechtine is involved in the second and third. The effect of the three pairings—god–god, god–human, and human–human—is to channel or filter the power of the gods into the human world so that Cú Chulainn can access it as a man.*[2] *(The early Irish did see parallels between Cú Chulainn and Jesus, and "The Death of Cú Chulainn" highlights these explicitly.)*

The fact that Cú Chulainn has so many foster-parents makes it clear how special he is to the people of Ulster, and partly explains his extraordinary skillset, which extends to poetry and lore. His ongoing relationship with his foster-kin, especially Fergus, develops further in the Boyhood Deeds, and is crucial to the main plot of the Táin.

The two foals in this story, like the foal in the First Branch of the Mabinogi, *are what are termed "cognate animals" that grow up with a hero. But these foals are not identified by name as Cú Chulainn's horses Líath Macha and Dub Sainglenn, who are otherwise said to come out of lakes: see "The Death of Cú Chulainn," pp. 306–07 below.*

---

1 See *The Celtic Heroic Age*, 12, 31, 35, 36; compare 223–25 ("The Story of Tuán Son of Cairell").

2 See *Coire Sois*, 7–8, 53–56.

The translation uses the Irish edited by A.G. van Hamel in Compert Con Culainn and Other Stories *(DIAS, 1933) 1–8.*

Conchobor and the lords of Ulster were at Emain Macha.

A flock of birds used to visit the plain to the east and eat the land bare: root, grass, and stem.[1] The Ulstermen were sick of seeing their land destroyed. One day they hitched up nine chariots to go after them, since it was their custom to hunt birds.

Conchobor rode in his chariot with his adult daughter[2] Dechtine: she was her father's charioteer. The Ulster champions—Conall, Lóegaire, and so on—were in their own chariots, and so was Bricriu.

The birds flew away home ahead of them, over Slieve Fúait, Edmand, and Brega. Ireland had no hedgerows, fences, or stone walls in those days, just wide open fields. (It was like that until the time of the sons of Áed Sláine,[3] when there were so many households in Ireland that they introduced borders.)

It was sweet and lovely to watch the birds fly and hear them sing. The flock was made up of 180 birds, all in pairs connected with a silver chain. Each group of twenty flew in a separate formation; there were nine altogether. Up front were two birds joined by a silver yoke.

Three birds split off during the day and went ahead of their pursuers to the end of Bruig na Bóinne, the ancient necropolis on the river Boyne.[4] That was where night overtook the Ulstermen, and snow

---

1 *A flock … stem* The 9th-century saga "The Battle of Mag Mucrama" (*Cath Maige Mucrama*, Ó Corráin #1015) alludes to this or a similar bird-flock that ravaged Ulster in its description of the cave of Crúachu in Connacht as "Ireland's entrance to hell," out of which come various creatures that lay waste the land. See *Cath Maige Mucrama*, ed. and trans. Máirín O Daly (ITS, 1975) §§34–37, and https://reader.exacteditions.com/issues/55068/page/3. This kind of "stripping bare" is a characteristic move in the power games between human rulers and the Otherworld*: see *Coire Sois,* 330–41. Here, in Tomás Ó Cathasaigh's analysis the "theme of the Waste Land implies the need for a fecundating hero who will restore vegetation to Emain Macha": this would normally have been a future king, but Conchobor can't be depended on for righteous judgments per p. 37 above, so the Ulster Cycle turns to Cú Chulainn as "exemplif[ying] the vigorous young male as the vital force in nature" (*Coire Sois*, 54).

2 *adult daughter* Another version of this text calls her his sister, which is what she clearly is in the *Táin*. See *Coire Sois*, 72.

3 *Áed Sláine* A historical King of Tara (d. 604): see https://www.dib.ie/biography/aed-slaine-a0048.

4 *the ancient … river Boyne* Added for clarity. This is the complex consisting of the Neolithic passage tombs at Knowth, Dowth, and Newgrange, associated in Irish tradition with the Otherworld.*

dumped down on them. Conchobor told his entourage to unhitch their chariots and go find shelter.

Conall and Bricriu went scouting. They found a new house standing by itself. [1] They went in and met a married couple, who offered hospitality. Conall and Bricriu went back to the group. Bricriu said it wasn't worth going to a house that had no bedding or food; plus, it looked cramped. The Ulstermen went there anyway, bringing their chariots. There wasn't much room for them in the house. Suddenly a pantry door popped open in front of them, and in due course they were brought some dinner. The Ulstermen got tipsy and were in a good mood.

Then their host told the Ulstermen that his wife was in labor in her pantry. Dechtine went to help her. She delivered a boy. At the same time, a mare at the door of the house gave birth to two foals. Then the Ulstermen took the boy and gave him the foals as a present, while Dechtine nursed him.

When the Ulstermen woke in the morning, all they could see east of the Bruig was their own horses and the woman's son with his foals: no house, no birds.

Then they went back to Emain.

They raised the boy until he was a toddler.

Then he got sick and died.

They mourned him. The loss of her foster-son* hit Dechtine hard.

When she came back from the funeral, she needed a drink. She asked for a drink out of a bronze vessel, and someone handed it to her. Every time she raised it to her mouth, a little creature tried to dart out of the drink onto her lip. When the drink was all gone, she took the cup from her mouth and the creature jumped in when she took a breath.

---

1 *a new … by itself* In another version of the story, called *Feis Tige Becfholtaig*, edited by Kuno Meyer, *ZCP* 5 (1905) 500–04 (recension 2 for Ó Corráin #1025, second half of the eighth century to first half of the ninth, appearing with Recension 1 of the *Táin* in Egerton 1782), they hear Otherworldly music and proceed to a house that is very grand inside, with a crystal throne. The head of the household (Lug, but not named as such) explains that the birds were actually fifty Ulster women who had been missing for three years, and presents them now in human form: they are led by Conchobor's sister Dechtine, who is pregnant (no threefold conception here). Then the story moves on to the talk about fosterage. The taking of women by the Otherworld* is a theme that continues in Irish folklore: see Angela Bourke, *The Burning of Bridget Cleary* (London: Pimlico, 1999).

That night she dreamed that a man came near and spoke to her. He told her that she was pregnant by him; that he had been the one who'd led them to the Bruig, and with whom they'd spent the night; that the child she had raised was his; that the same child was now back in her womb, and his name would be Sétanta; that he himself was Lug mac Ethnenn;[1] and that the foals should be raised for the boy.

The girl was actually pregnant. The Ulstermen were seriously disturbed about this because she was not known to be married at all. They guessed that Conchobor had gotten her pregnant when he was drunk, since she used to stay the night with him.[2]

Then Conchobor married his daughter to Súaltaim mac Roích. She was mortified to go to bed with him while she was pregnant. When it was time for bed, she mashed her innards together[3] so she became a virgin again. Then she went to her husband.

She got pregnant again.

She had a son.

Culann the smith took him and became his foster-father.* The boy would go on to kill his famous dog when he was playing, and said to him, "*I'll* be your dog, uncle.*" That's why the name Cú Chulainn ("Culann's Dog") stuck with him.

When the boy was born, the Ulstermen held a meeting in Emain Macha. They debated which of them would raise the boy, and appealed to Conchobor for judgment. Conchobor said, "You take the boy, Finnchóem."

His sister Finnchóem[4] took a good look at the boy. "This boy has

---

1 *Lug mac Ethnenn* One of the Túatha Dé Danann* or pagan gods of Ireland, Lug is the protagonist of the important 9th-century mythological saga "The (Second) Battle of Mag Tuired" (*Cath Maige Tuired*, Ó Corráin #1019): the standard edition and translation is by Elizabeth Gray (ITS, 1982), at https://celt.ucc.ie/published/T300010/. *Coire Sois*, 135–54, explains how that text functions as "exemplary myth": a template for human heroes including Cú Chulainn.

2 *stay the night with him* Although here there is suspicion of incest, David Stifter comments that in general, the "expression 'to spend the night' does not imply any sexual connotation. It was a common practice in medieval Ireland for many people (including a group of males) to sleep together for warmth. Sleeping with the king was a sign of highest honour[:] it was awarded to the chief poet, for example" (https://listserv.heanet.ie/cgi-bin/wa?A2=ind1604&L=OLD-IRISH-L&P=R1660).

3 *mashed her innards together* Or possibly "she sewed together her labia," according to Pierre-Yves Lambert ("La tuile gauloise de Châteaubleau (Seine-et-Marne)," *Études celtiques* 34 [1998–2000] 57–115, at 106)—but that of course would not have destroyed the fetus.

4 *His sister Finnchóem* Pronounced "FINN-hoyv." "His sister" added for clarity. She is the mother of the hero Conall Cernach, whose father is the poet* Amairgen below.

won my heart," she said. "I feel about him like I do about my own son, Conall Cernach."

"There's not much difference as far as you're concerned," said Conchobor, "between your son and your sister's son.*" Then Conchobor chanted [*a difficult poem*].

"You take the boy," Conchobor said again to his sister.

"She's not going to raise him," said Sencha, "I will—because I'm strong and cunning and brave and a skilled fighter and educated and wise. I'm not remiss in my duties. I address anyone even before the king speaks to them, I see to it that they're heard.[1] I set right the Ulstermen's legal judgments and I keep them level-headed. Only Conchobor outdoes me as a foster-father.*"

"He'll be no worse off if I take him," said Blaí the Guesthouse*-Keeper. "My messengers can connect me directly to Conchobor. I invite the men of Ireland in: I keep them fed for a week or ten days. I support their artistic and military pursuits. I give them a venue to display and vindicate their honor."

"Shameless blather," said Fergus. "He's chosen a strong man who's close to him: I'm the one who'll raise him. I'm strong and cunning and diplomatic. I'm not short of wealth or status. I'm formidable in courage and fighting skill."

"Listen to me," said Amairgen, "and don't turn away. I'm qualified to foster* a king. I can be praised for every distinction, for my bravery, for my intelligence, for my good fortune, for my age, for my eloquence, for the fame and courage of my children. He may be a prince, but I'm a poet,* worthy of a king's favor. I kill every chariot-warrior. I don't defer to anyone but Conchobor. I don't fraternize with anyone but kings."

Conchobor said, "There's no point to this. Finnchóem can take the boy until we reach Emain,[2] and the judge[3] Morann will decide what to do with him."

They left for Emain, and the boy traveled with Finnchóem.

---

1 *that they're heard* Literally, "I provide for their/his address," so it could also be that he makes the king's wishes known, or, as Thomas Kinsella has it, "I advise him before he speaks."

2 *until we reach Emain* This is inconsistent with the earlier statement that the Ulstermen were already meeting in Emain Macha to decide this.

3 *the judge* Added for clarity.

Then Morann decided after they reached Emain, and he said:

"Conchobor should have overall custody, since he's related to Finnchóem. Sencha can teach him eloquence and oratory. Blaí can provide for him. Fergus can take him on his knee. Amairgen can be his teacher. Conall Cernach can be his foster-brother.* Finnchóem can give him a mother's breasts. Chariot-warrior, king, and chief poet* should play equal parts in shaping him, because this boy will be loved by the masses. And in turn, this boy will avenge all attacks on your honor; he'll triumph at your river-crossings and win all your battles."

Then what they did with him was that Amairgen and Finnchóem took him to the hillfort of Dún Imbrith on Muirthemne Plain.

In the Táin, *Fergus says that* "when Cú Chulainn was four years old he went to join the boy-troop at Emain Macha. When he was five, he went to learn weapon handling and martial arts from Scáthach." *These episodes correspond to Cú Chulainn's "Boyhood Deeds" and to "The Wooing of Emer" respectively. The Boyhood Deeds are part of the* Táin *(which is where they belong, according to "The Unveiling of the* Táin*"), pp. 181–83 below. "The Wooing of Emer" follows here.*

(Yes, Cú Chulainn is ridiculously precocious. This too is a feature of the International Heroic Biography: traditional heroes develop either much faster or, in the so-called "Ash-Lad" paradigm, much slower than everyone else.)

The Wooing of Emer

*This tenth- or eleventh-century reworking of an eighth-century tale (*Tochmarc Emire, *Ó Corráin #1113) appears with Recension 1 of the* Táin *in* Lebor na hUidre. *It describes Cú Chulainn's courtship of Emer, his wife-to-be, and his time abroad as a student of the warrior woman Scáthach. As a matter of folklore rather than history, her fort has been identified with Dunscaith Castle on the Isle of Skye in Scotland, although this text substitutes the Alps (*Ailpi*) for Scotland (*Alba*).*

According to Fergus in the Táin, *Cú Chulainn is five years old at this point.*

The coded conversation with Emer and its drawn-out explanations are important as a demonstration of Cú Chulainn's intellect and his mastery of poetic language and traditional lore (particularly dindshenchas,* *the lore of place-names), at least some of which he must have learned from his foster-father* Amairgen. (The rarified language in this section is densely annotated—"glossed"—in the manuscript with explanatory comments.) This hero is not just a pretty face, a world-class athlete, and a budding sex machine, he is also profoundly learned, and (as in the Boyhood Deeds and "The Death of Aífe's Only Son," below) highly conscious and deliberate about creating his own legend. (And, of course, he is also a blood-soaked killer and—at least in this story—an unabashed rapist, making him not an uncomplicated protagonist.) Meanwhile, Emer is something like his intellectual equal: if he thinks of her as a trophy, she is at least not a subservient trophy.*

Cú Chulainn's time abroad is important not only because he perfects his repertoire of heroic feats, including his ultimate weapon, the gáe bolga,* *that Scáthach teaches only to him. The relationships he forms with fellow students who become his foster-brothers,* such as Fer Báeth and Fer Diad, are crucial background for the pathos of his having to fight them in the* Táin.

The translation uses the Irish edited by A.G. van Hamel in Compert Cú Chulainn and Other Stories, *16–68. On a few points I consulted an unpublished translation by Patrick K. Ford included in his Harvard coursepacks. For important commentary on this tale, see Amy Mulligan,* A Landscape of Words: Ireland, Britain, and the Poetics of Space, 700–1250 *(Manchester University Press, 2019), Chapter 2. A now-classic study of Cú Chulainn's conversations with Emer in this and other stories is Joanne Findon's* A Woman's Words: Emer and Female Speech in the Ulster Cycle *(University of Toronto Press, 1997).*

There was once an illustrious, preeminent king at Emain Macha, i.e., Conchobor son of Fachna Fáthach. His rule was idyllic for the Ulstermen. They had peace, prosperity, and pleasure. Forage, game, and seafood were plentiful. The Ulstermen had law, order, and good government during his reign. Nobility, prestige, and abundance flourished in the royal house at Emain.

Now, this is what that house was like, i.e., Conchobor's Red Branch. It was modeled on the great mead-hall (*Tech Mídchúarta*[1]) at Tara, i.e., with nine rows of sleeping-compartments* from the central fire to the outer wall.[2] All the interior partitions were bronze, thirty feet high. There were carved panels of red yew across the lower part, with a tile roof above. Conchobor's compartment was at the front of the house, with silver paneling, and bronze pillars that had gleaming gold tops and were inset with carbuncle gems, making night as bright as day. The silver paneling extended overhead[3] into the upper reaches of the house. Whenever Conchobor would hit the paneling with his royal scepter,[4] all the Ulstermen would turn his way.

Immediately surrounding Conchobor's sleeping-compartment were twelve sleeping-compartments for chariot-warriors.

There was room for all of Ulster's warrior elite to drink in that

1 *Tech Mídchúarta* Literally "mead-circling house," also known to archeologists as the Banquet Hall, on the Hill of Tara. As a historical feature, this dates from between the 5th and 8th centuries. The text's account of it here has been described in detail by Mallory, *In Search of the Irish Dreamtime*, 162–71, as the "Standard Irish Palace Description"; compare the very similar description of Bricriu's new house in §2 of "Bricriu's Feast."

2 *fire … wall* Literally just "from fire to wall." Early Irish houses were circular, with an open space and a fire in the center, and rings of sleeping-compartments* outside that. The "Standard Irish Palace Description" has seven rows, and this is even bigger. The archeological site of Emain Macha (Navan Fort) is actually dominated by a mound covering the mysterious so-called "40-metre structure," a huge circular building which, soon after it was built, was filled up with rocks, set on fire, and buried, possibly to manufacture a ritual site or Otherworld* abode (see Mallory, 161–73).

3 *overhead* Literally, "above the king."

4 *his royal scepter* See Kaarina Hollo, "Conchobar's 'sceptre': the growth of a literary topos," *CMCS* 29 (1995) 11–25.

house without crowding each other. The elite warriors had a grand, glorious, gratifying time there. Every gathering in that house had everything in vast abundance, including wonderful musicians. There were martial arts displays and music and reciting, i.e., warriors put on the displays, and poets* did the reciting, and harpists and *timpán*-players[1] provided the music.

One time, the Ulstermen were with Conchobor at Emain Macha, drinking from the Iron Gulf (*Iarngúalae*), Conchobor's ale-vat.[2] It would be filled with a hundred batches of beer in an evening. It would serve all the Ulstermen in one sitting.

The Ulster heroes used to perform feats on ropes that ran from one door to the other of the house in Emain. The house was 195 feet across. The heroes used to do three feats:[3] the spear-feat, the apple-feat, and the blade-feat. The heroes executing those feats were: Conall Cernach ("the Victorious") mac Amairgin; Fergus mac Roích the Overbold; Lóegaire Búadach ("the Triumphant") mac Connaid; Celtchar mac Uthechair; Dubthach mac Lugdach; Cú Chulainn mac Súaltaim; and Scél mac Bairdini, the namesake of Bairdine's Pass (*Belach mBairdini*) and door-guard of Emain Macha: his tales were proverbial,[4] because he was a great storyteller.

Cú Chulainn outdid them all at those feats with his speed and dexterity. The women of Ulster adored Cú Chulainn for his speed with the feats, his manual dexterity, his outstanding intellect,[5] his beautiful face, his fascinating appearance. For he had seven pupils in his kingly eyes, i.e., four in one eye, three in the other. He had seven fingers on each hand, and seven toes on each foot. He had, first of all, the gift of wisdom, as long as his hero's light[6] didn't come over

---

1 *timpán-players* The *timpán* was some sort of musical instrument: despite its etymology (Latin *tympanum*), it seems to have been a stringed instrument, not a drum or tambourine.

2 *Conchobor's ale-vat* Added for clarity.

3 *three feats* These seem to have involved juggling javelins, balls, and knives respectively. See pp. 119–20 below for detailed notes on Cú Chulainn's repertoire of feats, which include these three.

4 *tales were proverbial* Actually the text says "whence comes 'a *scél* ("tale") of Scél's'": his name is identical or homonymous with the word for "story."

5 *his outstanding intellect* Manuscript variant: "his speech."

6 *hero's light* This is a feature of his mutation* in battle, when his wisdom would be overwhelmed by bloodlust.

him; the gift of feats; the gift of *búanbach*;* the gift of *fidchell*;* the gift of reckoning; the gift of prophecy; the gift of discernment; the gift of beauty.

Cú Chulainn's three faults:

He was too young, because he hadn't sexually matured,[1] which made warriors who didn't know him more inclined to disrespect him.

He was too daring.

He was too beautiful.

The Ulstermen held a meeting about Cú Chulainn, because all their wives and daughters were infatuated with him, since he had no wife at the time. The conclusion they came to was to find Cú Chulainn a woman he'd be interested in wooing, because they thought he'd be less likely to debauch their daughters and seduce their wives if he had a wife to look after him. Also, they were concerned and afraid that Cú Chulainn would meet an untimely death, so that was another reason they were eager to find him a wife, so that he could have an heir: they knew he had to be the one to generate another like him.

Then Conchobor dispatched nine men to every province of Ireland to find Cú Chulainn a wife: to see if, in any of Ireland's strongholds or major settlements, they could find the daughter of any king, overlord, or guesthouse*-keeper that Cú Chulainn might be inclined to pick out and woo. All the messengers came back a year later, and they hadn't found a girl Cú Chulainn was interested in.

Then Cú Chulainn himself went to woo a girl he knew about in Lug's Gardens (*Luglochta Loga*[2]), i.e., Emer, daughter of Forgall the Wily. So Cú Chulainn himself, and his charioteer, Lóeg mac Ríangabra, left in his chariot. That was the one chariot the armies and chariot-horses of Ulster couldn't keep up with, because of the

---

1 *sexually matured* The expression *renga rodaim* literally translates to either "the loins" or "the reins" (see *eDIL*, s.v. *1 reng* 'a loin' and *2 reng* 'a cord') "of a great ox" (*ródáim*). The "reins" could be mustaches, so that this should be translated "he hadn't grown any facial hair" (compare the issue of his beardlessness in the *Táin*, p. 222 below), but the apparent consensus is that this is a genital euphemism, belied by Cú Chulainn's sexual exploits later in this story.

2 *Luglochta Loga* On the plain of Brega, apparently near what is now Lusk, County Dublin.

speed and swiftness of the chariot and the warriors riding in it.

So Cú Chulainn found the girl on the playing-field surrounded by her foster-sisters.* They were daughters of the landowners[1] living around Forgall's stronghold. They were all learning needlework and handicrafts from Emer. She was the one girl out of all the girls in Ireland that he saw fit to talk with and to woo, because she had the six gifts, i.e., the gift of beauty, the gift of voice, the gift of sweetness, the gift of needlework, the gift of wisdom, and the gift of chastity. Cú Chulainn said that unless an Irish girl was his equal in age and beauty and pedigree (and skill and dexterity[2]), she wouldn't go out with him, and she wouldn't be an acceptable wife for him unless she had those qualities. And now she was the one girl who satisfied all those conditions. That's why Cú Chulainn had come to woo her in particular.

Cú Chulainn put on his best clothes[3] that day to talk to Emer and show off his beauty to her. The girls were sitting in the viewing area outside the stronghold, and they heard him coming: the clatter of the horses, the creaking of the chariot, the tension of the straps, the screeching of the wheels, the straining of the hero, and the squealing of weapons.

"One of you," said Emer, "look and see who's coming."

"What I'm seeing," said her sister Fíal,[4] "is two horses,[5] both big, both beautiful, both fast, both sprightly, with ears pricked up and heads held high, spirited, sublime, sinuous, thin-mouthed, with curly coats and broad foreheads, dappled all over, slender-waisted, broad-chested, aggressive, with curling manes and curling tails.

---

1 *landowners* Normally this word means "guesthouse*-keepers"—commoners who achieve the honor-price* of nobles by maintaining a high standard of wealth and offering free accommodation to all comers—but it seems to have a more general sense here.

2 *skill and dexterity* Not in all the manuscripts.

3 *best clothes* Technically, his "fair clothes," to attend major gatherings like the fair (*óenach*) where Macha is made to race the king's horses.

4 *her sister Fíal* Edited for clarity from "Fíal, daughter of Forgall."

5 *two horses* The ensuing description of the horses, the chariot, Lóeg, and Cú Chulainn is practically identical to §§49–51 of "Bricriu's Feast" (see pp. 129–31 below). The runs of adjectives used to describe horses in the Ulster Cycle have been catalogued and translated by William Sayers, "Conventional descriptions of the horse in the Ulster Cycle," *Études Celtiques* 30 (1994) 233–49. I adopt some of his suggestions.

"There's a gray horse, wide in the haunches, fast, feisty, spirited, sprightly, spry as a lynx, long-maned, strapping, thunderous, thudding, mane arched, head high, chest broad. Its four hard hooves ignite the stony sod. It overtakes an amazing bird-flock, champion flyers. Look at it go—it pulls a breath's length ahead of them. Blazing sparks of fire shoot out from its brindled jaws. It's yoked on the right side of the chariot-shaft.

"The other horse is jet-black, stubborn, sturdy, slender in the leg, broad in the hoof, fleet and furious, curly-coated, broad-backed, strong in the haunches, rough, tough, rugged, hard-stepping, springing, thick- and curly-maned, bushy-tailed, curly-coated, wide in the forehead, fast. It rushes off in search of conflict, as the horses are driven throughout the land. It gallops on grasslands, doles out destruction, roars like the wind over fields and valleys. As it barrels through the land of oaks, it meets no obstacle.

"The chariot is sanded smooth, banded with metal rings, its bronze wheels bright. It has a bright silver chariot-pole banded with white-bronze,* a towering frame—truly gorgeous—with metal fastenings, an arched yoke embossed with solid gold, and two braided reins of tough yellow leather. The shaft and axle-tree are stiff as sword-blades.

"There's a dark, brooding man in the chariot, the most beautiful of all Irishmen. He's wearing a gorgeous, five-layer crimson cloak. An inlaid gold brooch keeps it fastened over his fair-skinned, heavily pulsating chest. He wears a long-sleeved linen jacket with a white hood, embroidered with flashing gold. His irises glitter with seven red dragonstone gems. His cheeks are blue-white and blood-red, and glow with jets of fire and steam. A luster of love overwhelms his face. It looks to me like a shower of pearls fell into his mouth. Each of his eyebrows is black as the side of a scorched ruin.[1] Resting on his thighs is a gold-hilted sword, and fastened to the copper frame of the chariot are a blood-dark spear well suited to his hand, and a jagged jabby javelin, both with shafts of reddish wood. Slung over his back he has a crimson shield with a silver rim, covered in golden animal designs. He does the hero's salmon-leap into the air, among lots of other feats, besides just being a warrior with his own chariot.

---

1 *scorched ruin* This sentence is in *eDIL*, s.v. *folaig*, "ruin." Henderson, in his translation of "Bricriu's Feast," has "the side of a black spit."

"There's a charioteer in front of him in the chariot, super-slim, lanky, and super freckled. The hair on his head is super red and super curly, and he wears a white-bronze* headband to stop it from falling over his face; in the back he has it in a gold clasp. He wears a cape with sleeves that open at the elbows, and carries a goad made of red gold."

Parts of the conversation that Cú Chulainn is about to have with Emer are deliberately obscure, but are explained later: Cú Chulainn interprets them for Lóeg on the drive back.

Cú Chulainn greeted the girls.

Emer raised her lovely face and recognized Cú Chulainn. Then she said, "We turn sunwise* to you," i.e., may God smooth the way for you.[1]

"Safety from adversity to all of you," he said, i.e., may you be safe from all harm.

"Where have you come from?" she said.

"From *Intide Emna*," he said, i.e., from the fields of Emain.

"Where did you spend the night?" she said.

"We stayed with the man who watches the cattle on the plain of Tethra," he said.

"What did you have for dinner there?" she said.

"We were served the ruin of a chariot."

"Which way did you come?"

"Between two foundations of the woods."

"Which way did you take after that?"

"That's easy:* from the cover of the sea, over the great secret of the Túatha Dé Danann,*[2] over the foam of the two horses of Emain,

---

1 *We turn sunwise ... smooth the way for you.* The Christian gloss is inexact. Emer's greeting refers to the way a chariot is supposed to veer right or left to honor or insult an approaching chariot: she says that they are figuratively "veering to the right" in front of him, in other words that they welcome his coming.

2 *Túatha Dé Danann** The text actually refers to them here as the "Men of Déa." The relevance of all the lore about the Túatha Dé Danann and their rivals the Fomoiri* to the conversation between Cú Chulainn and Emer has been discussed by Marie-Luise Theuerkauf, "The road less travelled: Cú Chulainn's journey to matrimony and the *dindshenchas* of *Tochmarc Emire*," in *Landscape and Myth in North-Western Europe*, ed. Matthias Egeler (Turnhout: Brepols, 2019) 213–38.

past the Morrígan's garden, through the great sow's back, over the glen of the great Dam, between the god and his prophet, over the marrow of the woman Fedelm, between the boar and his mate, over the washing-place of the horses of Dea, between the king of Ana and his servant, to Monnchuile of the four corners of the world, over the great crime, over the remains of the great feast, between big vat and little vat, to the daughters of the nephew of Tethra, king of the Fomoiri,* here in Lug's Gardens, that is, your gardens. Now tell me about yourself," said Cú Chulainn.

"That's easy,*" said Emer. "Tara among women, fairest of maidens, the soul of chastity (i.e., just as Tara stands above all other hills, I am chaste above all other women[1]). A *geis** that goes unheeded, a lookout who is unobservant (i.e., everyone has eyes for me because of my beauty, while I have eyes for no one). I'm a worm in the water, a very bashful woman (i.e., when someone spots it, the worm goes into deep water). [...][2] I'm a road not traveled on (i.e., because of her beauty). A king's daughter is a glowing ember of nobility (i.e., of honor). A path not to be attained on your single-minded race [...].[3] For I have mighty men trailing me (i.e., I have champions always breathing down my neck) in case anyone comes to carry me off against their will, without them and Forgall knowing what I'm up to."

"Who are these champions who guard you?" said Cú Chulainn.

"That's easy: two men named Luí; two named Lúath; Lúath and Láth Goible, son of Tethra; Triath and Trescath; Broin and Bolar; Bas son of Omnach; eight named Connla; Conn son of Forgall. They each have the strength of a hundred men and the feats of nine. As for Forgall himself, it would be hard to list all his powers: he's stronger than any laborer, wiser than any druid,* cleverer than any poet.* In spite of all your tricks, it'll be too much for you to take on Forgall himself: he's all-powerful when it comes to manly deeds."

---

1 *i.e., ... women* These parenthetical comments are interpretations in the manuscript of what Emer is saying, rather than explanations that she gives herself.

2 This gap is for an obscure phrase, *Tethra tethra da lua.*

3 *single-minded race [...]* The rest of this sentence is obscure, although it seems to say something about sleep (*súan*), ancient death (*senbath*), streams of poems (*srethaib cerd*), and the glories of warriors (*adbchlosaib erred*): the point might be that Emer doesn't think the life-course Cú Chulainn has chosen for himself, oriented towards gaining praise and glory, is compatible with courting her.

"Why don't you include me as one of those champions?" said Cú Chulainn.

"If your deeds are talked about," she said, "why wouldn't I include you?"

"Girl, I swear," said Cú Chulainn, "that my deeds will be mentioned among the most glorious instances of warriors' might."

"Just how strong are you?" said Emer.

"That's easy,*" he said. "When I'm fighting at my weakest, I can hold off twenty. A third of my strength is a match for thirty. I can fight forty single-handed. A hundred are safe under my protection.* Crossings and battlefields are abandoned out of fear and dread of me. Armies, droves, masses of armed men flee before the terror of my face and my mere expression."

"Those are decent accomplishments for a tender boy," she said, "but you have yet to reach the full strength of a chariot-warrior."

"I've had a good upbringing, girl," he said, "at the hand of my Uncle* Conchobor. It wasn't the way a peasant schools his children. Conchobor didn't raise me in a world bounded by flagstones and the kneading-trough, or between the fire and the wall, or on some field by myself, but among the chariot-riders and champions, jesters* and druids,* poets* and scholars, guesthouse*-keepers and food purveyors of Ulster, so that I possess all their habits and talents."

"Who was it that raised you to do all these magnificent deeds?" said Emer.

"That's easy," *says Cú Chulainn, naming the elder statesman Sencha, the guesthouse-keeper Blaí, the great warrior Fergus, the poet Amairgen, the king's sister Finnchóem (to whom he owes the hero Conall Cernach as a foster-brother*), and the druid Cathbad, and listing the skills and qualities they each imparted to him. Lastly, he mentions how the god Lug impregnated his mother Dechtine at Bruig na Bóinne. This section is not copied from Cú Chulainn's birth-tale, but gives similar information. (For a conversation supposedly in code, this part seems remarkably transparent.) Cú Chulainn then asks about Emer:*

"And what about you, though? How have you been raised in Lug's Gardens?"

"I was raised," she said, "with the traditional Irish virtues[1] of behaving with restraint, of guarding my chastity, of queenly bearing, of beauty in my appearance, making me the standard of comparison for every noble, beautiful figure among crowds of glorious women."

"Those are certainly fine virtues," said Cú Chulainn. "Now, how about it—shouldn't the two of us get together? Because I've never met a woman who could hold up her end of a conversation like this with me before."

"I have to ask: do you have a wife," she said, "taking care of the house while you're away?"

"No, I don't," said Cú Chulainn.

"I can't get married before my older sister, Fíal, whom you see here next to me. She's exemplary at handicrafts."

"She's not the one I've fallen in love with," said Cú Chulainn. "And I've never accepted a woman who has known a man before me, and I'm told she slept with Cairbre Nia Fer at one point."

While they were talking, Cú Chulainn saw the girl's breasts over the neckline of her dress. Then he said:

"That's a lovely plain, the plain under the yoke."[2]

That's when the girl said these words to answer Cú Chulainn:

"No one gets onto this plain," said Emer, "unless he kills fivescore[3] at every river crossing from the Ford of Scénnmenn on the Ollbine, to Banchuing Arcait,[4] where swift Brea makes Fedelm leap."

---

1 *traditional Irish virtues* Literally, "with the virtues of the *Féne*," a population-name for the Irish often used in early Irish law.

2 *the plain under the yoke* Kinsella's translation, "I see a sweet country [...] I could rest my weapon there" (27), apparently uses *eDIL*'s definition of *alchuing* (s.v. *alchaing*) as "rack for hanging weapons, etc." But more recently Amy Mulligan, *A Landscape of Words*, follows other scholars in preferring "yoke": "The double yoke was, quoting Cyril Fox, 'rounded and peaked to a single terret on each side of the bar', so that, as William Sayers interprets it, 'The plain is the girl's abdomen. The images of yoke and plain beyond, drawn from the cultivation of the land, recall the overall wooing journey, the road that no one enters and, more importantly, the myth of territorial sovereignty (cf. the rounded hills called *dá chich Anann* [the two breasts of Anu]), who assured the fertility of the land, man and beast.'" Importantly, the context calls for a remark that is *not* as transparently sexual as "hey, nice rack": as far as the bystanders are concerned, Cú Chulainn is admiring the landscape.

3 *fivescore* Not an exact translation, but the Irish is a poetic paraphrase for the number 100.

4 *Banchuing Arcait* Kinsella read this, plausibly enough, as "the 'Woman Yoke' that can hold a hundred" (27).

"That's a lovely plain, the plain under the yoke."

"No one gets onto this plain," she said, "unless, my fine young calf, he does a 'gruesome gremlin'[1] while carrying someone plus the weight of another, striking down three groups of nine men with one blow, but sparing one man in the middle of each."

"That's a lovely plain, the plain under the yoke."

"No one gets onto this plain," she said, "unless he fends off the prodding of Súan son of Roscmelc from Samain* to Imbolc,* from Imbolc to Beltaine,* and from Beltaine to Brón Trogain."

"So let it be spoken, so let it be done," said Cú Chulainn.

"So let it be affirmed, confirmed, accepted, agreed," she said. "One more question: tell me about yourself."

"I'm the nephew of the man who disappears into another in the woods of Badb," he said.

"What's your name, then?"

"I'm the hero of the plague that infects dogs."

Then, after those cryptic words, Cú Chulainn left them, and they didn't have any more conversation that day.

As Cú Chulainn was driving back through Brega, his charioteer, Lóeg, questioned him:

"Now," he said, "the words you and that girl, Emer, were saying—what did you mean by them?"

"Don't you realize," said Cú Chulainn, "that I'm courting Emer, and that's why we hid what we were saying, so the other girls wouldn't realize we were flirting, because if Forgall finds out, he won't consent to us getting together."

Cú Chulainn went over the conversation from the beginning and explained it to his charioteer to "shorten their road."

---

1 *my fine young calf ... gruesome gremlin* The expression *genid gráinde a lóeg bó briuine* (or *genid gráinde, a lóeg bó briuine*, as I've translated it), uses obscure poetic language to refer to Cú Chulainn's "heroic salmon-leap," as Cú Chulainn explains later on and the end of the story confirms. Van Hamel tried to explicate the original expression as "a paraphrase or 'kenning'": "*Eó* = 1. *a salmon*, 2. *a brooch*; the brooch may be called *the helmet's she-calf* (*loeg bó briuine*). *Err* = 1. *a hero*, 2. *a tail*: *the ugly goblin* (*genid gráinde*) may be said to designate the tail. Thus *a tail from a brooch* would mean *a hero from a salmon*, i.e., a hero's salmon-leap" (185).

The explanations are long and sometimes cryptic.

The obscure term Intide Emna *(the* intide *of Emain) refers to Cú Chulainn's starting point at Emain Macha, about which two stories are told. One is how Macha was made to race against the king's horses and gave birth to twins on the finish line: see "The Ulstermen's Paralysis," above, for more detailed versions. The other explains how Ireland was once ruled by three kings—Díthorbae, Áed Rúad (Áed "the Red-Haired"), and Cimbáeth—who agreed to rotating seven-year terms, with 21 sureties,* 7 druids,* 7 poets,* and 7 warlords to ensure the peaceful transfer of power and the righteousness of each reign. After 66 years of this, Áed drowned, and was succeeded by his daughter and sole heir Macha Mongrúad (Macha "the Red-Maned"). Díthorbae and Cimbáeth refused to share power with a woman and Macha defeated them in battle. Seven years later she refused to give up power to Díthorbae's five sons, claiming right of conquest. Instead, she married Cimbáeth and allied with him, and then approached the five sons at their campfire, disguised as a leper. One by one she led them away, ostensibly to have sex with her (they thought she had pretty eyes for a leper), but in fact she overpowered them and tied them up one after another, then made them her slaves and had them dig the earthworks for Emain Macha after she traced them with her brooch: according to this origin story, Emain Macha would be named for* eó imma múin Macha, *"a brooch around the neck of Macha."*[1]

Then Cú Chulainn and Lóeg stayed with "the man who watches the cattle on the plain of Tethra": this is Conchobor's fisherman, Roncu, because Tethra was a king of the Fomoiri, ocean demons sometimes analogized to the Vikings, so the "plain" of Tethra is the sea, and the "cattle" of the sea are the fish that Roncu catches.*

"We were served the ruin of a chariot" means that the food on offer was a foal, because there is a geis* *against riding in a chariot for three weeks after eating horse meat. This is because "a horse sustains the chariot," and eating horse meat compromises the integrity of that relationship. (It's*

---

1 For more extensive comments on these Macha stories, see Toner, "Macha and the invention of myth." The story about Macha and the sons of Díthorbae is found separately as Ó Corráin #1082.

unclear whether Cú Chulainn and Lóeg actually ate any. According to his death-tale, it would be taboo for Cú Chulainn to pass a cooking-pot without tasting the contents, but that geis* *isn't mentioned here.)*

"Two foundations of the woods" refers to the mountains Slieve Fúait and Slieve Gullion; they traveled through the woods between them.

*"The cover of the sea" is Muirthemne Plain, which was covered by the sea for thirty years "after the deluge," or else by a magical sea that was dispelled by the Dagdae of the Túatha Dé Danann.**

"The great secret of the Túatha Dé Danann" is where the Túatha Dé Danann secretly laid plans for the Second Battle of Mag Tuired against the Fomoiri. Cú Chulainn gives its current name as the Marsh of Dolluid, named after a son of Cairbre Nia Fer who was killed there.*

"Over the foam of the two horses of Emain" refers to an ancient king, Nemed, who had two horses reared for him by the Túatha Dé Danann in the Otherworld: when they released them, a stream burst from the Otherworld abode and covered the land for a year, and the place where that sea-foam was produced is called Úanub.*

*"The Morrígan's garden" is Óchtar nEdmainn, a place given to the Morrígan by the Dagdae, where she killed a relative of hers a year later, and pig-fennel (*feniculus porcinus*) grew in her garden as a result.*

"Over the great sow's back" refers to the ridge of Druimne Breg (or Druim nEbreg), because, when the Sons of Míl (the Gaels) were taking possession of Ireland from the Túatha Dé Danann, they were magically shown the shape of a sow on the hilltops.

*"The glen of the great Dam," which looks as if it could be "the glen of the great ox/stag (*dam*)," is actually supposed to be named after King Dam Dile, son of Smirgoll, son of Tethra, who lived there. The same location is identified as Glen mBreogain, said to be named for Breoga mac Breoguinn of the Sons of Míl, along with the plain of Brega.*

"Between the god and his prophet" refers to Óengus of the Túatha Dé Danann, also known as the Mac Óc *("Young Son"), who lived at Bruig*

na Bóinne, and the prophetic druid Bresal, who lived further west. Cú Chulainn passed between the two at a place named after Mairne, the wife of the Túatha Dé Danann* smith Goibniu.*

"Over the marrow of the woman Fedelm" refers to a part of the river Boyne. The name Boyne is from the goddess Bóann, wife of Nechtan, who was the custodian of a well that no one could drink from unless they were escorted by Nechtan's three cupbearers. Queen Fedelm, wife of Núadu, thought she was above this and would suffer no ill effects. She walked around the well counterclockwise out of disrespect. The well overflowed, crushing her legs, her right arm, and one eye: she fled to the sea with the water pouring after her, and different sections of the river were named after her thigh, forearm, and marrow.

"Between the boar and his mate" refers to Cleitech and Fessi, which are etymologically relatable to the animals.

"Over the washing-place of the horses of Dea" refers to where the Túatha Dé Danann washed their horses after the Battle of Mag Tuired, a place otherwise known as Ange after the king who owned the horses.*

"Between the king of Ana and his servant" refers to Cerna and Ráth Gniad, places named for the killing of King Cerna of Ana and his steward Gnia.

"To Monnchuile of the four corners" relates the placename Muin Chille or Uachtar Mannchuile to a farmer named Mann who took his cattle underground, into some kind of squared-off trench, to protect them during a time of cattle plague.

"The great crime" etymologizes Ailbine, the river Delvin. King Rúad mac Rigduinn of Munster set sail to meet with foreigners, and his ships got stuck in the middle of the sea for no clear reason. When lightening their cargo didn't help, they drew lots to throw someone overboard, and Rúad was chosen. Under the sea he found a plain with nine beautiful women who offered him gold to sleep with all of them: they said they had stopped the ships because they wanted him. When he did, one told him she would have a son, and he should stop there to pick up the boy on

his way home. He spent seven years abroad and went home by another route, so the women delivered his son to the bay of Ailbine, where the king and his men were, and played otherworldly music to them. The harbor was rocky and the boy seems to have hit his head on one of the rocks and died. The women started lamenting and called out "Ollbine," glossed as binne oll, *'great crime,' and so gave Ailbine its name.*

*"The remains of the great feast" refers to Taillne, where there was a great feast for Lug after his victory in the Second Battle of Mag Tuired and he assumed the kingship of the Túatha Dé Danann.**

"The daughters of the nephew of Tethra" means the daughters of Forgall, who is called the sister's son of Tethra, king of the Fomoiri.**

Cú Chulainn's self-identification as "the nephew of the man who disappears into another in the woods of Badb" refers to two rivers in Crích Rois (modern County Louth), the Conchobor and the Dofolt (glossed as do-fholt, *"hairless," i.e., bald), the one flowing into the other. Cú Chulainn is both the* nia *'nephew; sister's son' and* nia *'champion' of Conchobor. Crích Rois is "the woods of Badb" because it belongs to the Morrígan, who is the "carrion crow" (*badb*) of battle, also called Bé Néit, the war-goddess who is the mate of the war-god Néit.*

"The hero of the plague that infects dogs" means that Cú Chulainn is effectively a "rabid" warrior: "that is, I'm fierce and ruthless in battles and conflicts." *He doesn't specifically link this to his name Cú Chulainn. He continues:*

"When I said 'That's a lovely plain, the plain under the yoke,' I wasn't praising the plain of Brega, but the girl's physique. I could see the yoke-shaped curve of her chest through the gap in her shirt, and that's why I said 'the plain under the yoke' as a comment on the girl's breasts.

"When *she* said 'No one gets onto this plain unless they kill fivescore,' *fivescore* is poetic language for *one hundred*. That's the interpretation, and what it means is that it's not so easy to run off with the girl unless I kill a hundred men at every ford from the Ollbine to the Boyne, including Scennmenn the Wily, her father's sister, who'll turn into all kinds of things to wreck my chariot and cause my death," said Cú Chulainn.

"That 'gruesome gremlin' stuff she said meant she wouldn't come with me unless I did the hero's salmon-leap across three stockades to get to her. Because she has three brothers guarding her, Ibur, Scibur, and Catt, each in a nine-man squad, and I need to strike each group so that eight of them die without putting a scratch on her brothers, and then I need to carry her and her foster-sister* out of Forgall's stronghold along with their weight in gold and silver.

"When she mentioned the prodding of Súan son of Roscmelc,[1] what that means is that I have to go without sleep from Samain* on, which is *sam-fuin*, 'the waning (*fuin*) of summer (*sam*).' Because the year was once in two parts, summer from Beltaine* to Samain and winter from Samain to Beltaine. Or else Samain means ..."

Now Cú Chulainn explores possible etymologies for Samain (November 1), Imbolc (February 1), Beltaine (May 1), and Brón Trogain (August 1, otherwise called Lugnasad). He suggests "gentle sounds" for Samain, "sheep-milking" for Imbolc, "auspicious fire" lit by druids* or the placing of livestock under the protection of the idol "Bel" for Beltaine, and "sorrow of the earth" (at the coming of fall) for Brón Trogain.*

Cú Chulainn kept on driving and stayed at Emain Macha that night.

Emer's foster-sisters[2] told their parents[3] about the young warrior who had come in his splendid chariot, and the conversation he had

1 *Súan son of Roscmelc* Cú Chulainn doesn't comment on the name, but it translates to "Slumber, son of Shut-Eye," or maybe "Slumber, son of Eye-Gunk." It's not clear whether *benn*, normally "horn; prong, point," which I've translated "prodding," is supposed to be part of the name. Van Hamel took it as a reference to a sleeping-thorn (Modern Irish *biorán súain*, as at https://www.duchas.ie/en/cbes/4811622/4803053/5018439: "No sooner did he pull the sleeping-thorn out of her head than she woke up"), and suggested "who does not strike off the sleeping thorn, who does not avoid sleep" (145). Or it could even have sexual overtones: compare the English expression "in the arms of Morpheus" (according to Peter V. Macdonald in *Court Jesters* [Toronto: Methuen, 1985], 198, when a Canadian lawyer used this expression to accuse a truck driver of being asleep at the time of an incident, the answer was "I don't even know him. Does he live in Chetwynd?").

2 *Emer's foster-sisters* Replaces "the girls" for clarity.

3 *their parents* Literally "the landowners," mentioned above as the parents of the foster-sisters.

had with Emer, and that they didn't know what they'd said to each other, and that he'd driven away northward over Brega Plain. The landowners reported it to Forgall, including everything the girl had said to Cú Chulainn.

"It's true," said Forgall, "the mutant* from Emain Macha came and talked to Emer, and the girl fell in love with him, and that's why they were talking to each other. It won't do them any good," he said. "I will forestall them (i.e., I will interfere) so they won't succeed in getting what they want."

Then Forgall the Wily went to Emain Macha dressed in foreign clothes, posing as a messenger from a foreign king to talk to Conchobor. He brought him golden treasure from the Fairhaired Foreigners,[1] and all kinds of other goods. He—there were three men altogether—received a hearty welcome. After he'd sent away his escort on the third day, they regaled him with praise of Cú Chulainn, Conall, and other Ulster heroes. He said that was true, that the heroes performed amazingly, it was just that if Cú Chulainn were to go to Domnall the Soldierly in the Alps,[2] his skill would be even more amazing, and if he went to learn martial arts from Scáthach, he'd outclass the champions of all Europe. But, of course, his reason for suggesting this to Cú Chulainn was so he'd never come back. He figured that if Cú Chulainn got friendly with him,[3] the ruthlessness and temper of that warrior would lead to his death—or so he thought.

Cú Chulainn agreed to go and do that, and Forgall extracted guarantees from him to leave immediately.

Forgall went home, and the elite warriors got up the next day and got ready to do what they had promised. Cú Chulainn, Lóegaire Búadach and Conchobor set out, and some say Conall Cernach also came with them.

---

1 *Fairhaired Foreigners* The Norse, typically Norwegians or Icelanders in contrast to the Darkhaired Foreigners, the Danes, or the Gray Foreigners, the Anglo-Normans.

2 *the Alps* Cú Chulainn is normally said to have trained in Scotland (*Alba*): the Alps (*Ailpi*) are a confused or deliberate change to a setting that will better accommodate Cú Chulainn's long journey through unknown terrain.

3 *with him* While Forgall might be talking about the risk to himself if Cú Chulainn stays in Ireland to court his daughter, he most likely means the prospect of Cú Chulainn interacting with Domnall; one manuscript has "her friendship" instead of "his," which would be Scáthach rather than Emer.

Then Cú Chulainn crossed Brega to visit Emer. He talked to her before he set sail. She told him it had been Forgall who'd been to Emain and suggested he should go and study martial arts, so that he and Emer couldn't meet. She told him to stay alert everywhere he went to stop Forgall from destroying him. They both promised to stay chaste for each other[1]—unless one of them died in the meantime—until they met again. They said goodbye to each other and Cú Chulainn left for the Alps.

Then, when they reached Domnall, he taught them a trick (i.e., a feat) that involved heating a perforated flagstone with bellows: they would perform on it until the soles of their feet were black and livid. He taught them to climb up a spear and perform on its point.

Then Domnall's daughter fell in love with Cú Chulainn. Her name was Dornolla, which means "big-fisted" (*olldornae*). She was incredibly ugly. Her knees were huge, and she had her heels in front and her feet facing backwards. She had dark-gray bulging eyes. Her face was blacker than a bowl of jet.[2] She had a massive forehead. Her hair was a wild, bright red tangle coiled round her head. Cú Chulainn refused to go to bed with her, and she swore she'd take a handsome revenge.

Domnall said that Cú Chulainn's training wouldn't be second nature (i.e., ingrained) until he went to Scáthach, who lived to the east of the Alps. Then the four of them—Cú Chulainn,

---

1 *stay chaste for each other* Literally, "each of them promised their counterpart preservation of their *genas*." The translation "purity, chastity" would be obvious except for two things: *genas* can also mean "procreation, conception; sexual union?" (*eDIL*, s.v. *2 genas* in contrast to *1 genas*), and Cú Chulainn flagrantly violates his supposed promise. I suspect this of being deliberate wordplay on Cú Chulainn's part, where Emer understands him to be pledging to stay chaste and he willfully misunderstands himself to be pledging to keep up his virility (while naturally expecting *Emer* to stay chaste). As evidence that Cú Chulainn is capable of this kind of manipulation, look at how he treats the son he has with Aífe.

2 *blacker than a bowl of jet* This blackness, unless it refers to dirt or soot, is more likely meant as a stereotypical description of supernatural appearance than an identifier of what we now would recognize as race. However, associating blackness with unattractiveness can be read as proto-racist, regardless of the provenance. Unlike here, the word used in early Irish for the skin color of people from Africa was *gorm*, otherwise translated "blue": see Matthieu Boyd, "Celts seen as Muslims, Muslims seen by Celts in medieval literature," in *Contextualizing the Muslim Other in Medieval Christian Discourse*, ed. Jerold C. Frakes (New York: Palgrave Macmillan, 2011) 21–38.

King Conchobor of Ulster, Conall Cernach, and Lóegaire the Triumphant—traveled across the Alps. Then Emain Macha appeared in front of them, and Conchobor, Conall, and Lóegaire couldn't pass it by. Domnall's daughter had called up that mirage to separate Cú Chulainn from the group and cause his destruction.

Other versions say it was Forgall the Wily who called up the mirage to make them turn back, so that Cú Chulainn wouldn't get what he'd been promised in Emain, and he would be disgraced for turning back. Or else, if he did continue east to learn the martial arts, i.e., the accustomed and unaccustomed use of weapons, he'd be more likely to die if he was on his own.

Then Cú Chulainn willed himself to go ahead without them (i.e., that was his decision). The way forward was unclear and unfamiliar, because the girl had supernatural powers and had bedeviled him so that he got separated from the group. As Cú Chulainn made his way across the Alps, he was sad and depressed about losing his companions, and he didn't know where to find Scáthach. But he had promised his companions that he wouldn't return to Emain without finding Scáthach, or else he would die. So, realizing he was disoriented and clueless, he paused.

As he was standing there, he saw a big, terrible beast, like a lion, coming toward him. It watched him but didn't do him any harm. Whichever way he went, the monster cut him off, turning sideways in front of him. Then he hopped up on its back. He didn't try to steer it, but let it go where it liked. They traveled like that for four days, until they reached the edge of settled territory and saw an island where troops of boys were playing.[1] They laughed in shock at that vicious monster submitting to anyone. Then Cú Chulainn jumped off and parted ways with the monster, giving it his blessing.

He kept going, and happened upon (i.e., he arrived at) a big house

---

1 *playing* The Irish is *oc immáin lochdáin. Immáin* is "playing" or "wandering around"; *lochán* is usually a "small lake, pool" (*eDIL*, s.v. *lochan*), hence Meyer had "rowing on a small loch," but van Hamel thought it was a kind of game. ("Playing pool" would be a facetious translation, but setting that alongside "playing in a pool," which means something very different, shows the nature of the problem.) As Richard A.V. Cox and Colm Ó Baoill comment in their Scottish Gaelic translation of this tale in *Trì Seann Sgeulachdan* (Perthshire: Clann Tuirc, 2015), "if *immáin lochdáin* is some type of shinty [game], scholars don't (yet) know exactly what kind of game it was: cf. *lúthán* 'little feat or exploit' (DIL)" (64n62, my translation).

in a deep valley. He found a beautiful girl inside. The girl spoke to him and welcomed him: "It's nice to see you, Cú Chulainn," she said. He asked her how she knew him. She said they'd both been foster-children* of Wulfkin (*Ulbecán*) the Saxon, "when I was there and you were learning[1] eloquence from him." The girl gave him a drink and a meal, then he went on his way.

Then he met another remarkable warrior who offered him the same hearty welcome. They traded news, and Cú Chulainn asked him for information about Scáthach's stronghold. The young man gave him the information he needed to cross the unlucky plain that lay ahead of him. On the first half of the plain, a person would freeze, i.e., their feet would get stuck; on the other half, the grass would rise and trap them on its points. The man gave him a wheel and told him to cross half the plain by running the same way as the wheel, and he wouldn't get frozen. Then he gave him an apple and told him to follow the apple's track along the ground, and that way he could make it all the way across. Cú Chulainn took off (i.e., he went on) like that across the plain, and kept on going after that.

The young man had also told him there was a deep valley ahead of him with a single narrow path across it, and it was full of ghouls (i.e., horrors) that Forgall had sent there to destroy him, and then that would be the way for him to get to Scáthach's place, across a stony, terrifying height.

They had said goodbye to each other after that, Cú Chulainn and the young man. His name was Éochu Báirche, and he was the one who taught Cú Chulainn what to do to win honor at Scáthach's place. Then the same young man revealed to him what trials and tribulations he would suffer during the Cattle-Raid of Cúailnge; he told him what evils, exploits, and encounters he would inflict on the men of Ireland.

Cú Chulainn took that route across the unlucky plain and through the dangerous valley, as the young man had explained to him. The way he went took him straight into the camp where Scáthach's students were staying. He asked them where she was.

"On that island over there," they said.

---

1 *I was … learning* I follow Sayers, "Concepts of eloquence," 125, as opposed to "when I was there with you, [both] learning."

"Which way do I take to get there?" he said.

"The Students' Bridge," they said, "and no one gets across unless they've had warrior training."

Because the bridge was like this: it was low at both ends and high in the middle, and whenever anyone stood on one end, the other end would fly up at them and knock them flat.

What other versions of the story say here is that there was a crowd of Irish elite warriors there in the stronghold, learning feats from Scáthach: Fer Diad mac Damáin, Noísiu mac Uisnig, Lóch Mór mac Egomais, Fíamain mac Forai, and countless others. But this version doesn't mention them being there at this point.

Anyway, Cú Chulainn tried three times to cross the bridge, and failed. The men jeered at him. Then he mutated,* and jumped onto the start of the bridge. He made the hero's salmon-leap from there to the middle of it, and got to the other end of the bridge before it had time to rise. Then he hopped from there onto the island. He went up to the fort and knocked on the door with the butt of his spear so hard it went through.

Scáthach was told. "Ah," she said, "this is someone who's had training somewhere else."

And she sent her daughter to find out who the young man was.

So Scáthach's daughter Úathach[1] went to meet him. She looked at him but couldn't say anything: she was too turned on at the sight of the young man's stunning physique.

"That man has caught your fancy," said her mother, "I can tell."

"Too true," said the girl.

"Then get him into bed," she said, "and sleep with him tonight, if that's what you want."

"I wouldn't mind that at all," she said, "if he's into it."

Then the girl served him food and water, and stayed to entertain him. She showed him hospitality (i.e., welcome), disguised as a servant, i.e., taking advantage of the situation.[2] He (i.e., Cú Chulainn)

---

1 *Úathach* Pronounced "OO-uh-thock." The usual meaning is "horrible, dreadful," and perhaps in this case "spectral, ghostly," as if her beauty is ethereal and a little terrifying (*eDIL*, s.v. *1 úathach*, and compare *úath*). But "singular, exceptional" might be more flattering (s.v. *2 úathach*).

2 *taking advantage of the situation* Literally, "while getting *greimm* out of it/him," which Kuno Meyer read as "profiting by it"; van Hamel glossed *greimm* as "force, vigour"

was rough with her[1] and hurt her finger. The girl screamed. It roused (i.e., alerted) the whole stronghold: everyone got up. Then a mighty man, Cochair Cruibne, Scáthach's champion in battle, confronted him. He and Cú Chulainn attacked each other and fought for a long time. Then the champion resorted to his special moves, and Cú Chulainn reacted as if he'd studied them his whole life: he brought down the champion and cut his head off. Seeing that this made Scáthach sad, Cú Chulainn told her he would take over the man's duties and obligations, succeeding him as her champion and the leader of her army.

And then Úathach came along and chatted with Cú Chulainn.

Three days later the girl gave him some advice: if he was really there to achieve warrior status, he should go where Scáthach was teaching her sons, Cúar and Cett, and use the hero's salmon-leap to get up into the giant yew-tree where she was lounging. He should plant his sword between her breasts until she granted him three wishes: to teach him without holding anything back;[2] to let him marry her[3] without paying a bride-price; and to tell him what was in store for him, because she was a prophet.

---

vigour" without commenting on this specific instance. There are many options for *greimm* including "seizure, hold, grasp" (meaning II in *eDIL*), "bond, obligation, duty, service" (meaning III), "profit, use, advantage" (meaning IV), "a bite; a bit, a morsel" (meaning V); while the context would support something like "putting herself at his service," the syntax seems to call for something she derives from Cú Chulainn or the situation, hence my translation follows Meyer. Patrick Ford went another way with this entirely: "Then the maiden serves him with water and food and waits at his pleasure. She was bold toward him in the manner of a servant, i.e., by taking some of the food away. Cú Chulainn hurt her and broke her finger."

1 *was rough with her* The verb is *cráidid*, glossed by van Hamel as "hurt, violate" and in *eDIL* as "torments, persecutes; offends, injures," with many attestations that are not sexual. So this is vague: (i) Cú Chulainn might be physically abusing what he thinks is the waitstaff; (ii) this might be a consensual sexual event, or a prelude to one, during which Cú Chulainn hurts Úathach by accident; or (iii) it might be a sexually violent encounter that Úathach protests (or even enjoys up until he hurts her finger). (ii) would be my best guess since Úathach seems to have made advances (see previous note) and they seem to be on good terms afterwards, but Ford's interpretation would suggest (i).

2 *without holding anything back* Literally, "without neglect" or "without fail," but would Scáthach otherwise have been neglectful? However, this wish is probably why Cú Chulainn is able to learn what Scáthach never teaches anyone else—his secret weapon, the *gáe bolga*.*

3 *her* Úathach is probably referring to herself and not to Scáthach, although Cú Chulainn seems to end up having sex with both of them. The manuscripts seem to [continued …]

So Cú Chulainn took his weapons to where Scáthach was. He planted his feet on both sides of the weapons chest, drew his sword, pressed the point of it to her heart, and spoke: "Death looms over you," he said.

"I'll grant you three wishes," she said (i.e., the three things you have your eye on), "if you can say them in one breath."

"Oh, I will," he said—then he made her agree to them.

Other versions say here that Cú Chulainn took Scáthach to the beach and got intimate with her, and they slept together, and that then she chanted a prophecy to him of everything that was going to happen to him, saying "Hail, worn out but victorious," and so on. But that's not how it's told in this version.

Úathach slept with Cú Chulainn after that, and Scáthach taught him martial arts, i.e., to master weapons.

While he was studying with Scáthach and shacking up with her daughter Úathach, there was another remarkable man living in Munster, Lugaid mac Nóis, who was the grandson of the illustrious king Alamiach and a comrade of Cú Chulainn's, i.e., a foster-brother* of his. He went east with twelve chariot-warriors, all minor Munster royalty, to woo the twelve daughters of Cairbre Nia Fer, king of Tara,[1] but all of them were already engaged to other men.

When Forgall the Wily heard about this, he traveled to Tara and told Lugaid that he had the best girl in Ireland when it came to beauty, chastity, and handicrafts—and she was single. Lugaid said that sounded good to him. Then Forgall engaged the girl to him, and he also engaged twelve daughters of Brega landowners[2] to the twelve minor royals accompanying Lugaid.

Forgall escorted Lugaid to his stronghold for the wedding. But when Emer was brought to sit next to him, she grabbed his cheeks,

---

vary about whether the marriage will take place *with* a bride-price (which Scáthach would presumably pay instead of Cú Chulainn: King Rúad of the Isles makes the same offer later when it comes to his daughter Derbforgaill) or *without* one. But Kinsella's "a dowry for his marriage," if that means his marriage to Emer, seems to ignore the feminine possessive on *a hernaidmsi*.

1 *king of Tara* Added for clarity. The text has "Cairbre Nia Fer mac Rossa Rúaid."

2 *landowners* Or guesthouse*-keepers. See the note on p. 98 about the parents of Emer's companions.

putting his honor and his life at stake: she revealed that Cú Chulainn was the one she loved, and that she was putting Lugaid on notice,[1] and that anyone who took her as his wife would suffer loss of honor. Then Lugaid didn't dare sleep with Emer for fear of Cú Chulainn, and went home instead.

Now, in those days Scáthach was at war with other tribes, who were ruled by the princess Aífe.[2] Their armies met to do battle. Scáthach had bound Cú Chulainn (i.e., she tied him up), having previously given him a sleeping potion, so that he wouldn't go into battle and nothing would happen to him—she did it as a precaution. Cú Chulainn startled suddenly out of his sleep after one hour. The drink (i.e., the sleeping potion) would have kept anyone else out for twenty-four hours, but it was only an hour in his case. Then he went with Scáthach's two sons to face the three sons of Ilsúanach, i.e., they were Cúar, Cett, and Cruife, three of Aífe's warriors. He attacked the three of them on his own and defeated them.

There was a pitched battle the next day, and both armies advanced until the two forces stood face to face. Then the three sons of Éis Énchenn (Éis "Birdhead"), i.e., Cire, Bire, and Blaicne, three more of Aífe's warriors, went and engaged the two sons of Scáthach. They went on the path of feats. Then Scáthach let out a sigh, not knowing what would happen, because her two sons were short a man against their three opponents, and also because she was afraid of Aífe, who was the toughest warrior-woman in the world. Then Cú Chulainn went to join her sons, jumping onto the path, and he fought and killed their three opponents.

Aífe challenged Scáthach to fight. Cú Chulainn went to face Aífe, but first he asked about what she loved most. Scáthach said, "What

---

1 *putting Lugaid on notice* The Irish is *is fora gressi baí*, which Kuno Meyer took as "Forgall was against it" and most others, including Ford, translate as "she was under his [Cú Chulainn's] protection" (although the usual term for legal protection* is *snádud*, *fóesam*, or *commairce*). I follow Sharon Arbuthnot, who discusses this expression in "Gesture and verbal pronouncement in some Ulster Cycle tales," *Ulidia* 4, 139–49, at 140–42. She argues for "she was attacking his [Lugaid's] honour," reasoning that "Emer grabs Lugaid's cheeks [...] because the loss of honour he will suffer if he pursues a woman who is committed to someone else will be shown on that part of the body." She sees this as "a ritual for protecting oneself against foul play, and it succeeds without need of appeal to a third party."

2 *Aífe* Scáthach's sister, per "The Death of Aífe's Only Son," below.

she loves most is her two horses, her chariot, and her charioteer."

So Cú Chulainn and Aífe met on the path of feats, and started fighting there. Then Aífe disabled (i.e., broke) Cú Chulainn's weapon, leaving his sword no longer than his fist. Then Cú Chulainn said, "Oh no! Aífe's charioteer, her horses, and her chariot have fallen down the valley, and they're all dead!"

Aífe turned to look. Then Cú Chulainn lunged at her (i.e., he attacked her) and seized her under her breasts, and carried her over his shoulder like a sack until he rejoined his own side. Then he threw her on the ground and held a drawn sword over her. Aífe spoke:

"A life for a life, Cú Chulainn!" she said.

"Give me my three demands," said Cú Chulainn.

"They're yours if you can say them in one breath," she said.

"These-are-my-three-demands," he said, "give-hostages-to-Scáthach-and-never-bother-her-again-and-keep-me-company-for-a-night-in-front-of-your-stronghold-and-bear-me-a-son."

"I agree to all that," she said: "so shall it be done."

Then Cú Chulainn went with Aífe and slept with her that night. Then Aífe told him she was pregnant and would have a son.

"In seven years to the day, I'll send him to Ireland," she said, "and now leave a name for him."

Cú Chulainn left a gold thumb-ring for him and told her to have him come find him in Ireland when the ring fitted him. And he said to give him the name Connla, and told her he mustn't give his name to a single man, or let a single man turn him aside, or turn down a fight with a single man.[1]

Then Cú Chulainn headed back to his own side, the same way he had come. On the way, he met an old woman, blind in one eye. She told him to watch out and stay out of her way. He told her he had nowhere to stand except for the sea cliff that dropped away below him. She begged him to let her have the path. So he let her by, and hung on only by his toes. As she went by, she kicked his big toe to

---

1 *a single man* This lends itself to misinterpretation. For example, Kinsella's translation is that "Connla was to reveal this name to no man, that he must make way for no man, and refuse no man combat" (33). But the Irish is specific that these restrictions apply to an encounter with only one man (*óenfer*) at a time: he can reveal his name to a group (and perhaps also to a woman?). This becomes clear in "The Death of Aífe's Only Son," below. The Johnny Cash song "A Boy Named Sue," with lyrics by Shel Silverstein, is a surprisingly apt comparison to make to these restrictions.

make him fall off the cliff. He saw it coming and used his salmon-leap to get back up, then cut the hag's head off. She was the mother of the last three champions who had fallen to him, i.e., Éis Birdhead, and she had crossed his path because she wanted to destroy him.

Then Scáthach's army went home, taking the hostages they'd gotten from Aífe, and Cú Chulainn stayed put until he recovered.

Finally, Cú Chulainn had fully mastered all the martial arts he'd learned from Scáthach:[1] the apple-feat,[2] the thunder-feat,[3] the blade-feat, the lounging-feat,[4] the spear-feat, the rope-feat, the body-feat,[5] the cat's-feat, the hero's salmon-leap, the caber toss, the *gáe bolga,*[*] the sprint, the wheel-feat,[6] the support-feat,[7] the breath-control-feat, the hero's bark, the champion's scream, the controlled strike,[8] the stunning strike,[9] the wailing stroke,[10] climbing up a lance and standing upright on its point, the scythed chariot, the champion's

---

1 *all the martial arts ... from Scáthach* There are several similar lists of Cú Chulainn's feats in the literature. These are systematically considered by William Sayers, "Martial feats in the Old Irish Ulster Cycle," *The Canadian Journal of Irish Studies* 9.1 (1983) 45–80. I adopt his suggestions for some of the feats, and his detailed discussions are valuable in any case.

2 *apple-feat* Sayers: "'apple' meant any spherical object, including those employed as missiles" (50) (so look again at p. 113). If this feat involves juggling balls, Sayers suggests that the "blade-feat" involved juggling blades.

3 *thunder-feat* In the *Táin*, this is a massively destructive feat, killing hundreds at a time. It might be similar to the stunning-shot with a sling (see note below, and Sayers, 61), on a larger scale: a huge, debilitating noise.

4 *lounging-feat* Sayers: "It is suggested that this [...] consisted of a patterned series of moves about the body with a sharp-edged shield. The shield may also have been flipped in the air, thrown from hand to hand, and caught by the potentially injurious sharp rim" (52). The "lounging" would refer to the horizontal or sloping attitude of the shield.

5 *body-feat* Sayers: "some type of physical contortion" (53), distinct from Cú Chulainn's unique *ríastrad* mutation.[*]

6 *wheel-feat* This is described in the saga "Bricriu's Feast," §64, and involves flinging a chariot-wheel into the air as high as possible and catching it.

7 *support-feat* Van Hamel suggests an emendation to "rim-feat" (i.e., using his shield-rim as a weapon, which we see in the *Táin*, similar to how Sayers explicates the "lounging-feat" above), and Sayers to "eight-man feat."

8 *controlled strike* Van Hamel glosses this *béimm fo chomus* as "the stroke under restraint," but suggests that this is a substitution for "*béimm co fomus*, one of Cú Chulainn's tricks, which consists in cutting off his opponent's hair with a sword" (180).

9 *stunning strike* In "The Death of Aífe's Only Son" and the *Táin* itself, this involves a sling-stone fired so hard it concusses the air and knocks out people and animals; in this list of feats, Sayers thinks it could be a blow with the flat of the sword.

10 *wailing stroke* Sayers doesn't discuss this one. The *Táin* describes Conchobor's sword howling like a dog (p. 276), which might be comparable.

coil on the tips of spears.[1] Then he got a message to come back to his homeland, and he said goodbye.

And then Scáthach told him what was in store for him: she chanted to him using her ability to see the future,[2] and spoke the following words.

Scáthach speaks a difficult poem[3] predicting what Cú Chulainn will do in the Táin: *inflicting slaughter on the enemy, he will stand alone in great hardship while his cattle are driven off, and will suffer many wounds; Ailill and Maeve will revel in his injuries; the bulls Finnbennach and Donn Cúailnge will fight; Cú Chulainn will have only some 30 years to live.*

After that, Cú Chulainn launched his ship en route to Ireland. The other men aboard were Lugaid and Lúan, the two sons of Lóch; Fer Báeth; Láiríne; Fer Diad; and Drust mac Seirb.

They came to the house of Rúad, King of the Isles, on Samain* night. Conall Cernach and Lóegaire Búadach were already there collecting tribute, because in those days the Western Isles paid tribute to Ulster.

Then Cú Chulainn heard howls of grief in the king's fort up ahead.

"What's all that screaming about?" said Cú Chulainn.

"Rúad's daughter Derbforgaill[4] is being handed over as tribute to the Fomoiri,*" they said. "That's why there's such grief in the fort."

"Where's the girl?" he said.

---

1 *climbing up ... tips of spears* In this list, the "scythed chariot" interrupts what Sayers suggests is normally "a single complex feat: 'climbing a lance, straightening the body on its point, and the wheeling of a valiant hero'" (60), as on p. 111.

2 *her ability to see the future* The Irish is *imbas forosnai*, "knowledge that illuminates," an arcane practice that one law-text lists as one of the three primary qualifications of a poet.* There is a description of it in *Sanas Cormaic*, "Cormac's Glossary," attributed to Cormac mac Cuillenáin (d. 908), king-bishop of Cashel in Munster. Supposedly it entailed chewing raw meat from a pig, dog, or cat, conjuring (from a Christian perspective) false gods, and falling into a prophetic sleep. See *The Celtic Poets*, 46–47.

3 This poem is an expanded version of the early 8th-century poem "The Words of Scáthach" (*Verba Scáthaige*, Ó Corráin #1127), which has been edited and translated by P.L. Henry in *Celtica* 21 (1990) 191–207.

4 *Derbforgaill* Pronounced "DER-ver-gill." Added here for clarity: the first time she's named in the text is when Cú Chulainn recognizes her in Ireland.

"Down there on the beach," they said.

So Cú Chulainn went down to the girl on the beach. He asked her what was going on, and she told him everything.

"Where do these men come from?" he asked.

"From the island way out there," she said. "Don't stay here where those brutes can see you."

Then he stayed and faced them, and killed the three Fomoiri* in single combat. But the last one wounded him on the wrist. The girl gave him a strip of her clothing to bind it with. Then he left without telling her who he was.

The girl went back to the fort and told her father the whole story. Later Cú Chulainn came to the fort like any other guest, and Conall and Lóegaire welcomed him.

Many people in the fort bragged about killing the Fomoiri,* but the girl didn't believe them. Then the king got a bath[1] ready and sent everyone to her one at a time. Cú Chulainn came along like everyone else and the girl recognized him.

"I'll give you the girl," said the king, "and pay her bride-price myself."

"No," said Cú Chulainn, "have her follow me to Ireland a year from now, if she wants to, and she'll find me there."

After that, Cú Chulainn went back to Emain Macha and explained what he'd been up to. When he had rested, he headed for Forgall's stronghold to look for Emer. He tried for a whole year, but there were so many guards that he couldn't get through to her.

Now the year was up: "Today, Lóeg," said Cú Chulainn, "is when I was supposed to meet up with Rúad's daughter, but I don't know exactly where—that wasn't wise of me.[2] Let's go to the coast."

Then, on the shore of Loch Cúan, they saw two birds over the sea. Cú Chulainn put a stone in his sling and shot at the birds. The two men ran over after he hit one of them. When they got there, what they saw was two of the most beautiful women in the world: they were Derbforgaill, daughter of Rúad, and her companion.[3]

---

1 *a bath* This would be a pretext for the men to undress and reveal the wound and its telltale binding.

2 *wasn't wise of me* Literally, this sentence uses the first person plural ("we weren't wise," etc.), but I take it that Cú Chulainn is referring to himself rather than a joint decision.

3 *her companion* The Irish is *inailt*, which *eDIL*, s.v., gives as "foster-sister, [continued …]

"You've done an evil thing, Cú Chulainn," said Derbforgaill. "We came to see you, and yet you hurt us."

Cú Chulainn sucked out the stone, along with her clotted blood. "I can't marry you now," he said, "after drinking your blood. But I'll give you to my foster-son* here, Lugaid Red-Stripes." And so it was done.[1]

Then Cú Chulainn headed back to Forgall's stronghold: he had yet to find a girl to match the one there. He went back to Lug's Gardens, to Forgall's stronghold. That day the scythed chariot was gotten ready for him. And he drove it hard, i.e., a thunder-feat that would kill 309 men.[2] And that was one of three days that Cú Chulainn used the scythed chariot. And the reason it was called the "scythed" chariot is either because of the iron scythes sticking out of it, or because it was originally invented by the Syrians.[3]

Then he drove up to Forgall's stronghold, and did a salmon-leap out of the chariot across the three stockades, landing in the middle of the fort. There, inside the stockade, he struck three blows: each

---

fosterling; later a handmaid, a bondmaid, a female slave." The case for reading it primarily as 'foster-sister' in Old Irish texts is made by Máirín Ní Dhonnchadha, "*Inailt* 'foster-sister, fosterling'," *Celtica* 18 (1986) 185–91. Scholars (e.g., Kicki Ingridsdotter, Charlene Eska) have tended to understand "maidservant" here.

1 *so it was done* Lugaid's conception is mentioned in "Maeve's Series of Husbands," above, and "The Death of Maeve," below. The rest of the story of Derbforgaill, which involves a literal pissing-contest between her and the women of Ulster, is told in "The Death of Derbforgaill" (*Aided Derbforgaill*, Ó Corráin #967, first half of the 10th century), most recently translated by Kicki Ingridsdotter, "*Aided Derbforgaill* 'The Violent Death of Derbforgaill': A Critical Edition with Introduction, Translation and Textual Notes" (Ph.D. thesis, Uppsala University, 2009, https://www.diva-portal.org/smash/get/diva2:213892/FULLTEXT01.pdf). For commentary, see Charlene Eska, "The mutilation of Derbforgaill," in *Wounds and Wound Repair in Medieval Culture*, ed. Larissa Tracy and Kelly DeVries (Leiden: Brill, 2015), 252–66.

2 *309 men* See p. 119 above on the "thunder-feat." In this case it seems that Cú Chulainn uses his chariot to produce the sonic damage. The other two days when Cú Chulainn uses the scythed chariot would seem to be (i) the "Sixfold Slaughter" episode in the *Táin*, p. 244 below, where it is explicitly mentioned, and (ii) if he needs the chariot in order to do the version of the thunder-feat that kills hundreds, then at the battle in "The Death of Cú Chulainn," p. 304.

3 *the Syrians* The scythed chariot is called *in carpat serrdae*, and "from the Syrians" is *óna Serrdaib*, so *carpat Serrdae* would be "Syrian chariot," and there is no capitalization (in the modern sense; there are only large initials to start new sections) in early Irish manuscripts, so the phrase could be read either way. The wordplay with *scythe* would be very nice in English if the Scythians had been named as the inventors.

one took down eight men, and spared one man in the middle of each group of nine, i.e., Emer's three brothers Scibur, Ibur, and Catt.

Forgall tried to jump onto the outer wall to escape Cú Chulainn, but he fell, and lost his life.

Then Cú Chulainn picked up Emer and her foster-sister,* and their combined weight in gold and silver, and jumped back over the three walls with the two girls.

Cries of alarm were raised on every side.

Scennmenn charged at them. Cú Chulainn killed her[1] at the ford named after her, which is now called the Ford of Scennmenn.

They made it to Glondáth, where Cú Chulainn killed a hundred of the men who were after them.

"You've done a great feat (*glond*)," said Emer, "killing a hundred armed, able-bodied men."

"Its name will be Feat Ford (*Glond-áth*) forever," said Cú Chulainn.

Cú Chulainn made it to Crúfhóit. Its original name had been Whitefield (*Ráe Bán*). He struck so many huge, violent blows against the mob on that same spot that blood poured down in all directions.

"You've turned this hill into a gory sod today, Cú Chulainn," said the girl. Hence that place is called Gory Sod (*Crúfhóit*) i.e., a sod of gore.

Their pursuers caught up with them at Áth n-Imfúait on the Boyne. Emer got out of the chariot. Cú Chulainn chased them along the bank: the horses' hooves sent clods flying north across the ford. Then he chased them north, and the horses' hooves sent clods flying south. Hence it is called the Ford of Clods Everywhere (*Áth n-Imfúait*), because of the clods flying back and forth.

At every crossing from Scennmenn's Ford on the River Delvin (*Ollbine*) to the River Boyne in Brega, Cú Chulainn killed a hundred men, and made good on all the deeds he had promised the girl, and got away safely after all that, reaching Emain Macha as the night came on. Emer was introduced to Conchobor and the rest of the Ulster aristocracy inside the Red Branch, and they welcomed her.

---

1 *killed her* The text says "him," but, as van Hamel points out, Scennmenn was previously identified as Forgall's shapeshifting sister.

There was a bitter, sharp-tongued man there—Bricriu mac Carbada. He spoke up: "Cú Chulainn's sure going to have a problem with what happens tonight," he said, "which is that the woman he's brought with him has to sleep with Conchobor tonight, because he always takes precedence over the other Ulstermen when it comes to taking girls' virginity."

Hearing that made Cú Chulainn agitated, and he shook so hard he burst the seams on his seat cushion, and feathers went flying through the house. Then he stormed out.

"This is a big problem," said Cathbad, "because the king has a *geis** against not doing what Bricriu says, but Cú Chulainn will kill anyone who sleeps with his wife."

"Call Cú Chulainn to me," said Conchobor, "so I can try to soothe his rage."

Then Cú Chulainn came in.

"Off you go," said Conchobor, "and bring me back all the herds on Slieve Fúait."

Away went Cú Chulainn. He rounded up all the pigs and deer and other animals and birds that he could find on Slieve Fúait, and drove them en masse onto the green at Emain Macha. At that point his anger had subsided.

The Ulstermen held a meeting about the issue. They arrived at the recommendation that Emer should spend that night with Conchobor, with Fergus and Cathbad in the same bed to protect Cú Chulainn's honor, and the Ulstermen would bless the couple if Cú Chulainn agreed to it. He agreed to that, and that's what was done. Conchobor paid Emer's dowry the next day, and Cú Chulainn received his honor-price,* and then he moved in with his wife, and after that they were never parted until they died.

Cú Chulainn was made head of the boy-troop of Ulster after that …

This is followed by a longish poem listing the members of the boy-troop. See the Boyhood Deeds, pp. 181–97 for more about the boy-troop.

The Death of Aífe's Only Son

*This ninth- or tenth-century tale (*Aided Óenfhir Aífe, *Ó Corráin #980) follows on the events of "The Wooing of Emer," and appears with Recension 1 of the* Táin *in the Yellow Book of Lecan. According to what Fergus says in the* Táin *about his training with Scáthach, Cú Chulainn would seem to be twelve or thirteen years old at the time of this story. He has clearly told Emer something about his adventures covered in "The Wooing of Emer," including that he has a son named Connla. Now Connla comes to Ireland, with unfortunate results. While in Yeats's play based on this story, "On Baile's Strand" (1903), the tragedy is that Cú Chulainn doesn't know that it's his son until it's too late, in the early Irish text, Cú Chulainn knows exactly who it is and kills him anyway, over his wife's objections. This is an instance of the so-called "Sohrab and Rustum (Rostam)" theme, named after an episode in the Persian* Shahnameh *'Book of Kings' by Aboloqasem Ferdowsi.*[1] *In the International Heroic Biography, it seems standard for a hero to have to kill either his father or his son.*[2] *Cú Chulainn may be such a calculating hero that he engineers this situation to cross an item off the heroic checklist, making a spectacle of his willingness to sacrifice for Ulster while at the same time guaranteeing that he can never be superseded in the future by anyone, given the Ulstermen's logic in "The Wooing of Emer" that only Cú Chulainn can father his match. His attitude here contrasts painfully with the depth of his grief over Fer Diad in the* Táin. *But in "The Death of Cú Chulainn," he does seem to express regret for Connla.*

The translation uses the Irish edited by A.G. van Hamel in Compert Cú Chulainn and Other Stories, *9–15. Compare the version in* The Metrical Dindshenchas,* *Part IV, ed. and trans. Edward Gwynn (Dublin: Royal Irish Academy, Todd Lecture Series 11, 1924) 132–35, at https://celt.ucc.ie/published/T106500D.html.*

1 For the original Sohrab and Rostam episode, see Aboloqasem Ferdowsi (940–c. 1020), *Shahnameh, The Persian Book of Kings*, trans. Dick Davis (Viking Penguin, 2006) 187–214.

2 See Kim McCone, "The Death of Aífe's Only Son and the Heroic Biography," in *Ollam*, 3–17.

What was the reason Cú Chulainn killed his son? That's easy.*

Cú Chulainn went to learn weapons from Scáthach Úanainn daughter of Airdgemm, in Letha, until he had achieved mastery of feats thanks to her.

And Aífe daughter of Airdgemm met him and came away pregnant, and he told her she would have a son.

"Keep this golden thumb-ring," he said, "until it fits the boy. When it does, have him come find me in Ireland—and he mustn't let a single man turn him aside, or give his name to a single man, or turn down a fight with a single man."[1]

Seven years later, the boy came in search of his father.

The Ulstermen were gathered at Footprint Beach[2] (*Trácht Éise*) ahead of him. They saw the boy coming toward them over the sea in a bronze skiff, golden oars in hand. Inside the boat he had a pile of stones. He would load a stone in his staff sling,[3] and launch a stunning-shot at the birds, bringing them down unconscious but alive. Then he'd let them up into the air again. He did something with his jaw, with his hands cupped around his mouth, too fast for the eye to follow: he pitched his voice in their direction until it made them fall back down a second time. Then he revived them again.

"Well then," said Conchobor. "I pity whatever land that boy ends up in. If we had to face grown-ups from the island he comes from, they would grind us to dust, when a little boy does feats like that. Someone go meet him. Don't let him land, whatever you do."

"Who'll go and face him?"

"Who else but Condere mac Echach?"

"Why should Condere go?" said everyone.

"That's easy," said Conchobor: "If a situation calls for tact and eloquence, Condere is the man for the job."

"I'll go meet him," said Condere.

So Condere went, and meanwhile the boy made it to the beach.

"That's far enough, boyo," said Condere. "Tell us where you're going and who your people are."

---

1 *a single man* See the note to "The Wooing of Emer," p. 118 above.

2 *Footprint Beach* To be understood as "what is now Footprint Beach," since it gets its name only later in the story.

3 *staff sling* See http://www.lloydianaspects.co.uk/ancientWeaponry/theStaffSling.html for a modern reconstruction of this weapon.

"I don't give my name to a single man," said the boy, "and I don't stand aside for a single man."

"You can't land," said Condere, "until you give your name."

"I'll go where I'm going," said the boy. He turned away.

Then Condere said: "Turn to me, my boy. You're accomplished. You seem to have a promising bloodline. You would be the pride of Ulster's warriors. Keep your little jaws and little javelins away from the left side of your chariot,[1] and you can use them to build up the warriors of Ulster. Conchobor will take you under his protection.* Lend an ear, keep silent while I talk. Turn to Conchobor, the warlike son of Ness; to Sencha, the triumphant son of Ailill; to Cethern, the bloody-bladed son of Fintan, the fire that wounds battalions; to the poet* Amairgen; to Cúscraid with his vast armies. Welcome: Conall Cernach will take you under his protection, and treat you to the tales, songs, and laughter of a warrior band. Blaí the Guesthouse*-Keeper would be sad and sorry if you passed him by, warrior though he is, for it wouldn't be appropriate to shame so many people. So let it be said: I, Condere, got up[2] to confront the brave boy myself and stop him. But I've sworn to fight this boy with no beard or body hair," said Condere, "unless he does as the Ulstermen say."

"You've approached me nicely," said the boy, "so you'll have your conversation. I pitched my voice just right: I barked out unerring concussions from my young jaws. I fetched a lovely flock of birds by sending out far-flung javelins, with no need for a hero's salmon-leap. I showed off my feats of valor so that no one would try to box me in. Go ask the Ulstermen if they would rather come at me in single combat or in waves. Turn around now," said the boy, "because even if you had the strength of a hundred men, you wouldn't be fit to stop me."

"All right," said Condere, "someone else can come talk to you, then."

Then Condere went to the Ulstermen and told them that.

---

1 *left side of your chariot* Turning the left side of a chariot to someone is an insult, and normally a challenge to battle. Since the boy doesn't have a chariot, this is figurative and could be paraphrased "avoid using your little jaws or little javelins to give offense."

2 *I, Condere, got up* This follows van Hamel, who punctuates this whole paragraph as being spoken by Condere ("KON-there-uh"). Some others (see for instance https://iso.ucc.ie/Aided-aife/Aided-aife-text.html) take this one sentence as narration, not direct speech: "'So be it said.' Condere himself arose ..." While the verb is ambiguous, the 1sg emphasizing particle *-sa* (as against 3sg masculine *-som*) supports van Hamel's take.

"There's no way Ulster's honor will be carried off as long as I'm alive," said Conall Cernach.

Then he went to attack the boy.

"Pretty games, little boy," said Conall.

"They won't be any less attractive to use on you," said the boy.

The boy put a stone in his sling. He shot it into the air, i.e., a stunning-shot, roaring up at Conall with thunderous force. It knocked Conall head over heels. Before he could get up, the boy had tied his hands with his shield-strap.

"Someone else fight him!" said Conall.

But the boy made a laughingstock of the whole army that way.

Meanwhile Cú Chulainn was in a playful mood, going down to meet the boy, while Emer daughter of Forgall clung to his neck.

"Don't go down there!" she said. "It's your son that's down there. Don't commit *fingal** against your only son—steer clear, you impetuous, highborn boy. It's not fair play* or good counsel to go after your accomplished, overachieving son over there. Turn away from lacerating the sapling of your tree: Scáthach will be appalled by the news. If Connla turned the left side of his chariot to you, be the bigger man and let it go.[1] Look at me! Hear my voice! My advice is good. Let Cú Chulainn hear it! I know what name you'll get out of him, if Connla, the only son of Aífe, is the boy down there."

Then Cú Chulainn said, "Shush, woman! I'm not interested in a woman's advice when great deeds and glorious victory are at stake. Your womanly advice won't be followed. I'll be triumphant in deeds. Our overking's eyes will be gratified. The gore from Connla's body will settle on my skin in a fine mist of blood. He's a fine little javelin: sweetly spears will suck him dry. Even if that's who it is, woman, I'd kill him for the honor of Ulster."

Then he went down himself.

"It's a pretty game you're playing, little boy," he said.

"Yours is pretty nasty, though," said the little boy, "not letting me meet two of you at once so I can tell you my name."

---

1 *let it go* Van Hamel glosses this "it should be valorously dissolved." Again, since the boy doesn't have a chariot, Connla's "turn" should be understood broadly as "if the boy insults you."

"Did I need to bring a little kid with me?"[1] said Cú Chulainn. "You'll die, though, if you don't give your name."

"So be it," said the boy.

The boy came up to him. They traded blows. The boy sheared his hair off with his sword, i.e., a calculated blow.

"Enough of this charade!" said Cú Chulainn. "Now let's wrestle!"

"I can't reach your belt," said the boy. He stood up on two rocks, and shoved Cú Chulainn between two standing stones three times, while the boy didn't move his feet off the rocks until his feet sank into them up to the ankles. His footprints are still there. Hence the Ulstermen call that Footprint Beach (*Tracht Éise*).

Then they went into the sea, each of them trying to drown the other, and the boy dunked him twice.

Then Cú Chulainn went after the boy from the water and tricked him with the *gáe bolga*,* because Scáthach never taught anyone but Cú Chulainn to use that weapon. He shot it through the water at the boy: then the boy's guts lay at his feet.

"That," said the boy, "is something Scáthach never taught me. This is horrible—you've really harmed me!"

"True enough," said Cú Chulainn.

He took the boy in his arms, and carried him over and dropped him in front of the Ulstermen.

"Here you go, Ulstermen: my son," he said.

"How tragic," said the Ulstermen.

"True enough," said the boy. "If I'd stayed with you for five years, I'd scatter the men of the world before you on every side, and you would rule all the way to Rome. Since this is how it is, introduce me to the famous men here, so I can tell them all goodbye."

Then he hugged every man round the neck, one after the other, said goodbye to his father, and—just like that—he died.

They cried out for him in mourning: they made him a grave-mound and a headstone, and in his memory, for three days the Ulstermen wouldn't let any calf go to its mother.[2]

---

1 *bring ... with me* Cú Chulainn seems to be ironically mocking the *geis** he laid on Connla (see pp. 118, 126) (according to "The Wooing of Emer") not to reveal his name to any single individual: any additional person, even a noncombatant toddler, would have given Connla an out.

2 *any calf go to its mother* This is not explained; possibly the moos of pain and longing would make it seem as if the land itself were in mourning.

Other Stories about Cú Chulainn

Of the texts about Cú Chulainn that are not translated here, because their relevance to the Táin *is less immediate, the most significant is probably "The Wasting Sickness of Cú Chulainn and the Only Jealousy of Emer" (*Serglige Con Culainn & Óenét Emire, *Ó Corráin #1099, eighth or ninth century),*[1] *which fits in chronologically somewhere between "The Wooing of Emer" and "The Exile of the Sons of Uisliu." This story tells how, after being plunged into a coma for a year, Cú Chulainn is recruited by Otherworld* women to fight supernatural enemies. He becomes infatuated with one of the women, Fann, and brings her back with him: for a while he has her set up almost as a second wife, while Emer tries to kill her. When Fann finally gives up and leaves for the Otherworld, Cú Chulainn has to be restrained from chasing after her. The druids* give him a potion to make him forget all about her (which naturally limits the effect of this episode on his character development across the Ulster Cycle as a whole), and Emer gets a potion to forget her jealousy. Meanwhile, Fann's husband Manannán mac Lir casts a spell so that she and Cú Chulainn never meet again.*

"The Wasting Sickness" includes the interesting detail that Conall Cernach, Conchobor's son Cúscraid "the Stammerer of Macha," and Cú Chulainn each have a following of fangirls in Emain who inflict "blemishes" on themselves to look more like their heroes: the Conall fans have their necks askew, the Cúscraid fans deliberately stutter, and the Cú Chulainn fans gouge out an eye so they can look more like him in his mutant* battle-frenzy.*

*Emer gets back at Cú Chulainn (sort of) in "Emer's Elopement" (*Aithed Emire, *Ó Corráin #987, twelfth century),*[2] *a short text in which she falls in love with the Scandinavian prince Tuir Glésta when he comes to raid*

---

1 Edited by Myles Dillon, *Serglige Con Culainn* (DIAS, 1953), https://celt.ucc.ie/published/G301015/; translated by Gantz, 153–78 , and previously at https://www.google.com/books/edition/Heroic_Romances_of_Ireland/KukMrnlphFYC?hl=en&gbpv=0.

2 Edited and translated by Kuno Meyer, "Aithed Emere le Tuir n-Glesta mac ríg Lochlann," in "Irish miscellanies," *Revue Celtique* 6 (1883–85) 162–91 at 184–85, and now by Hanna van Gorcum, "*Aithed Emire:* a new edition" (bachelor's thesis, Utrecht University, 2013, https://studenttheses.uu.nl/bitstream/handle/20.500.12932/17316/Hanna%20van%20Gorcum%200482625%20Thesis%2020%20sep.docx?sequence=2&isAllowed=y).

Ulster. She sails off with him, but Cú Chulainn tracks them down, kills Tuir Glésta, and brings Emer home, complaining that "Ships at sea don't care who gets inside them, and women are the same, they don't care who enjoys them." This text reads like a later misogynistic revision of Emer's character; she is otherwise depicted as totally devoted to Cú Chulainn.

Two longer tales that could function as prequels to the Táin *but present significant continuity problems with the rest of the Ulster Cycle are "The Intoxication of the Ulstermen" (*Mesca Ulad*, Ó Corráin #1083, partly tenth century and partly twelfth century)*[1] *and "Bricriu's Feast" (*Fled Bricrenn*, Ó Corráin #1059, eighth century or later).*[2] *Since in both of them, Fergus, Dubthach, Bricriu, and the other Ulster exiles are still in Ulster (this ends in "The Exile of the Sons of Uisliu"), it seems appropriate to mention them here.*

"The Intoxication" starts with Ulster divided into three parts by Otherworld agents. These thirds are ruled by Conchobor, Cú Chulainn, and Fintan son of Niall Níamglonnach.*

Cú Chulainn and Fintan agree to give up their kingships and merge their territory with Conchobor's in exchange for preferential access to Conchobor at their feasts. On the way from Fintan's feast to Cú Chulainn's, the drunken Ulstermen drive their chariots all the way across Ireland and end up in the southwestern province of Munster, where Cú Roí mac Dáiri is hosting Ailill and Maeve. After an extended "Watchman Device" describing the Ulstermen's advance, Ailill and

1 Edited by J. Carmichael Watson, *Mesca Ulad* (DIAS, 1941), https://celt.ucc.ie/published/G301040/; translated by Watson, "Mesca Ulad," *Scottish Gaelic Studies* 5 (1938) 1–34; by Gantz, 188–218; and in *The Celtic Heroic Age*, 106–27.

2 Edited and translated by George Henderson, *Fled Bricrend, The Feast of Bricriu* (ITS, 1899); translated by Matthieu Boyd (2017) for the *Broadview Anthology of British Literature* website (https://sites.broadviewpress.com /bablonline, requires access code); also in Gantz, 219–55; in *The Celtic Heroic Age*, 76–105; and at https://irishtextssociety.org/texts/fledbricrenn.html in an unpublished edition and translation by Proinsias Mac Cana and Edgar Slotkin. For discussion, see *Fled Bricrenn: Reassessments*, ed. Pádraig Ó Riain (ITS, 2000), and my article cited below. "Bricriu's Feast and the exile of the sons of Dóel Dermait" (Ó Corráin #1060, 9th century) is a different text: see the edition and translation by Kaarina Hollo, *Fled Bricrenn ocus Loinges mac nDúil Dermait and its place in the Irish literary and oral narrative traditions* (Maynooth: Department of Old and Middle Irish, National University of Ireland, 2005).

Maeve invite them to stay, putting them in an iron house[1] *where they try to roast them to death. Alerted by Dubthach, the Ulstermen break free and slaughter the Connachtmen, sparing Ailill and his seven sons the Maines, then go back to Ulster to Cú Chulainn's feast, where Ailill (but not Maeve) visits them and receives gifts.*

This text presents Cú Chulainn as a king who chooses instead to become a warrior, and grows into that role despite what seems to be initial skepticism from the Ulstermen. A scene late in the battle is worth mentioning: Cú Chulainn is approached by the warrior Crimthann Nia Náir and the female satirist Riches, who exposes herself to him. As in the Boyhood Deeds,* *p. 196 below,* *Cú Chulainn is brought up short by female nudity, and his charioteer Lóeg has to kill Riches with a rock before Cú Chulainn will defend himself against Crimthann.*

"Bricriu's Feast" tells how Bricriu, in a mood to stir up trouble, builds a huge new house (conforming to the "Standard Irish Palace Description" as in "The Wooing of Emer," *p. 95 above)* *and invites the Ulstermen to a feast. As in "The Tale of Mac Dá Thó's Pig," the warriors compete for the Champion's Share of food and associated perks, such as whose wife gets to enter the hall ahead of the rest. Lóegaire Búadach, Conall Cernach, and Cú Chulainn are the top contenders. After they (and their wives, who have an extended word-battle) argue over it, they travel around Ireland to face different tests, some of which are impossible to situate before what happens in the* Táin. *Cú Chulainn is always #1, Conall #2, and Lóegaire #3, but Conall and Lóegaire make excuses and keep refusing to accept the results, and the tests continue. Lastly, the Ulstermen are challenged at Emain Macha by an ax-wielding stranger who offers them a "Champion's Bargain," which is the earliest example of the "Beheading Game" motif in the Arthurian tradition, made famous by* Sir Gawain and the Green Knight*: someone must cut off the stranger's head today, and he will cut off theirs tomorrow. Muinremor, Lóegaire, Conall, and Cú Chulainn each take him up on it, but when each of them beheads the stranger, he picks up his head and walks out. Only Cú Chulainn*

1 *an iron house* Compare Boyd, *The Four Branches of the Mabinogi*, 44, and see Patrick Sims-Williams, *Irish Influence on Medieval Welsh Literature* (Oxford University Press, 2011), 262–77, or his 2005 lecture "The Iron House in Ireland," https://www.asnc.cam.ac.uk/publications/Chadwick/HMC%20Vol%2016%202005%20Sims-Williams.pdf.

shows up the next night to keep his end of the bargain. The stranger (who is actually the Munster hero Cú Roí mac Dáiri in disguise) spares him, and announces that Cú Chulainn is the supreme warrior in Ireland.

In my opinion, these two texts are best understood as alternative traditions, medieval glosses, thought-experiments, or works of fan-fiction, which is not at all meant to be dismissive: they are fascinating investigations of major themes in the Ulster Cycle.[1]

See the headnote to "The Death of Cú Chulainn," p. 293 below, for some of Cú Chulainn's adventures after the Táin.

1 See Matthieu Boyd, "The timeless tale of *Bricriu's Feast,*" *North American Journal of Celtic Studies* 1.2 (2017) 133–54, and "From king to warrior in *Mesca Ulad,*" *PHCC* 37 (2019, for calendar year 2017) 60–76.

The Exile of the Sons of Uisliu

*This eighth- or ninth-century text (*Longes mac nUislenn, *Ó Corráin #1078) appears with Recension 1 of the* Táin *in the Yellow Book of Lecan and Egerton 1782, and with Recension 2 in the Book of Leinster. It explains why Fergus and other important warriors turn against Conchobor, attack Emain Macha, and go into exile with Ailill and Maeve, so that—in spite of their close ties to Cú Chulainn—they are on Maeve's side during the* Táin.

Conchobor's unwilling bride-to-be, the ill-omened Deirdre, runs off with the warrior Noísiu son of Uisliu and his two brothers. (A twelfth-century poem says that Noísiu's beauty caused the Táin, *as Paris's caused the Trojan War.*[1]*) Conchobor offers to reconcile with them, and they are invited back to Ulster under the formal legal protection* of Fergus, Dubthach, and Conchobor's son Cormac. What Conchobor does in spite of their protection is not only a deadly insult to the three of them, it violates early Irish law, so that the other Ulster exiles turn against Conchobor on principle. Conchobor is also responsible for the killing of Fergus's son, but this barely registers except as part of the larger issue.*

*Cú Chulainn is absent here. We have to imagine he is off on some adventure. The much longer Early Modern Irish (i.e., late medieval) story "The Fate of the Children of Uisneach" (*Oidheadh Chloinne hUisneach, *Ó Corráin #1080)*[2] *handles this differently. Conchobor first asks Conall Cernach and Cú Chulainn to offer their protection. He rejects them when they say that if they do it and Noísiu and his brothers come to harm, they will massacre everyone in Ulster for the offense, including Conchobor himself. Fergus is acceptable because he promises to kill whoever directly harms the brothers, but otherwise says that he will not come after Conchobor. Cú Chulainn steps in again at the end, taking Deirdre under his protection, but she leaps into Noísiu's grave and dies.*

---

1 The poem is *Clann Ollaman uaisle Emna*, "The nobles of Emain Macha are Ollam's descendants," most recently re-edited and translated by Michael Clarke in *Classical Antiquity and Medieval Ireland*, 307–20: "Strong Naoise is Alexander [=Paris], for whose beauty were (the wars of) Troy and the Táin."

2 See the edition and translation by Caoimhín Mac Giolla Léith, *Oidheadh chloinne hUisneach: The violent death of the children of Uisneach* (ITS, 1993); *Oidheadh Chloinne hUisneach: Reassessments*, ed. Kevin Murray (ITS, 2023); and Kate Louise Mathis. An older translation can be read at https://archive.org/details/oidhechloinneuisoosociuoft/page/n1/mode/2up.

The translation uses the Irish edited by Vernam Hull in Loinges mac n-Uislenn: The Exile of the Sons of Uisliu *(New York: MLA, 1949), at https://celt.ucc.ie/published/G301020B/, as well as the detailed review of Hull by Máirín O Daly in* Béaloideas *19.1/2 (1949) 196–207; the edition and translation by Anders Ahlqvist of "A rhetorical poem in* Longes mac nUislenn,*" in* Rhetoric and reality in medieval Celtic literature: studies in honor of Daniel F. Melia, *(CSANA Yearbook 11–12), ed. Georgia Henley and Paul Russell (Hamilton, NY: Colgate University Press, 2014) 1–7; and the opinions compiled by Kate Louise Mathis, "The Evolution of Deirdriu in the Ulster Cycle" (Ph.D. thesis, University of Edinburgh, 2010, https://era.ed.ac.uk/bitstream/handle/1842/9813/Mathis2011.pdf?sequence=1), 63–124. The poetry is especially difficult: where this translation differs from others (Kinsella, Gantz), it often adopts the suggestions of O Daly and Ahlqvist.*

What caused the exile of the sons of Uisliu? That's easy.* The Ulstermen were feasting at the house of Conchobor's storyteller, Fedlimid mac Daill. Fedlimid's wife was there to wait on everyone, on her feet despite being pregnant. Drinking horns and food made the rounds, and there was drunken shouting.

When it was bedtime, the woman made her way to bed. As she crossed the floor of the house, the child in her womb screamed so that the whole fort heard it. The scream had every man in the house on his feet, squaring off against the rest. Then Sencha mac Ailella made a pronouncement: "Don't move an inch! Let's have the woman brought to us so we can find out where that noise came from."

The woman was brought to them. Then her husband—that is, Fedlimid—said:

> "What is that quaver of wild wailing,
> woman," he said,
> "that rages in your lowing womb?
> Whoever has ears to hear is crushed
> by the sound between your sides—
> it thunders.
> My heart fears much terror:
> it gushes blood."

Then she hurried to Cathbad, since he was a seer:

"Listen to good-looking Cathbad,
a gracious prince,
a diadem potent and powerful,
exalted by druid* magic,
since I lack the wise words
to enlighten Fedlimid with knowledge,
because a woman never knows
what's in her womb,
even when it screams in there."

Then Cathbad said:

"What screamed in your womb:
a yellow-haired woman with yellow curls,
blue-gray exquisite eyes,
her cheeks dark purple as foxglove.
To the color of snow I compare
the flawless treasure of her teeth.
Her red-leather* lips resplendent:
a woman spawning slaying
among Ulster's chariot-fighters.
What screams inside your lowing womb:
a tall blonde woman with long hair.
Champions will vie for her.
High-kings will ask for her.
They are massing forces in the west,
under the aegis of Conchobor's province.[1]
Red lips like fine leather part

---

1 *They are … province* These lines are difficult. Hull's "with oppressive bodies of troops (?)" (which Tomás Ó Máille similarly read as "with mighty multitudes") is apparently taken by *eDIL* as a compound involving *1 tor* 'sorrow.' Since Cathbad's speeches anticipate the plot of the saga in a fairly specific way, this might be referring to Éogan mac Durthacht (whose realm of Fernmag is to the west of Emain Macha) preparing to come at Conchobor's behest to do his dirty work. O Daly disagreed with Hull and suggested that the subject here is still Deirdre: "She will be, after a search by large companies …" (brought back to Conchobor's province, etc.).

around pearly teeth.
High-queens will envy her
and her gorgeous, flawless form."

Then Cathbad touched the woman's belly, and the child quivered under his hand.

"It's true," he said. "There is a girl there. And her name will be Deirdre.[1] And she will bring evil."

Later, when the girl was born, Cathbad said:[2]

"Deirdre, you'll bring devastation
when you have a lovely face and fame.
The Ulstermen will endure it in your lifetime,
noble daughter of Fedlimid.

Ever after, fiery woman, you'll set jealousy ablaze.
In your prime—hear this—
the three sons of Uisliu will be exiled.

In your prime—a violent act—
they'll be killed in Emain.
People ever afterward will rue the loss inflicted
under the protection* of the great Mac Roích.[3]

Fateful woman, thanks to you
Fergus will be exiled from the Ulstermen;

---

1 *Deirdre* In Old Irish, *Deirdriu* (pronounced "DIRR-droo"): this name gets anglicized as *Deirdre* ("DER-dra" or "DEER-druh"), and for convenience the translation uses that form. The name is related to *derdrethar*, "rages, resounds," used twice to describe what she does in the womb: when Fedlimid speaks and when Cathbad touches her (which his naming of her immediately picks up on). The translation uses *quaver/quiver* to help track this. For the effect of the Irish, her name would need to be translated as something like Quevra.

2 *Cathbad said* Without getting into the details of the verse forms, it will be noticed that this next utterance by Cathbad is in stanzas. Máire Herbert has commented that "[t]he change of register from mantic *rosc* [accentual verse] to syllabic verse may be seen to mirror the passage of Deirdre from unseen, unborn threat to threat embodied in vulnerable human form."

3 *Mac Roích* I.e., Fergus. But Ó Daly suggested an emendation that would translate to "the destruction will be a cause for regret afterwards. Mighty sons of kings will fall." Ahlqvist approved.

and—a deed to weep over—
Fiachna son of Conchobor will die.

Fateful woman, for your crime
Gerrce mac Illadain will die,
and, an act that carries no less penalty,
Éogan mac Durthacht will be slaughtered.[1]

You'll do something grim and gruesome
in rage at Ulster's royal lord.
Your remains will be untraceable.[2]
The case will be notorious, Deirdre."

"Have her killed," said the warriors.

"No," said Conchobor. "I'll take her with me tomorrow, and she'll be raised the way I say, and be my consort."[3]

And the Ulstermen didn't dare set him straight about it. So that was done. Conchobor raised her, and she grew up to be by far the most beautiful girl in Ireland. She was raised in a separate enclosure so that none of the Ulstermen would see her till she slept with Conchobor. No one was ever allowed in there except her foster-father,* her foster-mother,* and also Leborcham: there was no keeping her out, since she was a female satirist.*[4]

---

1 *Éogan mac Durthacht ... slaughtered* This is not told in what follows, and in the *Táin* Éogan is apparently still alive. "The Death of Fergus," below, does say that Fergus eventually kills him.

2 *Your remains ... untraceable* Literally, "your little grave will be everywhere" (Hull) or "anywhere" (Ahlqvist). The sense may be that Deirdre's story "will in fact garner such great renown that countless places throughout Ireland will claim to be the site of her interment" (Kathryn Stelmach) or that "'your little grave will be in any place', i.e., in a random place / wherever it is made" (William Gillies).

3 *consort* Literally, "she will be the woman who will be in my company" (Hull). Hull thought this meant an extramarital relationship. To O Daly, "'she will be my wife' seems the natural translation in spite of [Hull's] scruples." This is a significant issue—how casual and exploitative are Conchobor's plans for Deirdre?—but the Irish doesn't seem conclusive. Conchobor might still be unmarried at this point since this saga never mentions Mugain, who is his queen in the *Táin*; but, as noted in "Maeve's Series of Husbands," p. 70 above, he could also legally have had multiple wives.

4 *Leborcham ... female satirist** The name is pronounced "LEV-ur-hum," meaning "long and crooked"—a Mother Gothel to Deirdre's Rapunzel. Although women in early Ireland could be fully accredited poets* considered responsible in the use of their skills (and Fedelm in the *Táin* seems to be an example of such), "[j]udging by the references

One time the girl's foster-father* was skinning a calf on the snow outside to cook it for her. Then she saw a raven drink the blood on the snow. She said to Leborcham, "I could love the man with those three colors—hair like the raven, I mean, and cheeks like the blood, and a body like snow."[1]

"You're in luck," said Leborcham. "He's not far from you. He's in the house nearby, that is, Noísiu son of Uisliu."[2]

"Then I won't be well again," she said, "until I see him."

Then at some point Noísiu was by himself on the earthwork ramparts—that is, of Emain—singing in a high tenor.[3] The tenor singing of the sons of Uisliu was lovely. Any cow or animal that heard it gave two-thirds more milk. Any person who heard it was filled with a sense of calm and well-being.

The sons of Uisliu[4] were also skilled warriors. Even if they were surrounded by the whole of Ulster, their parrying and self-defense were so outstanding that they would never be defeated as long as the three of them had their backs to each other.

They were also fast as hunting hounds, and used their speed to kill wild animals.

Anyway, when Noísiu was outside by himself, she snuck out pretending to want to get past him, and at first he didn't recognize her.

---

in the law-texts, it would seem that most women who composed verse were not legally recognised poets, but satirists who used verse for malicious purposes, in particular sorcery or witchcraft. [While illegal satirists are condemned in general, t]he law-texts reserve particular odium for the illegal satirist who is female" (*GEIL*, 49–50).

1 *three colors ... like snow* A classic trope: see Jessica Hemming, "Red, white, and black in symbolic thought," *Folklore* 123.3 (2012) 310–29, and "'I could love a man with those three colours': gazing and the tricoloured beloved," *CMCS* 68 (2014) 51–67. Of course, as Maria Tymoczko has pointed out, Deirdre is basing her ideal lover on a dead thing, which doesn't bode well for their relationship.

2 *Noísiu ... Uisliu* Pronounced "NOY-shyoo" or "NEE-shyoo," called *mac Uislenn* ("mock ISH-lenn") or "son of Uisliu" ("ISH-loo"); or elsewhere (as in "The Wooing of Emer" above), *mac Uisnig* ("mock ISH-nee"), "son of Uisnech" ("ISH-nock").

3 *high tenor* This translation follows Hull. The Irish is *andord*, literally "un-*dord*," *dord* being some kind of low-pitched droning, humming, or chanting. O Daly suggests it is "some sort of vocal signal, sometimes a war-cry or alarum, sometimes perhaps merely a halloo." The word is used for both the pleasant singing that Noísiu and his brothers do, and the high-pitched cry of Noísiu after his first conversation with Deirdre, although the point may be that Deirdre's overtures have corrupted the sound by breaking Noísiu's composure.

4 *The sons of Uisliu* Expanded for clarity. The sons consist of Noísiu and his two brothers, Ardán and Ainnle, although the brothers' names aren't mentioned until later.

"That's a good-looking heifer walking by," he said.

"The heifers grow big where there are no bulls," she said.

"You have the bull of the whole province," he said. "The king of Ulster, I mean."

"And if I could pick between the two of you," she said, "I'd choose a prime young bull like you."

"No!" he said. "What about Cathbad's prophecy?"

"Are you saying that to reject me?"

"Well, yes," he said.

Then she rushed at him and grabbed him by the ears.

"These ears will ring with shame and mockery,"[1] she said, "unless you take me away with you."

"Get away from me, woman!" he said.

"You'll get what's coming to you,"[2] she said.

Then he let out a high-pitched wail. Hearing it made all the Ulstermen jump to their feet. The sons of Uisliu went to intercept their brother.

"What's wrong with you?" they said. "It had better not be something Ulstermen will kill each other over."

He told them what Deirdre had done to him.

"This will turn evil," said his brothers.[3] "Even so, you won't be disgraced as long as we're alive. We'll take her to another country. There's no king in Ireland who wouldn't welcome us."

That was their decision. They left that night, that is, with a hundred and fifty warriors, and a hundred and fifty women, and a hundred and fifty dogs, and a hundred and fifty servants, and Deirdre in the mix as well.[4]

---

1 *These ears … shame and mockery* Literally, "These [will be] two ears of shame and mockery," but she is probably threatening to defame him so that shame and mockery are all he hears—not to mutilate or transform his ears so that people laugh at *them,* although some scholars have suggested so. In any case, what she threatens is the spell-like power of satire,* which presumably she learned from Leborcham.

2 *You'll get … to you* Literally, "you shall have that" (Hull), but what is "that"? His cry suggests that she is not agreeing to get away from him.

3 *said his brothers* Changed for clarity from "said the warriors."

4 *Deirdre in the mix as well* Deirdre may be using all these people for cover, but a large retinue is also an aspect of honor or public face. Unions where a woman openly leaves with a man or lets herself be stolen away against her family's wishes are recognized in early Irish law (*GEIL,* 70–71; Eska, *Cáin Lánamna*), so, open or secret, this form of departure has the effect of a wedding in defiance of Conchobor.

They spent a long time under the protection* of kings all over Ireland. Thanks to Conchobor's plotting, many attempts were made to destroy them, and they were driven southwest from Ess Rúaid and back northeast to Benn Étair (the Hill of Howth). Finally, the Ulstermen chased them over to Scotland, where they camped out in the wilderness. When they ran out of game in the mountains, they turned to raiding livestock from the men of Scotland. One day the locals set out to destroy them. At that point they went to the king of Scotland and he made them part of his household. He hired them as mercenaries, and they built their houses on the green. They built houses because of Deirdre, so that no one would see her and try to kill them over her.

Then at some point the king's steward came in early in the morning and poked around their house. He saw the couple sleeping. Then he went to wake the king.

"I could never find a woman worthy of you until today," he said. "Noísiu son of Uisliu has a woman with him who'd be worthy of the king of the western world. Have Noísiu killed as soon as possible, and the woman can sleep with you."[1]

"No," said the king, "but go proposition her on my behalf every day, in secret."

Whatever the steward told her, she would pass it on to her lover that very night. Since the king hadn't gotten anywhere with her, the sons of Uisliu were often ordered into dire straits, in hopes they would be killed.

But they were tough and survived every bloodbath, so nothing came of these attempts.

After talking to Deirdre,[2] the men of Scotland gathered to kill them. She told Noísiu. "Get out of here," she said. "If you don't leave tonight, they'll kill you tomorrow."

---

1 *can sleep with you* The Irish is *foath in ben lat-so*. We might have expected "and then you can sleep with the woman." The steward's point might be that if Deirdre were unattached she would naturally choose to sleep with the king.

2 *After talking to Deirdre* Literally, "after consultation with her regarding it" (Hull). We can only guess what the "consultation" involved. If Deirdre had been hinting that the king could have her if only the sons of Uisliu weren't around, she might have pretended to be in on the plot. Or she could have been given one last chance to accept the king's advances, before the sons of Uisliu would have to be killed. Scholars have suggested both.

She and the brothers[1] left that night and went to an island in the sea.

The Ulstermen were told about that.

"It's tragic, Conchobor," they said, "for the sons of Uisliu to die in hostile lands for a bad woman's crime. It would be better to show them leniency, to feed them, not kill them, and have them come back here instead of letting them fall to their enemies."

"So let them come," said Conchobor. "Have some sureties* go get them."

They received the message.

"We welcome it," they said. "We'll go, and let's have Fergus come with us as a surety, along with Dubthach and Conchobor's son Cormac."

The sureties went and escorted them up from the sea.

But Fergus was besieged with invitations to attend feasts. Conchobor had planned this, because the sons of Uisliu had sworn[2] that the first food they ate in Ireland would be Conchobor's. So Fergus's son Fíachu went ahead with them, and Fergus and Dubthach stayed behind.

The sons of Uisliu came to the green at Emain. Then Éogan mac Durthacht, king of Fernmag, came to make peace with Conchobor, since they'd been feuding for a long time.[3] Éogan was the one assigned to kill the sons of Uisliu. Conchobor was surrounded by his bodyguards so they couldn't get to him.

The sons of Uisliu were standing in the middle of the green, and the ramparts of Emain were lined with women. Éogan walked over to them with his troops. Then Fergus's son came to stand beside Noísiu. Éogan welcomed them with a thrust of his great spear, breaking Noísiu's back. Fergus's son put both arms around Noísiu, pulled

---

1 *She and the brothers* Expanded from "they" to make it clear that Deirdre isn't being left behind.

2 *had sworn* The Irish has only "said," but since keeping one's word is a matter of honor, their words have the force of an oath in governing their behavior. Similarly, for Fergus to turn down the invitations to feasts would be an offense against the honor of those extending them, and therefore not something he can do lightly. In "The Fate of the Children of Uisneach," Fergus is bound by a *geis** to attend a specific feast, which intensifies the conflict for him here. In "The Fate," Deirdre also has threatening dreams and visions on the way back to Ulster.

3 *Éogan … a long time* The warfare between Conchobor and Éogan is mentioned in the *Táin* as part of Cú Chulainn's Boyhood Deeds, p. 184 below.

him down, and threw himself on top of him, so that the blows that rained on Noísiu went through Fergus's son.

Then all the sons of Uisliu were killed, here and there on the green. No one made it out except on the point of a spear or the edge of a sword. And she was brought over to stand beside Conchobor, and her hands were tied behind her back.[1]

Fergus was told what happened. So were Dubthach and Cormac. They came at once and did great deeds. Dubthach killed Conchobor's son Maine.[2] Fiachna, the son of Conchobor's daughter Fedelm, was brought down with a single thrust. Fergus killed Traigthrén mac Traiglethain and his brother. These killings were an outrage to Conchobor's honor. Battle ensued, and in a single day a total of three hundred Ulstermen fell. Before morning Dubthach had slaughtered the young women of Ulster, and Fergus burned Emain. Then they went to seek refuge with Ailill and Maeve:[3] they knew those two would be prepared to support them, but as Ulstermen they took no pleasure in it. Three thousand went into exile. For sixteen years there was no end to the weeping and trembling they inflicted: they made Ulster weep and tremble every single night.

Meanwhile Deirdre spent a year with Conchobor. All that time she never smiled in laughter, or ate or slept enough, and she never

---

1 *And she … behind her back* Deirdre, of course, but she is not named. It might be that she is objectified and denied her personhood in this moment; it might be as though there is only one woman who matters in the world, a sense of scarcity that would explain why Conchobor could never let go of his grudge.

2 *Maine* Not to be confused with the seven sons of Ailill and Maeve who are named Maine. In "The Fate of the Children of Uisneach," the Maine in this story is a Scandinavian whose relatives have been killed by Noísiu, and he is the one who actually executes the brothers (beheading all three of them with a single blow) after they have been immobilized by Cathbad's magic. (Conchobor had told Cathbad they wouldn't be harmed, and Cathbad lays a curse on Emain Macha in retaliation for the lie.)

3 *they went … Ailill and Maeve* Later texts have Fergus go first to Eochaid Feidlech at Tara: see, for example, "The War of Fergus and Conchobor" (*Cogadh Fergusa agus Choncubhair*), edited and translated into French by Margaret C. Dobbs, "La guerre entre Fergus et Conchobar," *Revue Celtique* 40 (1923) 404–23, and translated by Patrick Brown at https://ulstercycle.wordpress.com/2009/11/07/the-war-of-fergus-and-conchobar/. For a full dossier on Fergus and his adventures, see Patricia Ní Mhaoileoin, "The heroic biography of Fergus mac Róich: a case study of the heroic-biographical pattern in Old and Middle Irish literature" (Ph.D. thesis, National University of Ireland, Galway, 2015, https://aran.library.nuigalway.ie/bitstream/handle/10379/5446/2015N%C3%ADMhaoileoinPhD.pdf).

lifted her head from her lap. When musicians were sent to distract her, she improvised this elegy:[1]

"You admire the warband
that swaggers into Emain after combat:
nobler still in striding home
were Uisliu's three heroic sons.

Noísiu with good hazel-mead:
I'd wash him by the fire.
Ardán with a stag or a fine pig,
tall Ainnle with a load on his back.

You may love the tasty mead
that the battle-glorious son of Ness drinks.
By the seashore, I once had
regular refreshment that was sweeter.

Noble Noísiu would prepare
the cooking-pit of a roving warband on the forest floor:
what the son of Uisliu cooked up
was more delicious than every honey-coated confection.

You always dote on the music
of pipers and horn-players;
today I declare
I have heard sweeter music.

Conchobor, your king, dotes
on pipers and horn-players;

---

1 *this elegy* On Irish women's lament poetry in general, see Kaarina Hollo, "Laments and lamenting in early medieval Ireland," in *Medieval Celtic Literature and Society*, ed. Helen Fulton (Four Courts, 2005) 83–94, and Angela Bourke, "More in anger than in sorrow: Irish women's lament poetry," in *Feminist Messages: Coding in Women's Folk Culture*, ed. Joan N. Radner (Urbana: University of Illinois Press, 1993) 160–82. On this lament specifically, see Marjorie Housley, "'The noble way you blushed': queering mourning verse in the Ulster Cycle," in *Knowing Sorrow: Grief, Gender, and Identity in the Middle Ages*, ed. Lee Templeton (Leiden: Brill, 2021) 142–64, which compares Deirdre's lament here with Cú Chulainn's lament for Fer Diad, below.

sweeter still I used to find—famously thrilling[1]—
the tune the sons of Uisliu would sing.

Noísiu's bass was like a rolling breaker:
his long-held notes were sweet music.
Ardán's baritone was good,
and Ainnle's high tenor coming to the mountain hut.

Noísiu: his gravemound is heaped.
He had a pitiful escort.
I poured out for him—his body was mobbed[2]—
the deadly drink he died from.

I loved his shearling cloak and handsome tunic.
A graceful man, although
it is sad that today I see no point
in waiting for the son of Uisliu to come from the green.[3]

I loved his mind, determined and direct;
I loved the warrior, noble and decorous.
After a journey past the forest eaves,
I loved to be bundled up[4] together in the dawn.

I loved the gray eye that women cherished,
baleful to enemies.

---

1 *thrilling* Hull had "fame of hosts (?)." The problem is *ell*, which Hull took as *3 ell*, "troop, flock"; I read it as *1 ell*, "a flush, a sudden emotion, a rush of feeling." Hence "fame of thrills," i.e., "famously thrilling."

2 *his body was mobbed* Hull had "host over a height (?)" for the parenthetical *drong tria alt*, which O Daly rejected without proposing an alternative, because the preposition means "through" not "over." *Drong* is a large group of people. The problem is *alt*, which has multiple meanings. I hesitantly take it as "shape, form" (*eDIL*, s.v. *1 alt* II.b.)—thus "a multitude [went] through his form"—with the sense that Noísiu was stabbed a lot by many people, which at least fits the context. The "drink" is metaphorical: Deirdre's sense of causing Noísiu's death.

3 *to come from the green* Speculative and probably wrong, but I haven't seen a better option. The end of the second line is *cid dind blai*, or *cid dinblai*, which Hull couldn't make sense of. *Cid* is "although it is"; the problem is the rest. (Kinsella's "a tall tree" seems to come from reading *dinnbile*, which is a stretch.) My translation is based on *de/di*, "from," with the article, and *blá*, "green, lawn, level field, plain" (*eDIL* s.v. *3 blá*), although the interaction of *cid* and *ba* is still a problem.

4 *bundled up* Speculative, on the basis of *custal* in *eDIL* ("held in, trussed, wrapped tightly," etc.).

After we toured the forest—a noble partnership—
I loved his tenor in the gloomy drizzle.

I don't sleep now,
or paint my nails.[1]
Joy, I cannot even contemplate
since it won't bring back the son of Tindell.[2]

I don't sleep:
I lie there half the night.
I rage against the crowds.
I don't eat, and I don't laugh.

Today I cannot spare the time for joy
in the society of Emain, once packed with nobles;
for serenity, solace, or soothing,
or a big house, or attractive ornaments."

And when Conchobor tried to soothe her, she improvised this elegy:

"Conchobor, what's wrong with you?
You brought up the sorrow under all my tears.
Long as I may live,
I'll never love you much.

What I found most beautiful under the sky,
what I loved most,
you took from me—a great crime—
not to see again until I die.

---

1 *paint my nails* This is the typical translation, but see Clodagh Downey, "Purple reign: the naming of Conall Corc," in *Approaches to Religion and Mythology in Celtic Studies*, ed. Katja Ritari and Alexandra Bergholm (Newcastle: Cambridge Scholars Publishing, 2008) 28–54, at 45–48. She proposes that this is instead "a circumlocution describing the act of eating, perhaps translateable literally as something like 'I do not defile/stain/taint my (finger)nails'. The phrase may furthermore contain the idea of the minimal degree of manual contact needed for eating: in other words, not only does Deirdre not eat, but she does not go so far as to touch her food."

2 *Tindell* Noísiu's mother. This way of identifying him might reflect a shift from the "manly" sphere of his activities while he was alive to the "womanly" sphere of Deirdre's experience without him, perhaps similar to how a mother would mourn him.

His absence grieves me.
This is how the son of Uisliu looks to me now:
a jet-black gravemound over a white body.
He was excellent beyond a multitude of men.

Purple cheeks prettier than a river meadow,
a red mouth, beetle-black eyebrows;
a row of pearly teeth suffused with beauty
like the noble sheen of snow.

What he wore was famous
among the Scottish warbands.
His gorgeous purple cloak—a perfect match
for its fringe of pure gold.

His tunic was satin, a valuable treasure,
with a hundred gems on it, a polished multitude.
To adorn it, it's clear:
fifty ounces of white-bronze.*

A gold-hilted sword in his hand;
two gray spears with piercing points;
a buckler rimmed with yellow gold
with a knob of silver on it.

Fine Fergus betrayed us,
bringing us over the sea.
He sold his honor for beer.
His great deeds have lapsed.

If Conchobor's Ulstermen
filled the plain,
I won't lie: I'd trade them all
to be with Noísiu son of Uisliu again.

Break my heart no more today.
I'll go soon to an early grave.
Grief is stronger than the sea:
I know it all too well, Conchobor."

"What do you hate most out of all you see?" said Conchobor.

"You, of course," she said, "and Éogan mac Durthacht!"

"Then you'll spend a year with Éogan," said Conchobor. Then he brought her over to Éogan.

The next day they went to the fair of Macha. She was behind Éogan in the chariot. She had sworn that no two men would ever share her.[1]

"Well, Deirdre," said Conchobor, "between me and Éogan, you look like a sheep making eyes at two rams."

There was a huge outcrop of stone ahead of them. She drove her head into it until her skull was in splinters and she was dead.

This was "The Exile of the Sons of Uisliu" and "The Exile of Fergus" and "The Death of the Sons of Uisliu and Deirdre."

*There is a sequel to this in "The Wooing of Lúaine and the Death of Athairne" (*Tochmarc Lúaine & Aided Athirne, *Ó Corráin #1116, second half of the twelfth century):*[2] *with Deirdre dead, Conchobor is inconsolable until he finds her match in a woman named Lúaine. They are engaged but Lúaine, rejecting the advances of the Ulster poet Athairne and his sons, is killed by their satire* before Conchobor can marry her, and he and the Ulster heroes avenge her. This text identifies the king of Scotland in the Deirdre story as Manannán son of Athgno, and says Noísiu and Deirdre had two children, a boy and a girl: Manannán fosters* them and attacks Ulster until Conchobor pays the boy compensation for his parents' death.*

---

1 *no two men … share her* Literally, "that she would never be with two men at the same time." Does she mean that she is a monogamous person, so the idea of being "shared" by Conchobor and Éogan outrages her beyond anything she has had to endure so far? Or is she still thinking of Noísiu and saying that no second man will have her—but in that case why did the issue not arise with Conchobor alone? Did he respect her grief for a whole year, and now intends for Éogan *not* to respect her grief? It is not clear how much sexual violence is actually threatened or practiced against Deirdre. Other sagas clearly mention the fact of rape, and sex in general; this one is more circumspect.

2 See the edition and translation by Whitley Stokes, "The wooing of Luaine and the death of Athirne," *Revue Celtique* 24 (1903) 270–87, 446 (add. and corr.), https://archive.org/details/revueceltiqu24pari/page/270/mode/2up, and the edition by Liam Breatnach which explores the difficult poetry, "Tochmarc Luaine ocus Aided Athairne," *Celtica* 13 (1980) 1–31.

The Pig-Keepers' Feud

*This ninth-century tale (*De chopur in dá muccida, *Ó Corráin #1035) appears with Recension 2 of the* Táin *in the Book of Leinster. The story accounts for the two great bulls at issue in the* Táin, *and explains why they have human intelligence and don't get along.*

There are elements here of the same kind of "Pythagorean" reincarnation as in "The Birth of Cú Chulainn." It may also be relevant that pigs have Otherworld connections: the description of the cave of Crúachu as a source of supernatural creatures*[1] *includes a story of pigs that defied any attempt to count them, until Ailill and Maeve came to do it in person (and one of them jumped out of its own skin to try to evade their authority); and in the Fourth Branch of the* Mabinogi,[2] *pigs are introduced to Wales as a gift from the Welsh equivalent of the Otherworld.*

The translation uses the Irish edited by R.I Best and Osborn Bergin in The Book of Leinster, *volume 5 (DIAS, 1967), 1121–24, reproduced at https://celt.ucc.ie//published/G800011E/text003.html. There is a previous translation by Kuno Meyer, "The begetting of the two swineherds," in Alfred Nutt,* The Celtic Doctrine of Re-birth *(Volume 2 of Nutt and Meyer's* The Voyage of Bran Son of Febal to the Land of the Living*) (London: David Nutt, 1897) 58–66, which includes some additional material as noted.*

Question: how did the Feud between the Two Pig-Keepers come about? That's easy.*

They were the pig-keeper of Ochall Oichni and the pig-keeper of Bodb,[3] king of the Otherworld abodes of Munster—the other was king of the Otherworld abodes of Connacht. Bodb's abode was the one on Femen; Ochall's was the one at Crúachu. They were good friends.

They had two pig-keepers, named Friuch and Rucht.[4] Friuch was

1 See p. 89, note 1 above.

2 See Boyd, *The Four Branches of the Mabinogi*, 71–74; compare 47.

3 *Bodb* Pronounced "BOTH-uv," with voiced *th,* Bodb is the brother of Óengus and the king of the Otherworld abodes ("fairy hills") of Munster; he features in "The Dream of Óengus" (see p. 153 below) and must not be confused with the war-goddess Badb.

4 *Friuch and Rucht* It's been suggested that these names mean "boar's bristles" and "grunting" respectively: see *eDIL*, s.vv. *friuch* and *2 rucht*, but then also *3 rucht*.

Bodb's pig-keeper and Rucht was Ochall's. They were good friends too. They each had pagan magic, and used to transform into any shape, just like Mongán mac Fiachna.[1]

Since they were good friends, when there was forage[2] in Munster, the pig-keeper from the north would come south with his scrawny pigs; and when there was forage in the north, the one from the south would go north.

They became a topic of contention: the Connachtmen said their pig-keeper was more powerful, and the Munstermen said theirs was.

One year there was lots of forage in Munster and the pig-keeper from the north brought his pigs south. His counterpart welcomed him. "They want to turn us against each other," he said. "The men here are saying you're more powerful than I am."

"Well, I'm not any *less*," said Ochall's pig-keeper.

"We can find out for sure," said Bodb's. "I'll influence your pigs so they don't get fat despite their feeding, while mine will." And that's what happened. Then Ochall's pig-keeper went home with his scrawny pigs: they were in such bad shape they barely made it. People laughed at him when he got back: "It was bad luck you went," everyone told him; "your counterpart's more powerful than you are."

"That's no big deal," he said. "We'll have forage again and I'll play the same trick on him." And that's what happened. Bodb's pig-keeper came north the following year, with his scrawny pigs, to visit him in Connacht, and Ochall's did the same thing to his pigs so they wasted away. Then everyone said they were both equally powerful. Bodb's pig-keeper went south with his pigs still scrawny.

Then Bodb fired his pig-keeper, and the one in the north also lost his job. They spent the whole of the next two years as crows[3]—one year in the north, in Connacht, at the hillfort of Crúachu, and the next at the Otherworld* abode on Femen.[4] The Munstermengathered

---

1 *Mongán mac Fiachna* A son of Manannán mac Lir of the Túatha Dé Danann.* At least one story equates him with Finn mac Cumaill. There is a collection of Mongán stories in *The Celtic Heroic Age*, 217–22.

2 *forage* Literally "mast": the accumulation of acorns, beech-nuts, chestnuts, and other food that pigs eat off the forest floor.

3 *crows* Or possibly hawks: see *eDIL*, s.v. *1 én*, explaining *sen-én*, 'ancient bird.'

4 *Femen* "FEV-en," a plain in the south of Ireland, shown on Map 1. The Otherworld abode is on Slievenamon Mountain (*Sliabh na mBan*, "The Mountain of the Women"), County Tipperary.

there one day. "Those birds in front of us aren't being exactly quiet," they said: "for a whole year they've been heckling each other and carrying on, right up till today."

While they were saying this they saw Ochall's steward coming up the hill toward them. His name was Fuidell mac Fiadmire. They welcomed him.

"Those birds in front of us are being so loud! You would think they were the same two birds we had in the north last year—that's exactly what they were doing all year long."

Here's what they saw after that: those two crows were there in human form, and they recognized them as the two pig-keepers. They welcomed them. "There's no sense in welcoming us," said Bodb's pig-keeper. "The two of us will cause the slaughter of loved ones, and great wailing."

"What have you been up to?" said Bodb.

"Nothing good," he said. "It's been two years since we left you: we were in the shape of birds, and you saw what we were doing right in front of you. We spent a whole year like that at Crúachu, and another at this Otherworld* abode on Femen. Now the men from the north and south have seen how powerful we are. Now we'll take the shape of water-monsters and spend the next two years under the sea."

Then they went away from them in different directions: one of them went into the river Shannon, and the other into the Suir, and they spent two whole years underwater. For a whole year they were seen gnawing at each other in the Suir, and the next they were seen in the Shannon.[1]

Then they were two stags, and they used to round up the other one's herds and run wild on the other's territory.

They became two *fían*-warriors,* wounding each other.

They became two phantoms, scaring each other.

They became two dragons, pelting down snow on each other's land.

1 *Then they went … the Shannon* A longer version of this text, appearing with Recension 1 of the *Táin* in Egerton 1782, expands on the exploits of the water monsters and the warriors they turn into: see Nutt, *The Celtic Doctrine of Re-birth*, 60–65. (This longer version has also been edited and translated into German by Ulrike Roider: *De chophur in da muccida: Wie die beiden Schweinehirten den Kreislauf der Existenzen durchwanderten: eine altirische Sage* [Innsbruck: Innsbrucker Beiträge zur Sprachwissenschaft, 1979].)

They fell out of the air and became two maggots. One went into the well of Glas Cruinn in Cúailnge, where it was drunk by a cow belonging to Dáire mac Fiachna. And the other one went into the spring of Garad in Connacht, where it was drunk by one of Maeve and Ailill's cows.[1] So those cows gave birth to[2] the two bulls, the White-Horned Bull (*Finnbennach*) of Aí and the Brown Bull (*Donn*) of Cúailnge.

As pig-keepers, they were Rucht and Rucne.

As birds, Ingen ("Talon") and Eitte ("Wing").

As sea creatures, Bled ("Whale") and Blod.

As *fían*-warriors,* Rinn ("Point") and Faebur ("Edge").

As phantoms, Scáth ("Shadow") and Scíath ("Shield").

As maggots, Crunniuc and Tunniuc.

Finnbennach of Aí and Donn of Cúailnge were their names when they were bulls.

*The text ends with an alliterative poem describing the two ferocious bulls. The "defective" late text "The Battle of Findchorad" (*Cath Findchorad, *Ó Corráin #1010) has preserved what scholars agree is a better version of this poem than the Book of Leinster has: see https://archive.org/details/zeitschriftfrc1314meyeuoft/page/400/mode/2up.*

1 *They fell ... cows* In the longer version, each maggot talks to the local ruler—Maeve of Connacht, and Dáire's father Fiachna in Ulster—and convinces them to feed them for a year before the cows drink them. Maeve's maggot, Crunniuc, actually advises her to marry Ailill, perhaps to avoid belonging to a woman (see p. 162).

2 *those cows gave birth to* Edited for clarity, from "So they were the origin of."

Other Prequels

“The Unveiling of the Táin*” lists other prequels that haven’t been translated here.*

“The Taking of the Otherworld Abode” is the short text* De Gabáil in tSíde *(Ó Corráin #1036, ninth century or earlier). This describes how Óengus (also known as the Mac Óc or “Young Son” because his mother’s pregnancy was magically accelerated), son of the Dagdae of the Túatha Dé Danann,* took possession of the Otherworld abode at Bruig na Bóinne. This story’s connection to the* Táin *is pretty tangential: Óengus is the protagonist of “The Dream of Óengus,” the second prequel listed here, and Bruig na Bóinne is involved in “The Birth of Cú Chulainn.”*

This story has been translated by Vernam Hull, “De gabáil in t-shída *(Concerning the seizure of the fairy mound),”* ZCP *19 (1933) 53–58, and by John Carey in* The Celtic Heroic Age, *145. On its status as a prequel, see Martina Maher,* “De gabáil int s[h]ída*:* remscél *or* remremscél*?” in* Ulidia 4, *150–61.*

“About the Mac Óc’s Dream” (De Aslingi in Meic Óic) *is more commonly known as “The Dream of Óengus” (*Aislinge Óenguso, *Ó Corráin #986, first half of the eighth century or earlier). This describes how Óengus gets help from Ailill and Maeve in his search for an enchanting—and enchanted—Otherworld woman, and then supposedly owes them his help on the Táin. (Conchobor’s physician Fíngin is also involved: he diagnoses Óengus with lovesickness.)*

This story has been translated by Kenneth Jackson in A Celtic Miscellany *(Harmondsworth: Penguin, 1971) 93–97; by Gantz, 107–112; by Kevin Murray at https://iso.ucc.ie/Aislinge-oenguso/Aislinge-oenguso-text.html; and most recently by Christina Cleary, “An investigation of the* remscéla Tána Bó Cúailgne *and an edition and translation of* Aislinge Óenguso *with textual notes” (Ph.D. thesis, Trinity College Dublin, 2018, http://www.tara.tcd.ie/handle/2262/83800). Its status as a* Táin *prequel is discussed by Hugh Fogarty, “*Aislinge Óenguso*: a* remscél *reconsidered,” in* Narrative in Celtic tradition: essays in honor of Edgar M. Slotkin *(*CSANA Yearbook *8–9), ed. Joseph Eska (New York: Colgate University Press, 2011) 56–67, and in Cleary’s thesis.*

"The Raid on Regamon's Cattle" is Táin Bó Regamna *(Ó Corráin #1108, eighth or ninth century). In this, the sons of Ailill and Maeve, the seven Maines, take an interest in Regamon, a Connacht landowner with seven attractive daughters and enough livestock to supply the army on the Táin. They conspire with the daughters to drive off Regamon's cattle in his absence, and when he comes after them in force, the daughters carry on to Crúachu with the cattle while the Maines hold him off. Ailill, Maeve, and Fergus come to the rescue and agree on terms with Regamon: they'll return his cattle, but his daughters will marry the Maines, and 140 cows will be paid as a dowry to support the army on the Táin.*

This story has been translated by A.H. Leahy in Heroic Romances of Ireland, *Vol. II (London: David Nutt, 1906) 83–99, online at https://archive.org/details/heroicromancesof02leah/page/82/mode/2up, and more recently into German by Johan Corthals.*

"Nera's Adventure" is Echtra Nerai *(Ó Corráin #1050, tenth century "but reworked"). In this, the Connachtman Nera takes up Ailill's dare to tie a loop around the foot of a hanged man on Samain* night. After some fun with the hanged man, Nera enters the Otherworld,* where he takes a wife and fathers a child, then comes back to warn Ailill and Maeve that the Otherworld is planning to attack them, which they can prevent only by invading it themselves—which they do, although then Nera disappears into it for good. Meanwhile, defying Cú Chulainn, the war-goddess Morrígan takes Nera's son's cow to be impregnated by the Brown Bull of Cúailnge: the resulting calf fights the Connacht bull Finnbennach and loses, and Maeve swears not to rest until she can watch the two bulls fight each other, which provides another motivation for the Táin than the one in the "Pillow-Talk" episode below. The bellow of the defeated calf gives Bricriu an excuse to mock Fergus's singing, and Fergus responds by implanting a* fidchell**-piece in Bricriu's head, which is referenced near the end of the* Táin *itself.*

This story has been translated by John Carey in The Celtic Heroic Age, *127–32, and can also be read at https://www.ucc.ie/en/media/academic/seanmeanghaeilge/cdi/texts/Meyer-Echtra-Nerai.pdf in the older translation by Kuno Meyer. For commentary, see John Carey, "Sequence and causation in* Echtra Nerai,*"* Ériu *39 (1988) 67–74, and Leonie Duignan, "The* echtrae *as an early Irish literary genre" (Ph.D.*

thesis, National University of Ireland Maynooth, 2010, https://mural.maynoothuniversity.ie/7801/).

"The Wooing of Ferb" is Tochmarc Ferbe *(Ó Corráin #1115, probably mid-twelfth century). Set seven years before the* Táin, *this describes the courtship of Ferb (pronounced "Ferve"), daughter of Gerg, by Ailill and Maeve's son Maine Mórgor (Maine "Most Filial"). Conchobor attacks and Maine is killed (although in the* Táin *itself, all seven of the Maines are living); Ferb laments him and Maeve counterattacks.*

This story has been translated by A.H. Leahy in The Courtship of Ferb *(London: David Nutt, 1902), and now by Rebecca Shercliff in her Ph.D. thesis, "A critical edition of* Tochmarc Ferbe*: with translation, textual notes and literary commentary" (University of Cambridge, 2018, https://www.repository.cam.ac.uk/handle/1810/288120): she refines Ó Corráin's dating of tenth to twelfth century.*

"The Raid on Flidais's Cattle" is Táin Bó Flidais *(Ó Corráin #1105, possibly ninth century, with a thirteenth-century second recension). This describes how Fergus and the Ulster exiles, and eventually Maeve and the men of Ireland, go after the cattle of the Gamanraid in Connacht, in what is now County Mayo. Flidais is the wife of their king Ailill and ends up as the wife of Fergus.*

This story has been translated by A.H. Leahy in Heroic Romances of Ireland, *Vol. II, 101–25, at https://archive.org/details/heroicromancesof02leah/page/100/mode/2up, and is now the focus of an active project: see https://www.northmayo.ie/tain-bo-fliodhaise-the-cattle-raid-of-mayo/, which includes a detailed summary of the plot.*

As noted, "The Unveiling of the Táin*" says there are 12 prequels but lists only 10. Obvious contenders for the remaining spots would be "The Exile of the Sons of Uisliu" (*Loinges mac nUislenn, *Ó Corráin #1078) and "The Death of Aífe's Only Son" (*Aided Óenfhir Aífe, *Ó Corráin #980), both translated above, and "The Cattle-Raid of Fráech" (*Táin bó Fraích, *Ó Corráin #1106), which is discussed below* *on p. 197, note 1,* *when Cú Chulainn fights Fráech in the* Táin.

*Yet another prequel is "The Raid on Dartad's Cattle" (*Táin bó Dartada, *Ó Corráin #1104, ninth century). In this, the Munster king Eochu Bec* *of Clíu is encouraged by a malicious Otherworld* couple (who give their names as "Victory and Defeat" and "Gathering and Destruction") to visit Ailill and Maeve in Connacht. Eochu agrees to provide cattle to support Ailill and Maeve's army in exchange for their protection, but on his way home he and his retinue of princes in fosterage* are attacked and killed by Connacht raiders acting on their own initiative. The Otherworld couple urge Ailill to send his son Órlám to take the cattle from Eochu's daughter, Dartad, since she is in love with him. But they also appear to the Munster champion Corb Cliach mac Tassaig and warn him to defend the honor of Munster against Connachtmen coming to take their cattle. Corb Cliach attacks Órlám, and Dartad is killed in the fighting: only Órlám and eight of his men make it back to Connacht with the cattle.*

This story has been translated by A.H. Leahy in Heroic Romances of Ireland, *Vol. II, 69–81, at https://archive.org/details/heroicromancesof02leah/page/68/mode/2up.*

The Body of the Táin

The Táin *is Ó Corráin #1103, as noted above. The translation uses the Irish edited by Cecile O'Rahilly in* Táin Bó Cúailnge: Recension I *(DIAS, 1976), at https://celt.ucc.ie/published/G301012.html (text) and https://celt.ucc.ie/published/T301012.html (translation); and* Táin Bó Cúalnge from the Book of Leinster *(DIAS, 1967), at https://celt.ucc.ie/published/G301035.html (text) and https://celt.ucc.ie/published/T301035.html (translation). Other sources are acknowledged in the notes.*

The Pillow-Talk

Recension 2 (the Book of Leinster version) starts with this episode, conventionally known as "The Pillow-Talk," which is not included in Recension 1. (See the manuscript image at https://www.isos.dias.ie/TCD/TCD_MS_1339.html#53.) A crucial issue here is the legal status of Ailill and Maeve's marriage. Tomás Ó Cathasaigh has analyzed it as "a marriage of equals," in which Maeve legitimately possesses the land, and Ailill is qualified to rule it. Maeve's accusation that Ailill is a "kept man" uses early Irish legal vocabulary: she calls him literally "a man on woman-property," whose honor-price was based on the woman's. Most women had no independent legal rights in early Irish law, but came under the authority of a male relative. One exception was if a woman was her father's heir, which could happen if he had no sons. (In Maeve's case, most or all of her brothers are dead: see pp. 69, 335–36.) She could keep those rights after marriage if her husband was an outsider to the jurisdiction, or if she brought all or most of the property to the marriage.*[1] *So the couple's argument is more than just an ego contest—it has legal substance. But Gregory Toner argues that once we know how the whole thing ends, Recension 2 of the* Táin *seems to be saying that "equality between king and queen is imprudent and potentially destructive."*[2]

One time, Ailill and Maeve were in their royal bed at Crúachu in Connacht, chatting as they rested on their pillow.

"I'll tell you what,[3] babe," said Ailill, "a woman has it good if she marries a nobleman."

"Sure," said the babe, "but where is this coming from?"

---

1 See *GEIL*, 70–73, and Eska, *Cáin Lánamna*.

2 See *Coire Sois,* 249–58, and Toner, "Reading the *Táin* from back to front," in *Táin Bó Cúalnge from the Book of Leinster: Reassessments*, ed. John Carey (ITS, 2020) 69–89, at 89.

3 *I'll tell you what* Ailill's remark starts with *fírbriathar*: this is literally "a true word," rendered "in truth" by O'Rahilly, hence my translation. It has also been taken to mean "a true saying," invoking common knowledge or even a proverb: "It's true what they say," as both Kinsella and Carson have it. Then the statement itself, *is maith ben ben dagfhir,* would sound proverbial—"A well-off woman is one well wed," for example—and Maeve's reply would be "what made you think of that?" The word translated 'babe' here is *ingen*, which, per *eDIL*, means "a daughter, girl, maiden, virgin; also freq. used of a (married) woman" as in this case; normally I make it 'girl' or 'daughter' depending on context. The same word is used to attribute Maeve's reply.

"Well, I was thinking how much better off you are today than when I married you."

"I was doing fine before you came along," said Maeve.

"That's not what I heard; that's not my understanding. You were living off a woman's inheritance and your neighbors were raiding and plundering it all away from you."

"That's not what it was like for me at all," said Maeve. "My father Eochaid Feidlech[1] was high-king of Ireland. He had six daughters: Deirbriu, Eithne, Éile, Clothru, Mugain, and me. I was the proudest and the finest of them. I was the best of them in generosity and gift-giving. I was the best of them in warfare and fighting and martial arts. I had fifteen hundred royal henchmen who were sons of foreigners and another fifteen hundred who were locals, and for every one of them I had ten more henchmen, and nine more henchmen, and eight more henchmen, and seven more henchmen, and six more henchmen, and five more henchmen, and four more henchmen, and three more henchmen, and two more henchmen, and one more henchman for every henchman.[2] That was my permanent household. And for that reason my father gave me one of the five provinces of Ireland: the province of Crúachu. That's why I'm called Maeve of Crúachu.[3]

"Finn mac Rossa Rúaid, king of Leinster, and Cairbre[4] Nia Fer, king of Tara, sent me marriage proposals. So did Conchobor, king of

1 *Eochaid Feidlech* She actually gives his pedigree going back ten generations: "Eochaid Feidlech mac Find meic Findomain meic Findeoin meic Findguill meic Rotha meic Rigéoin meic Blathachta meic Beothechta meic Enna Agnig meic Óengusa Turbig." Her sisters' names have been adjusted to match the spelling in "Maeve's Series of Husbands" and "The Death of Maeve," i.e., *Eithne* instead of *Ethi* here. Maeve's mother is rarely mentioned but "Fitness of Names" (II, 147) identifies her as Cróichen Chróderg, "Étaín's maid." Étaín ("EH-deen") is a supernatural woman who appears in "The Wooing of Étaín" (*Tochmarc Étaíne*, Ó Corráin #1114) and "The Destruction of Da Derga's Hostel."

2 *for every henchman* Assuming she means that for each of the original 3,000 there were (10 + 9 + 8 + 7 + 6 + 5 + 4 + 3 + 2 + 1) more, she had 168,000. If there were 10 for each of the original 3,000, and 9 for every one of *those*, and so on, she had trillions. These are by no means realistic numbers, and the way they're presented suggests that Maeve is trying to overwhelm Ailill with a sense of her grandeur. Her father's pedigree would serve the same function.

3 *Maeve of Crúachu* Crúachu is the royal site; the province is Connacht. Maeve's epithet distinguishes her from other Medbs of early Irish literature, like Medb Lethderg ("Red-side").

4 *Finn … Cairbre* Both sons of Ross Rúad, hence brothers of Ailill, but Maeve is making

Ulster, and so did Eochu Bec.[1] But I turned them all down, because I asked for a strange bride-price, that no woman before me had ever asked from any man in Ireland: that is, a husband without stinginess, jealousy, or fear.

"If my husband were stingy, we'd be a bad match, because generosity and gift-giving are one of my strengths. It would be a black mark against my husband if I were more generous, but not if we were the same, as long as both of us were generous.

"If my husband were a coward, we'd also be a bad match, because I single-handedly win at warfare and fighting and martial arts. It would be a black mark against my husband if I were braver, but not if we were the same, as long as both of us were brave.

"If my husband were jealous, it would still be bad, because I've never gone without a man waiting in the shadow of another.

"And I found a husband like that: meaning you, Ailill mac Rossa Rúaid of Leinster. You're not stingy, you're not jealous, and you're no slouch.

"I gave you a contract and a bride-price like you were a woman: a dozen outfits, a chariot worth twenty-seven *cumals*,* the width of your face in red gold, and the weight of your left arm in white-bronze.* And if anyone inflicts shame or grief or embarrassment on you, you have no right to compensation or honor-price* separate from what I have a right to, because you're a kept man."

"That's not what it was like for me either," said Ailill. "I had two brothers, one ruled Tara and one ruled Leinster—Finn was in Leinster and Cairbre at Tara. I let them rule because they were older, but I was no less generous with gifts than they were. And I never heard of any province in Ireland that was part of a woman's marriage-portion except for this one.[2] So I came and took the kingship here on the strength of my mother's claim, because my mother was Máta Muiresc the daughter of Mágu. And what better queen could I have than you, since you're the daughter of a high-king of Ireland?"

---

this about the social distinction of her suitors, not family rivalry; Ailill is about to count the fact that they're related to him as a point in his favor.

1 *Eochu Bec* Munster king, mentioned in "The Raid on Dartad's Cattle," p. 155 above.

2 *And I … this one* The translation here follows Ó Cathasaigh's analysis; others have taken it as "any province that was dependent on a woman," as though that were a weakness to exploit or an aberration to be rectified. "Maeve's Series of Husbands," above, varies from the narrative Ailill gives in this paragraph of how he and Maeve got together.

"Fine," said Maeve, "but the fact remains that I'm richer than you are."

"I'll be shocked if that's true," said Ailill, "because no one has more riches and treasure and wealth than I do, I know that for a fact."

Then they started having all their least valuable possessions brought out so they could determine who had more riches and treasure and wealth. First it was their cups, their vats, their iron pots, their jugs, their washbasins, and their tubs. Then their rings, their bracelets, their thumb-rings, their golden objects, and their clothes: purple, blue, black, green, yellow, dappled, gray, brown, checkered, and striped. Their huge flocks of sheep were brought in from the plains and meadowlands and fields. They were counted, assessed, and appraised, and turned out to be exactly the same in numbers and size. Now Maeve's sheep included a prize ram, worth a *cumal*,* but Ailill had one to match it. Their horses, steeds, and herds were brought in from their pastures and corrals. Maeve's herd included a prize horse, worth a *cumal*, but Ailill had one to match it. Then their huge herds of pigs were brought in from the woods and sloping valleys and the backcountry. They were counted, assessed, and appraised. Maeve had a prize boar and Ailill had one too. Then their herds of cows, their cattle, and their droves were brought in from the woods and wilderness throughout the province. They were counted, assessed, and appraised, and each had exactly the same in numbers and size. But Ailill had a prize bull. As a calf it had belonged to Maeve. Its name was Finnbennach, the White-Horned. It felt it was beneath it to belong to a woman, so it went to join the king's herd. Now Maeve felt as though she didn't have a penny to her name, since she didn't have a bull in her own herd to match it.

She sent for the herald Mac Roth and asked him to find out where there was another bull like that in all the provinces of Ireland.

"Actually," he said, "I know where to find a bull that's even better. It's in the province of Ulster, in the district of Cúailnge, at the house of Dáire mac Fiachna, and its name is Donn Cúailnge, the Brown Bull of Cooley."[1]

---

1 *Dáire … Cooley Dáire* is pronounced "DOY-ruh" (or "DAH-ruh"). *Donn* just means "Brown," so the bull's name is technically the Brown One of Cúailnge. Cúailnge is the Cooley Peninsula beside Carlingford Loch in modern County Louth in Northern Ireland: see Maps 3 and 4.

"Go there, Mac Roth, and ask Dáire to lend it to me for a year. When the year is up, he'll get it back with fifty heifers as a fee for the loan. And keep another offer up your sleeve: if the people there object to handing over such a valuable possession as the Brown Bull, then Dáire himself can come with it. He'll receive a chunk of the lush Aí Plain that's the size of his own land, a chariot worth twenty-seven *cumals*,* and he'll even get to pay my thighs a friendly visit."

So the heralds, a party of nine, went to the house of Dáire mac Fiachna. There was a warm welcome there for Mac Roth, which was only fitting since he was the chief herald of all. Dáire asked Mac Roth why he had come and Mac Roth told him, including the argument between Maeve and Ailill. "And I'm here to ask for a loan of the Brown Bull of Cúailnge to match the White-Horned. You'll be paid a fee of fifty heifers when the Brown Bull is returned. And wait, there's more: if you come too, you'll receive a chunk of the lush Aí Plain that's the size of your own land, a chariot worth twenty-seven *cumals*, and on top of that you'll get to pay Maeve's thighs a friendly visit."[1]

Dáire was thrilled, and bounced around until he burst the seams on his seat cushions.

"True as my conscience, even if the Ulstermen object, my treasure, the Brown Bull of Cúailnge, will be going to Ailill and Maeve in Connacht."

And Mac Roth was pleased to hear him say that.

Afterwards the heralds were waited on and the dirt floor was covered with fresh straw and rushes. They were served the finest food, and treated to a drinking fest that got them tipsy.

Two of the heralds struck up a conversation. "I'll tell you what," said one of them, "our host here is a prince of a man."

---

1 *there's more … friendly visit* Toner, "Reading the *Táin* from back to front," 83–85, sees the fifty heifers as reasonable compensation for the loan of the bull (which would presumably include its breeding services), but the rest of the offer as totally excessive, unless Maeve is scheming to take permanent possession of the bull through an offer of "concubinage" or "marriage" to Dáire. Early Irish law acknowledged polygyny (multiple wives), but not polyandry (multiple husbands); for Maeve to contemplate any kind of formal union with Dáire while staying married to Ailill is, Toner thinks, an example of her trying to act like a king.

"Isn't he though," said the other.

"Is there any finer man in Ulster?" said the first one.

"Yes," said the second, "the man he serves, Conchobor. If all the Ulstermen got behind him there would be no shame in it.[1] But it was more than generous of Dáire to give the nine of us envoys what would otherwise have taken four whole provinces to drag out of Ulster."

"I'd sooner watch that mouth of yours spit up blood and gore than what you said. If he hadn't agreed to give it up, we'd just take the bull by force."

Then a third herald joined in and asked what they were saying, and they repeated all of it, word for word.[2]

At that point Dáire mac Fiachna's steward came in with a man bringing alcohol and a man bringing food, and he heard what they were saying. He saw red, and put out the food and drink for them without telling them to help themselves or not to help themselves. He went straight to Dáire and said to him: "Are you the one who gave the heralds that magnificent treasure—I mean the Brown Bull?"

"I sure am," said Dáire.

"Then you're not master in your own house, because what they said is true: if you hadn't agreed to give it up, then they'd take it by force, with Ailill and Maeve's armies and the cunning of Fergus mac Roích."

"Then I vow by the gods I worship that that's the way they'll have to take it, because I'm all done with giving!"

That's how things stood until morning.[3]

The heralds got up early and came to see Dáire.

"Noble sir, show us where you keep the Brown Bull."

---

1 *If all … in it* The story assumes we know that there are thousands of expatriate Ulstermen living in Connacht who reject Conchobor's authority. They are led by Fergus mac Roích, who comes up shortly in the conversation between Dáire and the steward.

2 *word for word* Paraphrased for convenience: in the Irish, they actually repeat the conversation word for word. "He was saying 'our host here is a prince of a man,' and then he said 'isn't he though,' and then *he* said 'is there any finer man in Ulster?" etc. etc. This is more than a momentary indiscretion that the steward needs to overhear at the exact wrong second. The entire group is implicated.

3 *until morning* Toner points out that according to early Irish contract law, a contract could be rescinded only until sunset on the day it was agreed to, so Dáire may not be legally entitled to rescind it in the morning (87). This would make his actions a breach of contract and an insult.

"There's no way," said Dáire. "And if I made a habit of playing false with heralds, travelers, or passersby, none of you would still be alive."

"Why's that?" said Mac Roth.

"I've had more than enough cause," said Dáire. "You said if I wouldn't agree to give it up you would take it by force, with Ailill and Maeve's armies and the cunning of Fergus mac Roích."

"Come on," said Mac Roth. "Whatever some flunkies might say in the process of getting drunk and stuffing their faces with your food and drink, you can't pay any attention to it or take it seriously or hold it against Ailill and Maeve."[1]

"And yet, Mac Roth, I won't be giving you my bull now."

So the heralds turned back and went to Crúachu in Connacht. Maeve asked them to report, and Mac Roth told her how she wouldn't get the bull from Dáire.

"Why is that?" said Maeve.

Mac Roth explained why.

"There's no need to smooth off all the knots[2] in this, Mac Roth. Everyone knew that if he wouldn't agree to give it, we would take it by force. And now we will."

*

This is the beginning of Recension 1, which the translation follows from now on (short passages from Recension 2 are clearly marked). See the manuscript image at https://www.isos.dias.ie/RIA/RIA_MS_23_E_25.html#57. Section headings, in bold font here, are from the manuscripts. The translation "Now for X:" corresponds to X inso sís, *literally "Here below [is] X," and similar tags. Not all the headings have these.*

---

1 *against Ailill and Maeve* Toner notices how Ailill is implicated here: "Either the breach of contract with M[aeve] is taken also as bad faith against her marital partner, or Dáire's obstinate refusal in the face of the military threat from 'the army of Ailill and M[aeve]' is, in itself, a challenge to Ailill's honour" (88). This would explain why Ailill *has* to accompany Maeve on the cattle-raid. Toner thinks this might have been her plan all along.

2 *all the knots* A woodworking metaphor. Knots are the tough circular lumps in wood where a branch was attached to the treetrunk. Maeve means that either she is not interested in trying to wear away Dáire's resistance with further diplomacy, or she doesn't care about making the military option any less rough and ugly than it naturally is.

Now for *Táin Bó Cúailnge*:

The Connachtmen—that is, Ailill and Maeve—assembled a great army, and sent word to the other three provinces.[1] And Ailill sent messengers to the seven sons of Mágu,[2] i.e., Ailill, Ánlúan, Moccorb, Cet, Én, Bascall, and Dócha, each with three thousand men, and to Cormac Conn Loinges son of Conchobor, with the three hundred men he had who were being billeted in Connacht.

Then they all came and gathered at Crúachu on Aí Plain (*Crúachain Aí*).

Cormac's forces formed three groups as they approached Crúachu.[3]

The first group wore speckled cloaks wrapped around them. Their hair was cut close. They wore tunics down to their knees, and carried long shields, and every man had a spade-shaped thrusting spear in his hand, with a broad sharp head on a mid-weight shaft.

The second group wore dark gray cloaks and tunics with red embroidery that fell to their calves, and long hair hanging down their backs, and they carried white shields, and in their hands they carried five-pronged spears.

"That's not Cormac yet," said Maeve.

Then came the third group. They wore purple cloaks and hooded tunics with red embroidery that fell to their feet, and their hair was cut shoulder-length, and they carried curved shields with scalloped rims, and every man had a spear in his hand the size of a royal house-post.

"This time it's Cormac," said Maeve.

So the four provinces of Ireland assembled at Crúachu. Their prophets and druids* kept them there for two weeks, waiting

---

1 *the other three provinces* The southwestern province of Munster, the southeastern province of Leinster, and the central province of Meath.

2 *seven sons of Mágu* Compare p. 330 below. Cet and Ánlúan also featured in "The Story of Mac Dá Thó's Pig," according to which Ánlúan was killed (p. 85).

3 *Cormac's forces … approached Crúachu* The significance of this episode and other episodes involving the Ulster exiles is discussed by Tomás Ó Cathasaigh, "The Ulster exiles and thematic symmetry in Recension I of *Táin Bó Cúailnge*," *Studia Celtica Fennica* 14 (2017) 156–71, https://journal.fi/scf/article/download/60764/38327/108742.

for a sign. And Maeve said to her charioteer on the day they left: "Everyone who has to leave their loved ones and their friends today will curse me, because I'm the one who raised this army."

"Wait, then," said the charioteer, "and let me take the chariot in a sunwise* circle to make the omen stronger for our safe return."

He brought the chariot back around and they were about to set off, when they saw a teenage girl standing in front of them. She wore a speckled cloak with a gold brooch, and a hooded tunic with red embroidery. She wore shoes with gold buckles. She had a narrow chin and a wide forehead. Her beautiful black eyelashes cast a shadow on the middle of her cheeks. You would think her lips were fine red leather.* You would think that between her lips was a shower of pearls—that is, her teeth. She had three braids. Two were coiled up around her head, and the third went down her back and hit her calves. In her hand she held a weaving sword[1] made of white-bronze,* with gold inlay. She had three pupils in each eye. She was armed. Two black horses pulled her chariot.

"What's your name?" said Maeve.

"My name is Fedelm, poetess[2] of Connacht," said the girl.

"Where have you come from?"

"From studying poet*-lore in Scotland."

"And can you see the future?"[3]

"I actually can," said the girl.

"Then look for me and tell me what becomes of my expedition."

So the girl looked, and Maeve said: "Prophetess Fedelm, what do you make of my army?"

---

1 *weaving sword* This is a sword-shaped object normally made of wood. The pointed tip of the "blade" is used to pick up threads on a loom, and the blunt "hilt" to beat them into place. It is not to be confused with a weaver's *beam*, which is part of the loom and is much longer and thicker: the Bible famously compares the spear of Goliath to a weaver's beam.

2 *Fedelm, poetess* Pronounced "FETH-elm," with voiced *th*. The Irish for "poet" (*fili*, here compounded with *ban-*, "woman-") etymologically means "seer." Fedelm was studying *filidecht*, the craft of the *fili*, which would encompass poetry and divination (she is about to prophesy in verse).

3 *see the future* Literally, "Do you have *imbas forosnai*?" See the note to Scáthach's prophecy in "The Wooing of Emer," p. 120, note 2 above. What precisely Fedelm is doing, and how long it takes, when Maeve asks her to "look" is not clear from the text, but the repeated formal question "Prophetess Fedelm, what do you make of my army?" suggests that she is in a trance. She might or might not be registering Maeve's objections.

Fedelm answered, "I see it gory. I see it red."

"Impossible," said Maeve. "Conchobor mac Nessa is lying paralyzed in Emain, with all the Ulstermen and their best warriors. My messengers have come and told me. Prophetess Fedelm, what do you make of my army?"

"I see it gory. I see it red."

"That's not true," said Maeve. "Celtchar mac Uthidir is in Brookside Fort (*Dún Lethglaise*[1]) with a third of the Ulstermen, and Fergus mac Roích and his division[2] are in exile here with us. Prophetess Fedelm, what do you make of my army?"

"I see it gory. I see it red."

"Oh, big deal. There are always frictions and conflicts and bloody woundings every time you raise an army or have a lot of men in camp. Look again and tell me the truth. Prophetess Fedelm, what do you make of my army?"

"I see it gory. I see it red," said Fedelm, and then she said:

"I see a blond man who'll work weapon-feats,
his skin scored with wounds:
the hero's light above his head,
his brow a festival of talents.

He has a hero's seven pupils
gem-like in both eyes.
His spearpoints are bared.
He wears a red shirt with clasps.

He has the loveliest of faces.
He flusters the womenfolk.[3]

---

1 *Dún Lethglaise* Celtchar's fort at what is now Downpatrick, County Down, in Northern Ireland. The explanation of *lethglaise* as being "on one side of the stream" (as against other explanations involving a partly green mound, fetters, etc.) is from Thomas Charles-Edwards, *Early Christian Ireland* (Cambridge University Press, 2000) 65–67, which also reviews its history as a monastic site. Incidentally, Celtchar's patronymic is normally given as *mac Uthechair*.

2 *his division* "Division" is the standard translation of "thirty hundreds," i.e., 3,000 men, which has the extended meaning of "large force of warriors regardless of size."

3 *flusters the womenfolk* The Irish is *dobeir mod don banchureo. eDIL,* s.v. *mod,* sees the usage here as "perhaps an extension" of the meaning "function, work, service": "his

A young man of beauteous complexion,
in battle he takes on a dragon's dimensions.

In his rage he looks like
Cú Chulainn of Muirthemne.
I don't know if he *is* that Cú Chulainn
of fairest fame,
but I know this:
the army will be drenched in gore because of him.

I see a tall man on the plain,
bringing the army to battle.
In each hand he carries
four shortswords for doing incredible feats.

He attacks with his *gáe bolga**
and his sword with the ivory hilt and his spear.
He can inflict them on the army,
wielding each weapon its own special way.

This man in a red cloak as battle array,
he strides on every battlefield.
He attacks them over his left wheel-rim:
the mutant* destroys them.
I see his form has changed
from how he looked before.

---

beauty gives the women-folk no rest?" But Sarah Sheehan, "Feasts for the eyes: visuality and desire in the Ulster Cycle," in *Constructing Gender in Medieval Ireland*, ed. Ann Dooley and Sarah Sheehan (Palgrave Macmillan, 2013) 95–113, at 108, claims that here, "wordplay on *mod* foregrounds masculinity as a linguistic construct as well as the sexual difference that distinguishes the warrior from his appreciative audience; it also destabilizes heroic dignity through the bawdy sense of *mod/moth* that was available to the *Táin*'s audience," since *mod* is "a homophone of *moth* which, as *Sanas Chormaic* [Cormac's Glossary] notes, can refer to masculine gender as well as to the penis: '*Moth*: everything masculine, every masculine word, *et nomen virili membro*, that is, the virile organ'." On the reference to Cú Chulainn as a dragon, see Longman, "'What manner of man is this Hound?'," 16–17.

He's already started into battle.
Doom is coming if you don't take care.
I think the one who's coming for you is:
Cú Chulainn, son of Súaltaim.

He'll flatten your full forces,
cut you down in droves.
You'll leave him with a thousand heads.
The prophetess Fedelm gives it to you straight.

Gore will gush from soldiers' skins,
the hero will hand out full helpings of harm.
He will fell fighters; rout will take the men
of Clanna Dedad meic Sin.
There will be butchered bodies, women will wail
because of the Smith's Hound: oh yes, I see him."

It was the Monday after Samain* when they set out. This is the way they went: southeast from Crúachu, past Mucc Cruinb, past Terloch Teóra Crích, past Túaim Móna, past Cúil Silinne …

This is the start of a long list placenames describing the route all the way to Cúailnge. See Map 2 (the route in the Midlands) for the first part of the journey, and the images at https://www.isos.dias.ie/RIA/RIA_MS_23_E_25.html#58 and https://www.isos.dias.ie/TCD/TCD_MS_1339.html#56 for how the list is presented in the manuscripts (the repeated F. *is for the preposition* for, *"past")*.

From Finnabair in Cúailnge the armies of Ireland spread out across the province of Ulster to look for the bull. For they had gone past all these places on the way to Finnabair.[1]

Finit ("here ends") the preface. *Incipit* ("now begins") the story in proper order.

---

1 *Finnabair* This place at the end of the Cúailnge peninsula, starred on Map 4 and labeled *Finnabair Chúailnge* or Cooley Point, is named for Ailill and Maeve's daughter because of an event described much later, in the story of the Glennamain Massacre, so the text should be understood as saying "From the place *now known as* Finnabair in Cúailnge."

Now for the Story in Proper Order:

When they had come on the first stage of their journey from Crúachu to Cúil Silinne,[1] Maeve told her charioteer to harness her nine chariots so that she could drive around the camp and see who was reluctant to be out campaigning and who was eager.

Meanwhile, Ailill's tent was set up for him and all his paraphernalia was put inside, including beds and blankets. Then Fergus's tent was set up next to Ailill's. Next to him was Cormac Conn Loinges, son of Conchobor. Next to him was Conall Cernach. Next to him was Fíacha mac Fir Fhebe, the son of Conchobor's daughter. Maeve[2] was on the other side of Ailill, and Finnabair, the daughter of Ailill and Maeve, was next to her. This is not including servants and attendants.

Maeve came back from inspecting the army and said there was no point in anyone else going on the campaign as long as the division of Gaileóin[3] were going.

"Why are you putting them down?"[4] said Ailill.

"I'm not putting them down," said Maeve. "They're incredible warriors. When everyone else was putting up their shelters, they'd finished thatching their shelters and cooking their food. When everyone else was eating, they'd finished eating and their harpers were playing to them. So there's no point in bringing them. They'll take all the credit for the army winning."

"But they're on our side," said Ailill.

"They're not going with us."

"They can stay here, then."

"They're not staying either. They'll turn on us as soon as we get back, and steal our land."

"So tell me, what are we supposed to do with them, if you don't want them staying or going?"[5]

---

1 *Cúil Silinne* Near what is now Ardkillin Lough between Tulsk and Strokestown, County Roscommon.

2 *Maeve* The text specifies "Maeve, the daughter of Eochaid Feidlech," as though insisting on her station.

3 *division of Gaileóin* The Gaileóin (pronounced "GAL-yoyn") are from the southeastern province of Leinster, where Ailill was originally from.

4 *putting them down* This could also be legalistic: "Why are you defaming them?" The verb is *do-áinsea* 'disparages; condemns.'

5 *what are we … staying or going* In Recension 2, Ailill and Maeve's daughter Finnabair (who is totally silent in Recension 1) asks this question.

"Kill them," she said.

"I'm not going to lie, that's feminine logic right there," said Ailill.

"Bad idea," said Fergus. "I heard you whispering. It's not going to happen, not unless you kill all of us Ulster exiles. The Gaileóin are our allies."

"Be that as it may," said Maeve, "we could do it. I have two divisions that report to me, and my sons the seven Maines[1] have seven divisions. The odds are in their favor.[2] Maine 'Motherlike' (*Máthramail*), Maine 'Fatherlike' (*Athramail*), Maine 'Most Filial' (*Mórgor*), Maine 'Sweetly Filial' (*Míngor*), Maine 'Most Talkative' (*Móepirt*)—that is, Maine 'Honeyflower' (*Mílscothach*)—Maine 'Taciturn' (*Tái*),[3] and Maine 'Combines-Them-All' (*Cotageib Uli*), the one who looks like his mother and father and has the dignity of both."

"You're wrong," said Fergus. "There are seven kings from Munster here, who are also allies of us Ulster exiles. I'll fight you right here in camp, with those seven divisions, my division, and the division of Gaileóin. But it doesn't have to come to that. We'll position the Gaileóin so they don't upstage the rest of the army. We have seventeen divisions here, not counting camp-followers, women—because every king traveling with Maeve seems to have brought his wife along—and also boys. The Gaileóin are the eighteenth.[4] They can be split up across the whole army."

"I don't care," said Maeve, "as long as they don't stay in the tight formation they're in now."

So that's what they did. The Gaileóin were split up across the army.

The next morning they moved on to Móin Choltna, where they came across a herd of eighty deer. They surrounded them and killed

---

1 *the seven Maines* She has seven sons named Maine. See p. 74 above.

2 *The odds are in their favor* Literally, "their luck can protect them."

3 *Maine 'Motherlike' … Maine 'Taciturn'* As on p. 74 above, their nicknames here are glossed according to "Fitness of Names" (II, 135), which adds that Maine Mórgor took "great care of his father," while Maine Míngor took "gentle care of his mother." O'Rahilly's edition gives Maine Moépirt and Maine Andóe as different people, but according to "Fitness of Names" these are synonymous and both mean "talkative," in contrast to Maine Tái who is taciturn. The name Maine Tái is used in "Maeve's Series of Husbands," so I have substituted it here.

4 *eighteenth* I.e., division. If each division were literally 3,000 men, that would make the army 54,000 men.

them. Anywhere there was one of the Gaileóin, he was the one who got the deer: the rest of the army, collectively, caught only five. After that they came to Mag Trega where they made camp and cooked dinner.

They say that's where Dubthach began to chant:[1]

"Admit you haven't heard or hearkened yet
to Dubthach's trance-talk.
You have a hard campaign ahead of you,
over Finnbennach who belonged to Ailill's wife.

A warrior will come
to take back Muirthemne's cattle.
Ravens will drink blood off a battlefield
because some pig-keepers were friends once.

The solid river Cronn resists them,
it won't let them cross into Muirthemne
until the warriors' work is finished
on the mountain north of Ochaíne.

'Quick,' said Ailill to Cormac,
'come and get your son.'[2]
No one comes from the plains where the cattle graze
without hearing the noise of the army.

There will be a battle here in time,
with Maeve and a third of the army.
Men's corpses will be the result
if the mutant* comes at you."

---

1 *began to chant* This chant is discussed and translated by Tomás Ó Cathasaigh, "Dubthach's *laíd* in *Táin bó Cúailnge*," in *Lorg na leabhar: a Festschrift for Pádraig A. Breatnach*, ed. Caoimhín Breatnach, Meidhbhín Ní Urdáil, and Gordon Ó Riain (Four Courts, 2019) 149–65, and I follow his corrections of O'Rahilly.

2 *your son* This is a plural "your." I take it that Cormac is Cormac Conn Loinges, the notional leader of the exiles, and that he and all the exiles are being asked to restrain Cú Chulainn, as their foster-son. Incidentally, this verse (not formatted as poetry) is the first complete sentence of the Yellow Book of Lecan text of the *Táin*, at https://www.isos.dias.ie/TCD/TCD_MS_1318.html#383.

Then the war-goddess Nemain attacked them, and along with the oaf babbling in his sleep, that wasn't the quietest night they'd ever had. The warbands all got up immediately and the army was thrown into chaos until Maeve whipped them back into shape.

Then, after the army had been led astray over bogs and streams, they went and stayed at Gránard in northern Tethba. At that point Fergus, out of kin-love,* sent a warning to the Ulstermen. But they were all paralyzed except Cú Chulainn and his father Súaltaim.

Cú Chulainn and his father responded to Fergus's warning by advancing to Irard Cuilenn (which is now called Crossa Caíl)[1] and keeping a lookout for the army there.

"I expect the army will be here tonight," Cú Chulainn told his father. "Go warn the Ulstermen for us. I have to go meet Fedelm Noíchride"—the meeting was actually with her companion,[2] whom he was sleeping with on the side—"because I promised her I would."[3]

Before he left, he made a wooden hoop,[4] wrote in ogam* on the peg it was attached to, and stuck it on top of a standing stone.

Meanwhile, Fergus took the army on a long detour to the south[5] to give the Ulstermen time to rally their forces. He did that out of kin-love. Ailill and Maeve noticed what he was doing, and Maeve said:

> "Fergus, this is highly suspect.
> What type of trail are we taking?

---

1 *Irard Cuilenn … Crossa Caíl* Crossakeel near Kells in modern County Meath, labeled as Crossa Caíl on Map 2. The parenthetical is a manuscript gloss.

2 *companion* The problem of translating *inailt* is the same as p. 121, note 3 above: "foster-sister" or "maidservant." O'Rahilly says "handmaiden" but John Carey argues "foster-sister."

3 *because I promised her* Dooley, *Playing the Hero*, 161–66, discusses this episode and how, in Recension 2, Cú Chulainn makes it about showing men to be truer to their word than women, and Súaltaim and Lóeg moralize it in terms of women being a dishonorable distraction. Dooley sees it as an example of "the ability, born of long and easeful literary use, of the saga idiom to transform itself without effort into a story of women and their dangers," but also says that Cú Chulainn's liaison with Fedelm might be political, related to having her son Erc join the final battle on the side of the Ulstermen (see p. 273 below).

4 *a wooden hoop* A hoop like this, sometimes translated 'withe' or 'spancel-hoop' and usually made of flexible willow shoots or similar, might be used to hobble livestock, so its function in this scenario might be to "hobble" trespassers.

5 *a long detour to the south* From Gránard to Crossa Caíl on the map. There is a further turn to the south to the east of Kells, but they're not there yet.

We're wandering southward and northward,
past all these foreign parts.

Ailill with his troops
is afraid you'll betray him.
Until now he didn't notice
which way the route led.

If you're feeling some kin-love,*
stop leading the charge.
Maybe we can find someone else
to pick out a path."

Fergus answered:

"Maeve, why so worked up?
This is nothing like treachery.
The land that I'll be leading you across
is Ulster territory.

I'm not making all these detours
to handicap the army.
It's to avoid the great one
who guards the Plain of Muirthemne.

I'm not making these detours
carelessly, either,
but to keep us from meeting, even later on,
Súaltaim's son Cú Chulainn."[1]

---

1 Recension 2 breaks up these poems to create more back-and-forth between Maeve and Fergus, and gives the last word to Maeve in an additional verse claiming that Fergus has gotten rich while in exile, so it would be wrong for him to betray the army. Fergus then says she should find someone else to lead the army, but goes on doing it anyway. That night the army camps at Cúil Silinne and Fergus has a poetic dialogue with Maeve, warning her about Cú Chulainn and shooting down her predictions that her army will defeat him.

They advanced to Irard Cuilenn. The four sons of Irard mac Anchinnel, Eirr and Indell and their charioteers Foich and Fochlam, used to go on ahead to prevent the army's dust from getting on their brooches, rugs, and cloaks. They found the hoop Cú Chulainn had placed and noticed where his horses had grazed: Súaltaim's two horses had grazed the grass to the roots, while Cú Chulainn's had licked away the dirt under the grass all the way down to the rocks beneath.

The four men sat there until the army arrived, and their musicians kept them entertained. They handed the hoop to Fergus mac Roích. He read out the ogam* inscription.

Maeve arrived and said "What are you waiting for?"

"We're waiting," said Fergus, "because of that hoop over there. There's ogam on the peg, and what it says is this: 'No Invaders Past this Point—until one of you bends a single branch into a hoop like this one using only one hand. And my uncle* Fergus doesn't count.' Believe me," said Fergus, "Cú Chulainn is the one who put it here and his horses were the ones that grazed this plain."

He handed the hoop to a druid* and chanted this poem:

"This hoop here: what's it tell us?
What's its underlying secret?
How many put it here,
a few or many?

Will it wipe out the army
if they go past it?
Find out, you druids,
why it was left here."

The druid said:

"A champion put it there, a champ's quick chop,
befuddling warriors,
boxing in chiefs with their followers.
One man bent it using one hand.

Doesn't the king's army follow orders
unless they've broken with what's fair and true?
It was just so one of you could make a hoop
the same as the man who made it—
I don't know of any other reason
why this hoop was put here."

Then Fergus told them, "If you violate this hoop, or if you go past it, even if someone's holding onto it or it's been locked up in a house, it will alert the man who wrote the ogam* inscription, and he'll slaughter a bunch of you by morning unless one of you makes a hoop to match it."

"Look, we'd rather not have a bunch of men killed right away," said Ailill. "Let's cut through the outskirts of the big forest to the south of us. We won't go all the way through it or anything."

The warbands chopped down the woods to make way for the chariots. So that place was called Choppings (*Slechta*). The Partraige live there now.

But according to other versions, though, this is where the conversation between Maeve and the prophetess Fedelm comes in, the way we told it above, and it was after she answered Maeve that the forest was cut down:

"See for me," said Maeve, "what becomes of my expedition."

"It's hard for me," said the girl. "I can't see them all in the forest."

"That's fixable," said Maeve. "We'll chop the forest down."

So that happened, and that's why the place is called Choppings.

Then the army spent the night in Cúil Sibrille (i.e., Cenannas), and were caught in a heavy snowstorm. The snow came up to their waists and past the wheels of the chariots. They were up early the next day. They'd spent a restless night because of the snow, and hadn't had a chance to cook dinner.

See Map 3 (north Leinster and south Ulster) for what follows.

Cú Chulainn, on the other hand, slept in. He took the time to bathe and wash his hair. Then he came across the army's trail.

"If only I hadn't gone there," he said, "and betrayed Ulster! We've let the army get past to take the Ulstermen by surprise. Give us an estimate of the army," he told his charioteer Lóeg, "so we know how many there are."

Lóeg tried, and told Cú Chulainn, "To me it's all a muddle. I can't count them."

"It wouldn't be a muddle to me if I came over there," said Cú Chulainn.

"Get in the chariot, then," said Lóeg.

Cú Chulainn got into the chariot and spent a long time working out his estimate.

"Even you're not finding it easy," said Lóeg.

"It's easier for me than it is for you," said Cú Chulainn, "because I have three gifts: the gift of sight, the gift of understanding, and the gift of calculation. I've got it now. There are eighteen divisions here, but they're confusing to count because the eighteenth is split up across the army—that's the division of Gaileóin."

Then Cú Chulainn went around the army to the crossing at Áth Grencha. He cut down a forked branch with one swing of his sword, and stuck it in the middle of the crossing so that chariots couldn't pass on either side of it. Then Eirr and Indell and their charioteers Foich and Fochlam showed up. Cú Chulainn cut off their heads and stuck them on the four prongs of the branch. Hence the name "the Ford of the Fork" (*Áth nGabla*).[1]

The four men's horses ran back to the army, with their harnesses covered in blood. The army thought there must be a battle in progress up ahead of them. An advance company[2] came to reconnoiter the crossing. All they could see was the tracks of one chariot and the branch with the four heads, with an ogam* inscription on the side.

Then the whole army arrived.

"Do those heads belong to our men?" said Maeve.

"Not just our men," said Ailill. "Some of our best men."

Someone read out the ogam writing carved on the branch: "One

---

1 *Áth nGabla* Pronounced "awth nav-luh." Apparently located on the Mattock River in County Louth.

2 *An advance company* In Recension 2, they suspect the whole Ulster army is there and send Cormac Conn Loinges to investigate, on the basis that the Ulstermen wouldn't kill their king's own son.

man drove in this branch with one hand. You shall not pass until one of you pulls it out with one hand—not Fergus, though."

"It's amazing how fast those four were killed," said Ailill.

"That's not what you should call amazing," said Fergus. "What's amazing would be if the branch was cut off with one stroke—if the end shows a single cut, that'll make it all the more perfect. There's also the way it was driven in, because there was no hole dug for it: it was thrown one-handed from the back of a chariot."

"Get this crap out of our way, Fergus,"[1] said Maeve.

"Give me a chariot, then," said Fergus, "so I can pull out the branch and you can see if the end shows a single cut."

Fergus destroyed fourteen chariots in the process of pulling out the branch, and finally managed to do it from his own chariot. They could see that the end was a single cut.

"We need a better sense of the people we're invading," said Ailill. "Everyone make dinner. Last night wasn't relaxing for you because of the snow. And let's hear about some of the accomplishments and famous exploits of the people we're invading."

That's when they were told about Cú Chulainn's accomplishments.

It started with Ailill asking: "Did Conchobor do this?"

"No," said Fergus. "He wouldn't come near the border without bringing an army."

"Was it Celtchar mac Uthidir?"

"No. He wouldn't come near the border without bringing an army."

"Was it Éogan mac Durthacht?"

"No. He wouldn't come near the border without bringing thirty chariots mounted with scythe blades. The man who did this," said Fergus, "is Cú Chulainn. He's the one who would have cut down the tree with one blow, killed the four of them so fast, and come to the border with just his charioteer."

---

1 *Get this crap ... Fergus* Literally, "remove from us this obstacle, Fergus," but the point is that Maeve has only contempt for the obstacle; asking Fergus to deal with it is precisely what the invaders are not supposed to do. Recension 2 addresses the contradiction in a different way, by not having the inscription disqualify Fergus.

Now for the Praises of Cú Chulainn:

"What kind of man is this 'dog' we've been hearing about, that fights for Ulster?" said Ailill. "How old is this prodigy?"

"That's easy,*" said Fergus. "When he was four years old[1] he went to join the boy-troop at Emain Macha. When he was five, he went to learn weapon handling and martial arts from Scáthach. When he was six, received his adult weapons.[2] He's sixteen, currently."

"And he's the toughest Ulsterman there is?" said Maeve.

"Beyond any of them," said Fergus. "You'll never face a tougher warrior, a spearpoint that's sharper or faster or fiercer, a hero more harrowing, a raven more ravenous, anyone his age that's a third his match, a lion more savage, or anyone more qualified to be an impassable barrier, a sledgehammer, a walking death sentence, a horde-stopper. You won't find any man to match his growth, his fashion sense, the terror of him, his eloquence, his charm, his fame, his voice, his physique, his power, his grit, his acrobatics, his valor, his killing blows, his viciousness, his vigor, his victoriousness, his vengeance, his violence, his tracking skills, his accuracy, his hunting trophies, his speed, his ferocity, and his battle frenzy, launching a nine-men-killing combo from the points of spears. There's no one like Cú Chulainn."

"Big deal, as far as I'm concerned," said Maeve. "He has one body—he can be wounded, he's not beyond capture. Besides, he's only the age of a grown girl and won't have started acting like a man yet."[3]

---

1 *four years old* Literally, "in his fifth year." The other ages have been recast in the same way.

2 *received … weapons* This expression, literally "took arms" (as a rite of passage), is used for pp. 189–97 below, though it might seem hard to imagine that episode coming after his time with Scáthach in "The Wooing of Emer."

3 *the age of … yet* Ann Dooley interpreted this reference to "the age of a grown girl (*ingen macdacht*)" as "he is at the girly stage and his male strength hasn't come to him yet" (*Playing the Hero*, 254n11, though *fer-gníma* is literally 'male/manly deeds'), and Sarah Sheehan concurred that this "constructs the hero's youth as feminine" (see Longman, "'What manner of man is this Hound?'," 7–8). But the counterargument has been made that Maeve might be "subtly pointing out what a woman even of a young age can accomplish, versus a male coeval" (i.e., to her, it seems that a sixteen-year-old girl is basically an adult, while a sixteen-year-old boy is still a child). Compare Jennifer Dukes-Knight, 'The wooden sword: age and masculinity in *Táin Bó Cúailnge*," *PHCC* 33 (2013) 107–22, and *GEIL*, 81–91: in the historical context, a girl reached marriageable

"You're wrong," said Fergus. "It's no surprise to see him do something impressive today, since even when he was much younger, he already acted like a man."

Now for the Boyhood Deeds:

Well (said Fergus), he was raised by his mother and father at Airgdech[1] on Muirthemne Plain, where he was told inspiring stories about the boy-troop at Emain Macha. There are usually a hundred and fifty boys there playing sports. This is Conchobor's royal schedule: one-third of the day spent watching the boys, a third playing *fidchell*,* and a third drinking beer until he falls asleep. I say this even though he forced us into exile: there is no more amazing warrior in all of Ireland.[2]

Cú Chulainn asked his mother to let him go and join the boys.

"You're not going," she said, "until we find some Ulster warriors to escort you."

"I can't wait that long," said Cú Chulainn. "Point out which way Emain is?"

"Over there, to the north," said his mother, "and it's hard going. Slieve Fúait is in the way."

"I'll figure it out," said Cú Chulainn.

Then off he went, with his wooden shield, his toy spear, his shinty-stick,* and his ball. He kept throwing the spear in front of him and catching it by the point before it hit the ground.

He walked up to the boys without getting them to take him under their protection.* No one used to walk onto their playing field without being under their protection, but Cú Chulainn didn't know that.

---

age at fourteen with no further milestones, whereas a boy's legal capacity evolved from fourteen to twenty ("the age of beard-encirclement"), and the process was complete only when his father died and he came into his inheritance.

1 *Airgdech* Problematic. This could be Ardee in modern County Louth, which would make sense geographically (although the etymology of Ardee is normally *Áth Fhir Diad*, the ford where Fer Diad is killed), or else an equivalent to *Aircthech*, "Silvery (Place)." If we read *ocond Dairgdig* (instead of *ocond Airgdig*), we get "at the Oak-House," possibly with the generic sense "he was raised in a house made of oak."

2 *no more ... all of Ireland* On the evidence he has just given of what Conchobor does all day, Fergus's words sound brutally sarcastic. Recension 2 hastens to correct this impression: there, Fergus says that this is how Conchobor spends his free time, only after he finishes the daily business of governing and passing judgment.

"The boy's insulting us," said Follamain son of Conchobor, "though we can tell he's from Ulster."

They threatened him.

He charged at them.

They threw their hundred and fifty spears at him, and they all stuck in his toy shield. Then they threw all their balls at him and he trapped every single one against his chest. Then they threw their hundred and fifty shinty-sticks* at him and he fended them off so that they never touched him, and gathered up a bunch of them on his back.

Then he started to mutate.* You'd have thought every hair on his head had been pounded in with a hammer, the way it stood on end. You'd have thought there was a fiery spark on the tip of every hair. He closed one eye no bigger than the eye of a needle, and opened the other as wide as a mead-cup.[1] He unhinged his jaw all the way to his ear, and opened his mouth till you could stare into his guts. A hero's light shone from his forehead.

Then he attacked the boys. He knocked down fifty of them before they could make it to the gates of Emain. Nine of them ran past me and Conchobor. We were playing *fidchell** at the time. Cú Chulainn came leaping across the gameboard after them. Conchobor grabbed him by the forearm.

"These boys have been mistreated," he said.

"Can you blame me, Uncle* Conchobor? I came here straight from my mother and father's house, and they were mean to me."

"What's your name?" said Conchobor.

"Sétanta. My parents are Súaltaim and your sister Dechtine. I didn't expect to come here and be treated this way."

"Why didn't you make the boys take you under their protection*?"

"I didn't know[2] about that," said Cú Chulainn. "Can I leave it in your hands,[3] to put me under their protection yourself?"

---

1 *mead-cup* Or "a wooden cup" (*fidchúaich* as opposed to *midchúaich*).

2 *I didn't know* In Recension 2, Cú Chulainn answers that if he had known about the requirement to get the boy-troop's protection (which Conchobor describes as a *geis** of theirs), "I would have been on my guard against them" (O'Rahilly), which could be read as saying that he would have been better prepared to fight *instead* of asking for their protection.

3 *leave it in your hands* The Irish is "undertake my protection from them," where "undertake" is literally "take into your hand." Tomás Ó Cathasaigh, "The body in *Táin Bó Cúailnge*," in *Gablánach in scélaigecht: Celtic Studies in Honour of Ann Dooley*, ed.

"Agreed," said Conchobor.

Then Cú Chulainn went back to chasing the boys all over the house.

"What do you have against them now?" said Conchobor.

"Make me take *them* under *my* protection.*"

"I'll leave it in your hands, then."

"Agreed."

Then they all went out to the playing field, and the boys who had been knocked down picked themselves up: their foster-fathers* and foster-mothers* helped them.

Another time (said Fergus), when he was a boy in Emain, Cú Chulainn never slept.

"Tell me why you won't sleep," said Conchobor.

"I can't," said Cú Chulainn, "not unless my head and feet are level with each other."

Conchobor had stones set up at his head and feet and a separate sleeping-compartment* made for him.

Then one time a man went to wake him up and Cú Chulainn punched him in the forehead so hard that his forehead caved in on his brain, and with his forearm he knocked down one of the standing stones.

("Clearly," said Ailill, "that was the fist of a warrior and the arm of a champion!")

From then on (said Fergus), no one tried to wake him up until he woke up on his own.

Now the Death of the Boy-Troop:

Another time he was playing ball on the playing field east of Emain. He was by himself against the hundred and fifty boys. He kept defeating them that way in every game, all the time. Then Cú

Sarah Sheehan, Joanne Findon, and Westley Follett (Four Courts, 2013) 131–53, has shown that Cú Chulainn's deepening association with Conchobor and integration into Ulster society is reflected in his connection with the king's body: his hand, here; then his chest or lap (*ucht*) and his knee in the stories that follow. The English idiom "I leave it in your hands" isn't a perfect match, but it corresponds in an important way to what is said in the Irish.

Chulainn started punching them and fifty of them died. He ran away and hid under the bed in Conchobor's sleeping-compartment.*[1] The Ulstermen surrounded him, but Conchobor and I stood up in his defense. He threw the sleeping-compartment into the middle of the house along with the thirty warriors in it. Then the Ulstermen sat down around him, and we worked things out and made peace between the boys and him.

Now Éogan mac Durthacht's Battle against Conchobor:

The Ulstermen were at war with Éogan mac Durthacht. The Ulstermen went off to battle. Cú Chulainn was left sleeping.

The Ulstermen were defeated. Conchobor and his son Cúscraid the Stammerer[2] and countless others were left on the battlefield. Their howls woke Cú Chulainn. He stretched out so that the two flagstones around him were smashed. Bricriu over there was a witness (said Fergus). Then he got up.

I met him coming through the entrance to the stockade—I was badly wounded.

"Hey! How's it going, Uncle* Fergus?" he said. "Where's Conchobor?"

"I don't know," I said.

Off he went. The night was dark. He headed for the battlefield. Up ahead he saw a man missing half his head, carrying half of another man on his back.

"Help me, Cú Chulainn," he said. "I've been wounded, and I managed to get half my brother on my back. Take over for me for a while."

"Not happening," he said.

So the man threw the body at him. Cú Chulainn pushed it off. Then they wrestled. Cú Chulainn was thrown. He heard the

1 *under the bed ... sleeping-compartment* Since *imdae* here seems to refer to the whole sleeping-compartment, with room for thirty warriors, I take *adart,* technically a headrest or pillow, as meaning the bed.

2 *the Stammerer* "His son" added for clarity. "The Stammerer" is Cúscraid's conventional epithet, *Menn Machae* 'the Stammerer of Macha.' In "The Story of Mac Dá Thó's Pig," p. 83, it is explained that he cannot speak properly because the Connacht warrior Cet drove a spear through his throat.

war-goddess gibbering from the corpses: "Someone won't make much of a warrior if he lets phantoms walk all over him!"

Then Cú Chulainn got up and knocked the man's head off with his shinty-stick,* and started bouncing it across the field like a ball.

"Is my uncle* Conchobor on this battlefield?"

Conchobor answered him. Cú Chulainn went towards his voice and found him in a ditch, with dirt piled up on all sides to keep him hidden.

"Why have you come to the battlefield?" said Conchobor. "To die from fear?"

Cú Chulainn lifted him out of the ditch. Six of the strongest men in Ulster wouldn't have managed it so bravely.

"Go on ahead of me to that house over there," said Conchobor, "and start a fire for me."

Cú Chulainn set a big fire for him.

"Well then," said Conchobor. "If I had a roast pig, I'd pull through."

"I'll go get one," said Cú Chulainn.

Off he went. He saw a man at a cooking-pit in the middle of the woods, holding his weapons in one hand and roasting a boar with the other. The man was terrifying. Still, Cú Chulainn attacked him and took away his head and his pig. Then Conchobor gobbled up the pig. "Let's go home now," he said. They ran into Conchobor's son Cúscraid, who was also heavily wounded. Cú Chulainn carried him on his back and the three of them came back to Emain Macha.

Now the Death of the Twenty-Seven Men, and the Reason No One Dared to Wound the Ulstermen When They Were Paralyzed:

Another time, the Ulstermen were lying paralyzed (said Fergus). It doesn't affect women or boys or anyone outside the bounds of Ulster, or Cú Chulainn or his father. No one would dare shed the blood of anyone suffering from it because whoever does either contracts the same paralysis, or wastes away, or dies in short order.[1]

Twenty-seven men invaded us from the Islands of Faichi. They came into our back enclosure when we were paralyzed. The women

---

1 *lying paralyzed … short order* See the introduction to "The Ulstermen's Paralysis and the Twins of Macha," p. 54 above.

in there started screaming. The boy-troop was on the playing field. They came as soon as they heard the screaming, but when they saw the dark, dire-looking men, all of them ran away except Cú Chulainn. He threw stones at them and beat them with his shinty-stick.* He killed nine of them, and they left fifty wounds on him—then they went away. If a man did all that when he was five years old, it's no surprise to see him come to the borders and lop the heads off those four men.

Now the Killing of the Smith's Dog by Cú Chulainn, and Why Cú Chulainn Is His Name:

I know the boy well (said Conall Cernach)—all the more since he's a fosterling* of mine.[1] Not long after the feat that you just heard about from Fergus, he did another one.

Culann the smith invited Conchobor to a feast. He told him not to bring a huge crowd, because the feast wasn't being paid for with the proceeds of land and property, but from the efforts of his own hands and his smith's tongs.

So Conchobor took only fifty chariots' worth of the most respected and outstanding warriors.

He stopped by the playing field, because he made a habit of visiting the boys on his comings and goings, and getting them to greet him. There he saw Cú Chulainn playing ball against the hundred and fifty boys, and winning.

When the game involved taking shots on goal, Cú Chulainn filled the goal with balls and the boys had no hope of fending him off. When it was their turn to shoot, he made every save all by himself.

When they wrestled, he threw all the boys all by himself, and they couldn't muster the numbers it would take to throw him.

---

1 *I know the boy ... fosterling of mine* The Irish here has plural pronouns ("We know the boy [...] a fosterling of ours"), but this is fairly common with a singular sense, a cousin to the English "royal *we*." When Conchobor tells Cú Chulainn to go ahead of him and start a fire, for example, he says "go ahead of *us*," meaning himself. Of course, as described in "The Birth of Cú Chulainn," Cú Chulainn does have foster-relationships with many of the Ulster exiles. According to that text, Conall is a foster-brother rather than a foster-father to him.

When they played at yanking off each other's clothes, he stripped them all naked and they couldn't even take the brooch off his mantle.

Conchobor was amazed. He asked if Cú Chulainn's abilities would still be that much better than everyone else's when he came of age, and everyone said they would.

Then Conchobor spoke to Cú Chulainn. "We're on our way to a feast," he said. "Come with me—you're invited."

"I haven't had enough of playing yet,[1] Uncle* Conchobor," said the boy. "I'll catch up with you."

But when all of them got to the feast, Culann asked Conchobor: "Are you expecting anyone else to join you?" Conchobor said "no"—he forgot about the arrangement he had made with his foster-son.*

"I have a guard dog," said Culann. "It takes three chains to hold him, with three men on each. I got him from Spain.[2] Let him out to watch our herds and livestock, and close the stockade!"

Then the boy came along. The dog rushed at him. He kept on playing regardless: he kept throwing his ball in the air and throwing his shinty-stick* up to hit it, both on the exact same trajectory. And he threw his toy spear after them and caught it before it fell. Even as the dog was bearing down on him, he didn't let it interrupt his game.

Conchobor and his entourage were so horrified they couldn't move. They were convinced they'd never make it in time to save his life, even once the stockade was open.

When the dog got to him, he tossed aside his ball and shinty-stick and grabbed the dog with both hands: he put one hand on the dog's throat and one on the back of its neck, and slammed it on a nearby standing stone until it spattered limb from limb. Or according to another version, he fired his ball down its throat and all its guts came out the other end.[3]

---

1 *I haven't … playing yet* In Recension 2, Cú Chulainn says it is the other boys who haven't had their fill of playing. If we take him at his word, already he is starting to consider the good of the group in preference to his own.

2 *from Spain* Although a gloss on the *Táin* rejects it, saying the chronology doesn't line up, "The Death of Celtchar mac Uthechair" gives a competing account according to which this dog is the litter-mate of Ailbe from "The Story of Mac Dá Thó's Pig": see the headnote to that story, p. 75 above.

3 *according to … the other end* After a dramatic description of how the dog plans to swallow the boy headfirst down to his chest and then bite him in half, Recension 2 gives only the second option, with the ball.

The Ulstermen ran to him: some jumped the stockade and some went through the gate. They brought him to Conchobor, who hugged him to his chest.

They made a big fuss over him—the king's sister's son* had almost died!

Then Culann came inside.

"Welcome, little boy, for your mother's sake. As for me, though, I wish I never gave this feast. My work is in vain and my property is defenseless without my dog. The servant I lost—my dog, I mean—he kept my herds and livestock safe and sound. He protected them in the fields and at home."

"That's no problem," said the boy. "I'll raise a puppy from the same litter, and until it grows up and is fit to work, I'll be the dog that protects you and your livestock.[1] And I'll protect the whole of Muirthemne Plain. No one will make off with herds or flocks without my knowledge on my watch!"

"Then from now on your name will be *Cú Chulainn* ('Culann's Dog,' 'the Hound of Culann')," said Cathbad.

"I like it," said Cú Chulainn.

He did that when he was six years old (said Conall Cernach). It's no surprise what he has done now that he's sixteen.

A corresponding part of Recension 2:

> "If there is a puppy in Ireland descended from that dog, I'll raise it until it's as fit to work as its father. I'll be the dog that protects his herds and flocks and property in the meantime."
>
> "Good job passing judgment, little boy," said Conchobor.
>
> "I couldn't have given a better one," said Cathbad. "Why not call you Culann's Dog because of this?"
>
> "No," said Cú Chulainn, "I like my own name better—Sétanta mac Súaltaim."
>
> "Don't say that, little boy," said Cathbad. "The men of Ireland and Scotland will hear that name and they will have it on their lips forever."

---

1 *I'll raise a puppy … your livestock* Besides compensation in cows, this is a correct response in early Irish law to killing someone's guard dog (*GEIL*, 146).

"Then that can be my name. I'm fine with it."

And from then on that famous name has been attached to him, i.e., Cú Chulainn, since he killed the dog of the smith Culann.

Now for the Death of the Three Sons of Nechta Scéne:[1]

He did another exploit after that (said Fíacha mac Fir Fhebe). The druid* Cathbad was staying with his son—that is, Conchobor mac Nessa. He had a hundred zealous apprentices studying druid magic: that's how many Cathbad used to teach. One of the apprentices asked him what the day was lucky for. Cathbad said that if a warrior received weapons that day, his name would be supreme in Ireland forever for his feats of heroism, and the inspiring stories about him would last forever.

Cú Chulainn heard that and went straight to Conchobor to ask for weapons.

Conchobor said, "Who told you the day was right for it?"

"Grandpa[2] Cathbad," said Cú Chulainn.

"He would know,"[3] said Conchobor, and gave him a spear and shield. Cú Chulainn brandished them right there in the middle of the house, and they broke.[4] He worked his way through all fifteen sets of spare weapons that were kept in Conchobor's house to replace broken ones or for someone to receive their first set. Finally, he was given Conchobor's own weapons. They stayed intact. He brandished them, and blessed the king, saying, "Long live the kingdom and the people ruled by the man who owns these weapons!"

---

1 Georges Dumézil saw the killing of a threefold opponent (three brothers, in this case) by a hero associated with "thirdness" (Cú Chulainn is conceived three times per his birth-tale) as an instance of an Indo-European theme of "the third kills the triple." There is a recent comparative study of this section by Kim McCone: "Cú Chulainn's first arming and outing (*cét-gabál gaiscid*): Roman and Greek parallels for his slaying of three brothers (Horatius, the Curiatii and Heracles), 'woman trouble' (Horatius and Coriolanus), and immersions (Diomedes and Odysseus)," *ZCP* 69.1 (2022) 201–26.

2 *Grandpa* See *uncle** in the glossary.

3 *He would know* Conchobor literally says "We know him indeed" (O'Rahilly), meaning that he recognizes Cathbad as an authority in the matter.

4 *they broke* Not in the Irish, which says he "brandished them in the middle of the hall so that not one was left unbroken of the fifteen sets of weapons," etc. (O'Rahilly). But that could make it sound like he is using one set of weapons to destroy the rest, when actually he is trying out one set after another.

Then Cathbad came up to them and said, "Are those weapons that the boy's received?"

"Yes," said Conchobor.

"That's unfortunate," said Cathbad, "for his mother's son."

"What? Weren't you the one who told him so?"

"It certainly wasn't me."

"What did you lie to me for, you imp?" Conchobor asked Cú Chulainn.

"It's not a lie, king of warriors," said Cú Chulainn. "He predicted good luck to his apprentices this morning, and I heard him from the south side of Emain, and then I came straight to you."

"It *is* a lucky day," said Cathbad. "There's no doubt that whoever receives his weapons today will be renowned and famous. He just won't live long."

"That's wonderful!" said Cú Chulainn. "I'll be happy as long as I'm famous, even if I live for only one day on earth."

Later on,[1] another man asked the druids* what the day was lucky for.

"Whoever goes on his first chariot ride[2] today," said Cathbad, "his name will be supreme in Ireland forever."

Cú Chulainn heard that: he went straight to Conchobor and said, "Uncle* Conchobor, I need a chariot."

Conchobor gave him a chariot. He stuck his hand between the chariot's suspension-beams,* and the chariot broke. He broke a dozen chariots that way. Then he was given Conchobor's chariot. That one stayed intact.

He got into the chariot with Conchobor's charioteer. The charioteer, whose name was Ibor,[3] turned the chariot around on the spot.

"Get out now," said the charioteer. "These are valuable horses."

"I'm valuable too, boyo," said Cú Chulainn. "Just drive around Emain, and you'll be rewarded for it."

---

1 *Later on* Presumably on a different day, but Recension 2 has Cú Chulainn go off in the chariot on the same day after he gets his weapons, without Cathbad making a second prediction.

2 *first chariot ride* "First" is not in the Irish, which literally says "goes into a chariot," but it seems implicit; otherwise everyone who happened to ride in a chariot that day would be destined for fame.

3 *Ibor* Pronounced "IV-ur."

The charioteer drove off and Cú Chulainn made him go down the road so that he could say hello to the boys, "and so I can get their blessing." Then he asked him to drive back the way they'd come. When they got there, Cú Chulainn told the charioteer: "Now goad the horses[1] on."

"Which way?" said the charioteer.

"As far as the road goes," said Cú Chulainn.

They went to Slieve Fúait. They met Conall Cernach there. It was Conall's turn to guard the province that day. All the Ulster warriors were in daily rotation on Slieve Fúait, to extend protection* to any poets* who came along, and fight off invaders.[2] That way everyone was challenged and no one would go on to Emain unnoticed.

"I wish you prosperity," said Conall Cernach. "May you have victory and triumph."

"Go away, Conall. Go back to the fort and let me stand guard here in the meantime."

"Fair enough, if there's a poet who needs protecting. But if someone needs fighting, it's too soon for you to do that."

"Maybe that won't be necessary," said Cú Chulainn. "Meanwhile, let's go take a look at the sandbank at Loch Echtra. There are usually some *fían*-warriors* there."

"I'm game," said Conall.

---

1 *goad the horses* A goad is a spiked stick used to drive horses and cattle.

2 *extend protection ... fight off invaders* O'Rahilly's translation, "to protect anyone who came that way with poetry or with challenge to battle, so that he might be encountered and so that no one should go unnoticed into Emain," makes it sound like protection is being offered to those who come with a challenge to battle (in the nature of a safe-conduct to fight a duel, for example). But what Conall actually tells Cú Chulainn makes it clear that the man on guard is supposed to do the fighting on behalf of the province. The wording "extend protection" highlights the fact that this is legal, not just physical, protection. As a matter of early Irish law, most people needed to be formally taken under the protection of a counterpart of equal or higher status to travel to another community (*túath*). But poets could travel anywhere and expect to be safe, since their status didn't automatically lapse outside their home community. The poetry they would have to offer in this case is "presumably a panegyric [praise-poem] which is to be delivered at Emain in exchange for a reward. The subject of such a panegyric would of course be Conchobor: the poet's patron, after all, is the king or chief. The champion is excluded from panegyric in early Irish law [though] in the world of the *Táin* [...] such a restriction might not necessarily apply" (*Coire Sois*, 266). This is all made clearer in Recension 2, which adds that the border guard is responsible for doling out treasure to poets who would otherwise leave Ulster unsatisfied and apt to satirize* it.

So off they went. Cú Chulainn fired a slingstone and broke Conall's chariot axle.

"What did you throw that stone for, boyo?" said Conall.

"To test my marksmanship and calibrate my shooting," said Cú Chulainn. "And you Ulstermen make it a practice not to ride in a chariot that's unsafe. Go back to Emain, my dear* Conall, and leave me here to stand guard."

"All right, fine," said Conall. Conall didn't go any further after that.

Cú Chulainn went on to Loch Echtra and didn't run into anyone. The charioteer told him they should go to Emain to be back in time for feasting.[1]

"No," said Cú Chulainn. "What mountain is that over there?"

"Slieve Mondairn," said the charioteer.

"Let's go there," said Cú Chulainn.

Off they went, and when they reached the mountain, Cú Chulainn asked, "What's that bright pile of rocks up there at the top of the mountain?"

"Whitemound[2] (*Findcharn*)," said the charioteer.

"What plain is that?"

"The plain of Brega."

Then he told him the name of every major fort between Tara and Kells. He listed the meadows and crossings, monuments and settlements, hillforts and strongholds that went with them. Then he pointed out the fort of the three sons of Nechta Scéne[3]—their names were Fóill, Fannall, and Túachell.

"Are they the ones who say that there aren't more Ulstermen living than they've already killed?"

"That's them!" said the charioteer.

"Let's go meet them."

"That will put us in danger," said the charioteer.

"We didn't come all this way to avoid it," said Cú Chulainn.

Off they went. They unyoked the horses where a river ran into

---

1 *feasting* Recension 2 expands on this: the charioteer sits with the common people (messengers, jesters,* and so on) and is concerned about finding a seat.

2 *Whitemound* In Recension 2, Cú Chulainn makes them go up the mountain to the cairn, which gives them a view of the surrounding landscape.

3 *Nechta Scéne* Pronounced "NECK-ta SHKAY-nuh." She is their mother.

a bog, overlooking the fort of the sons of Nechta Scéne from the south.

Cú Chulainn took the hoop[1] off a standing stone. He threw it into the river as far as he could and let it float downstream, because that was a *geis*[*] violation for the sons of Nechta Scéne.[2] They noticed it and headed towards them. But after letting the hoop drift with the current, Cú Chulainn took a nap beside the stone. He told the charioteer, "Don't bother me for just a few people. You can wake me up if there's a lot." The charioteer was still terrified. He harnessed the chariot and pulled the rugs and skin coverings out from under Cú Chulainn, but didn't dare wake him because Cú Chulainn had told him in the first place not to wake him up for just a few people.

The sons of Nechta Scéne arrived.

"Who's here?" said one of them.

"A little boy who went for a chariot ride today," said the charioteer.

"I hope the first time he gets his weapons is a disaster," said the warrior. "Get him off our land, and stop the horses before they graze any more."

"I have the reins in my hand,"[3] said the charioteer. "There's no reason you should pick a fight with him," Ibor told the warrior, "and anyway, the boy's asleep."

"I'm no boy," said Cú Chulainn. "I see only one boy here, and he's about to fight a battle with a man."

"It will be my pleasure," said the warrior.

"Then it will be your pleasure to meet me at the crossing over there," said Cú Chulainn.

"Now pay attention," said the charioteer. "Watch out for the man you're about to face. His name is Fóill ('Sly'), and if you don't get him with your first thrust, you can keep trying all day long."

"I swear[*] by the god my people swear by, he'll never play that trick on Ulstermen again if this hand of mine can put my uncle[*]

---

1 *hoop* This hoop apparently serves a similar function to the one Cú Chulainn left in the army's path, p. 176. See the note there.

2 *a geis violation ... Nechta Scéne* The consequence of letting one's *geisi* be violated with impunity would be similar to the consequence of violating one's own *geisi*: usually death. The violation here might be disturbing the hoop, polluting the river, or a specific combination of the two.

3 *I have ... my hand* Equivalent to "Look, I'm already leaving."

Conchobor's stabbing-spear through him. I'll shank him like a boss."[1]

He hurled the spear at Fóill and broke his back with it.[2] Then he looted the corpse and took the head as a trophy.

"Watch out for the next man," said the charioteer. "His name is Fannall ('Swallow'). He skims over water as lightly as a swan or swallow."

"I swear he'll never play that trick on Ulstermen again," said Cú Chulainn. "You've seen how I cross the water in Emain."[3]

Then they met at the crossing. Cú Chulainn killed Fannall, took his head, and looted the corpse.

"Watch out for the next man coming for you," said the charioteer. "His name is Túachell ('Cunning'). That's no misnomer, since no weapon can bring him down."

"He won't know what to make of the *deil chlis*:[4] it'll turn him into a bloody sieve," said Cú Chulainn. He threw the spear at him and he collapsed. Then he sauntered up to him and chopped his head off. He brought the head back to the charioteer with what he looted from the corpse, and then he heard their mother, Nechta Scéne, scream in grief. He carried off his plunder and put the three heads into the chariot with him, saying, "I won't give up my trophies until I get to Emain Macha."

Off they went with the trophies. Then Cú Chulainn said to the charioteer, "You promised me great driving. We need it now, because of how the fight went, and the people coming after us."

---

1 *shank him like a boss* Literally, "there will be an outlaw's hand to him," meaning he will be killed with the same tenderness and concern he can expect from an outlaw. This seems to be established idiom: an Irish mention of Hercules says he had "a robber's hand" to describe him killing enemies in battle. See Vernam Hull, "*Lám deoraid*" and "A further note on *lám deoraid*," *ZCP* 18 (1929–30) 70–71 and 286.

2 *hurled the spear … with it* If Cú Chulainn followed through on his threat, this was the broad-headed stabbing-spear, not meant for throwing, which would make this killing all the more remarkable.

3 *how I cross … Emain* In Recension 2, Cú Chulainn explains that what he does is carry another boy on each shoulder and one on each hand, and not even his ankles get wet.

4 *deil chlis* Pronounced "dell hlish." Some kind of superpowered spear or spear-throwing technique, that possibly translates to "split-wood feat." If learned from Scáthach, it supports Fergus's chronology on p. 189. Recension 2 describes it as an iron ball, and Cú Chulainn uses it on his first opponent, Fóill, who apparently cannot be harmed by edged or pointed weapons. There is no particular reason to think that this was the original sense.

They drove on towards Slieve Fúait, and after Cú Chulainn harangued the charioteer, they sped so fast over Brega that the horses pulling the chariot outran the wind and birds on the wing, and Cú Chulainn could catch a stone from his sling before it hit the ground.

When they reached Slieve Fúait they came across a herd of deer.

"What are those weird cattle over there?"

"Wild deer," said the charioteer.

"Which would impress the Ulstermen more," said Cú Chulainn, "if I brought them in alive or dead?"

"Alive," said the charioteer. "Not everyone can catch them that way. There's no one who doesn't manage to bring them in dead. You won't be able to catch one alive, though."

"Sure I can," said Cú Chulainn. "Goad the horses into the bog."

The charioteer did that, and then the horses got stuck in the bog. Cú Chulainn jumped out of the chariot and grabbed the nearest deer, which was also the best-looking one. He lashed the horses through the bog and quickly pacified the deer. He tethered it between the two suspension-beams at the back of the chariot.

Then they saw a flock of swans ahead of them.

"Which would impress the Ulstermen more," said Cú Chulainn, "getting them alive or dead?"

"The most active and successful hunters capture them alive," said the charioteer.

Cú Chulainn aimed a small stone at the birds and hit eight of them. Then he threw a big stone, and hit twelve. He did it all with his stunning-shot.[1]

"Pick up the birds for me," Cú Chulainn told his charioteer. "If I go get them, the deer will jump on you."

"It's not that easy for me," said the charioteer. "The horses have gone crazy so I can't get past them. The iron wheels are too sharp for

1 *stunning-shot* The Irish uses a special term of uncertain meaning (*taithbéim*, translated "return-stroke" by O'Rahilly, and "stunning blow," "sticking blow," or "sparing blow" by others). But the gist is clear: this is a feat designed to knock out the target rather than kill it, possibly by concussing the air rather than hitting the target directly; it is also featured in the pre-tale "The Death of Aífe's Only Son," p. 125 above. (If it does hit the target, then in Cú Chulainn's case, since he tends to hurl stones hard enough to shatter skulls, this requires a precise calibration of force.)

me to climb over, and I can't get past the deer because its antlers take up the whole space between the suspension-beams.*"[1]

"Step off of its antlers, then," said Cú Chulainn. "I swear* by the god that Ulstermen swear by, I'll tilt my head and give it the eye so it won't dare move or turn its head at you."

So that's what they did: Cú Chulainn secured the reins and the charioteer went and collected the birds. Then Cú Chulainn tied the birds to the strings and cords of the chariot.

That's the way he came to Emain: a wild stag behind his chariot, a flock of swans fluttering above it, and three severed heads in the chariot with him.

"There's a chariot-warrior coming," said the watchman in Emain Macha. "He'll spill the blood of everyone in the fort unless we take precautions and send naked women out to meet him."

Cú Chulainn turned the left side of the chariot towards Emain: Emain had a *geis** against letting that stand.[2] And he said, "I swear by the god that Ulstermen swear by, unless you send a man out to fight me, I'll spill the blood of everyone in the fort!"

"Naked women, go and face him!" said Conchobor.

Then the women of Emain went to face him, led by Conchobor's wife Mugain, and they bared their breasts to him.

"These are the warriors who'll face you today," said Mugain.

Cú Chulainn hid his face. Then the warriors of Emain grabbed him and threw him in a vat of cold water. The vat exploded around him. The second vat boiled over with fist-sized bubbles. The third vat he went into after that, he heated so that it was a comfortable mix of hot and cold. Then he got out and the queen, Mugain, gave him a blue cloak with a silver brooch, and a hooded tunic. And then he sat down at Conchobor's knee, which became his regular spot from then on.

---

1 *It's not that easy ... suspension-beams* This makes a lot more sense looking at the chariot diagrams in Mallory, *In Search of the Irish Dreamtime*, 214–15, or in Raimund Karl, "Iron Age chariots and medieval texts: a step too far in 'breaking down boundaries'?" *e-Keltoi* 5.1 (2003) 1–29, at https://dc.uwm.edu/ekeltoi/vol5/iss1/1/. The charioteer could exit the chariot to the front, over the side, or out the back. The front is blocked by the horses, the sides by the wheels, and the back by the deer. In Recension 2, the problem is made more severe: the chariot is *moving* when Ibor is asked to get out.

2 *a geis against letting that stand* Literally, "which was a *geis* for it [Emain]": the Ulstermen had to treat it as an intolerable insult.

If a man could do all that when he was six (said Fíacha mac Fir Fhebe), it's no surprise if he routs and destroys, whether he's outnumbered or evenly matched, when he's sixteen today.

Now a Different Version Up to The Death of Órlám:

"Off we go now," said Ailill.

They advanced to the Plain of the Pig-keeper (*Mag Mucceda*).

Cú Chulainn cut down an oak tree before they got there, and wrote in ogam* on the side of it. What it said was that no one should venture past it until a warrior could leap it in a chariot.

They pitched their tents there, and tried leaping it in their chariots. Thirty horses were killed doing that, and thirty chariots were smashed. The place was called the Gap of Driving (*Belach nÁnae*) forever after.

The Death of Fráech

They stayed there until the next day. Then they sent for Fráech[1] ("Heather").

"Help us, Fráech," said Maeve. "Save us in our hour of need. Go find Cú Chulainn so you can fight him for us."

Fráech headed out early in the morning with eight other men and advanced to the Ford of the Stretcher (*Áth Fúait*). He saw Cú Chulainn bathing in the river.

---

1 *Fráech* Pronounced "FROYK" or "FRAY-uck." His mother is Bóann, the goddess of the river Boyne, which explains why the Otherworld* women reclaim his body. He stars in his own 8th-century saga, "The Cattle-Raid of Fráech" (*Táin bó Fraích*, Ó Corráin #1107), in which he courts Ailill and Maeve's daughter Finnabair, and they send him to retrieve a ring swallowed by a salmon, and to fetch some rowan berries from across a river with a monster in it. His aquatic prowess in that episode fits with the way he chooses to fight Cú Chulainn in the *Táin*. (The rest of the story involves a trip with Conall Cernach to retrieve Fráech's stolen cattle, wife, and children that were taken to the Alps.) See the translations in Gantz, 113–26, and by Wolfgang Meid as *The romance of Froech and Findabair, or, The driving of Froech's cattle: Táin bó Froích*, ed. Albert Bock, Benjamin Bruch, and Aaron Griffith (Innsbruck: Institut für Sprachen und Literaturen der Universität Innsbruck, 2015). Another version of his death is told in *The Metrical Dindshenchas*,* Part III, ed. and trans. Edward Gwynn (Dublin: Royal Irish Academy, Todd Lecture Series 10, 1913) 356–65, at https://celt.ucc.ie/published/T106500C.html.

"Wait here," Fráech told his entourage, "until I fight that man over there. He's no good in the water."

He took off his clothes and got into the water, heading for Cú Chulainn.

"Don't you come after *me*," said Cú Chulainn. "You'll die if you do, and I'll be sorry to kill you."

"I'm coming regardless," said Fráech, "so we can meet in the water, and I expect you to play fair[1] with me."

"Set whatever terms you like," said Cú Chulainn.

"We'll wrestle," said Fráech, "with one arm around the other."

They wrestled in the water for a long time, and Fráech went under.

Cú Chulainn pulled him up again.

"Will you let me spare you this time?" said Cú Chulainn.

"No," said Fráech.

Cú Chulainn pushed him under again, until he drowned.

His body washed up on the bank.[2] His entourage carried it back to camp. That ford was called the Ford of Fráech (*Áth Fraích*) forever after.

The whole camp mourned for Fráech mac Idaith. They saw a band of women in green tunics come for his body. They carried it away into their Otherworld* abode, and it was known as the Otherworld Abode of Fráech (*Síd Fraích*) after that.

Then Fergus leapt across the oak tree in his chariot.

They advanced as far as Áth Taiten. There Cú Chulainn brought down six of them, i.e., the six Dungail Irruis. Maeve had a puppy named Baiscne. Cú Chulainn threw a stone at it and took off its head.[3] So Baiscne's Ridge (*Druim Baiscne*) was the name of that

---

1 *play fair* Instead of *fir fer*, the usual term for fair play,* the Irish here has *cert* 'correct, right, proper, fitting; fair, just' (*eDIL*, s.v.).

2 *His body … on the bank* Following O'Rahilly's "He came to land." The verb here (*do-cuirethar* 'puts, brings,' with an infixed pronoun referring to Fráech) is deponent: passive in form but active in meaning. O'Rahilly and others read it as impersonal. But Cú Chulainn could also be the subject: "He brought him to land," a gesture of respect in allowing his body to be recovered.

3 *took off its head* Intertexually, this killing of a dog is interesting in light of Cú Chulainn's *geis** not to eat dog meat: see "The Death of Cú Chulainn," p. 303 below.

place from then on. "It makes you a complete laughingstock," said Maeve, "not to be hunting down that accursed loose thread who's out there killing you." So they went after him and broke the suspension-beams* of their chariots in the process.

The Death of Órlám

The next day they crossed Irard Cuilenn. Cú Chulainn let them go by. He came across the charioteer of Órlám, son of Ailill and Maeve, at Órlám's Gravesite[1] (*Tamlachta Órláim*), a little to the north of Dísert Lochat: he was cutting wood there.

According to another version, though, it was the suspension-beam of Cú Chulainn's chariot that broke, and he had gone to cut a new one when he met Órlám's charioteer. But according to this version, it was the charioteer who cut the beams.

"That's bold of the Ulstermen if they're the ones over there," said Cú Chulainn, "with a whole army after them." He went to set the charioteer straight, thinking he was one of the Ulstermen. He saw the man cutting wood: suspension-beams for a chariot.

"What are you doing here?" said Cú Chulainn.

"Cutting suspension-beams," said the charioteer. "We broke our chariot hunting that gazelle Cú Chulainn. Help me," said the charioteer. "You can decide if you're going to collect the beams or trim them."

"I'll trim them," said Cú Chulainn.

Then he trimmed the holly beams with his fingers, scraping off the bark and the knots, while the other man watched.

"I gave you a job that's beneath you," said the charioteer. He was terrified.

"Who are you?" said Cú Chulainn.

"I'm the charioteer for Órlám, son of Ailill and Maeve," he said. "What about you?"

"My name's Cú Chulainn," he said.

"Aah! I'm done for!" said the charioteer.

"Don't be afraid," said Cú Chulainn. "Where's your master?"

---

1 *Órlám's Gravesite* The placename anticipates the death of Órlám: it has that name *now* as a result of the story about to be told.

"He's on the mound over there," said the charioteer.

"Come along with me, then," said Cú Chulainn, "because I never hurt charioteers."

Cú Chulainn went up to Órlám. He killed him and cut off his head and shook it at the army. Then he put the head on the charioteer's back and said, "Take that with you, and carry it into camp like that. If you don't, I'll hit you with a stone from my sling."

When the charioteer came close to camp, he took the head off his back and told Ailill and Maeve what he had been through.

"This isn't like grabbing a baby bird out of the nest," she said.

"… And he told me that if I didn't bring the head back to camp on my back, he'd break my head open with a stone …"

The Death of the Three Sons of Gárach

After that, the three sons of Gárach lay in wait at the crossing. These were their names: Lon, Úalu, and Diliu. Mes Lir, Mes Lóech, and Mes Lethan were their three charioteers. They thought Cú Chulainn had gone too far in killing the king's two foster-sons* and his son and waving the head at the army. They were there to try and kill Cú Chulainn as payback, and so that they alone could be responsible for relieving the army of their distress. They cut three clubs for their charioteers so that the six of them could attack him together.

Then Cú Chulainn killed them all because they had broken the terms of fair play* against him.

Órlám's charioteer was standing between Ailill and Maeve at the time. Cú Chulainn shot a stone at him and smashed his head, making his brains spill over his ears. His name was Fer Teidil. So it isn't true that Cú Chulainn never killed charioteers. However, he didn't kill them if they hadn't done anything wrong.

The Death of the Marten and the Pet Bird

Cú Chulainn threatened in Méithe that whenever he saw Ailill or Maeve after that, he would shoot a stone from his sling at them. He did exactly that: he shot a stone that killed the marten that was on Maeve's shoulder south of the crossing, hence the placename Méithe of the Marten (*Méithe Togmaill*). And he killed the bird that was on

Ailill's shoulder north of the crossing, hence the placename Méithe of the Bird (*Méithe nÉoin*).

"Your opponent's not far off," Ailill said to the Maines. They stood up and looked around. When they sat back down, Cú Chulainn hit one of them and smashed his head.

"Sucks to be him," said Máenén the jester.* "Your boasting was uncalled-for. I would have cut his head off." Cú Chulainn shot a stone at him and smashed his head.

That's how the bunch of them died: first Órlám on the hill named after him, then the three sons of Gárach at their crossing, Fer Teidil at his resting-place, and Máenén on his hill.

"I swear* by the god my people swear by," said Ailill, "any man who makes fun of Cú Chulainn at this point, I'll cut him in half. Let's get marching day and night till we reach Cúailnge. The man will kill two-thirds of the army if he keeps it up."

Then the harpers of Caín Bile came from Ess Ruaid to entertain them with music.[1] They thought they had been sent by the Ulstermen to spy on them, so they hunted them until they fled before them in the shape of deer into the standing stones at Lía Mór in the north—they could do that because they were druids* with great arcane knowledge.

The Death of Lethan

The warrior Lethan waits for Cú Chulainn at the crossing of the river Níth in Conaille, and Cú Chulainn kills him: placenames in the area commemorate Lethan, his broken chariot, and his charioteer Mulcha.

---

1 *the harpers … music* Kinsella's "the magical sweet-mouth harpers of Caín Bile came out from the red cataract at Es Ruaid" is paraphrasing what he takes to be the meaning of the Irish names. Ciarán Carson has "the harpers of the Venerable Tree of Caín Bile came from the Red Cataract of Ess Ruad" for the same reason. The relevant meanings for *bile* are in *eDIL* s.v. *5 bil* ('mouth') and *1 bile* ('tree'). According to the *Metrical Dindshenchas*,* the rapids of Ess Ruad got their name from Ruad, daughter of Maine Mílscothach, who drowned there after hearing Otherworld* music (see Gwynn, *The Metrical Dindshenchas*, Part IV, 2–9, at https://celt.ucc.ie/published/T106500D/).

As the army continues to advance, the war-goddess "Allecto, that is, the Morrígan," *visits the Brown Bull in the shape of a raven and speaks an obscure verse portending slaughter.*[1] *The bull paws the ground at Tir Margéni in Cúailnge and then wanders off to Slieve Gullion with fifty heifers, followed by his herdsman, and throws off the 150 boys who used to play on his back, killing two-thirds of them.*

See Map 4 (north Louth and south Armagh) for what follows.

Cú Chulainn didn't kill anyone between Saili Imdoirchi in the region of Conaille and their arrival in Cúailnge. Then he set up on the mountain of Cuinche, because he threatened that wherever he saw Maeve he would whip a stone at her head. This was easier said than done because Maeve moved surrounded by half the army, with a roof of shields over her head.

Now the Death of Lócha:

Maeve had a maidservant named Lócha who went to fetch water surrounded by a bunch of other women. Cú Chulainn thought she was Maeve. He shot a stone at her from Cuinche and killed her on the plain named after her, whence the name the Plain of Lócha (*Réid Lócha*) in Cúailnge.

From Finnabair[2] in Cúailnge the army spread out and set the land on fire. They rounded up all the women, boys, girls, and cows in Cúailnge and brought them all to Finnabair.

"Mission not accomplished," said Maeve. "I don't see the bull in your possession."

"He's not in the province at all," said everyone.

They sent for Maeve's herdsman, Lóthar.

"Where's the bull," she said, "in your opinion?"

1 *verse portending slaughter* This has been edited and translated in Patrick L. Henry, "*Táin roscada*: discussion and edition," *ZCP* 47 (1995) 32–75, at 71–74. It seems to refer to Fiacc, "Raven," son of Fergus mac Roích, as the hero defending Ulster.

2 *Finnabair* Named after the character Finnabair due to later events: compare p. 170 above. The upcoming reference to Glen Gatt anticipates in the same way the naming of the place.

"I'm afraid to tell you," said the herdsman. "The night the Ulstermen went into paralysis, the bull went away with sixty heifers and he's now in Dubchaire in Glen Gatt."

"Go," said Maeve, "and take a hobble-hoop between each pair of you."

So they did, and hence the glen is called the Glen of Hobble-Hoops (*Glen Gatt*).

Then they brought the bull to Finnabair. As soon as the bull saw the herdsman—that is, Lóthar—he charged him and disemboweled him on his horns, and along with his 150 heifers he charged the camp and killed fifty warriors. That was "The Death of Lóthar on the Cattle-Raid."

After that the bull left the camp and they didn't know where he had gone and were demoralized. Maeve asked the herdsman[1] where he thought the bull was.

"I think he might be in the recesses of Slieve Gullion."

So they went back that way after ravaging Cúailnge, and didn't find the bull there.

The river Cronn rose against them as high as the treetops. They camped beside it and Maeve told some of her people to go across.

The Death of Úalu

In the morning an illustrious warrior named Úalu went and took a huge flagstone on his back to cross the river. But the current flipped him over on his back and he ended up with the stone on his belly. His grave and his headstone are on the road by the river: Úalu's Stone (*Lia Úalann*) is the name of it.

Then they went around the river Cronn up to its source, and would have gone between its source and the mountain except that Maeve wouldn't stand for it. She preferred to have them go across the mountain so that the track they made would last forever to insult the Ulstermen. Then they stayed there for three days and three nights digging their way forward: that was the Cúailnge Cow-Pass (*Bernas Bó Cúailnge*).

---

1 *the herdsman* Presumably not Lóthar, unless on his deathbed. This could be the bull's own herdsman Forgaimen (see p. 224), or Lóthar's newly-appointed replacement.

Then Cú Chulainn killed Cronn and Cóemdele, and he was just getting warmed up. A hundred warriors fell before him, that spear of kings, along with Roán and Roae, the two historians of the Cattle-Raid. He killed a hundred and forty-four kings beside that same river.

After that they came through the Cúailnge Cow-Pass with the livestock and cattle of Cúailnge, and spent the night in Glen Dáil Imda in Cúailnge. "Huts" (*Botha*) is the name of that place because they made huts for them there. The next day they advanced to the river Colptha. They made the ill-advised choice to try and cross it, and it rose up against them and swept a hundred of their chariot-warriors out to sea. The name of the area where they drowned is Chariot Meadow (*Clúain Carpat*). Then they went around the Colptha to its source at Belat Alióin, and spent the night at Liasa Liac. The name of that place comes from the fact that they made sheds for their calves there between Cúailnge and Conaille. Then they passed through Hobble-Hoop Glen (*Glen Gatlaig*). Then the river Glais Gatlaig rose against them. Its name had previously been Sechaire. It became Hobble-Hoop Creek (*Glais Gatlaig*) from then on because they used hobble-hoops to take their calves across, and they spent the night at Druim Féne in Conaille.

So those were their movements from Cúailnge to Machaire according to this version. But other authors and books give a different account of their movements from Finnabair to Conaille, that is:

Now for the Ravaging of Cúailnge:

When everyone had gathered with their spoils at Finnabair in Cúailnge, Maeve spoke. "We'll split our forces here," she said. "The cattle can't all go by one route. Let Ailill take half of them via the Midlúachair Road. Fergus and I will go via Bernas Bó nUlad."

"It's too bad about our half of the herd," said Fergus. "We can't get them over the mountain without splitting them up." So they did, hence the way they went was called The Ulstermen's Cow-Pass (*Bernas Bó nUlad*).

Then Ailill said to his charioteer Cuillius, "Spy on Maeve and Fergus for me today. I don't know why they've teamed up like this, and I'd appreciate it if you can bring me some proof."

Cuillius arrived when they were in Cluichri. The lovers stayed behind while the warriors went on ahead of them. Cuillius crept up to them, but they didn't hear the spy. Fergus's sword happened to be next to him. Cuillius pulled it out of the scabbard and left the empty scabbard behind.

Cuillius came back to Ailill.

"Well?" said Ailill.

"I'm afraid so," said Cuillius. "Here's your proof."

"Excellent," said Ailill. They grinned at each other.

"As you suspected," said Cuillius. "I found them sleeping together."

"She has the right," said Ailill. "She did it for his help on the cattle-raid. Take good care of the sword. Put it under your seat in the chariot in a linen wrap."

Meanwhile, Fergus got up and missed his sword. "Dammit!" he said.

"What's wrong?" said Maeve.

"I've wronged Ailill. Wait here while I take a walk in the woods," he said, "and don't be surprised if I'm gone a long time."

Maeve hadn't noticed that he'd lost his sword.

Off he went, carrying his charioteer's sword. He made himself a wooden sword in the forest. Hence the Ulstermen called that place The Forest of Overindulgence (*Fid Mórdrúalle*).

"Let's go on after the others," said Fergus.

The armies reconvened on the plain. They pitched their tents. Fergus was called to Ailill to play *fidchell*.* When Fergus walked into the tent, Ailill laughed at him.

Fergus said:[1]

1 *Fergus said* The conversation that follows between Fergus, Ailill, and Maeve is in difficult verse, introduced with both Irish and Latin tags (e.g., *Asbert Fergus* and *Fergus dixit*, both meaning "Fergus said"). The translation here is based on Patrick L. Henry, "*Táin roscada*: discussion and edition," *ZCP* 47 (1995) 32–75, and secondarily Karin Olsen, "The cuckold's revenge: reconstructing six Irish roscada in *Táin bó Cúailnge*," *CMCS* 28 (1994) 51–69, as well as O'Rahilly. Darach Ó Scolaí calls this the "Chess Game" sequence and suggests that although it is cryptic, "the fact that the [medieval] scribes chose not to rewrite this section allows us to conclude [...] that they thought that this episode *should not* be altered or omitted" (*Táin Bó Cúalnge from the Book of Leinster: Reassessments*, 127, his emphasis).

"It is lucky for the man being laughed at
if no one spills about the foolish offense of his egregious act.
By the point of my sword, the Blade of Macha, we will join forces
with fast-avenging swords when the Gaileóin cry out—
if a woman's victory had not complicated things.
We will have a rendezvous with bloody graves,
spears and a pinewood sword will face
a great force, great leaders:
an army vigorous
in battle as far as Cú Chulainn's[1] mountain.
It will scatter men's torsos."

Ailill said:

"Do not brag about battle, when you are swordless, and how you'll kill kings.
Your Leinster-style battle-cry might turn to dread.
Maeve swears to me she will protect us from the hordes herself.
Jealousy is a source of strife when it comes to women—
whatever slaughter they wreak, whatever plunder they take
from all over the world by the great deeds they do."

"Sit down, then," said Ailill, "and let's play *fidchell.*[*] You are welcome."

Ailill said:

"Play *fidchell* and *búanbach*[*] before a king and queen:
those games have been prepared for vast eager armies.
It is not unlikely you win the stake: you use the same hands
you use to pleasure queens and women.
I know the score: it is not unheard-of
for sweetly dominant women to make the first move to cheat.
And Finnabair could love brave Fergus for the mooing cows
that he could capture with troops from wealthy tribes:

---

1 *Cú Chulainn* He is referred to here as "Ness's grandson," not by name.

Fergus mac Rossa Roích, beautiful in the many ways a king is,
with a dragon's fury, a viper's breath,
the swipe of a lion in frontal attack."[1]

Then they started playing *fidchell*:* they moved the gold and silver pieces over the bronze board.

Ailill was heard saying:

"A king is above the threat of a copper spear-point bearing
death.
The clash on the frenzied gameboard is more chaotic:
it is a foot that scurries, mighty Maeve, a secret messenger to
Fergus
to hide the game you play."

Maeve was heard saying:

"Cease your classless chatter. A great lady does not lay down
her arms
for trivial premonitions about tender boys refusing
battle-glory.
I am not stingy, and I do not deny my people justice.
The herds we fight for are not short on cattle.
Fergus's feats will cleanse his honor."[2]

---

1 *Play fidchell ... frontal attack* Henry, "*Táin roscada*," 54–55, explains this verse as applying both to "Fergus's military role on the *Táin*" (represented by his skill at the boardgame) and "his amatory experience with M[aeve]": "The operation of the hands [...] is taken to be the common factor in the amatory and the stake-winning experiences. [After that] Ailill is saying that in his judgement M[aeve] is no doubt the prime mover in the affair with Fergus. [H]e turns to a reasonable and feasible aspiration for Fergus, namely the princess Fin[n]abair, who is the approved bait for *Táin* champions: she loves him—precisely for the kind of martial exploits expected so eagerly of him on the *Táin*; and Ailill's rising enthusiasm whets him to a standard rhetorical eulogy of Fergus."

2 *Ailill was heard ... his honor* Henry, "*Táin roscada*," 58–59, explains this exchange between Ailill and Maeve as follows (line references silently omitted): "Ailill forebodes lamentation and death on the Foray; he shows that he is aware of M[aeve]'s intrigue with Fergus. The board game is able to carry this symbolism as well as that of war. The effect of Ailill's dire prognostications can be to discourage the young warriors from [continued ...]

Then Fergus was heard. He said:

"Just so! I do not use a flood of words
to fight the gathered tribes.
And they will be visited with violent death;
and tricked out of their treasures;
and polished off with spearpoints;
and kings will compete for the spoils."

They stayed there that night, and the next morning they heard Ailill say:

"See now: a great champion faces the army
at the Cronn, Cú Chulainn's river.[1]
The men of Connacht[2] will give way before him.
Blood will burst from headless necks
in a gory, grave-strewn
clash of champions,
raising waves
to greet the beardless hero
who will come from Ulster."

Maeve was heard saying:

"Don't be difficult, arrogant Ailill:
don't insult a man for overlords he's given up.[3]

---

the terms of the age-old *comitatus* compact [...]: battling for 'mead', for the commemorative praise poem and for heroic reputation. M[aeve]'s reaction is sharp: she rebukes him for words unbecoming a nobleman; she has no intention of abandoning major imperial schemes on account of his trifling portents which can only dishearten the young warriors. These should remember that she is generous, just, and absolutely dependable [...] The spoils to be won on the foray are rich and Fergus's performance will cleanse the honor/face of any aspersions which can be cast at him. [...] This gives Fergus his cue: he will not fight with words [...] but with deeds; and these he specifies."

1 *Cú Chulainn's river* Again, he is referred to only as "Ness's grandson."

2 *men of Connacht* The text actually uses an archaic population name for the same region, Fir Ól nÉcmacht.

3 *don't insult ... given up* Henry: "do not insult a champion on account of high ones whom he has abandoned." I take it that this is referring to Fergus and his exile from Conchobor.

Herd the men together.
Carry off their women.
Drive cattle ahead of them in front of the army.
Swords will break over this.
Tell everyone:
to wield their weapons;
and drive the oxen;
and seize the women.
Great armies propose to come victorious
from the Cúailnge battlefield.
Still the armies sleep."[1]

Fergus was heard saying:

"Hang a trophy head in front of the wheels
to confront the swaggering champion's brutalities.
Have them swear by their tribes.
Have them pay homage to their queens.[2]
Have them fight the enemy."

Maeve was heard saying:

"Yes, that!
Do exactly that!"

Maeve said to Fergus: "You're in charge of the orders going out to all our armies. Take them forward. Ailill can report to you."

They set off for the river Cronn. They heard Maine son of Ailill speaking. Maine said:

"If you send me racing after the man of fine feats;

---

1 *the armies sleep* This could be referring to the Ulster armies lying paralyzed, but since this conversation is happening in the morning, it could also be that the Connacht forces are still asleep and need to get moving: this works with Fergus's orders in his reply.

2 *to their queens* "Queens" is a clear plural. Henry advises us to "[n]ote the sequence and military significance" of Fergus's instructions here, "and M[aeve]'s insistence upon them" (63), which results in a transfer of command from Ailill to Fergus.

along with my mother and father, with a mass of horned
cattle,
you'll keep him busy so that I can get to him with a knife from
my chariot.
You can use this awesome trick with the cattle to clear the
battlefield."

Fergus was heard saying:

"Brave lad. Don't go:
no one would predict that you'll succeed.
Your head will be taken off your body
by the beardless lad who beats the odds,
who rages on the battlefield.
He invokes the river;
woods move;
slaughter will be done at his coming.
With mighty water feats he'll drown
a whole mass of troops.
He will wound Ailill.
There will be many dishonored faces, Maeve,
on the severed heads he carries off the battlefield bristling with
spears."

"Let me go first with my exiles," said Fergus, "so that we don't violate fair play* against the lad, putting the cattle out in front of us, and the army behind them, and the women in the back."

Maeve was heard saying:

"Listen, Fergus!
On your honor and your life,
protect the cattle with your valiant forces.
Don't let the raging Ulstermen
come past Coba and from Gáirech into Aí Plain,
while you hold up the march."

Fergus was heard saying:

"Bah! Stupid Maeve! I'm not listening to you.
You won't find me skulking in the rank and file:
I am no weakling's son,
to duck the heat of battle in front of Emain.
I will not strike great blows against our allies.
Spare me your edicts.
Now they need me to inspect some siege equipment."[1]

Cú Chulainn came to meet them at the Ford of the River Cronn (*Áth Cruinn*).

"My dear* Lóeg," he said, "the armies are advancing on us."

Lóeg spoke:

"I invoke the gods," said the charioteer,
"that I'll do a great feat in front of chariot-warriors,
in a close-fitting cloak,
on slender horses
with silver trappings,
with golden wheels.
They'll carry us to many victories.
They'll overtake kings, if I can manage it.
Victory will come from their fast acceleration."

Cú Chulainn said:

"Watch out, Lóeg,
to keep a rein on Macha's gift of speed,
so the horses don't carry you
past the mob
to contend with the boastful woman in the plain beyond,

---

1 *inspect some siege equipment* This simplifies what Henry renders as "They are looking for me with one of the two outfits which break down ramparts on expeditions" (68). Henry's comment on this speech by Fergus: "The general, bent upon active service, turns brusquely on her imperial majesty and shrugs off her insinuations. The allied tribes have nothing to fear from him; she will not be able to find him among them, simply because he intends to press forward in the van [i.e., on the front lines, as in 'vanguard']. So she might leave him be; and here he breaks off, as active service units have arrived with assault equipment for his inspection."

who is deserting her son and my pine-sworded foster-father*[1]
and the chariot troops,
while Maeve's husband Ailill
is supposed to be coming with huge forces.

"I call on the waters to help me," said Cú Chulainn. "I call on heaven and earth and especially the river Cronn:[2]

"The solid river Cronn resists them,
it won't let them cross into Muirthemne
until the warriors' work is finished
on the mountain north of Ochaíne."

Then the river rose as high as the treetops.

Maine son of Ailill and Maeve came forward ahead of everyone. Cú Chulainn slaughtered him at the ford and thirty horsemen from his retinue drowned in the river. Cú Chulainn also killed thirty-two of their best warriors on the riverbank.

They pitched their tents at the ford. Lugaid mac Nóis uí Lomairc Allchomaig in a group of thirty horsemen came to talk to Cú Chulainn.

"Welcome, Lugaid," said Cú Chulainn. "If birds fly over Muirthemne Plain, I'll catch a barnacle goose for you and we can share another. Or if fish swim into the estuaries, I'll catch some lox—I mean, a salmon—for you and we can share another. Or you can have the three sprigs: a sprig of watercress, a sprig of laver,[3] a sprig of seaweed. You can have someone else take your turn at the ford."

"I appreciate it," said Lugaid. "I wish you all the best on behalf of my tribe, lad."

"It's a fine army you've got there," said Cú Chulainn.

---

1 *pine-sworded foster-father* Cú Chulainn is noting how Ailill has swapped out Fergus's sword for a wooden one.

2 *the river Cronn* A classic article on this episode is Joseph Falaky Nagy, "The rising of the Cronn river in the *Táin Bó Cúailnge*," in *Celtica Helsingiensia*, ed. Anders Ahlqvist et al. (Helsinki: Societas Scientiarum Fennica, 1996) 129–48, which considers it alongside the rising of the river Skamander in Homer's *Iliad*; see also John Carey, "The encounter at the ford: warriors, water and women," *Éigse* 34 (2004) 10–24, https://www.nui.ie/eigse/pdf/vol34/eigse34.pdf.

3 *laver* A kind of edible seaweed.

"You're outnumbered, but I don't see it going badly for you," said Lugaid.

"Just give me fair play* and a good clean fight," said Cú Chulainn. "My dear* Lugaid, is the army afraid of me?"

"I swear* to god," said Lugaid, "one or two men don't dare step outside the camp to take a piss without getting twenty or thirty more to go with them."

"It will be fun for them," said Cú Chulainn, "if I start to pelt them with my sling. You'd do well to remember your alliance with the Ulstermen, Lugaid, if they come for me with everything they've got. Anyway, tell me what you want."

"I want you to grant a truce to my men."

"All right, as long as they wear a mark. And tell my uncle* Fergus to have his men wear a mark, too. Tell the medics to have their group wear a mark and have them swear to preserve my life and send me food every night."

Lugaid left him. Fergus happened to be in his tent with Ailill. Lugaid called him outside and told him the news. Ailill was heard saying:[1]

"What are they plotting out there in the fields,
having secret conversations?
For Mac Roích to abscond from the tribes with a whole mass
of troops
does me no favors.
Announce it, make it known:
he'll take command in my presence.
As a reward for Maeve with the lovely arms
he'll provide me with great help:
I'll withdraw with a small force to special tents
while he takes it on himself to protect the camp from the
volleys of stones—
whoever this is who arrives and has come here to have secret
conversations."

---

1 *Ailill was heard saying* My translation of this difficult verse follows the text and German translation in Johan Corthals, "Zur Frage des mündlichen oder schriftlichen Ursprungs der Sagen*roscada*," in *Early Irish Literature — Media and Communication*, ed. Stephen N. Tranter and Hildegard L.C. Tristram (Tübingen: Gunter Narr Verlag, 1989) 201–20, at 209.

"I swear* to god, that won't work," said Fergus, "without asking the lad. Do me a favor, Lugaid, go and ask him if Ailill and his division can join my men. Take him an ox and a side of bacon and a barrel of wine."

So Lugaid went to Cú Chulainn and gave him that message.

"It's fine with me if he does that," said Cú Chulainn. So the two groups combined. They were there till nightfall. Cú Chulainn took out thirty of their warriors with his sling.[1]

Or they spent twenty nights there, as other books tell it.

"Your maneuvers will go badly," said Fergus. "The Ulstermen will recover from their paralysis and grind us into the mud and gravel. We're badly positioned to fight where we are. Move on to Cúil Airthir!"

Meanwhile, that night Cú Chulainn went to talk to the Ulstermen.

"Any news?" said Conchobor.

"They're kidnapping women," said Cú Chulainn, "driving off cattle, slaughtering men!"

"Who's kidnapping them? Who's driving them off? Who's slaughtering them?"

"The leader in killing and slaughter,[2] Ailill mac Máta, carries them off, along with fearless Fergus mac Roích, who wields a sword to cut down every single one of Conchobor's chariot troops—and he'll do it, too."

"It doesn't do you much good to tell us," said Conchobor. "Today we're still stricken, the same as before."

Cú Chulainn left them there, and went back to watch the armies moving out. He killed thirty of their warriors at Áth Durn.[3] Then they didn't stop moving till nightfall, when they reached Cúil Airthir. He killed thirty of them there, and they pitched their tents.

---

1 *took out thirty … with his sling* One way to make sense of this is that while Ailill and his men have joined Fergus, they aren't formally under Fergus's protection,* and might not be wearing the mark that tells Cú Chulainn not to kill them, so it doesn't really matter where they go.

2 *The leader in killing and slaughter* This is given as a gloss for an obscure expression that I haven't tried to translate separately. The way Cú Chulainn mentions only Ailill and Fergus is, of course, a pointed erasure of Maeve.

3 *killed thirty … Áth Durn* The beheading of these thirty men is anticipated by Ailill in a partly obscure verse omitted here. The name seems to mean "Ford of Fists/Blows."

In the morning, Ailill's charioteer, Cuillius, was washing the undercarriage at the ford. Cú Chulainn hit him with a stone and killed him. Hence the placename Cuillius's Ford (*Áth Cuillne*) in Cúil Airthir.

The army advanced. They spent the night on Druim Féne in Conaille, as previously stated, and Cú Chulainn caught up with them. He killed a hundred of them on each of the three nights they were there, pelting them with his sling from the hill of Ochaíne nearby.[1]

"Our army won't last long with Cú Chulainn hounding us like this," said Ailill. "Let's try to buy him off. I suggest a part of Aí Plain the size of Muirthemne Plain, the best chariot on Aí Plain, and enough equipment for twelve men. Or if he prefers, he can have this plain here, where he was raised, and 21 *cumals*.* Also his lost property and livestock will be restituted, and he'll be compensated for their value. And he can swear allegiance to me. He'll be better off, instead of serving under that petty lordling Conchobor."[2]

"Who'll deliver the message?"

"Mac Roth over there."

Mac Roth was Ailill and Maeve's messenger. He could go all the way round Ireland in a single day. Off he went to Delga, because Fergus figured that was where Cú Chulainn was.

"I see a man coming our way," Lóeg said to Cú Chulainn. "Blond hair, linen ensign, some kind of fancy staff[3] in his hand and an ivory-hilted dirk at his waist. He's wearing a hooded tunic with red embroidery."

"One of the king's warriors, I guess," said Cú Chulainn.

Mac Roth asked Lóeg whom he served under.

"That man down there," said Lóeg.

Cú Chulainn was sitting in snow up to his thighs with no clothes on, delousing his shirt.

---

1 *Druim Féne … Ochaíne nearby* Now Drumenagh Hill and Tipping's Wood in County Louth, still on Map 4.

2 *Conchobor* Added for clarity.

3 *fancy staff* Literally, "a staff/club of fury," which is also the name of the special club carried by the Dagdae, one of the Túatha Dé Danann.* Functionally, this seems to be a token of Mac Roth's office as herald or messenger.

So Mac Roth asked him whom he served under.

"Conchobor mac Nessa," said Cú Chulainn.

"Care to be more specific?"

"That's plenty," said Cú Chulainn.

"Well, where's Cú Chulainn?" said Mac Roth.

"What would you say to him?" said Cú Chulainn.

Mac Roth delivered the entire message as previously stated.

"Even if Cú Chulainn were around, he wouldn't accept that. He won't trade his mother's brother for another king."

Mac Roth came back later and offered him the noblest of the women they had captured, and the dry cows:* all he had to do was stop inflicting his sling on them at night. He could even keep attacking them during the day.

"I can't accept," said Cú Chulainn. "If you take away our low-grade women, our fine ladies will have to grind flour,[1] and if you drive off the dairy cows, we'll have no milk."

Mac Roth came back and offered him the lower-class women and the dairy cows.

"I can't accept," said Cú Chulainn. "Then the Ulstermen will sleep with their low-grade women and have low-grade children, and they'll slaughter the dairy cows for meat in the winter."

"Is there anything else you *will* accept?" said the messenger.

"Yes," said Cú Chulainn, "but I won't tell you what. I'll agree to it if someone else can tell you."

"I know what it is," said Fergus. "He's arranged it so that I have to be the one to explain it to you, but it's hardly in your favor. Anyway, the deal is this: he'll fight in single combat at a river crossing, and for the next day and night you won't be allowed to drive your cattle any further. He's stalling for time, hoping that the Ulstermen will send him reinforcements. And frankly I'm amazed it's taking them so long to shake off their paralysis."

"Well," said Ailill, "better we should lose a man every day than a hundred every night."

---

1 *grind flour* Literally, "work at querns" (a quern is a pair of stones for grinding grain by hand).

The Death of Etarcomol, and the Men of Ireland's Message Delivered to Cú Chulainn by the Mouth of Fergus

Then Fergus went to deliver the message that the invaders agreed to Cú Chulainn's terms.[1] Etarcomol, son of Ed and Leithrinn and foster-son* of Ailill and Maeve, tried to tag along.

"I don't want you to come," said Fergus. "It's not that I hate you, but I'd rather not see you fight Cú Chulainn. You're proud and self-important, and he's aggressive, quick to take offense, hot-blooded, headstrong, and prone to violent rage. No good can come of the two of you fighting."

"Can't you protect me from him?" said Etarcomol.

"Fine," said Fergus, "but only if you don't provoke him."

Off they went to Delga in two chariots.

Cú Chulainn was playing *búanbach** with Lóeg; he had his back to them. Lóeg was facing them, and said: "I see two chariots coming our way. There's a tall dark man in the first one, with dark bushy hair. He's wearing a purple cloak with a gold brooch, and a hooded tunic with red embroidery. He has a curved shield with a scalloped rim made of white-bronze.* He has a stabbing-spear in his hand with rings around it from the blade to the shaft. Resting on his thighs is a sword as big as a boat's rudder."

"That big rudder my uncle* Fergus carries is empty," said Cú Chulainn. "The only sword he has in his scabbard is made of wood. I hear Ailill snuck up when he was sleeping with Maeve, took away Fergus's sword, handed it to his charioteer, and put a wooden sword back in the scabbard."

Fergus came up to them.

"Welcome, Uncle Fergus," said Cú Chulainn. "If fish swim into the estuaries, I'll catch a salmon for you and we can share another. Or if birds fly over the plain, I'll catch a barnacle goose for you and we can share another. Or if all I can find is a handful of watercress or edible seaweed, I'll give you that and keep a drink cold in the sand for you."[2]

---

1 *that the invaders … terms* Added for clarity. The manuscript heading must consider this a sub-part of "The Death of Etarcomol," otherwise it has the events in the wrong order: the message is delivered first.

2 *Welcome … for you* The translation has been tweaked to clarify Cú Chulainn's intention here, which is to be as generous with Fergus as he can manage under the circumstances.

"I appreciate your welcome," said Fergus, "but we're not here for food. We know you're living off the land."

Then Cú Chulainn listened to what Fergus had to say, and Fergus started back. Etarcomol stayed behind and stared at Cú Chulainn.

"What are you looking at?" said Cú Chulainn.

"You," said Etarcomol.

"That shouldn't take too long."

"I can see that," said Etarcomol. "I don't know why anybody should be scared of you. You're not monstrous or terrifying and you don't outnumber anyone. You're just a pretty boy with wooden weapons and some cute tricks."[1]

"Even though you're badmouthing me," said Cú Chulainn, "I won't kill you for Fergus's sake. If you didn't have his protection,* I'd have sent you back to camp in bloody chunks with stringy bits attached, dragging on the ground behind your chariot."

"Lay off the threats," said Etarcomol. "As for the wonderful deal you made, about the single combat, I'll be first in line to fight you tomorrow."

Then off he went, but at Méithe and Ceithe[2] he turned around and said to his charioteer: "I boasted in front of Fergus that I would face Cú Chulainn tomorrow. But I can't stand to wait that long. Turn the chariot around."

Lóeg saw that and told Cú Chulainn: "The chariot's back, and has its left side turned to us."

"I can't let that stand,"[3] said Cú Chulainn. "Let's go down and meet him at the crossing to find out what he wants."

"I don't care to do what you're asking of me," said Cú Chulainn.

"You have no choice," said Etarcomol.

Cú Chulainn cut the ground out from under Etarcomol's feet, making him fall over with a chunk of turf on top of him.

"Get lost," said Cú Chulainn. "I'm not interested in bathing my hand in your guts. I'd have sliced you up several times over by now if it weren't for Fergus."

---

1 *cute tricks* Or, a reviewer suggests, "*ségda* could also convey the sense of feats that Cú Chulainn was lucky enough to execute successfully."

2 *Méithe and Ceithe* Apparently in modern County Louth. Compare p. 200.

3 *I can't let that stand* More literally, "It is not a challenge to be refused."

"I'm not going to leave you alone," said Etarcomol, "until I take your head or leave you mine."

"It will definitely be the latter," said Cú Chulainn.

Then Cú Chulainn slashed at him under the armpits so that all his clothes fell off. Still he didn't cut the skin.

"Now leave," said Cú Chulainn.

"No," said Etarcomol.

Cú Chulainn reached out and trimmed off his hair with the edge of his sword, leaving Etarcomol's head as smooth as if it had been shaved with a razor. He didn't even scratch the skin.

In the end, since the oaf was a nuisance and kept asking for it, Cú Chulainn chopped him in half with a blow that started at the top of his skull and went down through his belly button.

Fergus saw Etarcomol's chariot shoot past him with only one man in it. He turned around to scold Cú Chulainn.

"Curse you, you imp," he said, "for violating my protection.*[1] You must think I have a short club."[2]

"Don't be mad at me, Uncle* Fergus," said Cú Chulainn.[3] He bowed down and let Fergus's chariot drive past him[4] three times. "Ask his charioteer if I started it."

"He really didn't," said the charioteer.

"He said he wouldn't go away until he took my head or left me his," said Cú Chulainn. "Which would you rather have happen, Uncle Fergus?"

"What did happen," said Fergus, "since he was the one being obnoxious."

Then Fergus threaded a loop through Etarcomol's heels and dragged him back to camp behind his own chariot. Going over rocks, the two halves of the body would separate, and on level ground, they'd flop back together.

---

1 *violating my protection* This uses a legal term (*díguin*) for the offense, which would normally require compensation to be paid to the would-be protector.

2 *a short club* Fergus could be referring to his wooden sword, but it seems unlikely he would draw attention to it. The "club" is probably symbolic (Fergus's capacity to punish) or euphemistic (his penis, representing his manhood).

3 Some marginal comments are omitted here.

4 *drive past him* Or "over him," which would be an extreme gesture of submission, even if Cú Chulainn does have supernatural resilience.

Maeve looked at the corpse. "That young pup hasn't exactly been petted, Fergus."

"It's no skin off my nose," said Fergus, "if the lousy mutt wanted to go up against the big dog when he was no match."

Etarcomol got a grave and a headstone with his name written on it in ogam.* He was mourned. That night Cú Chulainn didn't attack them with his sling.

Now for the Death of Nad Crantail:

"Who have you got to face Cú Chulainn tomorrow?" asked Lugaid.

"They'll send him to you in the morning," said one of the Maines.

"We can't find anyone to go," said Maeve. "Let's ask him for a truce until we find him an opponent."

They got the truce.

"Where will you go looking for the man to face Cú Chulainn?" said Ailill.

"No one in Ireland seems up to it," said Maeve, "unless we can get Cú Roí mac Dáiri[1] or the *fían*-warrior* Nad Crantail."

One of Cú Roí's followers was in the tent. "Cú Roí won't come," he said. "He thinks enough of his men are here already."

"Someone go get Nad Crantail, then."

Maine Andoí went to see him and explained the situation.

"Come with us to uphold the honor of Connacht."

"I won't go unless I can have Finnabair."

But he went with them for the moment. His weapons were shipped by cart to the camp from the east of Connacht.

"Finnabair will be yours," said Maeve, "for going to face that man over there."

"I'll do it," he said.

That night Lugaid went to see Cú Chulainn. "Nad Crantail is coming to fight you tomorrow. Too bad for you: you won't hold out."

---

1 *Cú Roí mac Dáiri* A supernaturally powerful champion from Munster, who features in "Bricriu's Feast" (see pp. 132–33 above) as both an opponent and an advocate for Cú Chulainn. Cú Chulainn eventually kills him: see p. 293 below.

"Big deal," said Cú Chulainn. That was when he recited the verse "If Nad Crantail falls," etc.

The next day Nad Crantail left the camp carrying nine spikes of holly that were sharpened and scorched. Cú Chulainn was hunting birds beside his chariot. Nad Crantail threw one of the spikes at him. Cú Chulainn hopped up on the point of it and didn't let it interrupt his hunting. The same thing happened with the other eight spikes. When Nad Crantail threw the ninth one, the flock of birds flew off and Cú Chulainn went after them. He jumped up on the spike-points like a bird himself, going from one to the next to stop the birds from escaping. But everyone was sure he was running away from Nad Crantail.

"That Cú Chulainn of yours up and ran away from me," said Nad Crantail.

"Well, obviously," said Maeve, "if he was actually facing competent warriors, that imp wouldn't stand against them."

Fergus and the Ulstermen were distraught. They sent Fíacha mac Fir Fhebe to scold Cú Chulainn.

"Tell him," said Fergus, "that it was fine for him to attack the warriors as long as he did it bravely. But if he's going to run from just one man, he'd do better to hide: that kind of behavior is an embarrassment not just to him, but to every other Ulsterman."

"Who boasted that I ran away?" said Cú Chulainn.

"Nad Crantail," said Fíacha.

"If he had boasted about the feat I did in front of him, it would have been less inappropriate," said Cú Chulainn. "But he wouldn't be boasting if he'd had a weapon in his hand. You know I don't kill unarmed men. Let him come in the morning, between Ochaíne and the sea, and no matter how early he comes, he'll find me waiting. I won't run from him."

That ended the meeting, and when Cú Chulainn finished standing guard that night, he threw his cloak around him. He didn't notice that he was next to a standing stone as big as he was. He wrapped it in his cloak and bedded down beside it.

Then Nad Crantail arrived, with his cart full of weapons.

"Where's Cú Chulainn?" he said.

"Right over there," said Fergus.

"That's not what he looked like yesterday," said Nad Crantail. "You're Cú Chulainn?"

"So what if I am?" said Cú Chulainn.

"Well, if you are," said Nad Crantail, "you're a beardless boy. I'd sooner take a little lamb's head back to camp with me."

"You're right—I'm not Cú Chulainn at all. Go around the hill to meet him."

Cú Chulainn ran to Lóeg: "Smear a false beard on me. Their champion won't fight me if I'm beardless."[1] Lóeg did that for him, and he went to meet Nad Crantail on the hill.

"That's better," said Nad Crantail. "Now let's set some ground rules."

"Anything you want, as long as I know what they are."

"I'm going to throw a spear at you," said Nad Crantail, "and you're not allowed to dodge."

"Fine, no dodging, except straight up," said Cú Chulainn.

Nad Crantail threw his spear, and Cú Chulainn jumped over it.

"Curse you for dodging," said Nad Crantail.

"You're allowed to dodge upwards too," said Cú Chulainn.

Cú Chulainn threw a spear at him, but up high so that it came down through the top of his head and went straight through his body into the ground.

"Oof," said Nad Crantail. "You're the best warrior in Ireland! Listen, I have twenty-four sons back at the camp. Let me go and tell them about all my hidden treasures, and then I'll come back so you can behead me, because I'll die if this spear is pulled out of my head."

"Fine," said Cú Chulainn, "just as long as you do come back."

Nad Crantail walked into the camp.

"Where's the mutant's* head? Did you bring it?" everyone asked.

---

1 *won't fight me if I'm beardless* Sarah Künzler, *Flesh and Word: Reading Bodies in Old Norse-Icelandic and Early Irish Literature* (Berlin: De Gruyter, 2016) 125–41, and Longman, "'What manner of man is this Hound?'," 6–12, comment on Cú Chulainn's beardlessness. Interestingly, among the various etymologies of *Ulaid* (the Ulstermen) proposed in "Fitness of Names" (II, 138–39), one is "great grey ones," because when Conchobor and his warriors were all young and beardless, they put gray wool on their faces to help them fight off a vast Scandinavian invasion.

"Hold on, gentlemen, until I tell my sons what happened and go back to meet Cú Chulainn."

Nad Crantail went back to face Cú Chulainn and threw his sword at him.

Cú Chulainn jumped up so that the sword hit the standing stone and snapped in two. Then he mutated* like he did with the boys in Emain. He jumped on Nad Crantail's shield and chopped off his head. Then he hit him on the neck and split him down to the belly button. His body fell to the ground in four chunks. Then Cú Chulainn said:

> "If Nad Crantail has fallen,
> things will get nasty.
> It's too bad that right now
> I can't take on Maeve and a third of her army!"

Now for the Finding of the Bull According to This Version:

Maeve sends a third of the army to capture the Brown Bull, which they do without incident, except that Cú Chulainn kills the leader of the troops bringing it back to the camp.

Now the Death of Redg the Satirist:*

They reached the conclusion that Cú Chulainn would be less of a problem without his javelin.[1] On the advice of Ailill, the satirist* Redg went to ask Cú Chulainn for the javelin—that is, his spear.

"Give me your spear," said the satirist.

"No way," said Cú Chulainn. "I'll give you other treasures, though."

"Unacceptable," said the satirist.

Cú Chulainn wounded him because he wouldn't take what was offered: the satirist said he would dishonor him unless he got the javelin, so Cú Chulainn tossed him the javelin—straight through his head.

---

1 *They reached … his javelin* This sentence has been moved for clarity. It actually comes before the section heading in the manuscript.

"That's what I call rush delivery," said the satirist.*

Hence the place was called the Ford of Premium Rush Delivery (*Áth Tolam Sét*). The bronze head of the spear landed at another ford to the east: its name is the Ford of Shooting Bronze (*Umarrith*).

Cú Chulainn wins more single combats at places named after the people he kills, then goes back to defend Muirthemne, while Maeve makes a two-week foray to the north. She fights Finnmór, the wife of Celtchar mac Uthidir, destroys Dún Sobairche (now Dunseverick in County Antrim, Northern Ireland), and takes fifty women prisoner. Fords and hills are named after her everywhere she goes. She meets up with the men escorting the Brown Bull: a herdsman named Forgaimen is trampled to death and a hill is named after him.

Cú Chulainn stalls the army for a week, winning single combats and an unfair ambush. The army advances to Crónech (i.e., Focherd or Faughart, still on Map 4) under a truce, and Cú Chulainn kills 48 more people in single combat. Maeve arranges another truce, promising Cú Chulainn half her cattle.

Now Cú Chulainn's Encounter with Finnabair:

"Send Cú Chulainn a message," said Ailill. "He gets Finnabair and leaves the armies alone."

Maine 'Fatherlike' went to see him. First he ran into Lóeg.

"Who do you serve under?"[1] he asked. Lóeg wouldn't talk to him. He asked the same question three times.

"I serve Cú Chulainn," said Lóeg, "and don't fuck with me.[2] I might accidentally take your head off."

"This man is feral," said Maine, turning away from him. Then he went to talk to Cú Chulainn. Cú Chulainn had taken off his shirt

1 *Who do you serve under?* Literally, "Whose client/vassal/companion (*céile*) are you?"

2 *don't fuck with me* Beside being what an English-speaking soldier (or teenager) might actually say in this context, the translation closely matches the verb in Irish, which is defined in *eDIL*, s.v. *1 foirrgid*, as "presses hard, bears down, overpowers, often (but not necessarily) with notion of undue or wrongful aggression," with examples translated "overcome," "wr[eak] havoc," and "violate." The hatred directed at Maine contrasts sharply with the friendliness extended to Lugaid.

and was sitting in the snow up to his waist: the warrior was giving off such fierce heat that the snow around him had melted the length of a man.

Maine asked him three times whom he served under.

"Conchobor," said Cú Chulainn, "and don't fuck with me. If you bother me anymore, I'll pop your head off like popping the head off a blackbird."

"These two aren't so easy to talk to," said Maine. So he left and reported back to Ailill and Maeve.

"Lugaid should go talk to him," said Ailill, "and offer him the girl."

So Lugaid went and made the offer to Cú Chulainn.

"My dear* Lugaid," said Cú Chulainn, "this is a trick."

"A king has given his word," said Lugaid. "There will be no trickery."

"So be it," said Cú Chulainn.

Lugaid went away and gave that answer to Ailill and Maeve.

"Have the jester* go disguised as me," said Ailill, "wearing a king's crown on his head: he should stand far away from Cú Chulainn so he doesn't recognize him. And the girl will go with him so he can marry her to Cú Chulainn, and then they should hurry away without breaking character. And that way the ruse will probably stick, and he won't cause you any more delay until he comes to the final battle with the rest of the Ulstermen."

So the jester went with the girl to see Cú Chulainn and called to him from far away. Cú Chulainn went to meet them. But he realized from the way the man spoke that he was a jester. He threw a slingstone at him that he happened to be carrying, and it blew up his head and took out his brain.

Cú Chulainn walked up to the girl. He cut off her braids and shoved a stone through her cloak and her tunic. Then he shoved a stone through the middle of the jester. The two standing stones are still there: Finnabair's stone and the jester's stone. Cú Chulainn left them that way.

Ailill and Maeve sent some men to check on them because they thought it had been a long time. They were found in that position. Soon the whole camp had heard what happened. That was the end of their truce with Cú Chulainn.

Now for the Fight between Muinremor and Cú Roí:

When the army was there in the evening, they saw a stone thrown at them from the east and another one from the west coming to meet it. They collided in the air. The stones kept falling across Fergus's camp, Ailill's camp, and the Munstermen's camp.[1] This production went on until the same time the next day, while the army stood with their shields over their heads to fend off the debris, till the plain was filled with the stones. Hence the name the Stony Plain (*Mag Clochair*). It turned out to be Cú Roí mac Dáiri who had done that. He had come to help his followers, and he was in Cotail facing Muinremor mac Gerrcinn. Muinremor had come from Emain Macha to Ard Roích to help Cú Chulainn. Cú Roí knew there was no one in the army who could stand up to Muinremor. So they put on that production between the two of them.

The army begged them to simmer down. Then Muinremor and Cú Roí made peace and Cú Roí went home and Muinremor went to Emain Macha. And Muinremor didn't come back until the day of the final battle, while Cú Roí didn't come back until the fight with Fer Diad.

"Ask Cú Chulainn to give us permission to relocate," said Maeve and Ailill. They got permission and they relocated.

The Ulstermen's condition was over at this point. As they emerged from their paralysis, a bunch of them kept attacking the army until they became stricken all over again.

Now the Death of the Boy-Troop:

150 boys from the boy-troop of Ulster, led by Fiachna Fuilech mac Fir Fhebe[2]—said to be a third of the boy-troop, although according to the Boyhood Deeds this number would be all of them—attack the army and die in battle against an equal number of opponents. There is a brief description of the way Cú Chulainn mutates to avenge them, with the*

---

1 *the Munstermen's camp* The text actually calls them the Érainn, a population-group from Munster.

2 *Fiachna Fuilech mac Fir Fhebe* This character, "Bloody" Fiachna, is said to be the brother of Fíacha Fíaldána, "Fíacha the Brave and Generous" mac Fir Fhebe. He is an apparent duplicate of Fíacha or Fíachu mac Fir Fhebe, one of the Ulster exiles, who is elsewhere said to be the *father* of Fíacha Fíaldána.

significant note that in this state Cú Chulainn lashes out on all sides and can't distinguish friend from foe. There are more extensive versions of the death of the boy-troop and Cú Chulainn's transformation later on, so while these are both important episodes they are not translated here.

Now Rochad's Bloodless Fight:

Rochad mac Fathemain arrives to help Cú Chulainn. Finnabair is in love with him because he is the handsomest of the Ulster warriors, and the feeling is apparently mutual. Rochad and his men set up an ambush, but Fergus suggests calling him to a private meeting with Finnabair where he is taken prisoner and paroled, promising not to fight the army any more until the final battle. This is Rochad's "Bloodless Fight."

Now the Death of the Royal Mercenaries:

Maeve arranges another truce, and six royal mercenaries from Clann Dedad attack Cú Chulainn the next day. He kills them.

The Death of Cúr

Cúr mac Da Lath is asked to fight Cú Chulainn: if Cúr draws blood, his opponent dies within nine days. Maeve comments that this is a win-win: "If he kills Cú Chulainn, that means victory. And if he gets killed, it's a weight off the army, because it's unpleasant to be around Cúr, eating or sleeping." *Cúr dismisses Cú Chulainn as a beardless boy, but goes anyway, protected by his shield, and attacks Cú Chulainn while he's practicing his feats. There is a list of 21 feats, including the "heroic salmon-leap," the* gáe bolga,* *his mighty war-cry, standing up straight on the tip of a spear, and different acrobatics and methods of wielding balls, blades, shields, spears, etc.* *(See pp. 119–20)* *Cú Chulainn is so focused that he doesn't realize Cúr is attacking him. When Fíacha mac Fir Fhebe calls out a warning, Cú Chulainn takes the "apple-feat" (a real apple, or some kind of ball?) that he has in his hand, and hurls it through the center of Cúr's shield into his head. Then Fergus reminds the army that per their arrangement, they can't move on, and they go back to camp. The next day Cú Chulainn kills four more men in single combat.*

Now the Death of Fer Báeth:

"Go into the camp for me, my dear* Lóeg, and find out from Lugaid mac Nóis uí Lomairc who's going to come and face me tomorrow. Question him thoroughly and be sure to greet him."

So away went Lóeg.

"Welcome," said Lugaid. "It's no picnic for Cú Chulainn, the trouble he's in, all alone against the men of Ireland."

"Who's coming to face him tomorrow?"

"It's both of our comrade—curse his warrior skill![1]—who'll be facing him tomorrow: Fer Báeth. They're giving him Finnabair for it, and sovereignty over his own people."

Lóeg went back to Cú Chulainn.

"My dear* Lóeg isn't overjoyed with his answer," said Cú Chulainn.

Lóeg told him everything: how Fer Báeth had been called to Ailill and Maeve's tent, and they'd told him to sit next to Finnabair and explained how he was her favorite and he could have her if he fought Cú Chulainn. They thought he'd be a match for him since they'd both received the same training from Scáthach.

They served him wine till he was drunk, telling him what an honor that was because they'd brought only fifty wagonloads of wine with them. And it was the girl who kept serving him the wine.

"I don't want to go," said Fer Báeth. "Cú Chulainn's my foster-brother!* We're friends for life! … Whatever, I'll go face him tomorrow and I'll chop his head off."

"I'm sure you will," said Maeve.

Cú Chulainn told Lóeg to go and ask Lugaid to come and talk to him. Lugaid came to see him.

"So it's Fer Báeth who's coming to fight me tomorrow?" said Cú Chulainn.

"Oh, it's definitely him," said Lugaid.

"Wretched day," said Cú Chulainn. "I'm not going to live through it. The two of us are the same age, the same speed, the same weight—we'll have us a fight. Off you go, Lugaid. Tell him it's

---

1 *curse his warrior skill* Or "a curse on his weapons." See *eDIL*, s.v. *gaisced.*

beneath his honor as a warrior to meet me in combat. Tell him to come and meet me tonight so I can talk to him."

Lugaid told Fer Báeth, and since he wasn't backing down, he came over that night to rescind his friendship with Cú Chulainn. He brought Fíacha mac Fir Fhebe with him.

Cú Chulainn reminded him that they were foster-brothers* and had both had the same foster-mother,* Scáthach.

"I've got to do it," said Fer Báeth. "I promised Maeve."

"I guess you made your choice,"[1] said Cú Chulainn. He stormed off. He stomped on a sprig of holly in the valley there, driving it so far up his leg that the tip came poking out his knee. He yanked it out.

"Don't go away, Fer Báeth, till you see what I've found."

"Toss it over," said Fer Báeth.

Then Cú Chulainn threw it after Fer Báeth and it went through the nape of his neck and came out his mouth, which made him topple over on his back in the valley.

"What a toss!" said Fer Báeth. Hence that place was called the Toss of Muirthemne (*Focherd Muirthemne*).

Then Fíacha commented, "Your throwing is on point today, Cú Chulainn."

Fer Báeth died immediately there in the glen. Hence it was called Fer Báeth's Glen (*Glend Fir Baíth*).

Fergus speaks a poem about the death. Cú Chulainn sends Lóeg to visit the camp and confirm with Lugaid that Fer Báeth is dead.

Now the Encounter with Láiríne mac Nóis:

"One of you had better scurry off tomorrow to face your opponent," said Lugaid.

"There won't be anyone," said Ailill, "unless you resort to trickery.

---

1 *you made your choice* Loosely translated. *eDIL* (s.v. *selb*, II.b) quotes the eminent Rudolf Thurneysen's interpretation of this line as "Your possessions are now your bond" (my translation) meaning he has sold out his friendship for gifts and has to follow through on that commitment, but also suggests "Stick to your bargain" (s.v. *1 cotach*), while O'Rahilly has "Renounce your bond of friendship then."

Serve wine to every man who comes to see you, and tell him, 'This is the last of the wine we brought from Crúachu—we're really sorry you're having to get by on water here in camp.' And get Finnabair settled on his right and get someone to tell him, 'She'll be yours if you bring us the mutant's* head.'"

Night after night, they sent a message to one of the elite warriors and told him that. And Cú Chulainn killed all those warriors, one after another. They ended up not finding anyone to face him.

They sent for Láiríne mac Nóis, brother of the Munster king Lugaid. He was remarkably arrogant. They served him wine and sat Finnabair down on his right.

Maeve looked at the two of them. "I think they make an adorable couple," she said. "They'd be a good match."

"I won't stand in your way," said Ailill. "He can have her if he brings me the mutant's head."

"I surely will," said Láiríne.

Lugaid came in at that point: "Who have you got to go to the ford tomorrow?"

"Láiríne's going," said Ailill.

Then Lugaid went to talk to Cú Chulainn. They met in Fer Báeth's Glen and greeted each other in a friendly way.

"Here's why I've come to talk to you," said Lugaid. "There's this dopey, pompous mutt over there. He's my brother. His name's Láiríne. They're using the same girl as always to lead him on. I'm asking you as a friend, don't kill him. Don't leave me brotherless. The reason they're sending him after you is to make the two of us fight. It's fine with me if you give him a good ass-kicking, though, since he's coming here against my wishes."

The next day Láiríne came to face Cú Chulainn, and the girl came along to encourage him. Then Cú Chulainn fought him unarmed. He forced him to give up his weapons, then grabbed him with both hands and squeezed and shook him until the crap was beaten out of him. The ford was foul with his shit and his stench reeked to high heaven.

Then Cú Chulainn tossed him into Lugaid's arms. For the rest of his life, his bowels never recovered. He never stopped having chest pains. He couldn't eat without discomfort. But out of everyone who faced Cú Chulainn on the Táin, he was the only one who got away—even if it *was* a shitty escape.

Now the Morrígan's Conversation with Cú Chulainn:

Cú Chulainn saw a young woman coming towards him, wearing every color of the rainbow. She was incredibly gorgeous.

"Who are you?" said Cú Chulainn.

"The daughter of King Búan," she said. "I've come to see you. I've fallen in love with you because of the amazing stories that are told about you, and I've brought my treasures and my cattle with me."

"It's really not a good time. We're in bad shape—we're starving. It's not easy for me to get involved with a woman while I'm tied up with this conflict."

"I can help you with that."

"I didn't come here to chase tail."

"You'll be sorry," she said, "when I attack you in the middle of fighting some people. I'll be underfoot in the shape of an eel in the ford and trip you."

"That makes more sense to me than doing it as a king's daughter,"[1] he said. "I'll squeeze you with my toes till I break your ribs, and you'll carry that blemish* till I see fit to bless you."[2]

"I'll drive the cattle at you over the ford in the shape of a gray she-wolf."

"I'll fire a stone at you with my sling and make your eye go pop in your head, and you'll carry that blemish till I see fit to bless you."

"I'll come at you in the shape of a hornless red heifer leading the cattle. They'll charge you at many fords—fords and pools—and you'll never see me coming."

"I'll throw a stone at you and break your fetlocks, and you'll carry that blemish till I see fit to bless you."

She left him alone at that.

---

1 *than doing it as a king's daughter* Literally: "Likelier to me [i.e., in my opinion] indeed than (a) king's daughter." O'Rahilly says "I prefer that to the king's daughter," but there's no definite article, and I disagree with the sense.

2 *see fit to bless you* O'Rahilly: "until you get a judgment blessing." Other translators seem to have taken this as a reference to the final judgment and made it "forever." What makes sense for the plot is that Cú Chulainn himself needs to bless her.

Now for the Death of Lóch mac Mo Femis:

Maeve tries to bribe Lóch mac Mo Femis (or mac Emonis) to fight Cú Chulainn. Lóch considers it beneath his dignity to fight a boy. His brother Long goes instead, Cú Chulainn kills him, and Lóch swears revenge—if Cú Chulainn is actually a bearded man.

The seven Maines[1] *advance against Cú Chulainn, who shows himself in his fanciest clothes, and the women with the army, including Maeve, climb on the men's shoulders to look at him. They tell him to fake a beard using blackberry juice, because the grown men in the camp are supposedly mocking him and refusing to fight him. Cú Chulainn takes some grass and says a spell that makes him seem to have a beard. Now the women taunt Lóch, who is apparently still in mourning for his brother, and he agrees to fight Cú Chulainn in seven days. Meanwhile, Maeve sends a team of 7–10 men to attack Cú Chulainn every night, and he keeps killing them. Then she invites him to parley with her. Lóeg convinces him to take his sword, because he doesn't trust Maeve and* "because a warrior's not entitled to his honor-price* if he doesn't have his weapons: in that case he's only entitled to what the law gives a puny civilian." *At the parley Cú Chulainn is ambushed by 14 men and kills them all. He recites a poem of self-praise, then kills more men.*

Then Maeve started taunting Lóch. "Shame on you," she said. "The man who killed your brother is destroying our army without meeting any resistance from you. We're sure a bragging, needling imp like that won't be able to withstand the fury and rage of a hero like you, plus it was the same foster-mother* who trained you both."

So Lóch went to face Cú Chulainn to avenge his brother, since he was now under the impression that he had a beard. "Come to the upper ford," he said. "We won't be fighting in this ford polluted by Long's death."

When they got there, the Connachtmen[2] started driving the cattle across. "There will be a dearth of water (*tart eisc*) here today,"

---

1 *seven Maines* Earlier, the text describes how Cú Chulainn killed one of them, yet here they all are.

2 *the Connachtmen* Amplified from "the men" for clarity.

said the poet* Gabrán. Hence that place has been called Dearthwater Ford (*Áth Dairtesc*) and the Great Land of Dearthwater (*Tír Mór Darteisc*) ever since.

Then after Lóch and Cú Chulainn had come together at the ford and had started fighting and hewing and hacking at each other, the eel that was the Morrígan[1] made three coils around Cú Chulainn's legs and made him fall flat on his back[2] across the ford. Lóch attacked him with his sword until the ford ran gory with his blood.

"That's just horrible," said Fergus, "acting like that in the presence of the enemy.[3] One of you needs to taunt him, gentlemen," he said to his entourage, "so he doesn't die in vain."

Bricriu "Poisontongue" mac Carbada got up and started to taunt Cú Chulainn. "Your strength is spent," he said, "when you're letting small fry trounce you just when the Ulstermen are out of their paralysis and on their way to you. Apparently it's hard for you to play the hero while the men of Ireland watch. That's not the way to fight off a tough warrior."

Then Cú Chulainn got up and beat the eel, breaking her ribs, and the thunder-feat that the two warriors did in the ford sent the cattle charging east, overrunning the armies and picking up the tents with their horns.

The she-wolf attacked him and sent the cattle barreling westward, towards him. He fired a stone at her with his sling and made her eye pop in her head.

She shifted into the shape of the hornless red heifer and brought the cattle charging into the pools and fords. Then Cú Chulainn said: "I can't see the fords for the pools." He threw a stone at the hornless red heifer and broke her lower leg. Then he chanted a poem:

> "I'm here all alone, defending the herds,
> not holding them back but not letting them go.

1 *that was the Morrígan* Added for clarity.

2 *flat on his back* Dooley, *Playing the Hero*, 168, calls this "a dangerously vulnerable female position." The gender dynamics here could be compared to Beowulf losing his footing in the fight with Grendel's mother.

3 *just horrible ... the enemy* At first it sounds as if Fergus were going to lament the unfair treatment of Cú Chulainn, but surprisingly he faults Cú Chulainn for not putting up a better fight. The type of taunting or haranguing that Fergus calls for here is called *gressacht*: see the glossary under *satire*.*

I'm here as the cold hours pass,
alone against multitudes.

Someone tell Conchobor:
it's not too soon to come and help me.
The sons of Mágu have rustled their cows
and have divvied them up.

A lone man can resist,
but a lone log won't light.
If there were two or three,
they'd blaze like torches.

The men have almost wiped me out:
I've fought so many single combats.
I can't keep fighting their hand-picked warriors
while I'm here all alone."

Now Cú Chulainn had done to the Morrígan the three things he had promised to do to her,[1] and he defeated Lóch in the ford using the *gáe bolga*,* which Lóeg tossed downstream to him. He administered it anally, because Lóch's skin became hard like horn whenever he fought.[2]

"Step away[3] from me!" said Lóch.

Cú Chulainn let him go, and he collapsed on the other side of the ford. Hence the name Stepford (*Áth Traiged*) in Tír Mór.

1 *to do to her* The text adds "in *Táin bó Regamna*" (see p. 154 above) a saga that has a very similar episode in which the Morrígan promises to cause Cú Chulainn's death (cf p. 231 here). Dooley discusses the similarity briefly in *Playing the Hero*, 136–38.

2 *hard like horn whenever he fought* More literally, "Lóch had a horn-skin (*conganchnes*) while fighting against a man." Fer Diad also has this feature, and so did Celtchar's opponent Conganchness mac Dedad, mentioned in "Mac Dá Thó's Pig," p. 80 above.

3 *Step away* Recension 2 amplifies this: specifying that he is not asking for quarter or making a cowardly request, Lóch asks Cú Chulainn to let him fall facing east so that no one will think he died while running away. Cú Chulainn accepts this as an honorable ask, "a warrior's request."

In yet another violation of fair play, five men attack Cú Chulainn that same day. He kills them, and the placename records the event. Cú Chulainn pelts the army with slingstones to block their progress.*

Now the Healing of the Morrígan:

When Cú Chulainn was overcome with exhaustion, the Morrígan came along disguised as an old crone, one-eyed, half-blind, and milking a cow with three teats.

He asked her for a drink.

She gave him the milk from one teat.

"Health to the giver!" said Cú Chulainn. "Gods and ungods bless you." (Their gods were the ones with magic powers, and their ungods were the ones who farmed.)[1]

Then her head was healed and made whole.

Then she gave him milk from the second teat and her eye was healed.

She gave him milk from the third teat and her leg was healed.

Apparently, he said to her every time, "I see fit to bless you."

"But you said you'd never heal me," said the Morrígan.

"If I'd known that was you," said Cú Chulainn, "I never would have healed you."

After Fergus insists that Cú Chulainn be treated fairly, Cú Chulainn kills some more opponents in single combat. There's a list of the places they died that are named after them. Then Maeve sends a hundred men at once, Cú Chulainn kills them, and Maeve's remark about how they've been slaughtered inspires more placenames.

---

1 *Gods and ungods ... farmed* The translation of the parenthetical follows Dooley, *Playing the Hero*, 137, who comments that this gloss "could be compared with the position of the *Túatha Dé* (the magician gods) and the *Fir Bolg* (the farmers) of *Cath Maige Tuired*" (256n25), i.e., "The (Second) Battle of Mag Tuired," which tells about the Túatha Dé Danann* before the coming of the Gaels. It seems to exemplify an Indo-European theme of theomachy or war among the gods, where gods of magic and war defeat and assimilate fertility gods: the clearest comparison is to the Aesir and the Vanir in Norse mythology. The main antagonist of "The (Second) Battle of Mag Tuired" is Bres, a failure as a king who, like Cú Chulainn, is a sister's son* to the Túatha Dé Danann. In the aftermath of the battle Bres gives up secrets of agriculture to Cú Chulainn's supernatural father Lug. See *Coire Sois*, 135–51, and Mark Williams, *Ireland's Immortals*, 108–10.

Now the Scythed Chariot and the Great Rout on Muirthemne Plain:

Then the four provinces of Ireland camped at a place called the Great Rout[1] (*Breslech Mór*) on Muirthemne Plain. They sent their share of the cattle and plunder on ahead to a place called the Shelter of Ulster's Cattle (*Clithar Bó Ulad*). Cú Chulainn stationed himself near them on the mound of Lerga, and that evening his charioteer—that is, Lóeg mac Ríangabra—lit a fire for him.

In the distance he could see the fiery glint of the polished gold of his enemies' weapons shining over their heads as the sun set wreathed in cloud. The sight of the army—so many enemies, so many invaders—filled him with fury and outrage. He picked up his two spears, his shield, and his sword: he shook the shield and brandished the spears and waved the sword, and let out a full-throated heroic cry so bone-chilling that the bogeys, banshees, ghouls of the glens, and demons of the air[2] all yowled in reply. And the war-goddess Nemain threw the army into confusion.

The four provinces of Ireland made such a clatter as they faced off against their own spearpoints and hastily-seized weaponry that during the night a hundred of their warriors perished from terror and fright right there in camp.

Meanwhile, Lóeg saw a single man coming from the northeast, making his way straight towards him through the men of Ireland's camp.

"One man incoming, Cucuc,"[3] said Lóeg.

"What kind of man?" said Cú Chulainn.

---

1 *the Great Rout* Otherwise translated as the "Great Breach." But as elsewhere, the text seems to be using a placename that results from events about to be narrated: they camped at a place *now* called the Great Rout. The location would be south of Áth dá Fherta (since the army is about to be driven *back* there), around where the words Lugmad and (LOUTH) appear on Map 3.

2 *demons of the air* For a detailed investigation of these, see Kristen Mills, "*Demna aeóir* 'demons of the air," *Éigse* 41 (2021) 1–30, https://www.nui.ie/eigse/pdf/vol41/Eigse_Vol_XLI_2021_Mills.pdf.

3 *Cucuc* This renders the affectionate nickname *Cúcucán*, "Little Cúcuc," for Cú Chulainn. (Since *cú* also means 'dog,' this could also be taken as something like "Pupster.") When Lug uses *Cúcán* below, the translation is "Little Cú."

"That's easy:* he's a tall handsome man with long golden hair, all curly. He's wearing a green cloak with a bright silver brooch on his chest, and a tunic of royal satin with red-gold embroidery, that covers his pale skin down to his knees. He has a black shield with a hard boss[1] of white-bronze.* He's carrying a five-pronged spear with a forked javelin next to it. The way he plays and feints and juggles with them is incredible. But no one's confronting him and he's not confronting anyone, as if no one could see him."

"Right you are, kiddo,"[2] said Cú Chulainn. "That must be one of my friends from the Otherworld* coming to commiserate with me, because they know how hard it's been for me to stand alone against the four great provinces of Ireland on their cattle-raid of Cúailnge."

Cú Chulainn was correct. When the warrior reached him, he spoke to him and commiserated with him.

"Manly stuff, Cú Chulainn," he said.

"That's all you've got to say?"[3] said Cú Chulainn.

"I'm here to help," said the warrior.

"Who are you, anyway?" said Cú Chulainn.

"I'm your father from the Otherworld abodes, Lug mac Eithlenn."

"Well, my wounds are torturing me. I need healing."

"Then sleep for a while, Cú Chulainn," said the warrior. "Sleep deeply here on the mound at Lerga for three days and three nights, and I'll fight off the armies in the meantime."

Then he chanted to him in a low voice and Cú Chulainn drifted off to sleep, and slept until Lug could see that he was fully restored.

Then Lug spoke [*an obscure incantation,*[4] *urging Cú Chulainn to rise up and attack his enemies with supernatural help.*]

---

1 *boss* The boss is the metal part, typically a convex circle, in the center of a shield.

2 *kiddo* This translates *daltán*, 'little fosterling.'

3 *That's all ... to say* Following O'Rahilly's interpretation that Cú Chulainn is responding to the insufficiency of Lug's remark. There's a chance that what he's really saying here is "That was no big deal," referring to his efforts against the invaders (thus Ann Dooley's "Hardly that," *Playing the Hero*, 134), but given his physical condition at this point, it seems unlikely he would downplay his efforts.

4 *an obscure incantation* This is a difficult poem, and O'Rahilly doesn't venture to translate it all. The genre of *éle* 'incantation' is discussed by Jacqueline Borsje in "A spell called *éle*," in *Ulidia 3, Proceedings of the Third International Conference on the Ulster Cycle of Tales, University of Ulster, Coleraine 22–25 June, 2009. In Memoriam Patrick* [continued ...]

Cú Chulainn slept for three days and three nights—which stands to reason, considering how long he'd been awake. From the Monday after Samain* to the Wednesday after Imbolc,* he hadn't slept except to doze a little in the afternoon, with his head resting on the fist that clenched his spear, and the spear-shaft resting on his knee. He'd been hewing and hacking and slaying and slaughtering the four great provinces of Ireland all that time.

Then the Otherworld* warrior put plants and healing herbs and a curing charm in his many wounds and lesions and gashes and cuts, so that he recovered in his sleep and didn't feel a thing.

It was at this point that the boy-troop came south from Emain Macha: one hundred and fifty Ulster princes led by Conchobor's son Follamain. They engaged the armies three times, killing three times their number, and then they were killed too, all but Follamain mac Conchobair. Follamain swore that he would never go back to Emain till the brink of doom[1] unless he carried off Ailill's head with its golden crown. This was no easy task. The two sons of Beithe mac Báin, the sons of Ailill's foster-mother* and foster-father,* came up to him and wounded him so that he died at their hands. So that

---

Leo Henry, ed. Gregory Toner and Séamus Mac Mathúna (Berlin: 2013) 193–212, but Borsje doesn't try to complete the translation, stating that "more research is needed into its content." Complete translations have been attempted by Maria Tymoczko, *Translation in a Postcolonial Context*, 99, and Bernard Mees, *Celtic Curses* (Woodbridge: Boydell, 2009) 193, but scholars would probably agree with Borsje that these attempts are so far "not satisfactory."

1 *the brink of doom* The expression translated "forever" in this book is typically *co bráth* 'till doomsday/judgment,' which, even if Christian in origin, seems to be a fully normalized and unremarkable expression even when the characters are pagan. The expression here is an amplified version, *co bruinni m-brátha & betha*, "to the brink of doom/judgment and life," glossed as "till the day of doom" by *eDIL*, s.v. *bruinne*. There is limited evidence of pre-Christian Irish belief in the end times, nothing like the detailed prophecies of Ragnarök in Norse mythology: see https://www.capas.uni-heidelberg.de/en/i-shall-not-see-a-world-which-will-be-dear-to-me for an overview. For a medieval Irish Christian take on Judgment Day that appears in *Lebor na hUidre* along with Recension 1 of the *Táin*, see Uáitéar Mac Gearailt, "The Middle Irish homily *Scéla laí brátha*," *Apocrypha: International Journal of Apocryphal Literatures* 20 (2009) 83–114 and Elizabeth Boyle, "Eschatological justice in *Scéla laí brátha*," *CMCS* 59 (2010) 39–54 (http://thecelticist.ie/wp-content/uploads/2016/07/Eschatological_Justice_in_Scela_lai_bratha.pdf). For a whole collection of texts, see *The End and Beyond: Medieval Irish Eschatology*, 2 volumes, ed. John Carey, Emma Nic Cárthaigh, and Catríona Ó Dochertaigh (Aberystwyth: Celtic Studies Publications, 2014).

was “The Massacre of the Boy-Troop of Ulster and Follamain mac Conchobair.”

Meanwhile, Cú Chulainn was sound asleep for three days and three nights on the mound at Lerga. Then he woke up, rubbed his face and flushed bright red from head to toe. He was in high spirits, as if he were headed to a fair or a march or a romantic encounter or a feast or one of the great assemblies of Ireland.

“How long was I asleep?” said Cú Chulainn.

“Three days and three nights,” said the warrior.

“Then we're screwed!” said Cú Chulainn.

“Why is that?” said the warrior.

“No one's been attacking the invaders this whole time,” said Cú Chulainn.

“Not so,” said the warrior.

“How's that?' said Cú Chulainn.

“The boy-troop came south from Emain Macha—a hundred and fifty Ulster princes led by Follamain mac Conchobair—and they fought the armies three times during the three days and nights you were sleeping. They killed three times their number and were killed in turn, all but Follamain. Follamain swore he would take Ailill's head and it wasn't so easy, because he was killed too.”

“It's awful that I wasn't at my full strength. If I had been, the boys would never have died like that and neither would Follamain.”

“Forge on anyway, little Cú. There's no slight to your honor, no stain on your valor.”

“Stay here with us tonight,” said Cú Chulainn, “and we can both make the invaders pay for what they did to those boys.”

“No, I don't think so,” said the warrior. “No matter what amazing and heroic feats a man does in your company, he's not the one who gets the fame, renown, and glory for them: it all goes to you. That's why I won't be staying. But go inflict your own feats of valor on the army. They have no power over your life at this time.”

“What about the scythed chariot, my dear* Lóeg?” said Cú Chulainn. “Can you yoke it and do you have all the equipment for it? If you do, go ahead and get it ready—and if you don't, then don't, I guess.”

The charioteer got up and put on his combat outfit for charioteering. This outfit included a smooth skin tunic that was light and airy, supple and sheer. It was made of deerskin and tailored so that it didn't restrict his arm movements. Over that he wore a raven surcoat:[1] Simon Magus[2] had made it for Darius (or Nero[3]), King of the Romans, who had given it to Conchobor, who had given it to Cú Chulainn, who had given it to his charioteer. And now that same charioteer put on his crested, metal-plated, squared-off helmet: it was decorated with a plethora of colors and shapes and came down past his shoulders, but he found it more decorative than inconvenient.

He took the gold circlet, reddish-yellow like a band of glowing gold smelted over the edge of an anvil, that marked him as a charioteer as opposed to his master, and raised it to his brow.

In his right hand he took some switches to get his horses moving, and his ornamented goad. And he took in his sinistral grasp the means of checking his horses—basically, his left hand held the reins to control his driving.[4]

Then he dressed the horses in their inlaid iron armor, which protected them from forehead to foreleg. The chariot was covered with little barbs and spikes and spits and skewers, including the wheel-rims, so that every single corner, edge, apex and facet of that chariot was a meatgrinder.

Then he cast a protective spell over his horses and his companion, making them invisible to everyone in the camp while everyone in the camp stayed visible to them. And well he should, because on that day the charioteer would have to perform three great gifts of charioteering, i.e., keeping a perfectly straight course, plowing through obstacles, and jumping the chariot over gaps.[5]

---

1 *raven surcoat* Raven-black in color, for O'Rahilly; but since poets* are sometimes described as wearing feathered cloaks, actual feathers might not be impossible.

2 *Simon Magus* A magician baptized by St. Peter. See Acts 8.9–24 in the New Testament, and *Receptions of Simon Magus as an Archetype of the Heretic* by Alberto Ferreiro and Ephraim Nissan (Palgrave Macmillan, 2023), which discusses the idea that Simon could fly, possibly relevant if this is indeed supposed to be a feathered cloak.

3 *or Nero* A manuscript variant for Darius.

4 *sinistral grasp … his driving* The idea seems to be stated twice, once in elevated language, and again in a more standard way.

5 *three great gifts … over gaps* The translation here is based on William Sayers, "Three charioteering gifts in *Táin Bó Cúailnge* and *Mesca Ulad*," *Ériu* 32 (1981) 163–67.

That was when the champion and combat soldier, the one-man front line of the world's armies, Cú Chulainn, put on his combat gear of battle and contest and strife. The first layer of this consisted of twenty-seven waxed, rigid, densely-woven undershirts, which would be tightly bound to his pale skin with loops and ropes and bindings, so that he wouldn't lose control of his faculties[1] when his fighting frenzy came on. Over these he wore his warrior's combat vest[2] of toughened, tanned, tenacious leather, made from the best parts of seven yearling ox-hides, which covered him from the thin part of his side to the thick part of his armpit. He used to wear it to ward off spears and spearheads and barbs and javelins and arrows: they'd glance off as if they were hitting rock or stone or horn. Then he put on his sheer silk apron, with its border of variegated white gold, against his soft underbelly. Over the silk apron he put on his darker apron of supple dark leather made from the best parts of four yearling ox-hides, with his cowhide combat belt.

Then the royal hero picked up his weapons of battle and contest and strife. These included his eight shortswords along with his bright-faced ivory-hilted broadsword. He took his eight little spears and his five-pronged lance. He took his eight mini-javelins and his ivory-handled javelin. He took his eight little darts and the *deil chlis*.[3] He took his eight bucklers and the curved dark-red shield with a boss big enough to hold a prize boar, with its sharp, keen, razor-edged rim around it, so sharp and keen and razor-edged that it would shave a hair against the grain.[4] Whenever the warrior did the edge-feat with it, he did as much damage with his shield as with his spear and sword.

Then he put on his crested helmet of battle and contest and strife. It sounded like a hundred warriors, howling from every one

1 *twenty-seven … undershirts … lose control of his faculties* Ranke de Vries has a recent comment on these undershirts at https://leigheas.maynoothuniversity.ie/cu-chulainns-bizarre-adventures/; compare Longman, "'What manner of man is this Hound?'," 19–21.

2 *combat vest* In contrast to the belt associated with the leather apron, below, this "combat belt" or "battle-girdle" is effectively a leather breastplate, hence I translate "vest" instead of "belt."

3 *deil chlis* See p. 194, note 4 above, when Cú Chulainn uses this weapon in the Boyhood Deeds.

4 *shave a hair against the grain* More literally but (in my opinion) less logically, O'Rahilly has "cut a hair against the current," as if the hair were floating down a stream.

of its edges and facets. It used to cry with the voices of bogeys, banshees, ghouls of the glens, and demons of the air that were in front of Cú Chulainn, above him, and all around him wherever he went, advertising the imminent bloodshed of soldiers and champions. He wrapped himself in his protective cloak made of fabric from the Land of Promise,[1] a gift from his tutor in druid* magic.

Then Cú Chulainn started to mutate:* it turned him into something horrifying, multiform, weird, unrecognizable.[2] His whole body, all his limbs, joints, members, and extremities from head to toe, trembled like a tree—make that a bulrush—in a torrent. Violent contortions racked his flesh inside his skin. His feet and shins and knees went round the back; his heels and calves and thigh-muscles came to the front. The sinews of his calves bunched up on the front of his shins, in huge round knots the size of a fighter's fist. The sinews of his skull were hauled back to the nape of his neck, balled up like the heads of month-old babies, all immoderate, immeasurable, incommensurate, immense. His face collapsed in on itself.[3] He sucked in one of his eyes so deep that a wild crane couldn't have reached into his skull far enough to yank it out, while the other eye popped out on his cheek. His mouth was deformed, his lips drawn back in a rictus that bared his guts. His lungs and liver fluttered in his mouth and throat. He gnashed his jaws[4] and gargled out volleys of fire as wide as a ram's skin. The sound of his heart banging on his ribs was like the manic barking of a guard dog, or the roar of a lion attacking bears. The torches of the war-goddess, toxic clouds and blazing sparks of fire, were kindled in the air and smoke above his head by the fuming of the ferocious fury coming off him. His

1 *the Land of Promise* *Tír Tairngiri*, a heavenly aspect of the Otherworld,* sometimes situated overseas as opposed to underground.

2 *Then Cú Chulainn … unrecognizable* The most recent independent translation of the passage that follows is by Amy Mulligan, "The erasure of a warrior's body: Cú Chulainn, Isidore of Seville, and Irish independence," in *From Enlightenment to Rebellion: Essays in Honor of Christopher Fox*, ed. James G. Buickerood (Lewisburg: Bucknell University Press, 2018) 33–46, at 35–36.

3 *collapsed in on itself* Obscure. Speculative translation by O'Rahilly: "became a red hollow." Mulligan proposes "a wax-like concavity (?)."

4 *gnashed his jaws* Mulligan: "His upper palate struck a lion-felling blow (?) against the lower palate."

hair curled round his head like branches of red hawthorn used to fix the gap in a hedge. If a heavy-laden regal apple tree had been shaken over his head, almost none of the apples would have made it to the ground: they would have stayed impaled on his bristling hair. The hero's light rose from his forehead, as long and thick as a hero's fist and as long as his nose, and he swelled with rage as he deployed his shields and harangued his charioteer and pelted the army with sling-stones. Dark blood shot out the top of his head in a geyser as high and thick and sturdy and turgid and long as the mast of a great ship, and diffused into dark magical mist like the smoke of a royal guesthouse* preparing to welcome a king on a winter's night.

The mutated* Cú Chulainn jumped into his scythed chariot with its iron barbs, its slender blades, its hooks, its hardened spikes, its man-skewers, its harnesses loosened for action, and the barbs all over the suspension-beams,* lashings, loops, and fastenings of the undercarriage. The chariot looked like this: it had a streamlined, watertight cockpit,[1] high enough for feats, sword-straight, fit for a champion. It could carry eight sets of royal-tier weapons, and went as fast as a swallow, the wind, or a deer across the level plain. The chariot was drawn by two fast and furious and frenzied horses, with small round pointed heads, pricked ears, broad brows, fiery breasts: steady, splendid, easily harnessed to the beautiful shafts of Cú Chulainn's chariot.[2] One of them was strong, swift-leaping, battle-eager, arch-necked, mighty-hooved, close-rushing, kicking up clods. The other one was curly-maned, narrow-footed, slender-legged, lean-flanked, eating up the miles.[3]

---

1 *streamlined, watertight cockpit* O'Rahilly: "a framework of narrow and compact opening." Per *eDIL*, *tirim* 'dry,' which O'Rahilly translates 'compact,' affords a bunch of different possible meanings: level, cozy, shallow, etc. "Sword-straight" is also O'Rahilly's translation of an obscure expression.

2 *the beautiful shafts … chariot* The parts of the chariot named here (*fo grinnib áillib a fén*) are not included in the detailed survey of the Ulster Cycle chariot by Mallory, *In Search of the Irish Dreamtime*, 211–21, so the translation follows O'Rahilly.

3 *One of them … the miles* As on p. 98 above, the translation of the runs of adjectives for horses is informed by William Sayers, "Conventional descriptions of the horse in the Ulster Cycle."

Then Cú Chulainn did the thunder-feat that killed a hundred, and the thunder-feat that killed two hundred, and the thunder-feat that killed three hundred, and the thunder-feat that killed four hundred. He stopped at the one that killed five hundred, because he thought that was enough for his first foray against the four provinces of Ireland. That's how he showed up to attack his enemies, and he drove his chariot in a wide arc around the four great provinces of Ireland, engaging those hostiles with hostility. He set such a grueling pace that his iron-rimmed wheels dug into the ground, churning up enough raw material to build a fortress: sod and boulders and rocks and slabs and gravel piled up as high as the chariot wheels. He made this tactical encirclement of the four provinces so that they wouldn't be able to flee or scatter until he closed in to take revenge for the boy-troop.

Then he plowed over into the middle of their formation, spreading three ridges of enemy corpses around the outside of the army. Then he started butchering his enemies inside. They fell with the soles of their feet and their headless necks jammed up against each other, so thick was the carnage. He did that three times, leaving a six-layer blanket of corpses, i.e., three men's soles on three men's necks, all around the camp.

The name of this episode in the *Táin* is the Sixfold Slaughter. It is one of the three slaughters with a death toll beyond counting, the three being the Sixfold Slaughter, the Glennamain Massacre, and the battle at Gáirech and Irgáirech, except that in this case dogs and horses and humans perished indiscriminately.—Other sources say that Lug mac Eithlenn fought alongside Cú Chulainn in the battle of the Sixfold Slaughter.

No one knows, no one can count how many of the common soldiers died there. Only their leaders have been counted. These are their names:[1]

1 *These are their names* The formatting below follows the manuscript *Lebor na hUidre*, which presents these names in table form (see https://www.isos.dias.ie/RIA/RIA_MS_23_E_25.html#82), as does the Book of Leinster (https://www.isos.dias.ie/TCD/TCD_MS_1339.html#78).

Two (2) Crúaids
Two (2) Calads
Two (2) Círs
Two (2) Cíars
Two (2) Ecells
Three (3) Croms
Three (3) Cauraths
Three (3) Combirges
Four (4) Feochars
Four (4) Furachars
Four (4) Casses
Four (4) Fotas
Five (5) Cauraths
Five (5) Cermans
Five (5) Cobthachs
Six (6) Saxans
Six (6) Dáchs
Six (6) Dáires
Seven (7) Rochaids
Seven (7) Rónáns
Seven (7) Rúrthechs
Eight (8) Rochlads
Eight (8) Rochtads
Eight (8) Rindachs
Eight (8) Cairpres
Eight (8) Mulachs
Nine (9) Daigiths
Nine (9) Dáires
Nine (9) Dámachs
Ten (10) Fiacs
Ten (10) Fíachas
Ten (10) Fedelmids[1]

Cú Chulainn killed one hundred and fifty kings in that battle on Muirthemne Plain, along with countless dogs and horses, women, boys, infants, and rabble. Less than one in three of the men of Ireland escaped without a shattered thigh, a fractured skull, or an eye put out, or without being marked for life. But Cú Chulainn came away from the battle without a scratch on him, or on his charioteer or either of his horses.

Now the Description of Cú Chulainn's Appearance:

The next day Cú Chulainn came to look at the army and show off his benign and beautiful form to the ladies, young and old, and to the poets[*] and the men of art. He felt that his dark magical appearance of the night before hadn't been dignified or honorable, so now he came in broad daylight to show off his benign and beautiful side. He really was a beautiful young man, that Cú Chulainn mac Súaltaim, who had come to preen in front of the armies. He seemed to have three kinds of hair:[2] dark against his scalp, blood-red in the middle,

1 *Two (2) Crúaids ... Ten (10) Fedelmids* For clarity, instead of giving the Irish plurals of these names, English *-(e)s* is used as a plural marker (so "two Rónáns" instead of "two Rónáin"). Yes, there are two separate entries for the name Caurath. The total number of leaders listed, if the Cauraths aren't duplicates, is 186.

2 *three kinds of hair* This is not just gratuitous detail. As explained by Ranke de Vries in "Leeched knowledge: medical material in medieval Irish literature," a keynote presentation at the 2021 meeting of the Celtic Studies Association of North America, [continued ...]

and golden like a crown on top. It was nicely arranged, with three coils in the hollow at the nape of his neck. Every hair falling past his shoulders was like a gold thread: fine, flowing, flaxen, elegant, long-locked, luminous, lovely. His neck was framed by a hundred bright purple ringlets of flashing red gold; his head was surrounded by a hundred bright threads interspersed with carbuncle stones. His cheeks were flushed with four shades, i.e., yellow, green, blue, and purple. Seven pupils glittered like gems in each of his noble eyes. He had seven toes on each foot and seven fingers on each hand, and each separate toe and finger could grasp like a hawk's claws and grip like a griffin's.[1]

He'd put on his festive clothes that day. That is, he wore a fine, fetching, fitted, fringed, five-pleated purple cloak, and the bright silver brooch with gold inlay on his gleaming white chest was like a luminous lantern too flashing and flagrant for human eyes. Next to his skin he wore a silky satin tunic that came down to the top of his dark-red soldierly apron made of regal satin. He wore a dark red, dark purple shield with five gold circles on it, and a white-bronze* rim. An elaborate gold-hilted sword, with big red-gold knobs on the end of it, hung on his belt, ready for action. A long bright-edged spear stood beside him in the chariot, next to a sharp jabby javelin with rivets of burning gold. He held nine severed heads in one hand, and ten in the other, and he brandished them at the invaders. They were the spoils of one night's fighting.

Then the women of Connacht climbed over the warbands and perched on men's shoulders to look at Cú Chulainn. But Maeve hid and dared not show her face: instead she stayed under a cover of shields for fear of Cú Chulainn.

---

the three colors could correspond to the melancholic, sanguine, and choleric humors (involving black bile, blood, and yellow bile respectively), and hence to darkly morose, manic or exuberant, and viciously irritable temperaments that make up Cú Chulainn's personality. The one humor not represented is phlegm, associated with a phlegmatic—calm, stolid, and even slothful—temperament.

1 *a griffin's* O'Rahilly translates "the grip of a hedgehog's claws," based on a later glossary that equates this word to one that clearly means hedgehog: for the complications, see Longman, "'What manner of man is this Hound?'," 16.

Dubthach chants a poem prophesying slaughter, commenting on Cú Chulainn's appearance and the way the women stare at him but Maeve stays away; he advises killing Cú Chulainn in an ambush. Fergus is outraged: he answers with a poem criticizing Dubthach for killing the women of Ulster (see p. 143) Conchobor's son Fíacha, and Coirpre son of Fedelmid, and accusing him of stirring up trouble when Cú Chulainn is dear to the Ulstermen. Fergus also prophesies slaughter, enacted by "this army of human dogs," and flings Dubthach away from him.

Then Ailill, Maeve, Fergus, and the poet Gabrán discourse in poetry, the point of which seems to be that Maeve would like the Ulster exiles to take a more active role in fighting Cú Chulainn.*

Now the Bad Aim at Belach Eóin:

Fíacha Fíaldána Dimraith came to talk with his mother's sister's son, i.e., Maine Andóe ("Chatty" Maine). Dócha mac Mágach came with Maine Andóe. Dubthach Dóel Ulad came with Fíacha Fíaldána Dimraith. Dócha threw a spear at Fíacha and hit Dubthach. Then Dubthach threw a spear at Maine and hit Dócha. Dubthach and Dócha's mothers were sisters, too! That's where we get "The Bad Aim at Belach Eóin."

Or the Bad Aim at Belach Eóin happened like this, i.e., the armies arrived at Belach Eóin. Both sides stopped there. Diarmait mac Conchobuir from Ulster came down from the north. "One of you take a message," said Diarmait, "for Maine to come talk to me. He can bring one man with him and I'll bring one myself."

Then they met.

"I've come from Conchobor," said Diarmait, "to ask you to tell Maeve and Ailill to let all the cattle go, and pay restitution for everything they've done, and have the bull from the west come and meet the bull here so they can fight, as Maeve promised."

"I'll go tell them," said Maine.

Then he recited those terms to Maeve and Ailill.

"Maeve won't accept that," said Maine.

"Let's have an exchange of weapons then," said Diarmait, "if you prefer."

"Fine by me," said Maine.

They each threw a spear at the other and both of them died, and so the Bad Aim[1] at Belach Eóin is the name of that place. Then one army charged the other. Sixty men fell on each side. Hence the name Army Hill (*Ard in Dírma*).

Now the Death of Taman the Jester:*

Ailill's retinue put his royal crown on Taman the Jester. Ailill didn't dare wear it himself. Cú Chulainn winged a stone at the jester at Áth Tamuin and smashed his head off. Hence the placenames Taman's Ford (*Áth Tamuin*) and Taman's Burying-Ground (*Tuga im Thamun*).

The Death of Óengus mac Óenláime

Then at Moda Loga (which is the same name as Lugmad), Óengus mac Óenláime Gaibe (Óengus son of One-Hand-o'-Danger[2]), a brave Ulster warrior, drove the whole army back to the Ford of Two Barrows (*Áth dá Fherta*). He didn't let them past and pelted them with stones. And the learned say that he would have driven them before him to be put to the sword at Emain Macha, if only they had faced him in a series of single combats. They violated fair play* against him and killed him when he was outnumbered.

Fergus's Encounter with Cú Chulainn

"Let's have another one of you face me," said Cú Chulainn, "at the Ford of Two Barrows."

"Not me! Not me!" everyone called from wherever they were. "My people don't owe any scapegoat,[3] and even if they did, I wouldn't be the one to volunteer for scapegoating."

---

1 *Bad Aim* While the Irish word (*eDIL*, s.v. *imroll*) typically means a missed throw, as in the first version, it can also mean a mistake: these fatal hits were ill-advised or unintended.

2 *Óengus son of One-Hand-o'-Danger* See p. 81. His father's name is slightly different here.

3 *scapegoat* This translates the technical term *cimbid*, defined as follows in *GEIL*, 97–98: "He is a person who has committed a serious offence, which has not been paid for. The individual or kin whom he has wronged can seize him and hold him captive. [...] In

They begged Fergus mac Roích to go and face him. But he refused to go and face his foster-son,* Cú Chulainn. They gave him wine and got him massively drunk, then kept begging him to go and fight. He headed off at that point since they were laying it on so thick with their pleading.

Then Cú Chulainn said: "You're very confident in coming to face me, Uncle* Fergus, without a sword in your scabbard." (Because Ailill had stolen it out of there, as we said above.)

"It makes no difference to me," said Fergus. "Even if there were a sword in there, I wouldn't use it on you. Withdraw a ways for me, Cú Chulainn," he said.

"Then you withdraw for me another time," said Cú Chulainn.

"So be it," said Fergus.

Then Cú Chulainn retreated before Fergus back to Grellach Dolluid, so that Fergus would have to retreat before him on the day of battle.

Cú Chulainn got down from his chariot in Grellach Dolluid.

"Get after him, Fergus!" said everyone.

"No," said Fergus. "It's not that easy. He's too lively for me. I won't go until it's my turn again."

They moved on and camped in Crích Rois. Ferchú Loingsech ("Man-Dog the Exile"), who had been exiled by Ailill, heard of this and came to attack Cú Chulainn. He brought twelve men with him. Cú Chulainn killed them at Ferchú's Goblet (*Cingit Ferchon*). Their thirteen headstones are there.

The Encounter with Mann

Maeve sent Mann Muresci, son of Dáire of the Domnannaig, to fight Cú Chulainn. Mann was the brother of Damán, the father of Fer Diad. Mann was a brusque, brutal man, and his eating and sleeping habits reflected it. He was vicious and vulgar when he talked, like Dubthach Dóel Ulad. He was tough and tireless and strong-limbed

---

non-legal sources the word *cimbid* is used of a person who faces death on behalf of a group or tribe. [...] In religious writings, Christ is often portrayed as the *cimbid* for the sins of the world." "Tribute" in a *Hunger Games* sense would be a good match for the latter meaning.

like Muinremor mac Gerrcinn. He was brawny and belligerent like Triscoth, the strongman in Conchobor's household.

"I'll go unarmed and crush him with my bare hands, for I see no call to use weapons on that beardless imp."

Then he went to attack Cú Chulainn. He and his charioteer were on the plain keeping tabs on the army.

"One man incoming," Lóeg told Cú Chulainn.

"What kind of man?" said Cú Chulainn.

"Dark-haired, tough, beefy. And unarmed."

"Let him pass," said Cú Chulainn.

So Mann came up to them.

"I've come to challenge you," he said.

Then they wrestled for a long time, and Mann threw Cú Chulainn three times.

Then the charioteer started taunting him: "If you were fighting for the Champion's Share in Emain," he said, "you'd overpower all of Emain's warriors."

Then his champion's rage came over him and his warrior's fury mounted, and he slammed Mann against a standing stone and beat him into smithereens.

Hence the name *Mag Mandachta* i.e., *Mand Échta* i.e., the plain where Mann was killed.[1]

The next day Maeve sent 29 men to face Cú Chulainn in a bog. Fuiliarn is the name of the bog on this side of Fer Diad's Ford (*Áth Fhir Diad*). The 29 men, i.e., Gaile Dána with his 27 sons and his sister's son[*] Glas mac Delgna,[2] threw spears at him at the same time. Then, while they were all reaching for their swords, Fíacha mac Fir Fhebe came after them from the camp. He jumped out of his chariot when he saw their hands raised against Cú Chulainn, and he hacked off their 29 forearms.

---

1 This is where the *Táin* text ends in *Lebor na hUidre*, at the end of the page on https://www.isos.dias.ie/RIA/RIA_MS_23_E_25.html#84. The next page starts mid-sentence in "The Destruction of Da Derga's Hostel." The rest of Recension 1 comes primarily from the Yellow Book of Lecan.

2 *Gaile Dána ... Glas mac Delgna* In Recension 2, where Gaile Dána is called Calatín Dána (cf. p. 293), Maeve's excuse for sending all these men at once is that they are all descended from the same man, so they count as one for purposes of single combat.

Then Cú Chulainn said: "You've given me real help in need."

"Even this little," said Fíacha, "is against our terms of service as Ulstermen in exile. If any of them make it to camp, our division will be put to the sword."

"I swear,* etc.," said Cú Chulainn, "now that I've caught my breath, none of them will make it there alive."

After that, Cú Chulainn killed the 29 men, and Fíacha's two sons joined in—two brave Ulster warriors who had come to prove their strength against the army. That was what they achieved on the Táin until they came with Cú Chulainn to the final battle.

The stone in the middle of the ford still bears the marks of their shield-bosses, fists, and knees. And their 29 headstones were placed there.

Now Fer Diad versus Cú Chulainn:

At that point the four provinces of Ireland discussed among themselves who would be capable of getting Cú Chulainn off their backs. They proposed and decided and confirmed whom they should send to the ford to face Cú Chulainn. They all said it was the hornskinned man from Irrus Domnann, the assault impossible to withstand, the battle-stone of doom, Cú Chulainn's own dear foster-brother,* Fer Diad.[1] He had all the same feats as Cú Chulainn, with the sole exception of the *gáe bolga**—and they thought he could avoid even that, and protect himself from it, because he had a skin that was hard like horn, impervious to weapons and all kinds of blades.

Maeve sent messengers to Fer Diad. He didn't come back with them. Maeve sent poets* and men of art and satirists* after him, to satirize him, denounce him, and put him to shame, so there would be no shelter for him anywhere in the world unless he came to Maeve and Ailill's tent on the cattle-raid. Afraid they would disgrace him, Fer Diad came back with those messengers.

Finnabair, the daughter of Maeve and Ailill, was sat right next to him. She was the one who handed Fer Diad every goblet and cup,

1 *Fer Diad* Added here for clarity, since the text assumes we know who this is and starts using the name a few sentences later. The name literally means 'Man of a Pair': he is, in that sense, Cú Chulainn's other half. His homeland of Irrus Domnann corresponds to the barony of Erris in northwest County Mayo.

who gave him three kisses with every cup, who presented him with sweet-smelling apples over the neckline of her tunic.[1] She kept saying Fer Diad was her beloved, her favorite wooer of all the men in the world.

When Fer Diad was feeling full and fat and happy, Maeve said, "Well now, Fer Diad, do you know why you've been called to this tent?"

"I have no clue," said Fer Diad, "except that Ireland's noble men are here, so why would it make any less sense for me to be here too?"

"No, that's not it," said Maeve. "It's so we can give you a chariot worth twenty-one *cumals*,* enough equipment for twelve men, a part of fertile Aí Plain the size of Muirthemne Plain, the right to permanently stay at Crúachu and have wine served to you there, and permanent freedom from tax or tribute for your tribe and your descendants. You'll also get my leaf-shaped gold brooch weighing 200 ounces, 200 half-ounces, 200 coins' weight, and 200 quarter-ounces—and Finnabair, my daughter with Ailill, as your wife—and a free pass to my own thighs. And on top of that, if need be, you'll have the gods as a guarantee."

"Those grants and gifts are generous," said everyone.

"That's true," said Fer Diad. "They are generous—and as generous as they are, you'll keep them to yourself if I'm supposed to go and fight my foster-brother.*"

"Ah, gentlemen," said Maeve, in an attempt to stir up strife and dissension, "what Cú Chulainn said is true"—as if she hadn't heard Fer Diad speak at all.

"What did he say, Maeve?" said Fer Diad.

"He said, my darling," she said, "that he thought you couldn't help becoming the pick of his conquests[2] in any province he visited."

"It wasn't right for him to say that, because he's never known me to show weakness or cowardice, day or night. I swear,* etc., that I'll be the first to arrive at the combat ford tomorrow morning."

"Triumph and be blessed!" said Maeve. "I prefer that to finding any weakness or cowardice in you. Everyone feels kin-love* for their

1 *apples … her tunic* Not necessarily a euphemism for breasts: there could still be real apples, being handed over in a way that invites Fer Diad to make the connection himself.

2 *becoming … conquests* Following *eDIL*, s.v. *1 airigid*. But O'Rahilly has "that you should fall by his choicest feat of arms."

own people. Why is it any more appropriate for him to act in Ulster's interests since his mother was one of them, than for you to act in the interests of Connacht, because you're the son of a Connacht king?"

As they made their contracts and their agreement binding in this way, they composed the following chant.

Maeve and Fer Dia perform a duet in which she restates her offer, he anticipates that the fight will be hard and demands at least six sureties to enforce their bargain, she lists some options, he accepts and promises to kill Cú Chulainn, she promises to give him Finnabair, and they praise each other.*

An illustrious warrior from Ulster was there for that agreement: his name was Fergus mac Roích.[1] Fergus went back to his tent.

"I think it's tragic, what's going to happen tomorrow morning," said Fergus.

"What's that?" said his tentmates.

"The killing of my noble foster-son* Cú Chulainn."

"Really? Who would commit to doing that?"

"That's easy:* his own dear foster-brother,* Fer Diad mac Damáin. Why doesn't one of you go with my blessing and warn Cú Chulainn, for his own good, to maybe skip the ford tomorrow morning?"

"Honestly," they said, "even if you were the one at the ford, we wouldn't dare go to you there."[2]

"Well, boyo," said Fergus, "harness our horses and hook up the chariot."

His charioteer got up and fetched the horses and hooked up the chariot.

They drove off to the combat ford, where they met Cú Chulainn.

"One chariot incoming, Cucuc," said Lóeg.

Lóeg describes Fergus's chariot and horses. He mentions that Fergus has such a big, bushy beard that it would shelter fifty men in a storm. Cú

1 *his name was Fergus mac Roích* This line, introducing Fergus as if he's a new character, is a sign that the story of Cú Chulainn's fight with Fer Diad could have circulated independently from the rest of the *Táin*.

2 *wouldn't dare go to you there* The point is probably that such a warning would be taken as an insult, so the translation is adjusted from "wouldn't go."

Chulainn and Fergus exchange pleasantries, with Cú Chulainn offering to share his hypothetical food as in the Etarcomol episode. Fergus warns Cú Chulainn about Fer Diad and his impenetrable skin. Cú Chulainn answers Fergus that he plans to win regardless, and discusses it with Fergus in a poem, acknowledging Fer Diad's strength and predicting a hard fight from which he won't back down in spite of warnings.

"So much for my message," said Fergus.

"It's lucky," said Cú Chulainn, "that nobody else from your side dared to bring me that message.[1] But unless all four provinces of Ireland join forces at the same time, a warning about a single warrior means nothing to me."

Then Fergus went back to his tent. And now back to Cú Chulainn:

"What will you do tonight?" said Lóeg.

"What do you mean?" said Cú Chulainn.

"Fer Diad will probably show up freshly washed and shaved and scrubbed and groomed, and he'll bring the four provinces of Ireland along to watch the fight. I'd like you to go where you'll get the same treatment—to your wife Emer with the lovely hair, at the Rowan-Meadow of Two Oxen (*Cairthenn Clúana Dá Dam*) on Slieve Fúait." So Cú Chulainn went there that night and stayed with his wife. The story doesn't get into what he did after that, though; it tells us about Fer Diad, who went to his tent.

His tentmates' mood that night was sullen and sad. They were sure that when the two world champions met, they would both fall, or else their lord would be the one who fell, because it wasn't easy to fight Cú Chulainn on the cattle-raid.

Vast worries weighed on Fer Diad's mind that night and cost him his sleep. One of them was that he would lose all the treasures and the girl he'd been offered for the single combat. If he didn't fight that one man, he would have to fight six champions the day after.[2] But he had an even bigger worry: he was sure that if he ever faced Cú

---

1 *It's lucky … that message* O.R. Melling's paraphrase: "Only you could warn me of any man, Fergus, without dying for the insult" (*The Druid's Tune*, 184).

2 *six champions the day after* This refers to the six sureties* who were agreed to in the poetic dialogue with Maeve. It would have been their job to enforce his agreement to fight Cú Chulainn.

Chulainn at the ford, it would make him lose control over his own mind and soul.[1]

Fer Diad got up early the next day.

"Well, boyo," he said, "get the horses and hook up the chariot."

"If you want my opinion," said the charioteer, "it's no more promising for us to go on this adventure than not to go on it."

As Fer Diad talked to the charioteer, he composed this little chant to urge him on:

[FD:] "Let's go to this meeting
to fight this man,
till we reach that crossing,
that crossing where the war-goddess shrieks
overhead,
to meet Cú Chulainn,
wound his trim torso,[2]
run him through with a spear-point
and then he'll be dead."

[Charioteer:] "We'd do just as well to hang back.
The threats you exchange won't be pleasant.
Someone's going to grieve.
Your fight will soon be over.
Face the Ulstermen's foster-son,*
that meeting will bring harm.
It will be long remembered.
Woe to whoever takes that course!"

[FD:] "What you say is unacceptable.
A champion is not in the business of shame.
You mustn't show fear.
We're not going to hang back for your sake.
Hush now, boy.

---

1 *mind and soul* O'Rahilly has "he would no longer have power over his own body or soul," but "body" seems to be a mistake.

2 *wound his trim torso* O'Rahilly seems to be translating *tre chreitt cumaing*, the way this line reads in Recension 2, and I follow suit; but *tre cherd cumaing*, her text for Recension 1, might also translate to "through craft of violence."

We'll have to be brave in a bit:
it's better to be tough than timid.
Let's go to this meeting."

The charioteer fetched the horses and hooked up the chariot, and they drove out of the camp.

"Lad," said Fer Diad, "it's not right for us to leave without saying goodbye to the men of Ireland. Turn the horses and chariot around to face them."

The charioteer turned the horses and chariot to face the men of Ireland three times.

Meanwhile, Maeve went to take a piss on the floor of her tent.[1]

"Is Ailill asleep right now?" said Maeve.

"Hardly," said Ailill.

"Do you hear your new son-in-law saying goodbye to you?"

"Is *that* what he's doing?" said Ailill.

"Oh, yes," said Maeve. "But I pledge what my people pledge,[2] that the man saying goodbye like that won't be coming back on his own two feet."

"We've had good results from this engagement," said Ailill. "As long as he takes down Cú Chulainn, I'll be thrilled[3] even if they take each other down in the process. But it would make me happier if Fer Diad escaped."

Fer Diad advanced to the combat ford.

"Take a look, lad, if Cú Chulainn's at the ford," said Fer Diad.

"He isn't," said the charioteer.

"Take a really good look for me," said Fer Diad.

"Cú Chulainn isn't some inconspicuous speck that stays in hiding, wherever he goes," said the charioteer.

"It's true, then: Cú Chulainn never heard of a good warrior, or

---

1 *take a piss … her tent* The significance of this is discussed by Künzler, *Flesh and Word*, 344–46: she says that this mention of Maeve's "permeable" female body plays against Fer Diad's impenetrable horn-skin and compromises the heroic moment.

2 *I pledge … people pledge* The verb here is different from the one that's usual in this formula (see *swear** in the glossary), *1 luigid* in *eDIL* as opposed to *tongaid / toingid*.

3 *I'll be thrilled* Ailill talks about himself in the first person plural ("we'd be thrilled," etc.). The singular is used for clarity.

a good man, confronting him on this cattle-raid until today—and now that he *has* heard of one, he's left the ford."

"It's pathetic to criticize him in his absence. Because, do you remember how the two of you fought Germán Garbglas (Germán 'Rough-Gray') above the shores of the Tyrrhenian Sea, and how you left your sword in the middle of the enemy armies, and Cú Chulainn killed a hundred warriors to get it back and give it to you? And do you remember where we were that night?"

"I don't know," said Fer Diad.

"We were at the house of Scáthach's steward," said the charioteer, "and you were the first to go strutting and swaggering into the house ahead of the rest of us. The oaf whacked you in the small of your back with the three-pronged serving-fork[1] and tossed you out the door. Cú Chulainn came in and chopped him in half with one blow from his sword. Then I was your steward as long as you stayed there. If it were that day now, you wouldn't say you were a better warrior than Cú Chulainn."

"This is your fault," said Fer Diad, "because I wouldn't have picked this fight if you'd told me that to start with. Why don't you pull out the suspension-beams* from the chariot so that I can rest on them, and put the rug from the chariot under my head, so I can sleep for a while?"

"How awful," said the charioteer. "That's the sleep of a doomed man caught here between stags and hounds."[2]

"What, are you not capable of watching out for me and guarding me?"

"Of course I am," said the charioteer, "and unless they come out of the clouds and the air to attack you, no one will try attacking you from the east or west unless I see them and warn you."

The shafts of Fer Diad's chariot were pulled under his side and the

---

1 *the three-pronged serving-fork* Or, "his trident," since *áel* can be used for that (see *eDIL*, s.v. *2 áel*), but the lack of possessive, contrasting with 'his sword' in the next sentence, suggests that the steward is using an improvised weapon rather than one that is properly his.

2 *between stags and hounds* More literally, "a doomed one facing stags and hounds" (as O'Rahilly has it), but stags and hounds don't act in concert. Unless the doom is supposed to be so strong that even natural enemies are joining forces to implement it, the likely scenario is being caught between the hound-pack and the stags when they turn at bay: the early Irish equivalent of "between a rock and a hard place."

rug was tucked under his head. And yet he couldn't sleep, not even a little.

Now let's shift our focus back to Cú Chulainn. "All right, my dear* Lóeg, get the horses and hook up the chariot. If Fer Diad is waiting for us, he'll be impatient."[1]

The charioteer got up, fetched the horses and hooked up the chariot. Cú Chulainn got in and they drove off toward the ford.

As for Fer Diad's charioteer, he hadn't been on watch for long when he heard the rumble of an approaching chariot. As he woke his master, he chanted this poem…

The poem describes Cú Chulainn's fearsome approach in his chariot, describing him with heroic epithets. After that, under the heading "Now for the description of Cú Chulainn's chariot, one of the three main chariots in storytelling, on the Cattle-Raid of Cúailnge," *the charioteer gives Fer Diad a detailed description in prose of Cú Chulainn's magnificent chariot, horses, hairstyle, and charioteer.*

"You praise Cú Chulainn too much," said Fer Diad, "when he hasn't paid you a commission for it." And he described him as follows, and said:

[FD:] "It's time for you to help me—
whose side are you on?[2]
Shut up and stop praising.
Cú Chulainn's no impending doom.
If you see the champion of Cúailnge
with the feats he's so proud of,
I'll deal with him.

1 *impatient* Recension 2 explains this by saying that Cú Chulainn slept in until full daylight so that no one would accuse him of getting up early because he was nervous.

2 *whose side are you on* O'Rahilly has these lines as "It is time now for help for this is no deed of friendship (?)." My interpretation is that Fer Diad is telling the charioteer that his praise of Cú Chulainn isn't helping and isn't a friendly act towards him, therefore he should stop it and be supportive instead. In this poetic exchange, "we" seems to mean "I."

There's so much in it for me
he'll be finished off fast."

[Charioteer:] "If I see the champion of Cúailnge
with the feats he's so proud of,
he's not fleeing from us
but coming straight for us.
He may be masterful, but he's not miserly,
and for his quality, I praise him.
He runs, and not slowly,
but quick as a thunderclap."

[FD:] "You're practically picking a fight,
you've praised him so much.
Why have you taken his side
since he set out from home?
So far he's been challenged,
they've attacked him,
but all he's had to face
is some weak rabble."

It wasn't long until they met in the middle of the ford, and Fer Diad spoke to Cú Chulainn. "Where did *you* come from, Cúa?" he said. Because *cúa* is the word for "squinting" in Old Irish, and Cú Chulainn had seven pupils in his royal eyes, two of which were squinting. But he found that more decorative than disfiguring, and if he'd had any physical imperfection bigger than that, that's what Fer Diad would have used to taunt him. And as Fer Diad called attention to it, he composed a chant, and Cú Chulainn answered him throughout.[1]

[FD:] "Where did *you* come from, Cúa,
to fight with fresh strength?
Your flesh will be blood-red

1 *Cú Chulainn answered him throughout* It's unclear who is supposed to be speaking each of these verses. Some can be more clearly attributed than others. My attributions, [FD] and [CC], are only my best guess.

above your horses' panting.
Hopeless as starting a fire with one stick of
kindling:
woe to whoever takes the path you're on.
You'll need medical care
if you get home at all."

[CC:] "I have come, in the sight of warriors,
formations, and hundreds,
as a rampaging boar amid flocks of sheep[1]
to plunge you underwater:
raging against you, ready to test you
in a hundredfold match-up,
so that you reap the harm
as you fight for your life.

[CC:] "How will we meet?
Will we sigh over corpses?
In what pool will we wallow
as we fight at the ford?
Will it be on bloodstained spearpoints
or savage sword-blades
that you'll be cut down in front of your forces
if your time has come?"

[FD:] "Before sunset, before night,
if you're in harrowing need,
you can expect to tangle with the herd bull:[2]
the fight won't be bloodless.
The Ulstermen are calling for you.
They've got you out here unprotected.[3]

---

1 *boar … of sheep* Literally (and oddly), "a boar of pursuit abounding in flocks"; "of sheep" added to clarify my interpretation.

2 *with the herd bull* Reading *boirche* as a common noun (*eDIL*'s "perh[aps] 'the bull or stag that leads the herd'," s.v. *Boirche*), not as a placename or personal name, which would also be possible.

3 *unprotected* O'Rahilly translates "They have taken you unawares (?)." D.S. Nikolaev, "The evolution of poetical texts in *Táin Bó Cúailnge*," *Shagi/Steps* 2.4 (2016) 30–59, at 52,

They'll be appalled by what they see:
they'll be completely overrun.

[FD:] "You've put yourself in an exposed position.
You've come to the end of your life.
You'll be barraged with blades
to no subtle purpose:
a hero will strike you down.
The two of us will meet in battle.
You won't command three men
from this day till judgment comes."[1]

[CC:] "When we were with Scáthach,
with our typical boldness
we used to travel together,
we'd tour every country.
You were my heart's companion,
you were my tribe, you were my family:
I never found anyone dearer.
It would be tragic to lose you."

[FD:] "Spare me your warning.
You're the world's biggest boaster.
Don't expect to be bought off or let off easy,
because you're no paragon.
I'm well aware
you're just a nervous Nellie.
Oh heart of a fluttering bird,
with no courage, no stamina.

---

says that her translation is straightforward but the meaning is obscure unless "they" refers to Maeve's men, and indeed Recension 2 substitutes for this line "They've been stricken by an ulcer/cancer," presumably the *ces noínden* paralysis. The relevant word is in *eDIL* as "a state of heedlessness; being off one's guard, an unguarded condition" (s.v. *1 faill (b)*), and the idea that the Ulstermen have left Cú Chulainn exposed would fit the context.

1 *judgment comes* See the note on doomsday expressions, p. 238 above. The Irish here is *co tí in bráth*.

[FD:] "It compromises your honor
to shrink from our showdown
but before the rooster crows
I'll see your head on a spike.
Cú Chulainn of Cúailnge,
you're delirious, demented:
I'll do my absolute worst to you
because all this is your fault."

Then Cú Chulainn asked his charioteer to taunt him when he was losing and praise him when he was winning,[1] while he fought Fer Diad. So his charioteer said to him, "The man looms over you like the tail looms over a cat. He'll scrub you the way flax-tops are scutched in a pool. He'll smack you like a doting mother spanks her son." Then they went to their encounter in the ford, and did everything Scáthach had taught the two of them. Fer Diad and Cú Chulainn did incredible feats.

Then Cú Chulainn took a flying leap onto Fer Diad's shield. Three times, Fer Diad threw him off into the ford, so that the charioteer started taunting him again. Cú Chulainn swelled and blew up like an inflated bladder. His size increased until he was bigger than Fer Diad.

"Look out for the *gáe bolga*!"* called the charioteer. He tossed it downstream to him. Cú Chulainn caught it between his toes and administered it anally to Fer Diad. It went in as a single barb but exploded into twenty-four. That made Fer Diad lower his shield. Cú Chulainn caught him with his spear over the top of his shield, and it smashed his ribcage and went through Fer Diad's heart.

[FD:] "A mighty spear-shaft from your right hand!
My ribs are broken like spoils of war.
My heart is gore.
I fought well,
but I've fallen, Cúa."

---

1 *to taunt him ... winning* See the glossary under *satire** for the terms *gressacht* (taunting, haranguing) and *laíded* (encouraging praise) that apply here.

[CC:] "Alas, oh golden salmon,
oh brave Fer Diad,
oh handsome strong-smiter,
your arm was triumphant.

Our friendship was fair,
oh delight to the eye.
Your shield had a gold rim.
Your blade was a beauty.

Your bright silver ring
on your noble hand.
Your *fidchell**-set was precious.
Your cheeks a pretty purple.

Your curly yellow hair
was thick. The flexible, leaf-patterned belt
you wore round your sides
was a rare treasure.

Alas, dear calf,
that you fell to Cú Chulainn.
The shield you carried against the rigors of war
was no protection.
Our fight—
our sorrow from our furor.
The great hero was so fine.
Every army has been defeated
or trampled underfoot.
Alas, oh golden salmon.[1]
Oh, Fer Diad."

And likewise:

1 *dear calf … golden salmon* These animal expressions could also be translated metaphorically: *calf* as "dear one," *salmon* as "warrior."

It was all a game, it was all in fun,
until Fer Diad at the ford.
Alas for the golden pillar of might
thrown down at the ford.

It was all a game, it was all in fun,
until Fer Diad at the ford.
I thought my dear Fer Diad
would live forever after I am gone."

[*This episode is significantly amplified in Recension 2 and includes more poems.*[1] *The fight lasts five days. Cú Chulainn and Fer Diad alternate in offering each other the choice of weapons to use each day, and in the evening they embrace and camp together, and are given food and medical attention. On the first day, they rain projectiles on each other without drawing blood. On the second day, they throw spears at each other and begin to take damage. On the third day, they fight with spears from their chariots. On the fourth day, they fight with swords, carving huge lumps of flesh off each other. On the fifth day, they meet in the ford: Cú Chulainn performs his best, most original feats (some of which we are told he did not learn from Scáthach or Aífe or anyone else), and resorts to the* gáe bolga* *only after Fer Diad manages to stab him. The lament for Fer Diad is then developed at much greater length.*[2]]

The army marches south from the ford where Fer Diad was killed. Cú Chulainn lies there convalescing until a small group of Ulstermen take him to recover by bathing in the rivers of Conaille Muirthemne, 19 of which are listed by name. There is a kind of "table of contents" listing the episodes of the Táin *that are still to come. Prior to this, the army has posted the herald Mac Roth to warn them of any pursuit from the north.*

1 Ann Dooley has a detailed comparison of how the two recensions cover the Fer Diad fight, in "A hero for our time: *Táin* recensions I and II reconsidered," in *Táin Bó Cúalnge from the Book of Leinster: Reassessments*, ed. John Carey (ITS, 2020) 45–68, at 54–64.

2 *The lament for Fer Diad … greater length* This version of the lament is discussed in detail by Amy C. Mulligan, "Poetry, sinew, and the Irish performance of lament: keening a hero's body back together," *Philological Quarterly* 97.4 (2018) 389–408; compare Marjorie Housley, "'The noble way you blushed'" and Longman, "'What manner of man is this Hound?'." Ann Dooley responds to such readings in "A hero for our time," 64–68.

Now It's Time for Cethern's Hard Fighting:

"I see a chariot coming across the plain from the north today," said Mac Roth, "with a gray-haired man in it, unarmed except for a silver spike in his hand. You'd think there was a May mist over the chariot. He's jabbing his charioteer the same as the horses. He seems to be afraid of dying before he gets to us.[1] There's a brindled hunting-dog out in front of him."

"Who's that, Fergus?" said Ailill. "Could it be Conchobor or Celtchar?"

"No," said Fergus, "I think it's Cethern, the bountiful, bloody-bladed son of Fintan."

And so it was.

Then Cethern attacked them and inflicted major casualties, and became one himself: with his entrails flopping around his feet, he left the battle and came over to Cú Chulainn. Cú Chulainn felt sorry for his injuries.

"Get me a doctor," Cethern said to Cú Chulainn.

They made him a sickbed out of fresh rushes and got him a pillow. Then Cú Chulainn sent Lóeg to Fíacha mac Fir Fhebe in the exiles' camp to look for doctors. And he said he would kill them all, even if they were to camp out underground, unless they came to him to treat Cethern. The doctors were reluctant because Cethern wouldn't hesitate to injure anyone in the camp. Still, they came to see him.

So the first doctor to arrive examined Cethern.

"You won't survive," he said.

"Then neither will you," said Cethern. He punched him so hard his brains came out his ears.

He killed fifty doctors that way, or fifteen. The last one was only knocked out, and Cú Chulainn was able to rescue him.

---

1 *seems to be ... gets to us* O'Rahilly's more literal "for he thinks he will scarcely reach the host alive" (and the expression *Is ed hed lais* here is unclear, as she explains in a note) makes it sound like he's afraid that he'll be killed, whereas I take it that this is describing a sense of extreme urgency.

They sent for the seer-physician Fíngin, who was Conchobor's doctor, asking him to come and examine Cú Chulainn and Cethern.

"It wasn't a good move to kill the doctors," Cú Chulainn told Cethern. "Now none of them will come near you."

"It wasn't a good move for them to give me bad news," said Cethern. Because every one of the doctors who had examined him had said he wouldn't live, that he wasn't treatable, so then Cethern had punched them.

They saw Fíngin's chariot approaching, since he'd been told that Cú Chulainn and Cethern were in trouble.

"Examine Cethern for us," said Cú Chulainn, "but do it from a distance, because he just killed fifteen of their doctors."

So Fíngin approached Cethern and examined him from a distance.

"Examine me," said Cethern. "This first thrust I got is really painful."

"That's a proud, headstrong woman's[1] work," said Fíngin.

"That's probably true," said Cethern. "A tall, beautiful woman, with a pale, tender, oval face came up to me. She had long blonde hair, and two gold birds on her shoulders, and had a dark purple hooded cloak on. She had a shield over her back, five hands wide with gold overlay. She had a super-sharp, razor-edged light spear in her hand, and a sword with a horn hilt slung over her shoulder. She was an awesome sight. She was the first one who came at me and wounded me."

"Dammit!" said Cú Chulainn. "That was Maeve of Crúachu."

"Those are superficial, halfhearted acts of *fingal*.* They won't kill you," said the doctor.

"That's true," said Cethern. "A young warrior came at me—curved shield with a scalloped rim, bent-pointed spear, ivory-hilted sword slung over his shoulder. He wore a horsehair crest, and a brown cloak with a silver brooch. He lost a little blood to me himself."

---

1 *proud, headstrong woman* The word translated "headstrong" (*báeth*, as in the name Fer Báeth) could also be "impulsive, foolish, reckless" or "wanton, promiscuous," and a case could be made for any or all of these readings. Toner, "Reading the *Táin* from back to front," argues that from Recension 1 to Recension 2, Maeve "has been transformed from a lascivious and deceitful woman into a headstrong and ill-advised leader" (77).

"I know him," said Cú Chulainn. "That was Illann, son of Fergus mac Roích."

There are nine more rounds of this. Fíngin identifies some wounds as being caused by a certain number of a certain kind of person, Cethern gives a physical description including clothes, hair, and weapons, Cú Chulainn gives a name, and Fíngin sometimes comments further on the injury. Altogether, Cethern has been wounded by 23 people, beginning with Maeve and ending with Ailill and one of the Maines, and his heart is rolling around "like a ball of thread in an empty bag." *See Map 3 for the placenames in this section.*

"So what do you make of me, Dr. Fíngin?" said Cethern.

"I'm not going to lie," said Fíngin. "Don't go trading in your dairy cows for yearlings[1] now. As long as you were being attacked by twos and threes, it would have been easy to treat you. But when a whole army has left its mark on you, you'll be giving up the ghost no matter what."

And Fíngin steered his chariot away from him.

"You've written me off just like your colleagues," said Cethern. Then he punched him[2] so that he fell across the suspension-beams[*] of his chariot and the whole chariot clanged.

That's when Cú Chulainn said, "That's a nasty kick you gave an old graybeard."[3] Hence the placename the Rise of the Kick (*Óchtur Lúi*), which still exists in Crích Rois. "It would have been more appropriate to attack enemies instead of doctors."

Then the doctor gave Cethern a choice. He could lie sick for a year and then survive. Or, he could immediately have three days and

1 *cows for yearlings* *eDIL*'s suggested translation of this line, "thou must not give thy cows for strippers," lends itself to hilarious misunderstanding. Even per the usual sense of 'stripper' as applied to cows—one that is about to age out of giving milk—it seems to be not quite accurate: Cethern is being advised not to trade in his dairy cows for young ones (see *eDIL*, s.v. *dairt*) that haven't started giving milk yet. "If you do," Recension 2 adds, "you're not the one who'll enjoy them, and they'll bring you no profit"—because he'll be dead by then.

2 *he punched him* It clearly says that Cethern uses his fist (*dornd*) against Fíngin. Based on what follows, Recension 2 understandably says instead that he kicks him.

3 *an old graybeard* More literally, "It is vicious this kicking by you of an old, gray-haired [man]," reading *sengrantae* as *sen* 'old' + *grant* 'gray-haired.' Recension 2 takes Cethern to be the gray-haired man who is doing the kicking.

three nights of strength to attack his enemies—and that's what he chose.

Then Cú Chulainn looked for bone-marrow so the doctor could treat him. He made a marrow-mash from the bones of the cattle that he came across. Hence the name Marrow-Trough (*Smirommair*) in Crích Rois.

Cethern slept for a day and a night after drinking the marrow.

"I have no ribs," he said when he woke up.[1] "Put the ribs from the chariot-frame inside me."

"So be it," said Cú Chulainn.

"If I had my own weapons," said Cethern, "the things I would do would be remembered forever."

"In that case, what I'm seeing is a sight for sore eyes," said Cú Chulainn.

"What are you seeing?" said Cethern.

"It looks to me like your wife Finn Becc ('Little Blonde') daughter of Eochu coming toward us in her chariot."

Sure enough, they saw the woman bringing Cethern's weapons in her chariot.

Cethern grabbed his weapons, then attacked the army with his chariot-frame tied to his belly to give him more strength.

The camp was alerted by the "dead" doctor who had escaped from Cethern earlier on and had hidden with the corpses of the other doctors. There was such fear of Cethern that they put Ailill's crown on a standing stone. Cethern attacked the stone and drove his sword through it, all the way past his fist. Hence the placename Holey Stone (*Lía Toll*) in Crích Rois.

"This is a trick!" he said. "I won't stop until I see one of you wearing this crown of Ailill's." Then he attacked them all day long and into the night, until Maine[2] put the crown on his head and charged at Cethern in his chariot. Cethern threw his shield after him: it split him and his charioteer in half and went straight through the horses into the ground.

---

1 *when he woke up* Added for clarity.

2 *Maine* Recension 2 specifies that this was Maine Andóe.

Then the army closed in on Cethern. He kept up his attack until he went down fighting in the midst of them.

[In Recension 2, this is followed by a long lament by Cethern's wife.]

Now the army faces a series of Ulster champions.

Cethern's father Fintan, trying to avenge his son, attacks the army seven times. All his 150 men are killed except for Fintan and his son [named Crimthann in Recension 2]. They become separated, and Ailill saves the son in exchange for a truce with Fintan until the final battle. [Recension 2 labels this episode "The Tooth-Fight of Fintan," since the warriors who participated in it were found with the noses and lips of their enemies bitten off in their teeth.]

Menn mac Sálchada ("Glory son of War-Heel," featured in "The Story of Mac Dá Thó's Pig") attacks with 30 men, killing 12 and losing 12. He is left bloody and incapacitated, which is his "Red Embarrassment." The invading army lets him occupy their campsite, claiming that they never wronged him, since they never trespassed on his territory.

There is a second version, or a second instance, of "Rochad's Bloodless Fight" (cf p. 227). Rochad is the Ulster warrior in love with Finnabair. This time Ailill and Maeve arrange for her to spend the night with Rochad in exchange for a truce with him until the final battle. This causes problems:

The seven Munster kings were told what happened. One of them said, "That girl was offered to me, with fifteen sureties,* for coming on this expedition."

All seven of them admitted they had made the same deal. They went to take their revenge on Ailill's sons at Glennamain where they were bringing up the rearguard. Maeve came to the rescue. So did the division of Leinstermen. So did Ailill. So did Fergus. Seven hundred men died in the Glennamain Massacre.[1]

---

1 *Seven hundred men … Glennamain Massacre* This belies the earlier claim (p. 244) that the dead in this battle were beyond counting.

So that was Rochad's Bloodless Combat and the Glennamain Massacre, and when Finnabair heard about it—when she heard that seven hundred men were dead because of her—she died of shame on the spot. Hence the placename Finnabair-of-the-Mountain (*Finnabair Sléibe*).

Now the Funny Fight with Iliach:

At the Ford of Iliach's Grit (*Áth Feidle Iliach*), they faced Iliach, the grandfather of the champion Lóegaire the Triumphant.[1] Iliach was being cared for with filial piety by his grandson in Ráth Immail. He announced to the army that he was taking his revenge and would be the death of them.

This is how he appeared on the scene: in a chariot that was nothing but a frame without a rug or covering. Two old sorrel mares dragged the rickety thing. And he had filled it up with rocks to the same height as the clearance under it.[2] He would strike down everyone who came to stare at him. He was completely naked, well-endowed, with his scrotum dangling through the chariot-frame. The army noticed his appearance and made fun of the naked man. Dócha mac Mágach punished the rabble to stop them from jeering. And for that, Iliach told Dócha that at the end of the day he should take Iliach's sword and behead him with it, as long as Iliach had nothing left to give against the army.

Then Iliach noticed the marrow-mash.[3] He was told it had been made from the bones of Ulster cattle. So then he made another

1 *Lóegaire the Triumphant* Condensed for clarity. The text has: "Lóegaire Búadach son of Connach Buide son of Iliach" (pronounced "ILLY-ock").

2 *as the clearance under it* Literally, "until it was full up to the *focharpat*." O'Rahilly has "as high as the skin-coverings." David Stifter, "The Old-Irish chariot and its technology," in *Kelten am Rhein: Akten des dreizehnten Internationalen Keltologiekongresses*, vol. 2, ed. Stefan Zimmer (Mainz: Philipp von Zabern, 2009) 279–89, at 286, comments: "The hapax *focharpat* is attested only here. Although being perfectly transparent as a compound of *fo* 'under, below' + *carpat* 'chariot', its exact meaning remains unclear. Its superficial meaning '(thing) under the chariot' is counteracted by the context, which suggests something on top of the vehicle." My translation tries to make sense of the superficial meaning. Another approach would be that this sentence describes how the chariot sagged under the rocks. Why there are rocks at all is another question. They would seem to be needed as ballast since the chariot is so flimsy.

3 *the marrow-mash* Left over from Cethern's healing (p. 268)? Otherwise, the Connachtmen have apparently been making their own mash from the captured cows.

marrow-mash using the bones of the Connachtmen,[1] and the two mashes sat side by side.

Dócha cut his head off in the evening and took it to his grandson Lóegaire. He made peace with him and Lóegaire kept Iliach's sword.[2]

That is "Iliach's Funny Fight," because of how the army laughed at him.

Now the Charioteers' Barrage:

150 Ulster charioteers attack, kill three times their number, and die in battle.

Now the Trance of Amairgen:

Amairgen, in a trance or frenzy, throws stones at the army and forces them to hunker down at Tailtiu (now Teltown, County Meath, again on Map 3). As before with Muinremor, Cú Roí comes along and throws stones back at him. Cú Roí considers it inappropriate to attack a wounded man, so he targets only Amairgen and not Cú Chulainn. Amairgen lets the army go past Tailtiu in exchange for Cú Roí leaving; as soon as he does, Amairgen takes offense at the army's movements and starts throwing stones again, killing countless men.

Now Súaltaim's Repeated Warning:

Súaltaim of Súaltaim's Fort (*Ráth Súaltaim*) on Muirthemne Plain heard the commotion of his son Cú Chulainn fighting off the twelve sons and the sister's-son* of Gaile Dána.[3] He said: "Is the sky splitting, or the sea overflowing, or the ground breaking,[4] or is that the scream of my son outnumbered by enemies?"

---

1 *Connachtmen* The text actually uses an archaic population name for the same region, Fir Ól nEchmacht.

2 *Lóegaire kept Iliach's sword* The text doesn't use names here, but, following O'Rahilly, this is what it seems to be saying. Lóegaire would normally have needed to avenge his grandfather.

3 *Gaile Dána* See pp. 250–51 above.

4 *sky splitting … ground breaking* This has been read as a reflection of early Celtic belief in a threefold cosmos: the reference to sky, sea, and earth would encompass all that exists. Compare Conchobor's oath at the end of this section.

He went to join his son, but Cú Chulainn was less than thrilled to see him: he might be wounded, and Cú Chulainn wouldn't have the strength to avenge him.[1]

"Go warn the Ulstermen," said Cú Chulainn. "They need to meet the invaders in battle, right now. If they don't, they'll never get revenge."

Then his father noticed that there wasn't a spot on his body wider than the tip of a bulrush that was undamaged. Even his left arm, under his shield, had fifty wounds.

Súaltaim hurried to Emain and shouted: "They're slaughtering men, kidnapping women, driving off cattle!"

He shouted that once from outside the stockade, again from on top of the battlements, and a third time from the Mound of the Hostages inside Emain itself.

No one answered. The Ulstermen were banned[2] from speaking before Conchobor, and Conchobor never spoke before the three druids.*

"Who's kidnapping them? Who's driving them off? Who's killing them?" said one of the druids.

"Ailill mac Máta, with the help of Fergus[3] mac Roích. Your people have been overrun as far as Dún Sobairche. Their cows, their women, and their livestock have been pillaged. Cú Chulainn hasn't let the enemy into Muirthemne Plain or Crích Rois for all three months of winter. He wears wooden hoops to keep his cloak from sticking to his wounds, which he's been plugging with dry grass. He's in critical condition."

"This man is haranguing the king," said the druid. "He should die."

"So he should," said Conchobor.

---

1 *he might be wounded ... avenge him* O'Rahilly: "But Cú Chulainn was not pleased that he should come to him, for though he was wounded, Súaltaim would not be strong enough to avenge him." "Súaltaim" is not in the Irish here, and it would make more sense for Cú Chulainn to worry about incurring the impossible new burden of avenging his father: Cú Chulainn can protect himself, but, in his current condition, would struggle to protect others.

2 *banned* The word here is not *geis** but *airmert* (*eDIL*, s.vv. *airmert, airmit*), which seems to have a similar meaning.

3 *Ailill ... Fergus* Notice the apparently deliberate erasure of Maeve (as by Cú Chulainn on p. 214 above).

"So he should," said everyone.

"He's telling the truth, though," said Conchobor. "They've been pillaging Ulster from the Monday before Samain* till the Monday before Imbolc.*"

Súaltaim was not impressed with the response he was getting, and rushed outside. He fell on his shield, and the scalloped rim of the shield cut off his head. He carried his own head[1] back into Emain on top of the shield, and the head said the same as before.

"Well, there's no need to shout,"[2] said Conchobor. "I swear by the sea before them, the sky above them, and the earth below them, I will bring every cow back to its shed and every woman and boy back home, after I triumph over the Connachtmen in battle."

Now the Rallying of the Ulstermen:

Conchobor sends his son Finnchad to rally the troops, listing all the places he should visit and the heroes he should summon. (See https://www.isos.dias.ie/TCD/TCD_MS_1318.html#410 for this list in the Yellow Book of Lecan and https://www.isos.dias.ie/TCD/TCD_MS_1339.html#94 for the Book of Leinster.)[3] *The Ulster forces assemble at Emain Macha, but insist on waiting until Erc, the son of Cairbre Nia Fer and Fedelm Noíchride, can be brought from Tara to join them. Meanwhile, Conchobor and Celtchar attack the enemy rearguard, killing eighty*

1 *fell on his shield ... carried his own head* O'Rahilly has "The horse brought his head on the shield back into Emain," but no horse is mentioned—this is mistakenly translating what happens in Recension 2. There is a 3sg. active verb ('he/she/it carries') which could have the force of the impersonal, i.e., "Someone carried his head inside," but it seems just as likely (if we think of the Beheading Game in "Bricriu's Feast") that the now-headless Súaltaim is the subject, hence my translation. Severed heads that speak are fairly common in early Irish literature: two famous examples are Conaire in "The Destruction of Da Derga's Hostel" and Donn Bó in "The Battle of Allen" (*Cath Almaine*, Ó Corráin #1002).

2 *no need to shout* Literally, "a little too loud was that cry."

3 The little drawing of a head (is it Súaltaim's? Conchobor's? Finnchad's?) in the Book of Leinster elicits this comment from Roisin McLaughlin, "Text run-over imagery and reader's aids in Irish manuscripts," *Ériu* 71 (2021) 69–115, https://muse.jhu.edu/article/858943/pdf: "It is worth considering whether images which serve no apparent function as textual apparatus could have a thematic relationship to the text, although such a relationship could not be established with any certainty. In the Book of Leinster, a man's head has been drawn on p. 94a34 beside a section of *Táin Bó Cúalnge* which lists the names of the warriors of Ulster" (101).

men and capturing eighty women. Celtchar (or possibly Conchobor's son Cúscraid) predicts a bloody battle at Gáirech and Irgáirech, and on the night before the battle, while the war-goddess wreaks havoc on the army, Dubthach and Ailill (or possibly Cormac Conn Loinges) fall into a trance and chant predictions of slaughter.

This brings us back to Map 2, the Midlands.

Now the March of the Warbands:

While they were having these visions, the Connachtmen, on the advice of Ailill, Maeve, and Fergus, decided to send messengers to see if the Ulstermen had reached the plain. Then Ailill spoke: "Get up, Mac Roth, and go find out for us if they're on the same plain in Meath as we are. I've taken spoils and cattle from them and they can meet me in battle if they want to. But if they haven't made it this far I'm not going to hang around and wait for them."

So Mac Roth went to scout the plain. In due course he came back to Ailill, Maeve, and Fergus.

The first time Mac Roth had looked into the distance around Slieve Fúait, he had seen all the wild animals come pouring out of the woods, filling the entire plain.

"And when I looked again," said Mac Roth, "a dense mist had filled the glens and valleys, making the hills between them look like islands in lakes. Then I saw sparks of fire flashing in that huge mist, like I was watching an incredible display of every color in the world. After that came the lightning and the noise and the thunder, and a blast of wind—it almost ripped my hair off and threw me on my back, even though it hadn't been a windy day."

"What was that, Fergus?" said Ailill. "Identify it."

"Oh, that's easy,*" said Fergus. "That was the Ulstermen. They've come out of their paralysis. Now they're charging through the forest, and the overwhelming numbers and the magnitude and violence of their warriors is what made the forest shake. They're what the animals were running from. The dense mist you saw filling the valleys, that made the hills look like islands in lakes? That was the breath of those strongmen. The lightning and the sparks and all the colors you saw, Mac Roth," said Fergus, "those were the eyes of those champions flashing from their heads so you'd think they were sparks. The noise and the thunder and the violent uproar you heard, that was the whistling of swords and ivory-hilted dirks, the clatter of weapons, the creaking of chariots, the hoof-beats of the horses, the might of the chariot-warriors, the howl of the fighters, the noise of the soldiers, the absolute fury and towering rage of the warriors on their way to battle. They're so angry and worked up that they feel like they'll never get here."

"Let them come," said Ailill. "We have warriors ready to face them."

"You'll need them," said Fergus. "Nowhere in all Ireland, or anywhere in the western world from Greece and Scythia to the Orkneys and the Pillars of Hercules and Bregon's Tower[1] (*Tor Breogain*) and the Islands of Gades, will you find anyone who can resist the men of Ulster once they're up in arms."

Mac Roth goes back to observe the Ulstermen arriving at Slemain Mide, and, in the epic convention known as the "Watchman Device," brings back detailed descriptions of the heroes, their warbands, and their equipment. Fergus identifies them all with fulsome praise. The list includes Conchobor; Sencha mac Ailella; Cúscraid; Éogan mac Durthacht, king of Fernmag; Lóegaire Búadach; Muinremor; Feidlimid Cilair Cétaig; Connad mac Mornai; Rochad, now described as Finnabair's husband and as Maeve and Ailill's son-in-law; Fergus mac Léiti, king of Líne; Amairgen son of Écet Salach; Celtchar mac Uthechair; Feradach Finn Fechnach; Eirrge Echbél (Eirrge "Horsemouth"); Conchobor's sons Fíacha and Fíachna; the sons of Fíachna, Rus and Dáire and Imchad (Dáire was the original owner of the Brown Bull); Menn mac Sálchada; Fergna mac Finnchoíme (son of Finnchóem); and Furbaide Fer Benn (Furbaide "the Horned Man"). Then comes this description:

"Yet another warband came to the hill at Slemain Mide," said Mac Roth. "They were heroic, too many to count. They were unusually dressed, not like the other warbands. But their weapons and clothes

1 *Bregon's Tower* Tower built by Bregon son of Bráth at Brigantia [=La Coruña] in Spain, from which the Gaels supposedly first spotted Ireland: see *The Celtic Heroic Age*, 231. This survey of "the western world" corresponds to a similar survey of places in "Bricriu's Feast," §93.

and gear were amazing. In that warband was a big, proud force with a freckled boy leading it. His body was the ultimate perfection of the human form. Splendid troops were ranged in front of him.[1] He was carrying a white-bossed, gold-studded shield with a gold rim, and a light sharp spear that shimmered in his hand. He was wrapped in a purple fringed mantle, pinned on his chest with a silver brooch, and wore a white hooded tunic with red embroidery. Over his clothes he wore a gold-hilted sword."

Fergus fell silent. "I don't know of any boy like that among the Ulstermen," he said, "but I can think of one possibility, which is that those are the men of Tara with the sweet, amazing, magnificent boy Erc, the son of Cairbre Nia Fer and Conchobor's daughter.[2] Without asking his father's permission, he's come to support his grandfather. That boy," said Fergus, "is the reason why you'll lose this battle. No horror or fear can touch him as he charges at you through the center of your lines. The Ulster warriors will bellow bravely on their way to rescue their beloved lad, hacking through the forces in front of them. They will all experience a rush of kin-love* when they see the boy in that great conflict. Conchobor's sword will be heard making a noise like the howl of a guard-dog on his way to rescue the boy. Cú Chulainn will build three walls of bodies around the battlefield as he rushes toward that little boy. It will be kin-love that makes the Ulster warriors take on countless troops."[3]

"I find it fairly exhausting," said Mac Roth, "to tell you about everything I saw, but I've come back anyway to report to you."

"So you have," said Fergus.

"But Conall Cernach didn't come with his big warband,"[4] said Mac Roth. "And Conchobor's three sons didn't come with their three

1 *Splendid … of him* O'Rahilly doesn't translate this line. *eDIL*, s.v. *airgal (b)*, suggests "(may) splendid battle (be waged) before him!" but I prefer *(c)*, "line of battle, battalion."

2 Here I omit *Ní 'mmuscarat tairrid*, which O'Rahilly doesn't translate, and mentions in her notes as "Corrupt? Perhaps originally a marginal note; the text reads smoothly without it."

3 Recension 2 adds a metaphor that assimilates the warriors to the bulls they're fighting over: "That humongous drove will make a manly bellow as they rescue the calf of their own cow in the battle tomorrow morning."

4 *Conall Cernach didn't come … warband* This seems inconsistent, because (according to the *Táin*, anyway—"The Battle of Rosnaree," summarized on p. 291 below, tells a different story) Conall is with the Ulster exiles, unless the point is just that the Ulster forces aren't as complete as they could have been.

divisions. Neither did Cú Chulainn, since he was wounded fighting superior numbers. Except there was a warrior in a chariot by himself, and that was probably him arriving."

Mac Roth gives a description of the chariot and horses, the warrior, and the charioteer, and Fergus confirms that it is Cú Chulainn and Lóeg. Mac Roth wraps up his description, saying that from Fer Diad's Ford to Slemain Mide, all he saw were men and horses.

Conchobor makes camp and arranges a truce with Ailill until sunrise the next day. The Morrígan speaks in the twilight, cheering on and forecasting disaster for both the Ulstermen and their opponents, and Conchobor and Lóegaire chant more dire prophecies and calls to arms. The battle kicks off early in the morning, before any of the leaders are awake: Cú Chulainn sends his charioteer to wake them (or the poet Amairgen *chants a call to arms).*

"I woke them up," said the charioteer. "This is how they went into battle: totally naked, except for their weapons. Anyone whose tent faces east came charging west through the back of the tent."

"That's what I call help in need," said Cú Chulainn.[1]

But enough about the Ulstermen for now. As for the men of Ireland, the war-goddesses Badb, Bé Néit, and Nemain shrieked at them that night at Gáirech and Ilgáirech, and a hundred of their warriors died of fright. That was not the most peaceful night for them.

Now the Rallying of the Men of Ireland:

Overnight, Ailill sent Traigthrén to rally reinforcements for the men of Ireland, listing them at length in groups of three ("the three Conaires from Slieve Mis, the three Lesfinds from Lúachair," etc.): These three-man squads made up what was called the *Ferchuitred* ("Duty

1 In Recension 2, Conchobor now asks Sencha to hold the Ulstermen's advance until the omens are in their favor and the sun is shining fully on the battlefield. (Conchobor doesn't say so, but this would also give them a tactical advantage, since they're coming from the east, and the sun would be in their opponents' faces.)

Roster") of the men of Ireland, not including the ones Cú Chulainn had previously killed.

But now, back to Cú Chulainn. He said, "Take a look for me, Lóeg, and see how the Ulstermen are fighting now."

"They're holding the line bravely," said Lóeg. "If Conall Cernach's charioteer Óen and I drove our chariots from one wing of the army to the other, our horses' hooves and our wheels would never touch the ground."

"This is shaping up to be a huge fight," said Cú Chulainn. "Don't let anything happen without telling me," he told his charioteer.

"I'll do my best," said Lóeg. "Now the warriors from the west, where they are, are punching gaps through the line of battle heading east, and the same number of warriors from the east are punching through it heading west."

"It's awful that I'm not healed," said Cú Chulainn, "or the gap I made would be clear to see along with everyone else's."

Then the Connacht[1] reinforcements arrived in their three-man squads. As they joined in the battle at Gáirech and Irgáirech, there were also nine chariots of warriors from Irúath. In front of them there were three men on foot who kept pace with the chariots. Maeve let them go into battle only to drag Ailill out of harm's way if he was defeated, or to kill Conchobor if he was the one beaten.

Then Cú Chulainn's charioteer told him that Ailill and Maeve were begging Fergus to join in the battle. They told him it wouldn't be wrong, since they'd been so good to him while he was in exile.

"If I had my sword," said Fergus, "I'd make men's heads rain down on their shields as thick as hail on a bog where all the king's horses pull up short after they come galloping into the land."

Then Fergus swore this oath: "I swear,* etc., that I would hack men's jawbones from their necks, necks from shoulders, shoulders from elbows, elbows from forearms, forearms from fists, fists from fingers, fingers from nails, nails from craniums, craniums from torsos, torsos from thighs, thighs from knees, knees from calves, calves from feet, feet from toes, toes from toenails. Blood will fizz from their headless necks like a bee buzzing back and forth on a pretty day."

---

1 *Connacht* Added for clarity.

Then Ailill said to his charioteer,[1] "Bring me the sword that severs flesh. I swear* by the god my people swear by, if it's in any worse shape than when I gave it to you on that hillside in Ulster, all the men of Ireland couldn't save you from me."

Then Fergus was given his sword, and Ailill said, "Take your sword…"

Ailill chants a poem encouraging Fergus not to use his sword on the men of Ireland, and Fergus chants a greeting in praise of his sword and promises not to. Then the passage about the war-goddesses Badb, Bé Néit, and Nemain killing a hundred men during the night is repeated verbatim.

Then Fergus grabbed his weapons and headed into battle. Wielding his sword two-handed, he cleared a path for a hundred men through the enemy lines. Then Maeve grabbed her weapons and rushed into battle. Three times she triumphed, until a hedge of spears drove her back.

"I can't tell who's beating us to the north," Conchobor said to his entourage. "Keep fighting here while I go confront him."

"We'll hold this position," said the warriors. "Unless the ground breaks under us or the sky comes crashing down on us, we won't budge from here."

Then Conchobor went to face Fergus. He raised his shield against him, that is, the Ócháin, Conchobor's personal shield. It had four gold corners and four gold coverings. Fergus hit it three times but couldn't drive even the upper rim of the shield back onto Conchobor's head.

"Which Ulsterman is holding up this shield?" said Fergus.

"Someone better than you," said Conchobor, "who drove you into exile with the wolves and foxes, and will hold you off by force of arms while the men of Ireland watch."

Then Fergus aimed a two-handed avenging blow at Conchobor: the tip of his sword touched the ground behind him as he swung it back.

1 *said to his charioteer* We were told earlier, in one of the inconsistencies that characterizes Recension 1, that Cuillius was killed. Recension 2 specifies that Ailill's charioteer is now Fer Loga, who was his charioteer in "The Story of Mac Dá Thó's Pig."

Cormac Conn Loinges grabbed him and held back his arm with both hands.

"This is madness, madness I tell you, Uncle* Fergus!" said Cormac. "There's such a thing as being too paranoid. Friendship turns to hostility. You have no more friends here, only enemies.[1] These blows you strike are wicked, Uncle Fergus."

"I ask you," said Fergus, "whom am I to strike?"

"Attack those three hills up there. Turn aside and lash out wherever. Pay these men no heed. Remember the honor of Ulster which has not been lost. It won't be lost, not unless it's by your fault today.

"And go somewhere else, Conchobor," Cormac told his father. "Fergus will stop venting his rage on the Ulstermen here."

Fergus turned away. He killed a hundred Ulster warriors in his first onslaught until he ran into Conall Cernach.

"That's too much violence to inflict on your own people," said Conall, "just because a slut has a nice ass."

"Tell me, what should I do, true warrior?"

"Attack the hills over there and the woods around them," said Conall Cernach.

So Fergus slashed at the hills. With three blows he cut the tops off the three hills now called the Shorn Ones of Meath (*Máela Midi*).

Meanwhile, Cú Chulainn heard Fergus striking the hills, or Conchobor's shield.

"Who is striking those almighty blows in the distance?" said Cú Chulainn. "Gore chokes the heart. Rage ruins the world. It shakes up the hoops covering my wounds."[2]

Lóeg answered and said: "The one striking those blows is the pick of manhood, fearless Fergus mac Roích. Bloodshed, the death toll rising: that's Fergus for you. Because of his sword hidden in the chariot-pole, my lord Conchobor's chariot troops didn't make it to the great battle."

---

1 *There's such ... only enemies* O'Rahilly's translation: "That's a cautiousness that overreaches itself! Friendship proves hostile. Behold your enemies. Your friends have been destroyed."

2 *shakes up ... my wounds* The Irish is *Doscara trait túaga.* O'Rahilly has "Quickly it loosens the dressings of my wounds." The *túaga* are not the dressings but the wooden hoops that keep Cú Chulainn's clothes from sticking to his wounds; they powerfully fly off him a few sentences later.

Then Cú Chulainn said: "Hurry and take the hoops off my wounds. Men are drenched in blood. There will be swordplay. Men's days will be cut short."

The plugs of dry grass shot out of his wounds, sailing through the air as high as a lark, and the wooden hoops shot off him all the way to the Plain of Hoops (*Mag Túag*) in Connacht. They flew out of him every which way. His wounds made him convulse, and he slammed together the heads of the two slave-women[1] so that they were gray all over with each other's brains. Maeve had sent those women to get him to reopen his wounds: they'd been crying fake tears over him, telling him the Ulstermen had been defeated and Fergus had fallen in the thick of battle because Cú Chulainn hadn't joined in.

Cú Chulainn mutated,* and put on the twenty-seven shirts he used to wear, tied down with ropes and cords, to go into battle. He picked up his chariot—the frame and both wheels—and carried it on his back[2] as he went around the battlefield looking for Fergus.

"Over here, Uncle* Fergus!" said Cú Chulainn. He called three times but Fergus didn't answer. "I swear* by the god that Ulstermen swear by," said Cú Chulainn, "I'll scrub you the way flax-tops are scutched in a pool. I'll loom over you like the tail looms over a cat. I'll smack you like a doting mother spanks her son."

"What man in Ireland dares talk to me that way?"

"Cú Chulainn son of Súaltaim, and sister's-son* of Conchobor," said Cú Chulainn. "Now stand down."

"I did promise to do that," said Fergus.

"Then get away from me," said Cú Chulainn.

"Fine," said Fergus. "You stood down for me when you were riddled with wounds."

Then Fergus took his division out of the battle. Then the Gaileóin and the Munstermen left, which meant that the nine divisions of Ailill and Maeve and their seven sons were the only ones still fighting.

---

1 *the two slave-women* Recension 2 makes these two female satirists.*

2 *carried it on his back* This has been interpreted as Cú Chulainn hitching himself to the chariot, which would put him in the role of an animal, or as forming a kind of human-chariot hybrid like Cethern, a literal war machine or cyborg. See Aled Llion Jones, "Two by two: the doubled chariot-figure of *Táin Bó Cúailnge*," in *Ollam*, 19–34.

It was noon when Cú Chulainn entered the battle. As the sun went down behind the fringe of the forest, he defeated the last of the warbands, and all that was left of his chariot was a handful of ribs from the framework and a handful of spokes round the wheel.

Cú Chulainn came across Maeve leaving the battle.

"Spare me!"[1] said Maeve.

"It would serve you right if I killed you," said Cú Chulainn, but he spared her because he didn't use to kill women.

Cú Chulainn escorted the Connachtmen west to the river at Loin Ford[2] (*Áth Luain*), and made sure they crossed. He struck three blows with his sword down to the bedrock. Those are called the Three Bare Places of Loin Ford.

A corresponding part of Recension 2:

> Then Maeve covered the men of Ireland's retreat. She sent the Brown Bull, along with fifty of his heifers and eight of her attendants, around to Crúachu. Whoever did or didn't make it back, at least the Brown Bull would get there like she promised.
>
> Then Maeve got her period, and she said: "Fergus, cover the men of Ireland's retreat while I take a piss."[3]

---

1 *Spare me!* Patricia Kelly ("The *Táin* as literature," 82) cites *GEIL*, 212–13, to the effect that "pleading for quarter" is considered legal evidence that one party to a duel is in the wrong, and argues further that by not killing Maeve, Cú Chulainn may be acting consistently with early Irish Christian law-codes but "is simultaneously withholding acknowledgement of her as a legitimate participant in the battle, on the grounds of her sex."

2 *Loin Ford* Now Athlone, on the river Shannon on the border of Counties Westmeath and Roscommon; the "Loin Ford" etymology follows below. Compare the interestingly different account in Gwynn, *The Metrical Dindshenchas*,* Part III, 366–75, at https://celt.ucc.ie/published/T106500C.html.

3 *got her period … take a piss* This whole passage looks like an instance of "men writing women badly," and has been translated accordingly, but it presents some challenges. The key phrase in Irish is *a fúal fola*, which O'Rahilly translates "her issue of blood." Maeve then asks Fergus to take over *goro síblur-sa m'fúal úaim*, which O'Rahilly translates "that I may pass my water." On its own, *fúal* has the primary meaning "urine" and a secondary meaning "water (foul water, a puddle?)" (see *eDIL*, s.v. *1 fúal*). (Celtchar's persistent bladder problem in "The Story of Mac Dá Thó's Pig" is a *galar fúaile* 'sickness of the *fúal*.') *Fúal fola*, "*fúal* of blood," obviously refers to menstruation. What is not clear is how to interpret the other instances of *fúal* in this passage, unaccompanied by *fola*, in

"By my conscience," said Fergus, "this is terrible timing, and completely inappropriate."

"I can't help it," said Maeve. "I won't survive unless I take a piss."

So Fergus came and covered the men of Ireland's retreat. Maeve pissed until she made three trenches big enough for a household. Hence the place is called Maeve's Urinal (*Fúal Medba*).

Cú Chulainn came along while she was busy with this and didn't injure her: he wouldn't strike her from behind.

"Do me a favor today, Cú Chulainn," said Maeve.

"What's the favor?" said Cú Chulainn.

"Take this army under your patronage and protection* until they've gone west past the Great Ford (*Áth Mór*)."

"Granted," said Cú Chulainn. Cú Chulainn came around the men of Ireland and covered their retreat on one side, protecting them. The three-man squads on the duty roster covered the other side. Maeve came back into position and covered the rear, and that was how they escorted the men of Ireland west across the Great Ford.

Then Cú Chulainn took possession of his sword and cut the tops off the Three Bare Places of Loin Ford in response to the three Shorn Ones of Meath.

---

terms of (i) what the early Irish author understood to be involved in menstruation, hence what exactly is supposed to be filling the trenches; (ii) what Maeve thinks she is saying to Fergus; and (iii) what Fergus understands her to be saying. Since she uses only *fúal* and not *fúal fola* to Fergus, then (iii) Fergus probably thinks that Maeve is saying that she needs to urinate, and (ii) Maeve seems to want him to think that, whether or not (i) she herself, or the author, realizes that there might be a difference between the fluids she might feel pressure to expel. Patrica Kelly notes further that "the Old Irish term for menstruation is *galar místae*, 'monthly sickness'. This too points up M[aeve]'s failure on the battle-field, for another sign of 'the falsehood of [one party in] a duel' is to suffer an attack of illness (*galar*) after coming onto the field of combat" ("The *Táin* as literature," 82, citing *GEIL*, 212–13). But others have read this episode in other ways, e.g., contrasting Maeve's natural bloodshed with the blood of warriors shed by Cú Chulainn, both marking the landscape. For more on this episode, see Edel, *Inside the Táin*, 292–98; Künzler, *Flesh and Word*, 395–404; and Toner, "Reading the *Táin* from back to front," 70–77; and for a broader discussion focusing on slightly later sources, see Sharon Arbuthnot, "The medieval Irish vocabulary of sex and reproduction," *Kelten* 89 (2021), https://kelten.vanhamel.nl/k89-2021-arbuthnot-irish-literature-medieval-medicine.

With the army now in full retreat, Maeve said to Fergus, "Oh, Fergus, what a shitshow."[1]

"That's what usually happens to a herd of horses led by a mare.[2] They're so far up the ass of the woman[3] who misled them, they get taken for all they're worth."

In the morning after the battle, the Brown Bull was taken away to face the bull Finnbennach at Tarbga on Aí Plain. (Tarbga means "bull-sorrow" or "bull-battle." It was a hill previously named Roí Dedond.) Everyone who had survived the battle did nothing but watch the two bulls fight.

Bricriu Poisontongue had been recuperating in Connacht after Fergus had fractured his skull with *fidchell**-pieces.[4] The two bulls

---

1 *What a shitshow* This is a loose translation of what she says, which is "*Correcad lochta & fulachta* here today, Fergus." There is serious disagreement about the meaning, beyond the obvious that Maeve is unhappy with the outcome of the battle. Options include "Men and lesser men meet here today" (Cecile O'Rahilly); "Camp confusions have come on us here today" (Ann Dooley); "The pot was stirred, Fergus, and today a mess was made" (Ciarán Carson, following Dooley); "We have had shame and shambles here today, Fergus" (Thomas Kinsella); "The proof of the pudding is in the eating" (Doris Edel). See Toner, "Reading the *Táin* from back to front," 75–77, and most recently Wolfgang Meid, "Varia IV. *Táin bó Cúailnge*: the final verbal exchange between Medb and Fergus," *Éigse* 41 (2021) 260–67. Meid's reading, "Good ones and not so good ones have been fighting each other today," is consistent with O'Rahilly's. He proposes that Maeve is too proud to openly admit defeat: if so, her comment would mean something like (my paraphrase) "Now we see who are the better men," without actually saying which those are but implicitly finding fault with Fergus; then Fergus responds to the reality of the defeat, blaming Maeve for not putting a man in charge and also for his own failures at being that man, since his sexual attraction to her confused him about picking a side.

2 *led by a mare* Toner, 76n25, points to a study by Konstanze Krueger et al., "Movement initiation in groups of feral horses," *Behavioural Processes* 103 (2014) 91–101, which finds that whereas forming a herd "is exclusive to alpha males," mares can sometimes initiate herd movements; so, for what it's worth, Fergus isn't referring to something that never happens in nature. But, as Patricia Kelly puts it, "the implication is that a 'stallion' would have been a more suitable choice of leader, and Fergus's patronymic mac Roeich 'son of great horse' marks him out as an ideal candidate" ("The *Táin* as literature," 79).

3 *the ass of the woman* The various references to *tóin mná*, "a woman's ass" or "chasing tail" (here and on pp. 280 and 231 above) intersect with a usage of the same phrase "in a legal context which lists the kinds of men whose honour price is dependent on their wives. One of these is [...] 'a man who follows his wife's buttocks across a boundary,' i.e., a man who marries a woman from outside the *túath*. This is a dishonourable union, as normally a woman's honour price is assessed as half that of her husband" (Patricia Kelly, "The *Táin* as literature," 80, citing T.M. Charles-Edwards, "The social background to Irish *peregrinatio*," *Celtica* 11 [1976] 43–59, at 47).

4 *after Fergus ... fidchell-pieces* This event is described in "Nera's Adventure" (see p. 154

ran over Bricriu as they clashed, and he died from it. That is "The Death of Bricriu."

The Brown Bull impaled his leg on the other bull's horn. He went a day and a night without pulling it off, until Fergus harangued him and smacked him on the flank with a stick.

"What a disgrace," he said. "Were you brought here to dishonor your clan and your species, you scrappy old calf, after so many died for you?"

Then the Brown Bull yanked his leg away and broke it in the process, but his opponent's horn popped off onto the mountain beside him, which is still called Horn Mountain (*Slíab n-Adarca*). Then he hoisted up Finnbennach for a day and a night, and plunged into the lake beside Crúachu. He came out with his opponent's loin and shoulder-blade and liver dangling from his horns.

The Connachtmen formed a mob to kill him, but Fergus wouldn't allow it, and said to let him go wherever he felt like going. Then the bull headed home to Ulster. On the way he took a drink at Whiteshoulder (*Finnléithe*), where he dropped the shoulder-blade; the place was named Whiteshoulder as a result. He took another drink at the Loin Ford (*Áth Lúain*), where he dropped his opponent's loin. That's where we get Loin Ford. At Irard Cuilenn he bellowed, and was heard all over Ulster. He took a drink at Liverland (*Troma*), where his opponent's liver fell off his horns—that's where we get Liverland. He went on to Bull's Brow (*Taul Tairb*) and rested his forehead against the hill at the Ford of Two Barrows (*Áth Dá Fherta*). That's where we get Bull's Brow on Muirthemne Plain. Then he went up the Midlúachair Road to Cuib—Cuib was where he used to hang out with Dáire's dry cows*—and pawed up a trench. That's where we get Trench Field (*Gort mBúraig*). Then he went on until he dropped dead at Bull Ridge (*Druim Tairb*) on the border of Ulster and Uí Echach. Hence the name Bull Ridge.

Ailill and Maeve made peace with the Ulstermen and Cú Chulainn. For the next seven years, no one in Ireland was killed as a result of their feud. The Connachtmen went home, leaving Finnabair

above): Bricriu made fun of Fergus's singing by comparing it to a bellowing calf, and Fergus reacted violently.

with Cú Chulainn,[1] and the Ulstermen went back to Emain Macha in triumph. *Finit.* Amen.[2]

Recension 2 ends like this. The Brown Bull has been traveling around Ireland with the disintegrating corpse of Finnbennach, and then:

He tossed his head violently and shook off the Finnbennach over Ireland. He threw his thigh to Waterford (*Port Láirge*). He threw his ribcage to Dublin, known as "The Ford of the Hurdles" (*Áth Cliath*). After that he faced north, recognized the land of Cúailnge, and headed for it.

There were women and boys and children there, crying over the Brown Bull. They saw the brow of the Brown Bull coming towards them: "Here comes a bull's brow!" they said. Hence the name Bull's Brow (*Taul Tairb*) ever since.

Then the Brown Bull attacked the women and boys and children of Cúailnge and wreaked slaughter on them.

Afterwards he turned his back to the hill and his heart broke like a nut in his chest.[3]

This concludes the account and the story and the ending of the *Táin*.

A blessing on everyone who faithfully memorizes the *Táin* as is, and doesn't add any other form to it.

---

1 *leaving Finnabair with Cú Chulainn* Another inconsistency: earlier it was said that Finnabair died after the Glennamain Massacre. "This last paragraph in which the death of Finnabair is ignored is purely a scribal addendum," notes O'Rahilly.

2 See https://www.isos.dias.ie/TCD/TCD_MS_1318.html#419 for the end of the text in the Yellow Book of Lecan, just above the big initial B which begins *Táin bó Dartada* (see p. 155 above).

3 *broke ... chest* The Stowe version finishes this off with "he threw up his heart in a black gush of blood from his mouth." For other examples of the "nut" expression, see Liam Mac Mathúna, "Lexical and literary aspects of 'heart' in Irish," *Ériu* 53 (2003) 1–18. It is otherwise used for emotional heartbreak, which suggests that the bull is overcome with remorse at the killing he did on his rampage, as opposed to just dying of overexertion. McLaughlin, "Text run-over imagery," 99, notes the drawing in the bottom margin at https://www.isos.dias.ie/TCD/TCD_MS_1339.html#104: "There may be a thematic connection between this image of a warrior, seemingly in flight, and the description of the charging bull. It may also be significant that such a distinctive symbol is found at the end of one of the most important early Irish sagas."

Then, in Latin:[1]

But I, who have copied this history (*historia*) or, more accurately, this tale (*fabula*[2]), give no credence to some of the things in this history or tale. Because, in fact, some of the things in it are the illusions of demons, while some are poetic figments. Some are realistic. Some are not. Some are for the amusement of idiots.

1 This Latin colophon (concluding statement) is specific to the Book of Leinster: see it at the URL in the previous note. Pádraig Ó Néill, "The Latin colophon to the 'Táin bó Cúailnge' in the Book of Leinster: a critical view of Old Irish literature," *Celtica* 23 (1999) 269–75, argues that this desire to "subject the *Táin* to the rigorous criteria of Christian historiography and rhetoric [...] betrays a new, critical, attitude towards native Irish literature, one which presages the end of the compact between the two learned classes of native *filid* [poets*] and monastic *literati*. The explanation for this change almost certainly is to be sought in the ecclesiastical reforms, especially the introduction of foreign religious orders, which were being effected in the Irish Church during the second half of the twelfth century."

2 *fabula* This word is the origin of English *fable*, but it means a work of folklore, myth, or literary fiction rather than a story with a moral. In the tradition of Plato's *Timaeus* and Macrobius' *Commentary on the Dream of Scipio*, a medieval Christian might be trained to plumb a pagan *fabula* for underlying truth. Importantly, this colophon discounts *some* of the things reported in the *Táin*, not *all*.

Aftermath

The Táin*'s immediate aftermath is represented by "The Battle of Rosnaree on the Boyne" (*Cath Ruis na Ríg for Bóinn, *Ó Corráin #1021, second half of the twelfth century),*[1] *which appears with Recension 2 of the* Táin *in the Book of Leinster. Depressed and outraged by the attack on his territory, Conchobor wants to launch a revenge expedition in the winter following the* Táin. *Cathbad convinces him to wait for spring, and in the meantime Conchobor rallies his network of allies. These include Scandinavians from Norway, the Shetland Islands, the Orkney Islands, the Faroe Islands, and the Western Isles of Scotland, where Conall Cernach, as in "The Wooing of Emer," has been off collecting tribute. In this text, rather than being with Fergus and the Ulster exiles, Conall is still on Conchobor's side, and says that if he had known about the invasion, he would already have taken revenge in full. The Scandinavians land in Ireland and the Ulstermen welcome them with feasts.*

Meanwhile, a proposal comes to Ailill and Maeve from their Munster allies to offer reparations to Ulster—1:1 replacement of all buildings and livestock destroyed or taken during the Táin *invasion, and payment in gold to Conchobor himself—if Conchobor will agree not to attack any of the men of Ireland. Maeve is totally opposed to this, but Ailill (assuming her objection is to Connacht footing the entire bill) says that since four provinces of Ireland were involved in the attack on Ulster, all four provinces should share the cost, and Maeve agrees to that. The proposal is sent to Ailill's brothers Finn, King of Leinster, and Cairbre Nia Fer, King of Tara, and their messengers present it to Conchobor. Conchobor rejects it, saying he will agree to no settlement until he has camped everywhere in Ireland, in other words until he has conquered the whole island. He starts by marching south to attack Finn and Cairbre, and fights the titular battle of Rosnaree on the Boyne against the two of them. Conall saves the Ulstermen from being defeated, and Cú Chulainn kills Cairbre. Finn retreats back to Leinster. Cairbre's son Erc (who is also Conchobor's grandson, since his mother was Conchobor's daughter Fedelm, and was on Conchobor's side in the* Táin*) submits to Conchobor, and is allowed to keep control of Tara and Meath under Conchobor's overlordship.*

Patrick Wadden comments that the reader who was expecting a

1 Edited and translated by Edmund Hogan, *Cath Ruis na Ríg for Bóinn* (Dublin: Royal Irish Academy, Todd Lecture Series 4, 1892), at https://archive.org/details/toddlectureserie04royauoft/page/2/mode/2up.

rematch between Ulster and Connacht "cannot help but feel unfulfilled, even cheated" by what happens here, but explains that with the Scandinavian involvement and Ulster's domination of the midlands, this text is reflecting twelfth-century political conditions.[1]

Erc makes peace with Cú Chulainn by marrying his daughter Fínscoth,[2] *but this peace is only temporary: see "The Death of Cú Chulainn," below.*

1 Patrick Wadden, "*Cath Ruis na Ríg for Bóinn*: history and literature in twelfth-century Ireland," *Aiste* 4 (2014) 11–44.

2 See Leenane, "The role of Cú Chulainn," 181–83, 267–68. Fínscoth is not well attested (one text calls her a daughter of Conchobor), and, other than Connla from "The Death of Aífe's Only Son," the various children who come to be attributed to Cú Chulainn "might be invented or reflect otherwise undocumented traditions or later developing ones" (267).

The Death of Cú Chulainn

This is an eighth-century text (Ó Corráin #960) variously referred to as Aided Con Culainn, *"The Death of Cú Chulainn," and* Brislech Mór Maige Muirthemni, *"The Great Breach/Rout/Defeat on Muirthemne Plain" (the same title as the episode of the* Táin *that is otherwise referred to as the Sixfold Slaughter, but obviously referring to a different battle). Except for the first short section, it appears with Recension 2 of the* Táin *in the Book of Leinster.*

Cú Chulainn's antagonists in this tale are Lugaid mac Con Roí, Erc mac Cairpri, and the children of Calatín. They are making war on Cú Chulainn to avenge their fathers. In Emer's final lament, she says their preparations took 16 years: that would make Cú Chulainn around 33 at this point, which (probably not coincidentally) is the age of Jesus at his crucifixion.

Lugaid is the son of the Munster hero Cú Roí mac Dáiri. How Cú Chulainn killed his father is told in the eighth-century text "The Death of Cú Roí."[1]

Erc mac Cairpri is the son of Cairbre Nia Fer. As a boy, he featured in Mac Roth's report on the Ulster troops before the final battle in the Táin (p. 276). *How Cú Chulainn killed his father is told in "The Battle of Rosnaree" (see p. 291).*

The children of Calatín are sextuplets, three boys and three girls, who were born posthumously to Calatín Dána, one of Cú Chulainn's opponents in the Táin (p. 250). *They were raised by their mother to seek revenge.*

Bettina Kimpton says that this tale "emphasizes the importance of social bonds, calls attention to the ambivalent value of war, promotes the idea of unity, and connects the representation of Cú Chulainn with that of Christ. By these means, the theme of vengeance is balanced in the text by that of social reciprocity and cohesion, and is transformed into an expression of Christian salvation."

Conchobor is mentioned in this text but doesn't play an active role.

---

1 *Aided Chon Roí,* Ó Corráin #962 (first half of the 8th century with later reworking), edited and translated by R.I. Best, "The tragic death of Cúrói mac Dári," *Ériu* 2 (1905) 18–35, at https://archive.org/details/riujournalschoooacadgoog/page/n32/mode/2up. See also "*Amra Con Roí* (*ACR*): discussion, edition, translation" by P.L. Henry, *Études Celtiques* 31 (1995) 179–94, at https://www.persee.fr/doc/ecelt_0373-1928_1995_num_31_1_2069.

Why that is might be explained by "The Death of Conchobor," below, which says that Conchobor was convalescent for 7 years before he died.

This translation uses the Irish edited by Bettina Kimpton in The Death of Cú Chulainn: A Critical Edition of the Earliest Version of *Brislech Mór Maige Muirthemni* with Introduction, Translation, Notes, Bibliography and Vocabulary *(Maynooth: School of Celtic Studies, NUI Maynooth, 2009).*[1] *The beginning of the text is messy since the first part is missing from the Book of Leinster: Kimpton supplies some of it from Trinity College Dublin manuscript H.3.18.*

The sons of Calatín[2] studied druid* magic, and strategy (i.e., warfare[3]), and great destruction, and attraction spells.

The daughters of Calatín studied occult knowledge, and lore, and sorcery (i.e., witchcraft).

And their mother blinded them all, making them purblind (i.e., fully blind or blind in one eye).

This was to increase their ferocity (i.e., their pain or longing) to avenge their father with the craft they had learned.

"Well, it wasn't child's play for my father to mess with (i.e., to attack or assault) Cú Chulainn; probably (i.e., definitely) it won't be child's play for me if I try it, either."

"And when will we go after him?" said Erc.

"That's easy:* not until we make three weapons (i.e., three pieces of equipment) to use against him," said the sons of Calatín, "which is a matter (i.e., work or study) of seven days."

"Then it's time," said Erc and Lugaid, "for us to rally the men of Ireland."

"Not yet," said the sons of Calatín, "because this matter of seven days (i.e., seven days' work) is actually a matter of seven years": one

1 There is an earlier translation by Maria Tymoczko in *Two Death Tales from the Ulster Cycle* (Dublin: Dolmen Press, 1981). Other translations—John Carey's in *The Celtic Heroic Age*, 134–43, and Patrick Brown's—skip the poetry. The text in van Hamel, *Compert Con Culainn and Other Stories*, 69–133, is a later version, not the same as Kimpton's.

2 *of Calatín* Added for clarity, along with "of Calatín" in the next sentence, and "their mother" after that (the manuscript says only "she"; very seldom this "she" has been interpreted as Maeve).

3 These parenthetical remarks are the text's own glosses in H.3.18.

day a year[1] was spent making the spears. After that, Maine, a venomous man, was the one who assembled and ground (i.e., honed or sharpened) them.

The Ulstermen issued an order (i.e., a proclamation) advising Cú Chulainn not to leave Emain Macha without an escort.

"Cú Chulainn will attack: watch out for him."

The Book of Leinster text seems to pick up immediately after this, as Cú Chulainn objects to being kept home:

"... I haven't let the weeping of women and boys get to me until today." Then the fifty queens advanced and bared their breasts at him. They were the ones who had come up with the idea of baring women's breasts in the first place, i.e., during his Boyhood Deeds, holding back Cú Chulainn at Emain. And they didn't let him go into battle that day.

"I see your attraction spell has failed to bring Cú Chulainn here today, sons of Calatín,"[2] said Lugaid. "It's a long time to make men wait here after they came all the way from Munster.[3] This attraction idea of yours is bad. It will be a long time till Cú Chulainn comes."

"We'll bring him here tomorrow."

The next day, the children of Calatín conjured up armies around Emain Macha so that the whole place seemed to be burning up in one big cloud of smoke, and the Ulster armies were overwhelmed,[4] and the weapons fell off their racks. Cú Chulainn got the bad news.

---

1 *one day a year* The Fourth Branch of the *Mabinogi*, from medieval Wales, involves a similar restriction on the making of a spear, only during Mass on Sundays: see Boyd, *The Four Branches*, 86–87.

2 *sons of Calatín* The Irish uses different words for "sons of Calatín" (*a maccu Calatín*, here) and "children of Calatín" (*clann Chalatín*, below). It seems the attraction spell is a specialty of the sons, as are the specially-prepared spears that feature later, while all of them are involved in conjuring the illusions around Emain Macha, and the sisters appear as the dog-cooking witches.

3 *all the way from Munster* The specific placenames have been distilled for clarity. It literally says "It has been a long time to be at Béolu Menbolg for the man who is here from Dún Chermnai, and from Belach Con Glais, and from Temair Lóchra, and from Combur Tri nUisce" (Kimpton). The listed places are all in the southwestern province of Munster.

4 *the Ulster armies were overwhelmed* Kimpton's literal rendering of the Irish is "so that Emuin Macha was overthrown to the detriment of the hosts." The text doesn't say here that the *ces noínden* paralysis kicks in, but it clearly does: when [continued ...]

Then Leborcham[1] said:

"Up you get, Cú Chulainn, off you go.
Save Muirthemne Plain from the Leinstermen.
Well-raised child of Lug,
turn to your heroic battle-feats.
Cú Chulainn, off you go,
and repulse
the invasion of Muirthemne.
Mighty omens: warriors bound for battle.
Don't let yourself be outdone by Cormac,
the rallying-point away from Conchobor:
you and Conall aren't close,
because you don't support Cormac.[2]
It's not filial piety[3]
that drives Lugaid, with his grand alliance,
to kill you in revenge for what you did.
Equip yourself, you glorious brawler,
grandson of Cathbad, and off you go. Up you get."[4]

Cú Chulainn is dead, the text says the Ulstermen are still shaking it off. The magical armies are probably only illusions accompanied by an illusion of burning. The King Cycle tale "The death of Muirchertach mac Erca" (*Aided Muirchertaig meic Erca*, Ó Corráin #978, second half of the 12th century), translated by Whitley Stokes in *Revue Celtique* 23 (1902) 395–437 (https://archive.org/details/revueceltiqu23pari/page/395/mode/2up), seems like a useful parallel: in that, armies are conjured out of stones and turf for Muirchertach to fight, but others see him attacking only the ground (409–15).

1 *Leborcham* This seems to be the same character as Deirdre's friend the female satirist in "The Exile of the Sons of Uisliu."

2 *Cormac* Kimpton, who translates "Let not Cormac overcome you, who is invoked far from Conchobar. You are not near to Conall, for you do not accept Cormac," doesn't identify Cormac. I take it that this is Cormac Conn Loinges, son of Conchobor, the nominal leader of the Ulster exiles in Connacht. Conall Cernach is with him according to the *Táin*.

3 *not filial piety* This translation follows Kimpton: the word here (see *eDIL*, s.v. *2 goire*) has the specific sense of filial piety and a son's legal obligation to care for his (foster-) parents; it can also have a broader sense of 'piety,' 'dutifulness,' 'service,' and such. If it's being used here in the narrow sense, the point could be that Lugaid, although he is there to avenge his father, is motivated more by bloodlust and ambition than by duty, so he would not, for example, accept compensation in lieu of pursuing his vengeance.

4 *Up you get* This way of closing a poem by quoting the words it starts with is, when it isn't built into the poem (a technique called *dúnad*, "closing"), a way to mark the end in manuscripts that may not use line-breaks.

Then Cú Chulainn said:

"Lay off me, woman.
I'm not the only beneficiary of Conchobor's province.
The enemy may be tough, but I won't fight alone:
it's a bad call to exhaust myself on top of exhaustion.
I'm not a warrior who's eager and hungry for battle today."

Then Niab, Celtchar's daughter, Conall Cernach's wife, said:

"That's as it should be, as far as you're concerned,
Cú Chulainn.
Conall's chariot won't protect you.
Handsome, perfect Conall
is out there sacrificing for Ulster,
in muddy fords,
lamb-headed,[1]
wherever you see him,
because you've given up fighting.
Nothing counts as a great deed
beside the great circuit
of Amairgen's son."[2]

---

1 *lamb-headed* The Irish clearly says this, but it's less clear what it means. Kimpton points out the parallel to Nad Crantail's comment on Cú Chulainn's beardlessness in the *Táin*: "I'd sooner take a little lamb's head back to camp with me," p. 222 above. In "The Intoxication of the Ulstermen," the Ulster heroes travel with a character named Úanchenn ('Lamb-Head'), an incredibly violent eleven-year-old boy who has to be restrained by 77 men with chains. This seems to correspond to Cú Chulainn's own potential for violence in the Boyhood Deeds: see Boyd, "From king to warrior in *Mesca Ulad*," 71–72. I presented on this issue of "lamb-headed" at the 2023 meeting of the Celtic Studies Association of North America, finding various other parallels. My proposal was ultimately that the expression is used for a hero who is self-sacrificing on behalf of his people, even if it could also just refer to curly hair.

2 *Amairgen's son* Conall. Niab (pronounced "neev") is trying to promote Conall's reputation at Cú Chulainn's expense, which is a lot like the women's word-battle in "Bricriu's Feast." She seems to be arguing that even though Conall is away in exile, he is still actively fighting for Ulster's interests—perhaps she even thinks of them as Ulster's *real* interests, separate from Conchobor's.

"Really, woman," said Cú Chulainn. "I might be doomed, but I still have no equal. I'll preserve my honor. No one is going to do my fighting for me. I'm not avoiding my death."

Then Cú Chulainn leapt for his weapons. And he put on a cloak, which came undone and made him drop his brooch. Then Cú Chulainn said:

> "I don't hold it against the cloak
> for giving me a warning.
> I *do* hold it against the brooch
> for stabbing me,
> and making me lose my grip
> on the sharp-edged shield
> that will scatter the enemy,
> making it land on my foot.[1]
> I'll die soon, of an untimely wound
> that will be inflicted on me by the best of men.
> South of Muirthemne Plain, they'll be
> wailing out of pity when I'm gone."

Then he put on his cloak, and picked up his shield with its scalloped edge. And he said to Lóeg mac Riangabra, "Harness the chariot for us, my dear* Lóeg."

"I swear* by the god my people swear by," said Lóeg, "if everyone in Conchobor's province came to pitch in, they couldn't drag Líath Macha to the chariot. He's never gone against you before today. He's not being his usual delightful self with me. Come talk to Líath yourself, if you like."

Cú Chulainn went to him. And the horse turned his left side to him three times. And the Morrígan had sabotaged the chariot the

---

1 *I don't hold it … my foot* This is the best sense I can make of the Irish, which Kimpton translates as "The mantle which brings a warning is not a culprit. The brooch which wounds the flesh is a culprit, so that the shield before which spoils/warriors will be scattered falls through the foot by a separation of the sharp edge from my right fist." Patrick Brown has Cú Chulainn say "This cloak is not my enemy […] Nor is the brooch that pierces my foot. It's giving me a warning. Shields will be shattered, blades broken before my right fist." This is attractive, but the contrast between *Ni bidba bratt* (the cloak is not to blame) and *Is bidba delg* (the brooch *is* to blame) seems clear. The brooch would have been of the penannular or pseudo-penannular type, with a long spike of a pin that could plausibly cause injury.

night before, because she didn't want Cú Chulainn going into battle—she knew he would never make it back to Emain Macha. Then Cú Chulainn said to Líath Macha:

"It isn't normal, Líath,
for your left side to be to me.
That's a fierce challenge you're putting up—
and the penalty for that is death.[1]
I can't take my mind back
to the open plains
where we used to ride for days.
Now the chariot's coming apart:
long red reins,
horse and wheel,
frame and yoke,
and the seat where I always sat.
Badb has favored us,[2]
here in Emain Macha. It isn't normal."

Then Líath Macha came and dropped big swelling tears of blood at Cú Chulainn's feet.

Cú Chulainn jumped into the chariot and raced south along the Midlúachair Road. He saw a woman up ahead: Leborcham, daughter of the slaves Auae and Adarc, who was part of Concobor's household.

Then Leborcham said:

"Don't leave us, don't leave us, Cú Chulainn.
Your face is honorable.
Your cheek is noble.[3]

---

1 *death* Rather than intending to kill the horse himself, Cú Chulainn seems to realize from its behavior that it too is fated to die.

2 *Badb has favored us* Badb ("BATH-uv," with voiced *th*), which also means "carrion crow," is another name or aspect of the war-goddess. (Cú Chulainn encounters her in this form in the Boyhood Deeds, pp. 184–85, when he rescues Conchobor from the battlefield) Cú Chulainn's comment here could be sarcastic, since the war-goddess's "friendly" gesture was to damage his chariot, or an expression of legitimate surprise that she is trying to protect him, given how antagonistic she was towards him in the *Táin*.

3 *Your face ... noble* The point here is not just that Cú Chulainn is too [continued ...]

Your suffering face
is handsome and glowing.
If it's your fate to be destroyed,
are we not supposed to mourn?
Woe to our women!
Woe to our sons!
Woe to our hopes!
We will always lament you.
But you will march
regally on to the battle,
where noble ones will die.
There'll be wailing on Muirthemne Plain
when you are gone."

And the 150 women in Emain Macha joined in loudly to say the same.

"It would be better not to leave them," said Lóeg, "because you've never gone against the wishes of the women on your mother's side before today."

"No, I really haven't," said Cú Chulainn.

"Suck it up and leave, Lóeg.
A charioteer accepts.
A warrior protects.
A hero makes the tough calls.[1]
Men are about manliness.
Women are about wimpishness.

Take us forward to battle. Don't let people feel sorry for you if it doesn't help."

---

handsome to die; relying on the semantic linkages between honor and the face or cheeks in Old Irish, she seems to be saying that in spite of Niab's comments, his "face" (his honor) is intact, so he doesn't need to go fight to defend it.

1 *makes the tough calls* Kimpton translates this "with a champion, advising (*comairle*)," but *comairle* can mean 'decision, resolution,' 'handling, management,' and 'sagacity, prudence' as well as 'advice, counsel, admonition' (*eDIL*). It fits the context better for Cú Chulainn to say that being a champion or hero (*cuinnid*) is about relying on one's own judgment rather than giving or taking advice, since he is explicitly refusing to take advice from the women or Lóeg.

The chariot veered away to the right. And the women screamed and howled and clapped their hands with grief. They knew he'd never come back to Emain Macha.

The living words of Cú Chulainn on the day he died:

Cú Chulainn utters a portentous and challenging poem, which makes sense in an impressionistic way but isn't easy to translate word-for-word, although Kimpton makes the best of it (38). These are his "living words" as opposed to his "ghost words" spoken after his death. Cú Chulainn says that the women are sad for him, and many Ulstermen will mourn him. Witches, blind in their left eyes, will initiate his death. In his single chariot, he will charge the enemy three times in defense of Ulster. No one will weep over that because they won't be there to see it. His enemies will violate fair play and gang up on him in pursuit of their revenge. He will ask his horse to help him defeat satirists,* and cleanse Muirthemne Plain of the aspersions that they try to cast on him. He will be wounded in the belly, and drink from a refreshing stream before a marvelous feeling clouds his pain. The end of the poem predicts the coming of the Antichrist and the Last Judgment, and seems worth including here in spite of the difficult language:*

"...In your own times you will face
mass death of livestock,
scant protection.
Did I not wield fame in battle?[1]
A tight-fisted man
will be born
soon before the world's destruction.
He'll take away freedom.[2]

---

1 *fame in battle* This seems like an incongruous statement, but the logic of it might be that a powerful reputation can be weaponized, and the Antichrist will take advantage of his worldly fame to lie to and manipulate people. It seems that Cú Chulainn is becoming uneasy with what had been the major goal of his early life, to be famous at all costs.

2 *take away freedom* Literally, "His clientship will be base" (Kimpton). Base clientship (see *GEIL*, 29–32), a legal status of tenant farmers that contrasted with free clientship, was a step above serfdom: the point would seem to be that under the Antichrist, free clientship will no longer be an option. Of course, the Antichrist is a liar, and as a matter of law, "a dishonest lord is demoted to the rank of commoner. If a lord makes an [continued ...]

His time will be dark.
He'll deceive a multitude,
corrupting many.
He will know
when the time has come to unleash his lies.
He will spread falsehood,
destroy truth.
Battles will break out:
a leader captured;
limbs hacked off;
bones broken;
skin sliced;
eyes gouged;
pride-perverted laws.
Gold as tribute,
silver on trees,[1]
gems from rockslabs
will fill the greed
of a crystal mountain.[2]
Generosity will be offensive;
dissembling will be noble.
For we know what will become of him
on the day the world will be annihilated,.

---

unjust decision (*gúbreth*) against a client, the client is entitled to leave him without paying the normal heavy fine for desertion" (27).

1 *silver on trees* Kimpton doesn't explain this, but it could be alluding to Jeremiah 10.2–4: "Thus saith the Lord: Learn not according to the ways of the Gentiles: and be not afraid of the signs of heaven, which the heathens fear: For the laws of the people are vain: for the works of the hand of the workman hath cut a tree out of the forest with an axe. He hath decked it with silver and gold: he hath put it together with nails and hammers, that it may not fall asunder" (Douai-Rheims).

2 *a crystal mountain* The translation of this sentence is basically Kimpton's. The "crystal mountain" doesn't seem to be biblical and, although the seafaring Saint Brendan spots one "crystal mountain" that is surely an iceberg, this could be referring to the Otherworld* (see Howard Rollin Patch, "Some elements in mediaeval descriptions of the Otherworld," *PMLA* 33.4 [1918] 601–43, at 609–10: "[c]rystal and glass and ice are obviously used everywhere in Otherworld descriptions"). The point could be that the Otherworld will align with the powers of evil in the end? Other early Irish texts, like "The Adventure of Connlae" (*Echtrae Chonnlai*, Ó Corráin #1042, 7th century), align the Otherworld with Christianity, though, so this idea should be approached with care.

by the One who exalts humanity for your sake,
to redeem creation.
But worship the Son with his law.
It is seven times better for you.
And I, in my pride,
have reflected on his law:
I would do better
if only I were allowed to live.—You all are sad."

The story continues:

The foster-mother* who raised him[1] had her house along the way he always used to travel south and back. She always had a cup ready with a drink for him. He stopped for a drink, said goodbye to his foster-mother, and kept going down the Midlúachair Road and past the Plain of Mugain. Here's what he saw: three witches, blind in their left eyes, waiting for him on the road. They were cooking a lapdog with poisons and spells on spits of rowan. It was one of Cú Chulainn's *geisi** not to stop and partake from a cooking-pot. It was also a *geis* for him to eat the flesh of his namesake.[2] He started to race ahead in hopes of getting past them. He knew they weren't there for his benefit.

Which is why one witch called over to him, "Come visit, Cú Chulainn."

"The hell I will," said Cú Chulainn.

"The food's just a dog," she said. "If this were some big cookout you would visit. Because it's something small, you won't. No one can do great things if they won't tolerate or accept small ones."

So he stopped by, and the witch handed him the shoulder of the dog with her left hand. He took it from her hand and stuck it

1 *The foster-mother who raised him* This would seem to be Finnchóem according to "The Birth of Cú Chulainn," but she isn't named here.

2 *one of Cú Chulainn's ... his namesake* "The flesh of his namesake" is dog meat, given his status since boyhood as "Culann's Dog." See Matthieu Boyd, "On not eating dog," in *Ollam*, 35–46. The early Irish didn't normally eat dog, and the dog-eating *geis* seems secondary to the cooking-pot one, since otherwise it was fine—at least in the *Táin*—for Cú Chulainn to kill dogs. Compare p. 198 above, when Recension 1 has Cú Chulainn kill Maeve's puppy Baiscne; in both Recensions 1 and 2 the list of casualties he inflicts in the Sixfold Slaughter episode also includes dogs.

under his left thigh. The hand that took it, and the thigh he tucked it under, cramped up from top to bottom so they lost their usual strength.

Cú Chulainn advances until Lóeg spots the enemy army. Meanwhile, their leader Erc sees Cú Chulainn and describes his horses, equipment, and hairstyle in extravagant detail. The army surrounds Erc with a protective shieldwall and he makes a speech that mingles praise for Cú Chulainn, calling him "the son of (a) god, the son of (a) man" *(which begins to invite comparisons with Jesus), with dire predictions of what Cú Chulainn will do to his enemies; still, Erc is confident that he will be defeated. Erc's troops are in distress:* "How can we prepare? How will we resist his feats?" *Erc advises them to form a single massive unit with a shieldwall on every side. He also advises them to stage a fight between two of their own men, and have a satirist* on hand to demand Cú Chulainn's spear, which has otherwise been prophesied to kill a king. They should also scream, apparently to provoke Cú Chulainn's anger so that he doesn't challenge them to single combat like he did in the* Táin, *but plunges in to attack them all.*

Then Cú Chulainn came toward the warbands, and performed three thunder-feats from his chariot, i.e., one that killed hundreds, and one that killed three hundred, and one that killed 27, to clear the armies off Muirthemne Plain. Cú Chulainn closed in on the warbands and went to town on them with his weapons: he wielded his spears and shield and sword and feats until Muirthemne Plain was covered with their head-chunks and skull-chunks and arm-chunks and leg-chunks and ragged red bones in numbers like the sand of the sea, and the stars in heaven, and dew in May, and snowflakes, and hailstones, and leaves in a forest, and buttercups on the Plain of Brega, and the grass under the hooves of a herd of horses on a summer day, and the field was gray with their brains after he got through with his furious assault on them.

After that, he caught sight of the two men attacking each other and did nothing to separate them.

"It disgraces you, Cú Chulainn," said the satirist, "not to break up this fight."

So Cú Chulainn jumped down and punched them both in the head, so their brains came out their ears and noses.

"Well, you broke them up," said the satirist.* "They can't hurt each other now."

"They wouldn't have quieted down if I'd just asked them," said Cú Chulainn.

"Give me that spear, Cú Chulainn," said the satirist.

"I swear* what my people swear, you don't need it any more than I do. The men of Ireland are attacking me here, and I'm attacking *them*."

"I'll satirize you if you don't," said the satirist.

"I've never been satirized for stinginess or ungenerosity." Then Cú Chulainn threw the spear at him, butt-first, and it went through his head and killed nine men behind him.

Cú Chulainn broke through the enemy formation. Then Lugaid son of Cú Roí grabbed one of the spears that the sons of Calatín had prepared.

"What will fall by this spear, sons of Calatín?" said Lugaid.

"A king will fall by that spear," said the sons of Calatín.

Then Lugaid threw the spear and hit Lóeg mac Riangabra, spilling his guts on the chariot-cushion.

"I'm hurt bad," said Lóeg.

Cú Chulainn pulled out the spear and Lóeg said his goodbyes. Then Cú Chulainn said, "I'll be both a chariot-warrior and a charioteer today."

Again Cú Chulainn breaks through the enemy formation. Again he sees two men fighting and a satirist with a hazel wand looking on. This time Cú Chulainn shoves the two men into a rock so that they splatter to pieces. The conversation with the satirist is repeated and amplified:

"Give me that spear," said the satirist.

"I swear what my people swear, you don't need it any more than I do. It's up to my hand, my courage, and my skill at arms to sweep the four provinces of Ireland off Muirthemne Plain today."

"I'll satirize you," said the satirist.

"I don't have to grant more than one request per day, and I've already paid for my honor today."

"I'll satirize the Ulstermen for your crimes," said the satirist.*

"They've never been satirized before," he said, "to accuse me of stinginess or ungenerosity. For the short time I have left, there won't be any satirizing today."

Cú Chulainn throws the spear at the satirist and kills him and nine men behind him, as before. Erc takes one of the special spears and asks the sons of Calatín what it will do. They say it will kill a king. Erc says they made the same prediction about the spear that Lugaid threw, and they insist they were correct: it killed "the king of the charioteers of Ireland," *Lóeg. Erc says he won't kill the same kind of king again.*

Then Erc threw the spear and hit Líath Macha. Cú Chulainn pulled it out, and they said their goodbyes to each other. Then, still wearing half the yoke from the chariot, Líath Macha left him, and went to the Gray's Pool (*Linn Léith*) in Slieve Fúait. That's where he had come from to join Cú Chulainn, and that's where he went after he was wounded.[1] Then Cú Chulainn said, "A pair of horses will drive with one yoke here today."[2] With that, Cú Chulainn stuck his foot under one end of the yoke, and plowed through the army like before.

---

1 *after he was wounded* Kimpton translates "after being slain," but the Irish *íarna guin* could mean "after his slaying" or "after his wounding," and only the latter makes sense in terms of Conall Cernach's meeting with the horse later on, even if the wound is mortal. The idea that Cú Chulainn got his horses out of lakes is reflected in "Bricriu's Feast," §31: "Cú Chulainn had had his first encounter with his famous horse, the Gray One of Macha, on the banks of the Gray One's Pool by Slieve Fúait. It had come out of the lake, and Cú Chulainn had crept up to it and wrapped both arms around its neck. Then the horse had gone galloping around the whole of Ireland while they struggled, until in the evening Cú Chulainn had come back to Emain with the horse now broken in. Then he had gone and gotten his other horse, the Black One of Saingliu, from the Pool of the Black One of Saingliu in exactly the same way" (my translation). Although the term isn't used for them initially, Cú Chulainn's horses seem related to the folklore of the "waterhorse" (Old Irish *ech usci*, Modern Irish *each uisce* anglicized *aughisky*, Scottish Gaelic *each-uisge*). See Bo Almqvist, "Waterhorse legends (MLSIT 4086 & 4086B): the case for and against a connection between Irish and Nordic tradition," *Béaloideas* 59 (1991) 107–20, and Matthias Egeler, "Horses, lakes, and heroes: *Landnámabók* S83, *Vǫlsunga saga* 13, and the Grey of Macha," *Viking and Medieval Scandinavia* 10 (2014) 53–64.

2 *A pair of horses ... today* This does seem to be what the Irish says, but there is only one horse left (Dub Sainglenn); perhaps Cú Chulainn is referring to himself as the other "horse." Patrick Brown understandably goes with "My chariot must be yoked to a single horse today."

A third pair of men fighting. Cú Chulainn treats them "no worse" than the previous four. This conversation with the satirist goes:*

"Give me that spear," said the satirist.

"You don't need it any more than I do."

"I'll satirize you," said the satirist.

"I've paid for my honor today. I don't have to grant more than one request per day."

"I'll satirize the Ulstermen for your crimes," said the satirist.

"I've paid for their honor," he said.

"I'll satirize your family," said the satirist.

"Well, I'm not going to let slanderous news about me spread to lands I've never been, because I don't have much time left."

Cú Chulainn threw the spear at him, butt-first, and it went through his head and through 27 other men.

"That's a gift made in anger, Cú Chulainn," said the satirist.

Now Lugaid takes the last of the special spears and asks the sons of Calatín what it will do. They say again that it will kill a king, and explain Erc's cast as having hit "the king of the horses of Ireland," *Líath Macha. Lugaid says he won't kill the same kind of king again.*

Then Lugaid threw the spear and hit Cú Chulainn, spilling his guts on the chariot-cushion. Then Dub Sainglenn left him, wearing half the yoke, and went to Black Lake (*Loch Dub*) in the land of Muscraige Tíre.[1] That's where he had come from to join Cú Chulainn. That's where he went back to, and it made the lake boil.

After that, the chariot stood alone on the plain. Cú Chulainn said, "I'd like to go to the lake over there and get a drink."

"We'll allow it," they said, "as long as you come back to us."

"If I don't," said Cú Chulainn, "I order you to come and get me."

Then he gathered up his entrails in his arms and wandered off towards the lake. When he reached the lake he swung his hand out from his chest and flung his guts away. Then he took a drink and washed off the gore. Hence the lake was called Handout Lake[2] (*Loch*

---

1 *Muscraige Tíre* Part of Munster, now in Counties Tipperary and Kilkenny.

2 *Handout Lake* Otherwise translated as "Hand-boon Lake" by Patrick Brown and "Lac du bienfait de la main" by Georges Dottin. *Lámraith* would be analyzed [continued …]

Lámraith) on Muirthemne Plain. Another name for it, now, is Loch Tonnchuil. After that he sprinted away and ordered them to come to him.

He went a long way west of the lake, and his vision failed. He went towards a standing stone on the plain, and looped his belt around it so that he wouldn't die sitting or lying down, but standing. The enemy surrounded him, but didn't dare come close—they thought he was alive.

"Shame on you," said Erc mac Cairpri, "for not taking his head as revenge for taking my father's."[1]

Líath Macha came back to defend Cú Chulainn for as long as his soul was in him and the hero's light kept shining from his forehead. After that, Líath Macha lashed out with three bloody attacks, killing fifty with his teeth and thirty with each hoof. That's how many of the enemy he killed. Hence the expression "no keener than Líath Macha's victorious charges after Cú Chulainn was killed."

After that a carrion crow landed on Cú Chulainn's shoulder. "There wouldn't usually be birds on that stone," said Erc mac Cairpri. So, after that, Lugaid pulled Cú Chulainn's hair back and cut off his head. Then Cú Chulainn's sword dropped out of his hand, cutting off Lugaid's hand so it fell to the ground. They cut off Cú Chulainn's hand as payback.

The army left, taking Cú Chulainn's head and hand with them, and went to Tara. That's where his head and hand are buried, under a shield of earth.[2] Cenn Fáelad[3] mac Ailella has a poem about that...

---

as *lám* 'hand, arm' compounded with *rath* 'grace; the granting of a favor, a mark of favor, a boon; good luck, fortune, prosperity' (*eDIL*, s.v. *1 rath*). The idea seems to be that he is generously bestowing his guts on the lake and that the name commemorates his action.

1 Omitting some comments about the burial arrangements for his father's head.

2 *shield of earth* The Irish is *lán lainne a scéith di úir*: literally "the whole of the cover of his shield from soil," i.e., a layer of earth equivalent to the full coverage of his shield. Mallory, *In Search of the Irish Dreamtime*, 258, translates this "the whole panel of his golden shield" and states that this is one of "only two references to grave goods in the Ulster tales," the other one also being a reference to warriors being buried with their shields. Kimpton reads *úir* as 'earth, soil' while Mallory takes it as a form of *ór* 'gold,' less convincingly: *lán lainne a scéith óir* would fit his reading.

3 *Cenn Fáelad* Pronounced "KEN FWEE-luth," with voiced *th*. After being wounded in battle and losing his "brain of forgetting," he was known for synthesizing Irish poetry, early Irish law, and Christian learning in the 7th century: see https://www.dib.ie/biography/cenn-faelad-a1593 (Boyd, "Modeling impairment and disability," has more).

...followed by the poem. It summarizes the battle and Cú Chulainn's death and credits him with killing 32+40+200+120+160+80=632 men, plus 30 kings and 144 chiefs (so 806 in all).

The army went south to the river Liffey. When they reached the river, Lugaid said to his charioteer, "My full belt feels like it's weighing me down.[1] I'd like to bathe." He went out ahead of the army to bathe, while the army moved on. He caught a salmon between his shins and tossed it up to his charioteer, who immediately lit a fire to cook it.

After that, the Ulster armies had shaken off their paralysis and started moving south from Emain Macha toward Slieve Fúait. Now, Cú Chulainn and Conall Cernach had made a pact as fellow warriors, that if either one were killed the other would avenge him.

"If I'm killed first," said Cú Chulainn, "how fast will you avenge me?"

"The day you die," said Conall, "I'll avenge you by evening. And if I'm killed first, how fast will you avenge me?"

"Your blood won't be cold on the ground," said Cú Chulainn, "before I avenge you."

So when Conall came in his chariot ahead of the Ulster forces,[2] he encountered Líath Macha, gushing blood on his way to the Gray's Pool. Then Conall said:

"You can't manage a yoke
going to the Gray's Pool:
you'll go there propelled by your wounds,
by your bodily injuries,
spattered with the blood of man and horse
and Lugaid's arm.

1 *full belt ... weighing me down* A warrior's "belt" was more of an element of body armor, and (if you recall Conall's treatment of Ánlúan's head in "Mac Dá Thó's Pig") it could also be used to hang or store trophies.

2 *when Conall came ... the Ulster forces* If the point of what Niab said earlier was that Conall was still with the exiles, his obligation to Cú Chulainn would seem to take precedence over any such considerations.

Lugaid son of Cú Roí mac Dáiri:
he killed my foster-brother* Cú Chulainn."

Then Conall and Líath Macha went on and visited the battlefield. They saw Cú Chulainn (headless) by the standing stone. Líath Macha went and laid his head on Cú Chulainn's chest.

"Líath Macha is grieved by that corpse," said Conall. Then Conall went and put his foot against the hedge of fallen shields.[1] "I swear* what my people swear, this hedge befits a great man."

"You have named this place," said a druid.* "That will be its name forever: Greatman's Hedge (*Airrbe Rófhir*)."

Then they went after the enemy.

Lugaid was still there bathing.

"Keep an eye on the plain," he said to his charioteer, "so that no one can come up on us unseen."

The charioteer looked out. "There's a lone rider coming toward us," he said, "at a high rate of speed. You'd think the ravens of Ireland were above him. You'd think there were snowflakes speckling the plain in front of him."

"That rider is no friend of ours," said Lugaid. "It's Conall Cernach on Derg Drúchtach ('Dripping Red'). The birds you saw above him are the sods from the hooves of that horse. The snowflakes you saw speckling the plain in front of him are the foam from his horse's mouth and off the bridle bit. Look again," said Lugaid, "to see which way he's heading."

"He's heading for the ford—the way our army went."

"Let that horse pass us by. We don't want to confront it."

But when Conall reached the middle of the ford, he looked over.

"That's quite a salmon,"[2] he said.

He looked again: "That's quite a charioteer," he said.

He looked a third time: "That's quite a king. I'd better pay him a visit."

1 *of fallen shields* Patrick Brown's suggestion, but a convincing one: Kimpton makes this "hedge" sound like a shrubbery.

2 *quite a salmon* Kimpton supplies this line of dialogue to account for how the text mentions a second and third look, but describes only two in total; presumably there had to be a first look.

He rode up to them.

"A pleasure to see a debtor's face," he said.

"If someone owes you something," said Lugaid, "go and collect."

"You owe me," said Conall Cernach, "for killing my friend Cú Chulainn, and I'm here trying to prosecute a claim on you for it."

"Inappropriate," said Lugaid. "It won't be considered valor on your part to fight me here, not until I've taken my victory-spoils back to Munster with me."

"Fine," said Conall, "as long as we don't travel together or make conversation."

*Lugaid proposes different southbound routes for each of them to follow. Their paths intersect at Silverwood Plain (*Mag nArgetrois*), in the Nore River valley now in Counties Laois and Kilkenny: Lugaid arrives first and Conall throws a spear at him, pinning his foot to a standing stone, which gets the name Lugaid's Stone. Lugaid moves on to (what will be called as a result of this episode) Lugaid's Barrow (*Fertae Lugdach*) at the Bridge of Ossory (*Droichit Osraige*):*

There they met.

"I want fair play[*] from you," said Lugaid.

"How so?" said Conall Cernach.

"Fight me one-handed, since I have only one hand myself."

"Granted," said Conall Cernach. Then his arm was roped to his side.

They fought for several hours[1] and neither was any closer to victory. When Conall realized that, he looked over at his mare, the Derg Drúchtach. She had a head like a dog,[2] and used to kill men in battles and contests. On cue, the mare advanced on Lugaid and took a bite out of his side, so that his entrails fell round his feet.

"Dammit," said Lugaid. "That's not fair play, Conall Cernach."

---

1 *for several hours* The Irish seems to say "for two hours," but the word *tráth*, which originally referred to the canonical hours—approximately three hours apart—could mean a length of time up to a day. Here *eDIL* suggests "for the space of two of the watches of the day."

2 *a head like a dog* Edward Pettit discusses the affinities of this in "Three variations on the theme of the dog-headed spear in medieval Irish: Celtchar's *lúin*, Conall Cernach's *Derg Drúchtach*, Lugaid's *flesc*," *Studia Hibernica* 42 (2016) 65–96.

"I only made you that guarantee on my own behalf," said Conall. "I didn't make any on behalf of animals and the legally incompetent."

"I know very well that you won't go until you take my head," said Lugaid, "because I took Cú Chulainn's. Take the credit for taking my head, then—raise it over yours[1]—and wield my kingship on top of your kingship, and my weapons on top of your weapons. I'd rather you be the best warrior in Ireland than anyone else."[2]

With that, Conall Cernach cut off his head. He took it with him to meet the Ulstermen at Roiriu in Leinster. Someone put the head on a stone and they left it behind. They reached Gris. Then Conall Cernach said, "Did anyone bring the head?"

"No," said everyone.

"I swear* what my people swear," said Conall Cernach, "that's not half a crime."[3] Hence the place was called Half-Crime (*Midbine*) at Roiriu. They went back to find the head, and here's what they saw: the head had dissolved the stone and fallen through it.[4]

The Ulstermen didn't allow themselves to enter Emain Macha with their spoils of victory that week. But Cú Chulainn's soul

1 *raise it over yours* Added to clarify the double sense of the Irish. The text says that Conall should take "my head upon your head," which Kimpton translates figuratively, as "May you take [...] my head on your own behalf," which seems perfectly appropriate since the earlier "I only guaranteed it to you on my own behalf" uses the same idiom. But what follows makes it clear that Lugaid is also expecting Conall to physically place the severed head on top of his own as a trophy, and suffer the magical consequences.

2 *than anyone else* Added for clarity.

3 *half a crime* The Irish is *Ní midbine sin*, which is obviously negative (Kimpton translates "that is not a small crime"), so the placename Midbine seems to commemorate but not confirm this statement. It would be more straightforward if, as Patrick Brown has it, Conall had said "That *is* half a crime."

4 *fallen through it* There are other instances of this stone-dissolving severed head motif. One involves Conall and the king Mes Gegrai, in "The Siege of Howth" (*Talland Étair*, Ó Corráin #1109), ed. and trans. Whitley Stokes, *Revue Celtique* 8 (1887) 47–64, https://archive.org/details/revueceltique08pari/page/46/mode/2up (Stokes's translation of the invitation is "Put thou my head above thy head and add my glory to thy glory") and more recently by Caoimhín Ó Dónaill as *Talland Étair: A Critical Edition with Introduction, Translation, Textual Notes, and Vocabulary* (Maynooth: Department of Old and Middle Irish, National University of Ireland, 2005). The other involves later traditions about the god Lug's confrontation with his grandfather Balor: see Jeremiah Curtin, *Hero-Tales of Ireland* (Boston: Little, Brown, & Co., 1911) 293–94, and Brian Ó Cuív, "*Cath Maige Tuired*," in *Irish Sagas*, ed. Myles Dillon (Dublin: Mercier, 1959) 24–37. In both cases, the winner deliberately sets the head on a rock and watches it fall through.

did—he appeared to the fifty queens he had insulted the day before he went into battle. Here's what they saw: Cú Chulainn in his ghostly chariot in the sky over Emain Macha. Then Cú Chulainn chanted to them and said after his death:

"Emain, Emain,
a sovereign Sovereign will come to us.
Tonsured priests will settle in the lands of Emain.
They will come from the Alps of Europe.[1]
I call forth a boat I will expect from heaven,
bringing Patrick's[2] populace across the bright sea.
They'll make a solemn prayer to the King of high heaven
for him to receive us in Zion.
We'll go to the Day of full Judgment.
A fine man will set up
to the east of me on this very plain.[3]
That will do until we meet again, Emain."

The ghost-words of Cú Chulainn on the day he perished:

"The little lamb is slain, Emain.
The protector is slain, Emain.
He was pierced with a spear, Emain.
He fell in battle, Emain.
Though your calf was one against many,
he crushed men.
The little lamb is slain, Emain.
I will speak of a great slaughter of great men.
I have a long way to ride,
since I've been defeated early.
Amid the lamenting cry of a fair woman,

---

1 *the Alps of Europe* Here, unlike in "The Wooing of Emer," the Alps might be an anachronistic reference to the monasteries founded by the Irish on the Continent, like St. Gall in Switzerland.

2 *Patrick* Called *Succet* in the text. This was Patrick's name at birth according to his 7th-century hagiographer Muirchú moccu Machthéni.

3 *to the east ... this very plain* This refers to Armagh, the seat of the archbishopric associated with Saint Patrick.

Dechtine's dear one,
people's protector,[1]
rides along fair paths
to the fort of happiness.
A noble god used to protect me
when he would come to the champion of chariot-warriors.
I will speak of a great slaughter.
When I fought one on one, alone,
I would invoke the fair son of Eithne;[2]
in every situation, on every side, he was there.
Aífe's son was buried.[3]
Lóeg is dead:
there couldn't be a heavier disaster. [...]"[4]

Cú Chulainn said *de adventu Christi* ("of the coming of Christ"):

"Christ rides point through the lands of the powerless and
unknowing.
He will rule in person;
he looks after his people.
Death is in store for the fair King, the Lord,
below us, above us,
the world's inheritance,
a fort of the destitute, a fort for us unto the clouds on high.
A sister's son* of men[5] will come.

---

1 *people's protector* My choice among the alternatives proposed by Kimpton (64). Cú Chulainn is talking about himself here in the third person: the "fair woman" referred to two lines above would be Emer, and the "fort of happiness" (*dún subae*) two lines after this would seem to be heaven.

2 *son of Eithne* Cú Chulainn's supernatural father, Lug. Cú Chulainn might be toying with the idea that what he thought was Lug's help was the Christian God's all along. The word translated "situation" (*cruth*) has the primary meaning 'form, shape, appearance,' and only secondarily 'misfortune, distress' (which Kimpton prefers).

3 *Aífe's son was buried* This refers to Connla, fathered by Cú Chulainn: see "The Wooing of Emer" and "The Death of Aífe's Only Son." In contrast to Cú Chulainn's attitude in those texts, his comment here sounds like a note of regret.

4 Omitted here are some lines about Conall for which Kimpton proposes "My warrior-helper Conall [will hasten to me], whom a swift fleet keeps [away] from the Ulstermen, with a chariot-riding host, with a messenger, on [the] dark waters from Mag nÉo into Mag Cride" (46, 64).

5 *A sister's son of men* The sister's son relationship, which is the relationship Cú Chulainn

His law will fill every place.
He will put a stop to your deception.
Jesus will vanquish hell
for the tribes of Adam's offspring astray
in an ephemeral realm
guided by a hand towards which they may be envious and bitter,
at which they may rejoice,
at which they will speak the law of heaven.
What king is this, what pent-up flood[1] whom armies will speak of?
Our Lord who enlightens us: the King who has redeemed the earth
for a Kingdom that in no way, shape, or form lacks the virtues of heaven.

After victory in battle the King will sit
fully enthroned
above lofty kingdoms,
as one, as two, as three,[2]
through his power that I can't examine, I can't tell of, I can't say.

The warning before his death
will be a dismal sight for humankind.
The stars in heaven will tremble,
the bright, red sun will lapse,[3]

---

has to the people of Ulster, is the relationship Jesus was understood to have to humanity and specifically to the people of Israel, since the Virgin Mary was a "sister" of both humans in general and Jews in particular. See *Coire Sois*, 65–94, and Matthieu Boyd, "The poems of Blathmac, son of Cú Brettan, and *The Dream of the Rood*," *SMART: Studies in Medieval and Renaissance Teaching* 19.2 (Fall 2012) 49–80.

1 *flood* Compare Isaiah 59.19.

2 *as three* This line refers to the mystery of the Trinity: the Christian God as Father, Son, and Holy Spirit. The previous line *La forlínad suide* ("fully enthroned"), translated by Kimpton "with fullness of seats"—unless it is meant to refer to seating for the saved or the elect (compare Ephesians 2.6)—could be rendered in a funny way as "with ample seating" on God's throne for all the persons of the Trinity.

3 *sun will lapse* See Matthew 27.45, Mark 15.33, and Luke 23.44 for the darkness during the Crucifixion.

the blue track of the firmament will be overrun,
the lustrous moon half-hidden
at the time of his wake.

Jesus most high and most humble,
through his harrowing of hell,
through his establishment of rule,
through his setting free the kingdom,
through his myriad armies,
through his heavenly omnipotence
that embraces the heavens, humanity, and all creation,
and everlasting life. Christ."

Líath Macha went to say goodbye to Emer, and laid his head in her lap. And he went around her three times in a sunwise* circle, and then went sunwise around Dún Imrid and Dún Delgae.[1]

Now Emer delivers a long lament for Cú Chulainn addressed to Líath Macha: she describes Cú Chulainn as a great protector, a golden being favored by Otherworld kings.* "His fearsomeness protected me. His courage sustained me. My handsome combat-conquering husband cared for me [...] Tell me, what chance is there of any renown or merit or mettle, or prowess, prodigality, prominence, or exploit, since circumstances have conspired against combat-conquering Cú Chulainn?"

She memorializes the events of the battle, saying it happened "on a Wednesday on the first day of autumn," *and tells how the one-eyed witches cooked a gray dog for his destruction.*

She lists, by name and class, 871 men killed by Cú Chulainn ("eight Láths, eight Níaths..."; specific numbers of druids, charioteers, poets,* kings, old men, young men, middle-aged men, and so on). He took 800 right hands and 800 left eyes, leaving the enemy survivors "blemished.*"*

She lists 15 Ulster heroes by name, from Conchobor to Fergus, and laments that none of them were there to protect Cú Chulainn, and that all of Ulster's warriors weren't with him when he died.

1 *Dún Imrid and Dún Delgae* Forts belonging to Cú Chulainn on Muirthemne Plain. The second location is now Dundalk in County Louth.

She says that she is devastated by the loss, that there is nothing left for her:

> "Surely every heart that loved him should burst.
> Surely every ear that heard him should never forget him.
> Surely every tear ever shed should forever lament him.
> Surely every eye that has seen him should weep showers of
>   blood,
> for it is the end of the world in sorrow with him gone,
> for I won't be seen now with another husband.
> Men's faces won't be jolly and generous at my wedding,
> for I won't find a husband like Cú Chulainn."

Her lament ends with how Conall avenged Cú Chulainn and references some more of Cú Chulainn's exploits, including being "victorious in single combats after being taken away by fairy women" *(referencing the events of "The Wasting Sickness of Cú Chulainn") and his courtship of her and exploits with Scáthach (referencing the events of "The Wooing of Emer"); she mentions that the magical attacks on him were 16 years in preparation. She calls on the world to lament with her, and the text concludes at the end of her poem:*

> "Wretched is the state of the world
> since we will not meet another day
> Líath, Líath."

Finit. Amen.

*Cú Chulainn makes an encore appearance in "Cú Chulainn's Ghostly Chariot" (*Síaburcharpat Con Culainn, *Ó Corráin #1100)*[1] *which is in*

1 Frustratingly, the latest work on this text, by Feargal Ó Béarra, "A critical edition of *Síaburcharpat Con Culaind*" (Ph.D. thesis, National University of Ireland, Galway, 2004), is still unpublished and inaccessible. There is a translation by Johan Corthals into German. Otherwise the English translation is by John O'Beirne Crowe, under the title "The Demoniac Chariot of Cu Chulaind," in "Siabur-charpat Con Culaind," *The Journal of the Royal Historical and Archaeological Association of Ireland*, 4th series, 1.2 (1878, for 1871) 371–448, at https://books.google.com/books?id=aSYNAAAAYAAJ&pg=PA375#v=onepage&q&f=false (and on various other sites): his translation was revised by Eleanor Hull, as "The Phantom Chariot of Cuchullin," in *The Cuchullin Saga in* [continued ...]

the manuscript Lebor na hUidre *along with Recension 1 of the* Táin. *This describes Saint Patrick's mission to the pagan king of Tara, Lóegaire mac Néill. Lóegaire idolizes Cú Chulainn, so Patrick brings him out of hell to testify to his suffering and humiliation there. Cú Chulainn tells of his raids on Scandinavia (*Lochlann*) and on the Otherworldly* "Shadow Fortress" (*Dún Scáith*)*[1] *and its monsters, and his grueling swim back (which might remind modern readers of Beowulf's swimming-match with Breca). He says that everything he suffered on that expedition was nothing compared to even one night in hell:* "My prowess was epic, my sword was hard: the Devil crushed me with one finger into the red embers." *Lóegaire is moved to convert, and Cú Chulainn's soul, as a reward for helping, goes to heaven. This and the death-tales choose different ways of resolving the tension that audiences in early Christian Ireland must have felt between admiration for the exploits of the Ulster Cycle heroes and the sense that without privileged insight or special intervention, they were all damned. In the twelfth-century Latin* Vision of Tnugdal,[2] *by an Irish monk abroad, Fergus and Conall are seen in hell, propping open the jaws of the beast Acheron.*

Irish Literature (London: David Nutt, 1898) 275–87, at https://books.google.com/books?id=8zRh-BJSDeoC&pg=PA275#v=onepage&q&f=false. The uncredited translation in *Ancient Irish Tales*, ed. Tom Peete Cross and Clark Harris Slover (New York: Henry Holt & Company, 1936, rpt. Barnes and Noble, 1996) 347–54, seems to be adapted from Hull. For analysis, see Elva Johnston, "The salvation of the individual and the salvation of society in *Siaburcharpat Con Culaind*," in *The individual in Celtic literatures (CSANA Yearbook 1)*, ed. Joseph Falaky Nagy (Four Courts, 2001) 109–25, and Joseph Falaky Nagy, "Excavating Loegaire mac Néill," in *Saltair saíochta, sanasaíochta agus seanchais: A festschrift for Gearóid Mac Eoin*, ed. Dónall Ó Baoill, Donncha Ó hAodha, and Nollaig Ó Muraíle (Four Courts, 2013) 181–89.

1 This place is otherwise associated with his mentor Scáthach, and a proposed location is Dunscaith Castle on the Isle of Skye in Scotland. This raid by Cú Chulainn has been compared to the one by Arthur in the Middle Welsh poem *Preiddeu Annwfn*, "The Spoils of Annwfn."

2 *The Vision of Tnugdal*, trans. Jean-Michel Picard, intro. Yolande de Pontfarcy (Four Courts, 1989); Latin text at https://celt.ucc.ie/published/L207009/; see also Ní Mhaoileoin, "The Heroic Biography of Fergus mac Róich," 121–27.

The Death of Conchobor

*This tale (*Aided Chonchobair, *Ó Corráin #963) exists in different versions, from the second half of the eighth century to the eleventh. It appears with Recension 2 of the* Táin *in the Book of Leinster. Like "The Death of Cú Chulainn," it tries to rehabilitate its title character as a hero worthy of respect by Christians.*

The first part of the story, which mentions Cú Chulainn, seems to happen prior to "The Exile of the Sons of Uisliu," because Conall is still in Ulster. Cú Chulainn might be young at this point, and not have fully eclipsed Conall as top hero.

The text doesn't say how much time passes between Cet's raid on Emain and his wounding of Conchobor, but it seems likely that the events of "The Exile of the Sons of Uisliu," the Táin, *and even "The Death of Cú Chulainn" happen in the interim, since both Conall Cernach and Cú Chulainn are no longer around to rescue or avenge Conchobor. (Annalists dated Cú Chulainn's death to 2 CE and Conchobor's to 33 CE, "clearly to associate these heroes with Christ": see John V. Kelleher, "The* Táin *and the Annals,"* Ériu *22 [1971] 107–27.)*

The translation uses the Irish edited by Chantal Kobel, "A Critical Edition of Aided Chonchobair *'The violent death of Conchobar'; with Translation, Textual Notes and Bibliography" (Ph.D. thesis, Trinity College Dublin, 2015, https://www.tara.tcd.ie/handle/2262/80099), Version A, 219–345, which improves on the earlier edition by Kuno Meyer in* Death-Tales of the Ulster Heroes, *4–11, and the embedded poem as edited and translated by Kobel, 157–218, building on Johann Corthals, "The* retoiric *in* Aided Chonchobuir,*"* Ériu *40 (1989) 41–59.*

The Ulstermen got very drunk one time at Emain Macha. Huge arguments and competitions broke out among them, i.e., Conall and Cú Chulainn and Lóegaire the Triumphant.

"Bring me the brain of Mes Gegrai," said Conall, "so I can give my competitors a piece of my mind."

In those days the Ulstermen had a custom of taking out the brains of every warrior that they killed in single combat and mixing them with lime to make a hard ball. And whenever they got into arguments or competitions, the brain-balls would be brought to them to brandish as trophies.[1]

"Well, Conchobor," said Conall, "until my competitors perform a deed like this in single combat, they're not fit to compete with me."

"Very true," said Conchobor.

So the brain went back on the shelf where it usually sat.

The assembly broke up the next day and everyone went their separate ways. Conchobor's two jesters* by the fire had seen the big fuss over the brain. The next day they took it outside to play.

Then Cet mac Mágach came on a raiding tour of Ulster. This Cet was the most brutal menace in Ireland. He came striding across the green at Emain, carrying the heads of three Ulster warriors.

As the jesters were playing with Mes Gegrai's brain, one of them called to the other, saying "Look out! Look out!"[2]

"A king will fall because of it," said the other.

Cet overheard them. He snatched the brain out of their hands and took it with him, because he knew it had been foretold[3] that Mes Gegrai would avenge himself after his death.

In every battle and skirmish the Connachtmen fought against the Ulstermen from then on, Cet would carry the brain tucked into his belt, to see if he could manage an illustrious kill with it against the Ulstermen.

One time Cet came east on a raid and rustled cattle from Fir Rois. The Ulstermen who came in pursuit caught up with him and he held them off until Connachtmen showed up from the other side to rescue him. Battle lines were drawn, and Conchobor himself went into battle.

---

1 *to brandish as trophies* Literally, "so that they were in their hands." There is no historical evidence for such brain-balls. Conall's killing of the Leinster king Mes Gegrai is told in "The Siege of Howth" (see p. 312, note 4 above). He had the brain extracted so that Mes Gegrai's widow could keep the head, after it had cured him of being cross-eyed. "The Wasting Sickness of Cú Chulainn" (see Gantz, 155) has the Ulstermen using the tongues of their enemies as trophies instead.

2 *Look out!* Literally, *"Asso, asso,"* glossed as 'behold' by *eDIL*. A plausible scenario is that the jesters are playing catch, and the first one's admonishment to keep eyes on the ball triggers a flash of prophetic insight from the second. They don't seem to have noticed Cet at this point.

3 *he knew it had been foretold* "The Siege of Howth" mentions no such prophecy, so the meaning is probably that Cet recognized the jesters' exchange as prophetic, not that he already knew there was a prophecy.

That's when the women of Connacht begged Conchobor to step aside so they could admire his figure. No one on earth had ever cut the figure that Conchobor did—the physique, the form, the fashion; the size, the stature, the symmetry; the eyes, the hair, the brightness; the wisdom, the manners, the eloquence; the equipment, the clothing, the splendor; the weapons, the wealth, the dignity; the virtues, the valor, the lineage. That Conchobor was utterly flawless. Actually, though, it was Cet who had put the women up to it.

So Conchobor went off by himself[1] so the women could admire him. But Cet slipped in among the women. He loaded Mes Gegrai's brain in his sling and flung it so that it hit Conchobor in the head and sank two-thirds of the way in. Conchobor collapsed. The Ulstermen hurried up and carried him away from Cet.

Where Conchobor fell was on the bank of the ford of Daire Dá Báeth. His grave is there, with a standing stone at his head and another at his feet.

The Connachtmen were routed as far as the Hawthorn of Hound Heights (*Sciaid Aird na Con*). Then they drove the Ulstermen back east to the ford of Daire Dá Báeth.

"Get me out of here!" said Conchobor. "I'll give the kingship of Ulster to whoever carries me home."

"I'll carry you," said Cenn Berraide ("Shorn Head"), his manservant—he put a rope around him and hoisted him on his back as far as Ardachad on Slieve Fúait. Then Cenn Berraide's heart gave out. This is the reason for the saying "Cenn Berraide's reign over Ulster," i.e., he had the king on his back for half a day.[2]

The battle went on for a whole day after the king left. Then the Ulstermen were defeated.

Meanwhile Conchobor's doctor was sent for, i.e., Fíngin. He was the one who could tell from the smoke rising from a house how many people inside were sick and from what sickness.

"All right," said Fíngin, "if the stone is removed from your head, you'll be dead any minute. If it isn't removed, though, I can heal you, and you'll carry a blemish.*"

---

1 *off by himself* Against protocol: as a matter of early Irish law, a king "must always be accompanied by a retinue" or lose his honor-price* (*GEIL*, 19).

2 *Cenn Berraide's reign … half a day* This seems to be a proverbial expression for a short span of time. The name is pronounced "KEN BER-ith-uh," with voiced *th*.

"It's easier for us to cope with the blemish* than with him dying," said the Ulstermen.

So Fíngin healed his head, stitching it with gold thread to match the gold of Conchobor's hair. And the doctor told Conchobor to watch out, i.e., not to get angry, not to ride a horse, not to have vigorous encounters with women,[1] and not to run. He spent the rest of his life, seven years, in that predicament: he lacked the capacity to do anything but sit in his seat.

That is, until he heard that Christ had been crucified by the Jews.[2] At that time a great trembling seized all creation, and heaven and earth trembled at the enormity of what had been committed then, i.e., Jesus Christ, the Son of the Living God, being crucified when he was guiltless.

"What's this?" Conchobor asked his druid.* "What great deed is being done today?"

The druid told him the truth,[3] that Christ had been crucified.

"This is monumental," said Conchobor.

---

1 *vigorous encounters with women* Meyer had *ná etraiged mnái [⁊ná rocaithed biad] co anfeta*, which he translated "that he should not have connexion with a woman, that he should not eat food greedily." But Kobel dismisses the bracketed language, which is in only one manuscript, as a scribe's addition, leaving *na etraiged mnái co ainféta*. She cites interpretations of *co ainféta* as "tumultuous[ly], turbulently," and "provides a modernised translation [...] 'he should not have sexual relations [with] a woman' in contrast to Meyer's translation in order to convey the sense more clearly" (326). But she doesn't discuss whether Conchobor is banned from all sex or only vigorous sex—if *na etraiged mnái* was enough for the former meaning, *co ainféta* seems like an important qualifier.

2 *by the Jews* The antisemitic trope of "Jewish deicide"—that the Jews were collectively responsible for killing Christ, a position explicitly denied in the 1965 "Declaration on the Relation of the [Catholic] Church with Non-Christian Religions" (a.k.a. *Nostra Aetate*)—developed in the formative Christian Church on the basis of Matthew 27.25. It was conceptually satisfying for the early Christian Irish since the death of Christ could be read in terms of Irish values both as an act of treacherous rebellion against an overlord with whom the Jews had contracted for the land of Israel (through God's covenant with Abraham in Genesis 12, 15, and 17), and also as an act of *fingal*,* since Jesus was a sister's son* of the Jews. "That the ideology which underlies the *Táin* was charged with meaning for the Irish people in the eighth century is shown by [the poet] Blathmac's recasting of the life of Christ within the framework of that ideology" (*Coire Sois*, 218). This wasn't a matter of animosity for the Jewish community in Ireland since there wasn't any such until the 11th century or later. See *Coire Sois*, 65–94; Boyd, "The poems of Blathmac"; and Anna Matheson, "Was there a Jewish presence in medieval Ireland?," *Jewish Historical Studies* 51 (2019) 301–25, https://www.jstor.org/stable/48733615?seq=1.

3 *told him the truth* Literally, "'That's very true,' said the druid. 'It is a great deed, Christ being crucified.'"

"Now, that man," said the druid,* "was born the same night as you, that is, on the eighth day before the Calends of January, although the year was different."

That was when Conchobor believed. And he was one of the two men in Ireland who believed in God before the coming of the Faith. Morann mac Maín[1] was the other one.

Conchobor now speaks this poem, in which he imagines giving his life to save Christ from his enemies.[2]

"Alas that I didn't get to meet the High King!
Mankind would have seen me appear as a ruthless warrior.

You, my mouth, with a harsh and militant call to arms, will provoke
victory in noble combat, the bitter slaughter of a vicious horde.

To render noble help, defending Christ with spears, would have eased my foolish outcry:
I would have struck back hard against the persecution of the perfect Lord.

It was a great story that people are keening a King's crucifixion.
It would be so much greater if I were to trade my own beautiful body for that unique, miraculous High King's.

I would have been seen to do a manly deed, defying packs of enemies,
as a strong man above them, standing by the Lord and helping.

---

1 *Morann mac Maín* The judge mentioned in "The Birth of Cú Chulainn." Cormac mac Airt, king of Tara, is supposed to have been a third prescient believer. His story is told in Tomás Ó Cathasaigh, *The Heroic Biography of Cormac mac Airt* (DIAS, 1977).

2 Except for a little interpretive license, the translation here closely follows the careful work of Corthals and Kobel in making sense of this challenging poem, but substitutes "I" for what I take to be Conchobor's use of a "royal *we*," and makes some other choices among options they propose.

Wouldn't I have stood by a forgiving God, to help him?
Wouldn't I have fought in an unequal fight, and died? Any
equal opposition, I'd have overcome.

Christ, our heavenly Hero, was not unwilling to be made to
suffer,
although he had an earthly body—our holy, mighty Christ.

What's the use, when I can't reach him now, of my grim talk of
despair,
despairing that I can't avenge God?
The ones who crucified the King, Creator of the heavens, are
scum.

I'm struck down in my pride of mind, without reaching the
King.
Christ's crucifixion leaves me devastated. If I had risen to his
aid, I would have died:

it would have been easier for me not to go on living after the
High King's ordeal.
The noble King, he suffered the cross and the crown of thorns
to redeem humanity's wrongdoing.

For his sake I would go to my death, a lord of action:
may I shed the apprehension of death, and may it be nothing.

Pure heavenly Hero—if only my heart had urgently gone
before him,
when I heard about my High King's awful lamentation.[1]

For, my Lord, with these words with which I couldn't manage
to truly help the King,
my Lord heals me: deadly sorrow combines with the fear of
God.[2]

---

1 *awful lamentation* This could refer not to others' lamention of Jesus, as before, but to his own lamentation in Matthew 27.46 and Mark 15.34.

2 *the fear of God* Kobel follows Corthals in reading this line as "deadly sorrow together

It humbles me to go to my rest without avenging the Creator."

Conchobor composed this poem when Bachrach, a Leinster druid,* told him how Christ had been crucified, when Conchobor asked "What are these incredible signs?" etc.

Or it might have been Altus, the consul Octavian[1] sent to the Gaels to collect tribute, who told Conchobor that Christ had been crucified.

In one manuscript (Meyer, Death-Tales, *10–11) the text goes on like this:*

"All right then," said Conchobor. "I'll take down a thousand armed men to rescue Christ."

Then he leapt for his two spears and brandished them so violently that they splintered in his fists. And he took his sword in his hand and attacked the woods around him until he turned them into a plain, i.e., Mag Lámraige in Fir Rois. Then he said, "This is how I'd avenge Christ on the Jews and the ones who crucified him, if I could get at them."

His fury made Mes Gegrai's brain pop out of his head, and his own brain gushed out over him, and he died from it. And it's because of that that everyone says: "Conchobor dwells in heaven thanks to the wish that Conchobor made for himself."

The last thing Conchobor said was: "Whoever carries me home without stopping," he said, "will inherit my kingship…"

---

with great (religious) fear of (its) cause." This is the "sorrow according to God" (*tristitia secundum Deum*) of 2 Corinthians 7.10, which "worketh penance, steadfast to salvation," as opposed to Conchobor's earlier, more sinful despair (*tristitia saeculi*: the "sorrow of the world" which "worketh death") and possible fear of death. Conchobor's foreseeable death after speaking this poem is framed as martyrdom, not suicide. For more on this, see Reinoud Otten, "'Men Dare Not Offer Prayers for Them': Perceptions of Suicide in Medieval Ireland" (M.A. thesis, Utrecht University, 2023, https://studenttheses.uu.nl/handle/20.500.12932/44784) 33–41.

1 *Octavian* Otherwise known as Caesar Augustus (63 BCE–14 CE). Biblically, Jesus was crucified under the next emperor, Tiberius (42 BCE–37 CE); and indeed Version C (Kobel, 378–80) makes Altus an envoy of Tiberius.

Now this version has the episode with Cenn Berraide.

God revealed Mes Gegrai's brain to Búite mac Bronaigh, and now Búite has it as a pillow: everyone who goes to their death with Mes Gegrai's brain on top of them is bound for heaven. And it's said it will be carried south to the Leinstermen, and then they will gain the supremacy. So that concludes "The Death of Conchobor."

Other versions (Kobel, 347, 380) say explicitly that Conchobor was baptized by the blood bursting from his wound; one adds that his soul went to hell only to be released immediately as part of Christ's Harrowing of Hell.

*The saga "Da Coca's Guesthouse***" (*Bruiden Da Choca, *Ó Corráin #995, first half of the twelfth century)*[1] *covers the disputed succession after Conchobor's death. Presented with a choice between Fergus, Cúscraid, and Cormac Conn Loinges, the Ulstermen choose Cormac, who returns from exile with Ailill and Maeve only to fall afoul of his* geisi* *and reignite the feud with Connacht, which leads to his death in the titular guesthouse.*

*After this comes a further sequel, "The Battle of Airtech" (*Cath Airtig, *Ó Corráin #1001, first half of the twelfth century)*[2] *in which the kingship is offered to Conall Cernach after Cormac's death, and Conall (after lamenting Conchobor and offering advice on how to govern) bestows it on Cúscraid. Cúscraid finally makes peace with Fergus, who returns from exile with his wife Flidais to take over Cú Chulainn and Súaltaim's former holdings on Muirthemne Plain. (It says he lives there until Flidais dies, then goes back to Ailill and Maeve for the events described in "The Death of Fergus," below.) Controversy arises over some land that, according to this text, Maeve had turned over to Conchobor*

---

1 Edited and translated by Gregory Toner, *Bruiden Da Choca* (ITS, 2007); at https://archive.org/details/revueceltique21pari/page/150/mode/2up in an older translation by Whitley Stokes. The story is largely modeled on the better-known King Cycle saga "The Destruction of Da Derga's Hostel."

2 Edited and translated by R.I. Best, "The Battle of Airtech," *Ériu* 8 (1916) 170–90, at https://archive.org/details/eriu_1916_8/page/170/mode/2up. A recent comment on the text is Emmet Taylor, "What heroes fear: the tragedy of the old hero in *Cath Airtig*," *Kelten* 93 (2022), at https://kelten.vanhamel.nl/ 93-2022-taylor-irish-cath-airtig-heroes-old-age.

to compensate him for his warriors' deaths during the Táin. *She refuses to let it pass to Conchobor's heirs, and war breaks out yet again. The Ulstermen win the titular Battle of Airtech but can't wipe out the Connachtmen entirely. And so their rivalry continues.*

The Death of Fergus

*This twelfth-century tale (*Aided Fergusa meic Róich, *Ó Corráin #971) appears with Recension 1 of the* Táin *in the Yellow Book of Lecan. Like some parts of the* Táin *itself, this story shows that Ailill and Maeve's relationship is not always as jealousy-free as Maeve says in "The Pillow-Talk."*

How Fergus is killed is remarkably similar to Baldr's death in Norse mythology.[1]

The translation uses the Irish edited by Kuno Meyer in Death-Tales of the Ulster Heroes, *32–35.*

How did Fergus die? That's easy.*

Fergus went into exile in Connacht after his honor was violated in the matter of the sons of Uisliu, because he was one of the three sureties* they'd been given for their safety, along with Dubthach Beetletongue and Conchobor's son Cormac Conn Loinges. They were all in exile in the west for fourteen years, and they never stopped bringing tears and trembling to the Ulstermen: they brought them tears and trembling every night.

He—that is, Fergus—killed Conchobor's son Fiachra, and Geirge mac Illeda, and Éogan mac Durthacht. He led the Táin. There were many exploits he performed while in Ailill and Maeve's household, and he and his men were out in the field more often than at home.

The exiles numbered three thousand. Fergus's best friend in Ailill's household was the blind poet* Lugaid, i.e., a brother of Ailill's.

After their military exploits they stayed by the lake on Aí Plain. They made a big camp there, with games and gatherings.

One day the whole army went to bathe in the lake.

"Go down there, Fergus," said Ailill, "and dunk the men!"

"They're no good in water," said Fergus. He went down anyway.

Maeve's heart couldn't stand her not going in as well.

As Fergus went into the lake, all the rocks and gravel on the bottom came up to the surface.

---

1 See Snorri Sturluson's *Edda*, trans. Anthony Faulkes (London: Everyman, 1995) 48–51, at http://vsnrweb-publications.org.uk/EDDArestr.pdf; Ní Mhaoileoin, "The heroic biography of Fergus mac Róich," 114–21; and now Kim McCone, "The deaths of Baldr and Fergus mac Roig," *ZCP* 71 (2024) 179–86.

Maeve climbed onto Fergus's chest and wrapped her legs around him, and the lake hid what they were doing.

Ailill was seized with jealousy.

Then Maeve came back up.

"It's lovely what that stag and doe[1] are doing in the lake, Lugaid," said Ailill.

"Why not kill them?" said Lugaid, who had never missed his aim.

"Take a shot at them for me!" said Ailill.

"Turn me to face them," said Lugaid, "and give me a spear."

Fergus was washing in the lake with his chest facing them. And Ailill had his chariot brought up so he had it nearby. And Lugaid threw the spear so that it went through Fergus and came out his back.

"Bull's-eye!" said Lugaid.

"That's true," said everyone, "Fergus has gone tits up!"[2]

"How tragic," said Lugaid, "that I've killed my foster-brother* and friend without meaning to."

"Bring me my chariot!" said Ailill.

The whole army fled, every man for himself, exiles and Connachtmen all making for the shore.

Fergus pulled out the spear and threw it after Ailill: it skewered the hunting dog between the chariot's two suspension-beams.* Then Fergus got out of the lake and stretched out on the hill beside the lake, and immediately his soul left him, and his grave is there still.

This has been "The Death of Fergus."

---

1 *stag and doe* Carey, "The encounter at the ford," 19–21, juxtaposes Ailill's way of referring to Fergus with an impotence charm in which a "stag of flood" (*dam tuli*) is bound by a "wanton woman," which he argues is "a charm which can be used both to render a man sexually incapable and to deprive a fighter of the power of movement." In general, he finds that "warriors, women and water" are a "risky conjunction."

2 *tits up* The word here (*bruinne*) is the same as 'chest' in "with his chest facing them."

The Death of Ailill and Conall Cernach

*This probably twelfth-century tale (*Aided Ailella & Chonaill Chernaig, *Ó Corráin #956) occurs with other Ulster Cycle death-tales in Edinburgh, National Library of Scotland, Advocates ms. 72.1.40. It assumes knowledge of "The Death of Fergus." Here Ailill is again said to be "without jealousy"—the jealousy is on Maeve's side.*

The translation uses the Irish from the new edition by Anouk Nuijten, "Critical Editions of Aided Ailella 7 Chonall Chernaig *and* Aided Cheit maic Mágach *with Translations, Texual Notes and Commentary" (Ph.D. thesis, University of Cambridge, 2021, https://www.repository.cam.ac.uk/handle/1810/324456). There was a previous edition and translation by Kuno Meyer in* ZCP *1 (1897) 102–11, 503, at https://research.ucc.ie/celt/document/G301019 (text) and https://research.ucc.ie/celt/document/T301019 (translation).*

There was a mighty Ulsterman, Conall Cernach son of Amairgen: he was the best warrior in Ireland. He was remarkably brutal, i.e., he was a man who never walked away from a fight, as long as there was a spear in his hand, without taking a Connachtman's head. He had it in for the Connachtmen in a big way, because they'd killed his (three[1]) brothers. And yet there wasn't one of the Connachtmen whose son or brother or father he himself hadn't killed.

He killed three sons of Ailill and Maeve, and he was also the one who killed Bélchú[2] of Breifne and his three sons. And he was the one who killed the seven sons of Mágu of the Connachtmen, i.e., Ánlúan, Docha, Mac Corb, Finn, Scannlán, Cet, and Ailill.[3] And

1 *three* In one manuscript of the text but not the other. Meanwhile, "The Siege of Howth" identifies two of Conall's brothers, one of them a seven-year-old foster-son* of Cú Chulainn, as being killed in battle by the Leinstermen.

2 *Bélchú* This story is told in "The Death of Cet mac Mágach" (*Aided Cheit maic Mágach*, Ó Corráin #958), translated by Meyer, *Death-Tales of the Ulster Heroes*, 36–46, and in Nuijten's thesis, 116–21. According to this, Conall didn't personally kill Bélchú, but got his sons to murder him by switching beds with him, a reversal of Aarne-Thompson tale type 1119, "Ogres Kill Their Own Children" (compare Thompson motif K499.8, "Trickster dupes rival by exchanging beds"). Then Conall killed the sons.

3 *the seven sons of Mágu … Ailill* "Son of Mágu (*mac Mágach*)" has been dropped from all the sons' names for easier reading. Their names are given at the start of the *Táin* as Ailill,

he was the one who killed Ailill son of Máta Muiresc. (Ailill was a Connachtman since Máta Muiresc was his mother; he was also a son of Ross Rúaid of Leinster. And he'd gone west to defend the kingship of Leinster, and took over the kingship of Connacht on the basis of his mother's claim, and there, in his mother's land in the west, he was called by his matronymic.[1])

But Conall Cernach fell prey to weakness and frailty in the end, after his foster-kindred[2*] were killed, i.e., Conchobor and Cú Chulainn, and he fell prey to grief and frailty and debilitating sickness, and barely had the strength to move his legs. And he thought about whose household he should go to for care and feeding.

"Ailill and Maeve!" he said. "They're the couple who'll be able to look after me. Now, I already hate them with a passion, but even so, I have to go there."

Then he traveled to Crúachu by himself. And he went into the stronghold where Ailill and Maeve were, and Ailill welcomed him.

"Welcome, Conall," said Maeve. "And yet, you've always hated our side with a passion."

"Be good to me," said Conall, "I'm a good warrior.[3] There's flocks[4] in it for whoever is good to me."

"Of course you'll be welcome," said Maeve.

Ánlúan, Moccorb, Cet, Én, Bascall, and Dócha, which doesn't entirely match. Cet and Ánlúan featured in "The Story of Mac Dá Thó's Pig," Dócha in two episodes of the *Táin* (pp. 247, 270–271); Cet again in "The Death of Conchobor."

1 Parentheses added for clarity: this is background information about Ailill, separate from the overview of Conall. The statement that Conall killed Ailill is a little confusing because the text is about to tell us how it happened, but lists it along with his previous accomplishments.

2 *foster-kindred* The Irish is *iar marbad a c[h]umalta*, which Nuijten translates as "after his foster-brothers were killed" (55). *Comalta* does mean "foster-brother," but can also be used "with wider connotation," as *eDIL* has it, and Conchobor, as Conall's uncle, would have been his foster-father.

3 *good to me … good warrior* One of the manuscripts is damaged here: see Nuijten (71–72). She translates the first part of what Conall says (*Maith do denum forom*) as "Good is your behaviour towards me" (55), apparently taking *do* as the 2sg possessive, whereas I take it as the preposition *do*: literally, "Goodness for doing towards me," i.e., "the situation calls for you to be good to me," because Conall goes on to explain what's in it for them.

4 *There's flocks* Nuijten (72) cites a suggestion by Thomas Owen Clancy that this *alma* 'herds, flocks' could also be read as *almsa* 'alms.' The verb is singular, hence my translation.

"I'll need my own house, up on top of the rampart."[1]

So they built him a house, and brought him a pig and a cow and Maeve and Ailill's leftovers and twelve loaves of bread and a ram and a cauldron of broth, and he ate them all in one sitting. He tunneled under the rampart, and used to go out and raid Connacht every night until he was full, and be back in his house before morning.[2]

They fed him like that for a whole year, always the same amount. And every day he would regale the Connachtmen with descriptions of how he'd killed their sons and brothers and fathers. The Connachtmen would bring him their spears to trim and rivet, and he would finish them before the cows got up.

Now, Maeve was a woman of vast power, honor, and dignity, and vast desires when it came to everything, so every day she'd have thirty men back-to-back, or one visit from Fergus. But her husband, Ailill, was the same age[3] as she was, a man without a blemish, i.e., without jealousy, fear, or stinginess. Ailill was handsome and strong and had good judgment: for example, when he'd be playing *fidchell** with someone, Maeve's servant used to come and call him to hook up with her. And Ailill would say this: "Hold on a bit till we finish the game."

He used to see other women behind her back, and that made her jealous, so she brought in Conall Cernach to keep tabs on him, to stop him from doing that against her will.

Early one May morning, Ailill was hooking up with a woman by the edge of the stockade.[4] Conall was on the ramparts riveting a spear. Then Maeve came out, because she knew about the sex: there was a hazel-branch moving beside the couple, and Maeve saw it.

"Well, Conall," said Maeve, "until today you've been 'Conall the Victorious.' Conall Pathetic and Odious[5] is more like it: that's your

---

1 *on top of the rampart* The other manuscript has "against the rampart," like a lean-to.

2 *used to go out … before morning* Conall's enormous appetite is a plot point in "The Story of Mac Dá Thó's Pig." My translation here is a paraphrase of "used to get his fill from the Connachtmen": Nuijten (73–74) agrees that what's going on here is that after his daily serving of food, he's still hungry, so he goes out at night and plunders the countryside.

3 *the same age* By contrast, "Maeve's Series of Husbands," (p. 73) presents him as much younger than she is.

4 *edge of the stockade* The other manuscript specifies "in a whitethorn bush in the forest near the south side of the fort."

5 *Victorious … Pathetic and Odious* Maeve renames him from *Conall Cernach* to *Conall cláen trúag*, which sounds similar in a way that my translation is meant to reflect. As

name from now on. When you were 'Victorious,' no one would have dared to go against your guarantee. That outrage today reflects directly on you."

Then Conall said: "Actually, this is about revenge for Fergus!" And he aimed the spear at the couple, sending it clear through Ailill's body, or, alternatively, Ailill was in an empty house, and Conall hit him through the roof.[1]

Everyone came and got Ailill out of there.

"Whodunnit?" said everyone.

"Conall dunnit," said Ailill.

"Dammit, that's not true at all," said Conall.

"It is too," said Maeve.

"*If* it is," he said, "it was revenge for Fergus!"

"You've done yourself a bad turn, Conall," said Ailill, "by doing *me* a bad turn. Now get out of my sight[2] before I die, because the Connachtmen will kill you as soon as I'm dead."

"I just need to make it to my chariot parked out front of the fort," said Conall.

"I'll hang on till then,"[3] said Ailill.

Conall made it to his chariot. Then Ailill immediately died, and then after that the Connachtmen let loose on Conall. He killed a

---

Nuijten points out (80–81, 192–94) there is complex wordplay involving the double meanings of *cernach* (which can also mean 'angular') and *cláen* ('crooked,' either physically or morally), and traditions that Conall had a crooked neck, about which see William Sayers, "Portraits of the Ulster hero Conall: a case for Waardenburg's Syndrome?" *Emania* 20 (2006) 75–80, and p. 355 below.

1 *through the roof* Nuijten's edition seems to say he hit him *upwards* (*suas*) through the roof, but it's hard to see how. Meyer more logically had "or maybe he wounded him in an empty house through the thatch above."

2 *get out of my sight* Ailill literally tells Conall to get out of his face/cheeks, which of course have a connection with personal honor. Nuijten says: "I suggest taking *inchaib* [cheeks] in a less literal sense, instead translating it as 'protection, security, guarantee'. *eDIL* notes that the combination *d(i) inchaib* is often taken as 'by the guarantee of; by means of'. I would propose to translate *do m'inchaib* as 'under my guarantee', in the sense that Ailill allows Conall to flee under his protection, until he dies, after which he is not able to offer his protection anymore" (84). I agree with her about the situation; the question is just how openly it's stated.

3 *I'll hang on till then* Substituting the unambiguous reading of the other manuscript for what Nuijten translates as "You will not die because of that," but nonetheless interprets as having the implication "that by promising Conall not to die before the latter reaches his chariot, he grants Conall a head-start before the Connachta begin their pursuit of him" (86).

lot of them. He had a *geis** against fording a river without leaving the water clear and sparkling.[1] There were miners washing ore in the river upstream, and he got caught in the sediment, which slowed him down in front of everyone.[2] That's where they killed him, after he slaughtered more Connachtmen. The three Red Dogs of Mairtine from the land of the Fir Maige were the ones who cut off his head. And they were of the Erna[3] and belonged to Ailill's household, and they took Conall's head in revenge for Cú Roí.[4] And while they were slaughtering him is when Maeve showed up in pursuit. Maeve said: "His pale head, which they carried off," etc.[5]

They took it with them, Conall's head, to avenge Cú Roí, whose head the Ulstermen had taken north with them, and Conall's head is still in the west. It has room inside it for four yearling calves, or for four people to play *fidchell,** or for a couple to bed down. The Ulstermen received a prophecy that it will be carried north again and that they will recover their old strength as soon as they drink milk out of it. And there is a saying, "The Ulstermen's destruction caused the Ulstermen's destruction."[6]

This has been "The Death of Ailill and Conall Cernach."

---

1 *clear and sparkling* Nuijten's literal version: "There was a geis on him to go into a ford without filtering [it] after him" (61). On the principle that most heroic *geisi* have a social purpose, the point of this would be to limit the environmental damage caused by warriors' violence: Conall is not supposed to leave any water undrinkable. See next note.

2 *slowed him down ... everyone* Meyer thought this meant that "the troubled water reached him, so that it held him fast before every body." Nuijten has "the unfiltered water came to him, so that that detained him before everyone." Nuijten's version leaves room for the possibility that Conall was delayed not by a magical effect of the dirty water, but by having to stay there and clean it, because he knew his *geis* would kill him if he left it like that. The place is supposedly Ballyconnell, County Cavan (see Nuijten, 152).

3 *the Erna* A Munster tribe. "Maeve's Series of Husbands" identifies Ailill as "son of Máta, son of Sraibgend of the Erna," so according to some traditions, they would have had a connection to Ailill. On the three "Red Dogs" specifically, see Burgess, "Disintegrating Lugaid Ríab nDerg," 329–30; stories say they helped Maeve become queen of Connacht.

4 *for Cú Roí* See Best, "The tragic death of Cúrói mac Dári," for how he died.

5 *Maeve said ... etc.* Presumably this refers to some kind of poem or chant commemorating the event.

6 *Ulstermen's destruction* The Irish is *dith Ulad le dith Ulad*. Nuijten (95) discusses how this pivots on two ways of reading *dith Ulad*: in other words, the destruction that was caused by the Ulstermen caused the Ulstermen to be destroyed. This dovetails with the Christian ethics of Matthew 26.52: "all that take the sword shall perish with the sword."

The Death of Maeve

*This perhaps eleventh-century tale (*Aided Meidbe, *Ó Corráin #977) appears with Recension 2 of the* Táin *in the Book of Leinster, and with "The Death of Ailill and Conall Cernach" in the Edinburgh manuscript. Ó Corráin calls it "[a] brief tale of the crimes of queen M[aeve]'s family": "This looks like a clerical exemplum of the evils of paganism by one who had read the deeds of the [Greek] House of Atreus, but the reader is given no context." The story has facts about Maeve and her sisters in common with "Maeve's Series of Husbands," pp. 68–74 above, but many of the details are different. Here Maeve kills her sister Clothru to become queen of Connacht, rather than getting the province as a gift from her father; Clothru is the mother of Furbaide; and no background is given for how Clothru was impregnated by Conchobor. The gathering at Loch Rí might suggest that the epic feud between Ulster and Connacht is finally coming to an end.*

*The translation uses the Irish edited by Vernam Hull, "*Aided Meidbe*: The Violent Death of Medb,"* Speculum *13.1 (1938) 52–61.*

What caused the death of Maeve, daughter of Eochaid Feidlech from Tara?

The three sons of Finn were Conall Anglonnach, Eochaid Finn, and Eochaid Feidlech. Then Eochaid Feidlech had three sons and three daughters. The three sons were Bres, Nár, and Lothar, that is, the three Finns of Emain, or the three Blond Triplets (*Finn Emna*[1]). The three daughters were Eithne Úathach (Eithne "the Terrible"), Maeve of Crúachu, and Clothru of Crúachu. Eithne the Terrible was called that because she used to eat children, so that children always loathed the mention of her name.[2]

1 *Finn Emna* Sources differ about whether *Emna* here refers to Emain Macha (giving the first option: the Finns of Emain) or not (the second option: the Fair, or Blond, Triplets). See *eDIL*, s.v. *1 emon*.

2 *Eithne the Terrible … her name* This explanation conflates Maeve's sister Eithne with another Eithne, daughter of Ernbrand, from the text "The Expulsion of the Déisi," who was fed little boys to accelerate her growth, because of a prophecy that she would help the Déisi seize their future territory. See *Coire Sois*, 287–91, and "Fitness of Names" (II, 122–23).

Now Clothru was queen in Crúachu before Maeve wrested control of it from Eochaid by force. The three Finns were trying to steal the kingship from their father. Clothru tried to intervene and prevent them, but they declared war on Eochaid anyway. Then she came up to them.

"Are you meaning to insult your father?" she said. "What you're doing is unjust."

"It's necessary," said the young men.

"Do you have any offspring?"

"Not many," they said.

"Since you've embraced injustice, you'll probably die. Come to me," she said, "since it's my time to conceive, and let's find out if you can leave me any of your offspring."

And they did. Each one took his turn with her, and it had a positive outcome, i.e., Lugaid of the Red Stripes, son of the three Blond Triplets.

"Now," she said, "leave Dad alone. It's unjust enough to have had sex with your sister without waging war on your father."

That kept them from winning the battle.[1]

Now, Clothru used to spend the tributes she received from Connacht on Clothru's Island (*Inis Clothrann*) in Loch Rí.[2] They say what happened is that Maeve killed her and her side was cut open[3] with swords to give birth to Furbaide son of Conchobor.

---

1 *kept them from winning the battle* About how this works, see Kicki Ingridsdotter, "Motivation for incest: Clothru and the battle of *Druim Criaich*," *Studia Celtica Fennica* 10 (2013) 43–65, and Boyd, "Aspects of sexual violence in early Irish literature," 79–84.

2 *Loch Rí* Now Lough Ree, north of Athlone: see Map 1.

3 *was cut open* The passive leaves it vague whether Maeve did the cutting open but Burgess, "Disintegrating Lugaid Ríab nDerg," 181–82, takes it that she did: Burgess says that Maeve "played midwife to the sister who fell by her hand." Burgess also quotes a passage from the 10th-century *Betha Adamnáin*, "The life of Adomnán (of Iona)," where Adomnán judges that a woman murderer should be executed by "someone whom no mother bore": this might have been meant to communicate, like John 8.7, that no one should dare, but in fact there is a young man there who, like Shakespeare's Macduff, says he was brought out through his mother's side and so has standing to perform the execution. The same idea might be involved here too: "Brought into the world not by maternal travail, but savagely unleashed from his mother's lifeless body by the incisive stroke of a sword," says Burgess, the "unborn" Furbaide would have special standing to hit Maeve in a way that Cú Chulainn couldn't manage with his sling.

Maeve took over the kingship of Connacht after that, and brought in Ailill to rule with her. She used to spend the tributes from Connacht on Clothru's Island, and it was a *geis** for her not to bathe every morning in the spring at the entrance to the island.

In due course Furbaide went to Clothru's Island and drove a stake, the same height as Maeve, into the flagstone where she used to bathe. He tied a rope to the top of it and stretched it across Loch Rí, taking the free end home with him. After that, whenever the young men of Ulster used to play, this was Furbaide's game: he pulled his rope taut between two stakes, and shot along it. He never gave up until he could hit an apple sitting on top of the stake on the island.

One time there was a big gathering of the Connachtmen and the Ulstermen around Loch Rí, and they came together from the west and from the east. Early in the morning, Maeve took the opportunity to bathe in the spring above the lake.

"What a vision of beauty over there," said everyone.

"Who's that?" said Furbaide.

"Your mother's sister," said everyone.

He was eating a piece of cheese.[1] He didn't waste time looking for a stone—he put the cheese in his sling. When Maeve turned to face him, he hurled the cheese and smacked her in the head with it, killing her with one shot to avenge his mother.

This has been "The Death of Maeve."

---

1 *cheese* This is one of those details in early Irish literature that seems random and comical, but Karen Burgess, in a paper entitled "Sinister cheese: terrible *tanach* in Irish tradition," presented at the 16th annual University of California Celtic Studies Conference in 1994 but sadly unpublished, argues that it has serious purpose. Burgess says that "cheese is no ordinary foodstuff—rather, it is food in transition. It is milk gone bad—the product of a maternal breast, the archetypical sustainer of life—now curdled and mouldering, in a state of decomposition. It is the antithesis of new milk, and, as such, the natural embodiment of opposition. [... C]heese is truly liminal food—it is always somewhere between two states. It is one thing on its way to becoming something else. As such, cheese is the ideal food of marginalized individuals. [...] As food in transition—specifically, as food which is being transformed by nature, which is decomposing—the affinities between cheese and death are clear." She adds that "The so-called 'culinary triangle' (cooked-raw-rotted) proposed by anthropologist-philosopher Claude Lévi-Strauss may be of some help in unravelling this apparent contradiction." (I prefer the quoted wording, but see Burgess, "Disintegrating Lugaid Ríab nDerg," 177–81, for similar content.)

Glossary of Terms and Concepts

Beltaine Pronounced "BEL-tin-yuh." One of the quarter-days in the traditional calendar, marking the beginning of summer in the human world: May 1. Although not as notoriously as at Samain,* the boundary with the Otherworld* might be more permeable at this time.

blemish A term with legal significance, especially as it relates to kings: "A king is expected to have a perfect body, free from blemish or disability. The sagas provide a number of instances of a king losing his kingship through some disfigurement" (*GEIL*, 19). For more on this, see Boyd, "Modeling impairment and disability in early Irish literature."

búanbach A boardgame, possibly something like backgammon. Like *fidchell** below, it functioned as a form of recreation or a test of intellect. See Mallory, *In Search of the Irish Dreamtime*, 248–50, and the classic article by Eoin Mac White, "Early Irish Boardgames," *Éigse* 5 (1947) 25–35, at https://www.unicorngarden.com/eigse/eigse01.htm.

cumal A *cumal* ("KUH-val") is a unit of value, equivalent to three dairy cows or one enslaved woman. The word originally had the literal meaning "enslaved woman," but it is used in many other contexts.

my dear When starred, this translates *popa* ("POB-uh"), which *eDIL* characterizes as "a respectful form of address to an elder or superior, but occas[ionally] familiarly to an inferior," when Cú Chulainn is talking to a friend or foster-brother,* or to his charioteer Lóeg. When he speaks to elders, like Conchobor or Fergus, the translation is "uncle.*"

dindshenchas Pronounced "DINN-HEN-uh-hus." One of the special types of lore (*senchas*, "SHEN-uh-hus") that poets* were expected to master, consisting of stories related to the names of places. The *Táin* has a lot of *dindshenchas* embedded in it.

Gwynn's five-volume edition and translation of *The Metrical Dindshenchas* is an important primary text, and Marie-Luise Theuerkauf, *Dindshenchas Érenn* (Cork: Cork Studies in Celtic Literatures, 2023), surveys the genre and has a useful chart (122–24) relating the *dindshenchas* to early Irish saga texts including the *Táin*. Mulligan, *A Landscape of Words*, and Sarah Künzler, *Memory and Remembering in Early Irish Literature* (Berlin: De Gruyter, 2024) are important studies.

druid A pagan priest, soothsayer, and loremaster. The most common functions of druids in Ulster Cycle tales are to pronounce on auspicious days and issue prophecies. Druid magic is stereotyped in some early Irish texts, particularly saints' lives, as diabolical.

dry cows Cows that are not producing milk, typically in the 2–3 months before giving birth. Cows that *are* producing milk are traditionally known as milch cows, but since "milch" might be unfamiliar language for most twenty-first-century readers, this translation uses "dairy cows" for that.

fair play This translates *fír fer* (pronounced "feer ver"), literally "truth of men," the rules for honorable combat. The general principle was that combatants ought to meet in equal numbers and on equal terms. See further Philip O'Leary, "*Fír fer*: an internalized ethical concept in early Irish literature?" *Éigse* 22 (1987) 1–14.

***fían*-warrior** This translates *fénnid*, a warrior in a *fían* ("FEE-an"), which was a roving warband living outside a settled community, usually by hunting in the wilderness and by raiding. There was an early Irish legal principle that a man came into his full legal rights only on his father's death (*GEIL*, 82–83). Instead of living as a lowly *fer midboth* ("man of middle huts") on his father's land, a young man might choose to join a *fían* in the interim. Another reason to join a *fían* was to protest an injustice or to seek revenge, as Conchobor's mother Ness does in one version of his birth-tale. (See also Matthieu Boyd, "Melion and the wolves of Ireland," *Neophilologus* 93.4 [2009] 555–70.) Some men were long-term "professional," even lifelong, *fían*-members. Along with the druid Cathbad in the same version of Conchobor's birth-tale, the hero Finn mac Cumaill is an example of such, as is Cú Chulainn's opponent Nad Crantail in the *Táin*. Further reading: Kim McCone, "The Celtic and Indo-European origins of the *Fían*," in *The Gaelic Finn Tradition*, ed. Sharon J. Arbuthnot and Geraldine Parsons (Four Courts, 2012), 14–30.

fidchell A boardgame, functionally equivalent to chess as a test of intellect. (Compare *búanbach** above, and see the references there.) Pronounced "FITH-hyell," a compound of *fid* 'wood' and *cíall* 'sense, wits.'

fingal In the early Irish justice system, killing members of one's own family was considered especially heinous. The relevant kin-group was the *fine* (pronounced "FINN-uh"), the descendants of a common great-grandfather. Killing within the kin-group caused a legal problem, in that the killer was both required to compensate the family and entitled to compensation as a member of it, and any revenge killings would quickly eat up the family from within. "The Death of Aífe's Only Son" is a clear instance of *fingal*, although it doesn't provoke the furious backlash one finds in a tale like "The Kin-Slaying of Rónán" (*Fingal Rónáin*, Ó Corráin #1056, translated in *The Celtic Heroic Age*, 274–82). In Christian terms, suicide is considered a type of *fingal*: see Otten, "Perceptions of Suicide," 5–6, 25–28.

Fomoire, pl. Fomoiri Pronounced "FOV-wi-ruh," pl. "FOV-wi-ri," anglicized as "Fomorians." The Fomoiri are supernatural beings who are rivals and antagonists of the Túatha Dé Danann,* especially in connection with the Second Battle of Mag Tuired. Etymologically, they are ocean demons: their name is normally understood as *fo* 'under' plus either *mor* 'phantom' or *muir* 'sea.' ("Fitness of Names" I, 185, suggested "evil people who used to plunder on the sea" or "good people who used to live on sea-islands," the latter sense from *fó* 'good' plus *muir*.) They are often analogized to the Vikings and associated with the Western Isles of Scotland. On the terminology, see Simon Rodway, "Mermaids, leprechauns, and Fomorians: a Middle Irish account of the descendants of Cain," *CMCS* 59 (2010) 1–17, at 16–17; for further discussion, see Williams, *Ireland's Immortals*, and

John Carey, "The nature of the Fomoiri: the dark other in the medieval Irish imagination," in *Myth and History in Celtic and Scandinavian Traditions*, ed. Emily Lyle (Amsterdam University Press, 2021) 25–48.

fosterage, foster- As noted in the Introduction, foster-relationships were important in early Ireland and in early Irish literature, and led to lasting alliances and close emotional ties. Fosterage could be arranged for a fee or out of personal affection. The words for foster-parents are the "mommy" and "daddy" words *muimme* and *aitte*; the word for a foster-child or "fosterling" is typically *dalta* (translated here as "student" in the context of Scáthach's martial-arts academy); for a foster-brother (e.g., when Fer Diad and Cú Chulainn talk about each other), it is *comalta*, "co-fosterling." As in "The Birth of Cú Chulainn," having many foster-parents or foster-siblings was a sign of prestige. One of the questions the king of Tara's daughters supposedly asked Saint Patrick when he preached to them about Jesus was "Was he fostered by many?" (*The Celtic Heroic Age*, 210). See *GEIL*, 81–91, and Thomas C. O'Donnell, *Fosterage in Medieval Ireland: An Emotional History* (University of Amsterdam Press, 2020).

gáe bolga Pronounced "GUY BOL-guh." Cú Chulainn's special weapon of last resort, which is thrown and explodes into multiple barbs. The meaning is seemingly "bag-spear," but see Sayers, "Martial feats," 55–56, on the etymological difficulties, so I leave it untranslated. Edward Pettit, "Cú Chulainn's *gáe bolga*—from harpoon to stingray-spear?" *Studia Hibernica* 41 (2015) 9–48, explores the traditions surrounding it. Longman, "'What manner of man is this Hound?'," calls it "a brutal, desecrating weapon, inflicting damage from the inside that violates and disrupts the demarcation between internal and external" (18). Although perhaps not all would agree (the way Cú Chulainn uses it on Lóch and Fer Diad, as a result of their impenetrable skin, might not be *inevitably* sexual), it has been analyzed as phallic by Dooley, *Playing the Hero*, 168; by Sarah Sheehan, "Fer Diad deflowered: homoerotics and masculinity in *Comrac Fir Diad*," in *Ulidia 2: Proceedings of the Second International Conference on the Ulster Cycle of Tales, National University of Ireland Maynooth, 24–27 June*

2005, ed. Ruairí Ó hUiginn and Brian Ó Catháin (Maynooth: An Sagart, 2009) 54–65; and now by Longman.

geis Pronounced "gesh." The plural is *geisi.* (The Modern Irish is *geas*, pronounced "gyass," plural *geasa.*) This term, elsewhere often translated "taboo," is a supernatural obligation or restriction: something a person must do, must avoid, or must not allow to take place. It is usually specific to the individual, although some stories about kings, notably "The Destruction of Da Derga's Hostel," distinguish between a king's personal *geisi* and ones that are associated with the kingship. Also, "The Wooing of Emer" mentions what seems to be a general *geis* against riding in a chariot for three weeks after eating horse meat.

Reasonably soon after a person violates their *geis* or *geisi*, they almost always die, whether the violation is a cause or only a sign of their impending doom. A deadly double bind could be produced by contradictory *geisi* or by a *geis* conflicting with poetic satire.*

According to his death-tale, Cú Chulainn has two, ultimately conflicting *geisi*: not to pass a cooking-pot without stopping to partake, and not to eat dog meat ("the flesh of his namesake," given his identity as "Culann's Dog"). Conall Cernach has a *geis* not to leave the water fouled when he crosses a river; Maeve has one[1] not to marry a man who is stingy, jealous, or cowardly. In "The Wooing of Emer," Cú Chulainn saddles his son Connla with obnoxious *geisi* that inevitably force a confrontation (which follows in "The Death of Aífe's Only Son"). It could be argued that many heroes' *geisi* have an important social purpose—for example, stopping at every cooking-pot forces Cú Chulainn to strengthen the social bonds that restrain and guide his violence.

guesthouse The Irish is *bruiden* ("BRITH-en," with voiced *th*), conventionally translated "hostel" (which is let stand in "The Destruction of Da Derga's Hostel" as the standard translation of that title). The guesthouse was a vehicle for social mobility.

1 *Maeve has one* Her three requirements for a husband are famously mentioned in the "Pillow-Talk" introduction to Recension 2 of the *Táin*, but it's only in "Maeve's Series of Husbands" that she is said to have a *geis* against marrying a man who doesn't meet them.

In early Irish law, an unusually rich commoner could elevate himself to the status and honor-price* of a lord, a process which normally took several generations, by running a free public guesthouse and accepting a legal obligation to provide unlimited hospitality to all comers. He would lose his elevated status as a *briugu* or guesthouse-keeper if he turned anyone away. See *GEIL*, 36–38. Mac Dá Thó is a king, not a *briugu*; for him, the idea would seem to be to boost his status and reputation as a king by practicing public generosity (limited, in his case, by the rule about one stab of the fork).

honor-price This translates *díre* ("DEER-uh") or *lóg n-enech* ("LOAG NEN-uck," literally "the price of one's cheeks," i.e., face). As mentioned in the Introduction, honor-price was an expression of one's legal status, including the compensation one was entitled to receive.

There were various criteria used to calculate honor-price. For commoners, it was based on wealth (how much livestock they owned, the size of their house, etc.). For lords, it was based on the number of tenant farmers or "clients" they had. For kings, it was based on the number of polities (*túatha*) they controlled. Poets* and Christian clerics had their own separate hierarchies and their honor-price was based on where they ranked. The honor-price of wives and dependent professionals (a champion, herald, charioteer, and so on) was a fraction of their husband's or employer's (half for a first wife, a third for a second wife; half for many of the professionals), which could still be very high if they were attached to a king. (A woman didn't have an independent honor-price except in special circumstances, such as if she was her father's sole heir or her husband was a foreigner: see the comment on pp. 36 and 159.) The amount of the honor-price ranged from a single dairy cow for a standard farmer, to 42 cows for the king of a province like Ulster or Connacht. But a king could lose his honor-price and be downgraded to commoner status for things deemed inconsistent with his royal dignity, such as doing manual labor, traveling around without a retinue, cowardice in battle, being the target of poetic satire* without doing anything about it, or violating a *geis** (see *GEIL*, 18–21). Lóeg tells Cú Chulainn in the *Táin* that a warrior's honor-price would be downgraded if he was unarmed.

Killing someone required payment of a flat fee called *éraic* (pronounced "EH-rick" and conventionally translated "body-fine") plus the honor-price of everyone in the victim's kin-group, who could enslave or execute the killer if they weren't paid. Killing someone with powerful relatives could get very expensive very quickly.

Imbolc Pronounced "IM-bollug." One of the "quarter-days" in the calendar: February 1, whose Christian association is with the feast of Saint Brigit (February 2). See Tatiana Mikhailova, "February 1st in Ireland (*Imbolc* or *Lá Fhéile Bríde*): from Christian saint to pagan goddess," *Yearbook of Balkan and Baltic Studies* 3.1 (2020) 85–108, https://www.folklore.ee/balkan_baltic_yearbook/vol3/05.pdf. The invasion of Ulster in the *Táin*, and the Ulstermen's paralysis, lasts until this date.

jester This usually translates *drúth*, which can refer to a developmentally disabled person or a professional entertainer who imitates one. (Other early Irish terms for "jester" include *óinmit*, which is the word used in "The Death of Conchobor," and *crossán*.) In the sagas, the *drúth* apparently has special status as the alter ego or expendable sacrifice for a king, which would explain why jesters in the *Táin* are specifically chosen to wear Ailill's crown. See *GEIL*, 64–65 and 91–95, and Matthieu Boyd, "Competing assumptions about the *drúth* in *Orgain Denna Ríg*," *Ériu* 59 (2009) 37–47.

kin-love As mentioned in the Introduction, this translates *condalbae*. Tomás Ó Cathasaigh in particular has argued for the importance of this as a positive value in the *Táin*: see *Coire Sois*, 9, 90, 194.

mutant This translates *(in) ríastarthae*, a name for Cú Chulainn based on his *ríastrad* transformation. Kinsella rendered it "the Warped One."

mutate, mutation This translates *ríastrad* ("REE-uh-struth," with voiced *th*), a physical transformation unique to Cú Chulainn in his battle-frenzy. See the descriptions on pp. 182 and 242. Kinsella famously rendered it "warp-spasm." It has been extensively discussed, e.g., in Künzler, *Flesh and Word* (citing many prior references); Mulligan, "The erasure of a warrior's body"; Longman, "'What manner of man is this Hound?'"; Ron J. Popenhagen, "Cú Chulainn unbound," in *The Medieval Cultures of the Irish Sea and the North Sea*, ed. Charles W. MacQuarrie and Joseph Falaky Nagy (Amsterdam University Press, 2019) 59–77; and, for a comparative perspective, Ralph O'Connor, "Monsters of the tribe: berserk fury, shapeshifting and social dysfunction in *Táin Bó Cúailnge*, *Egils saga* and *Hrólfs saga kraka*," in *King and Warrior in Early North-West Europe*, ed. Jan Erik Rekdal and Charles Doherty (Four Courts, 2016) 180–236.

ogam *Ogam* (pronounced "OG-um" or "AW-hum": the *g* is softened, hence the modern spelling *ogham*) was an early writing system of notches and slashes, attested mostly for personal names incised on standing stones. It would have been a major project to write a whole sentence in *ogam* the way Cú Chulainn supposedly does, and none of the surviving inscriptions are nearly that long. The "Ogham in 3D" Project at the Dublin Institute for Advanced Studies (https://ogham.celt.dias.ie) is an outstanding resource on the subject: see https://ogham.celt.dias.ie/menu.php?lang=en&menuitem=03 to practice writing in *ogam*. Otherwise, the standard reference is Damian McManus, *A Guide to Ogam* (Maynooth: An Sagart, 1991).

Otherworld This translates *síd,* which means "Otherworld" and "peace": see *Coire Sois*, 19–34 for the connection. The Otherworld was a place of peace and plenty, which righteous human rulers could bring into being in the human world as well. It was the home of the Túatha Dé Danann* after they yielded Ireland to the Gaels. The poem *A Bé Find, in rega lim* ("Fair lady, will you go with me") from "The Wooing of Étaín," translated in the *Broadview Anthology of British Literature* vol. 1, 3e, 33, paints a vivid picture of the idyllic conditions.

When the word seems to refer to a landscape feature or is used in the plural, the translation is "Otherworld abode(s)" so that there is still a clear connection. Older translations tended to refer to *síd*-mounds as "fairy hills" or "elfmounds." In some texts, the Otherworld is located overseas instead of underground.

poet *fili*, pl. *filid* (pronounced "FILL-uh" and "FILL-ith," with voiced *th*, respectively; the Modern Irish is *file*, pl. *filí*). The translation "poet" is reductive: they might be considered "poet-professors," in that besides their poetic compositions, which would presumably have focused on panegyric (praise-poetry) and satire,* the poets were also expected to master storytelling, genealogy, place-name lore (*dindshenchas**), and history. In "The Wooing of Emer," Cú Chulainn models this medley of poetic disciplines in his conversation with Emer—presumably that was part of his training in fosterage* with the Ulster poet Amairgen. Etymologically, the word *fili* means "seer," and at the beginning of the *Táin*, Maeve meets a female poet, Fedelm, who functions primarily in this role of predicting the future; she and Cú Chulainn's teacher Scáthach possess the technique of divination called *imbas forosnai*. Poets had their own ranked hierarchy, and their honor-price* was portable so they could travel freely outside their home *túath* without needing to come under anyone's protection.*

protection With a few exceptions, such as poets,* early Irish people's legal rights were linked to their home polity, the *túath*. (Usually translated "tribe" or "petty kingdom," the *túath* was the basic early Irish political unit of a few thousand people ruled by the lowest grade of king. See *GEIL*, 3–7.) When people traveled, they were expected to come under the formal legal protection of someone of equal or greater honor-price* in the *túath* they were visiting. The Irish for this is usually *snádud* (pronounced "SNOTH-uth," with voiced *th*), *commairce* ("KOM-er-kyuh," anglicized *comrick*), or *fóesam* ("FOY-suv"); *GEIL*, 213n156, has a suggestion that *commairce* applies if the protector is physically absent, *fóesam* if they are present. Protection automatically applied to guests at someone's home, and could also be extended *ad hoc*, such as when Conchobor invites the sons of Uisliu to come back to Ulster in "The Exile of the Sons of Uisliu" and Fergus guarantees their safety. Killing someone under protection was a legal offense, *díguin* (pronounced "DEE-hwin"), that impugned the honor of the protector, who would have to be paid their honor-price* on top of the standard fine and compensation to the kindred for the killing. See *GEIL*, 140–41.

There is overlap between legal protection and the ability to protect others physically. When Cet opposes Muinremor in "Mac Dá Thó's Pig" (p. 82), the fact that he has killed and taken heads on Muinremor's land with impunity discredits Muinremor as an incompetent protector. When Cú Chulainn says, in "The Wooing of Emer" (p. 102), "a hundred are safe under my protection," he's making a speech about his fighting abilities, but the word is *comairce*: "a hundred are safe under my guarantee of protection," speaking to his daunting reputation, would seem equally accurate.

red leather The word is *partaing*, a conventional image usually translated "Parthian leather," which was famously dyed crimson. Lips like *partaing* and teeth like a shower of pearls are recurrent images of beauty in early Irish literature. *Partaing* has also been controversially understood as a reference to the redness of Irish crabs: see Peter Schrijver, "Varia: V. Non-Indo-European surviving in Ireland in the first millennium AD," *Ériu* 51 (2000) 195–99; G.R. Isaac's reply in "Varia: I. Some Old Irish etymologies, and some conclusions drawn from them," *Ériu* 53 (2003) 151–55; and Schrijver again, "Varia: I. More on non-Indo-European surviving in Ireland in the first millennium AD," *Ériu* 55 (2005) 137–44.

Samain Pronounced "SAV-win." The modern form is *Samhain*, "SAH-win" or "SOW-in." This is the pagan festival on November 1: the time corresponds to Welsh *Nos Calan Gaeaf* and to the Christian celebration of All Souls and All Saints Days. In early Irish literature, the boundaries between the Otherworld* and the human world are uniquely permeable at this time; various significant and frightening events happen on Samain night.[1]

1 "Nera's Adventure," summarized on p. 154, is a striking example. Compare the role of May Eve in the First Branch of the *Mabinogi* (Boyd, *The Four Branches of the Mabinogi*, 32–33).

Samain, or "the Monday before Samain," is also the start of the invasion of Ulster in the *Táin*.

Samain is often now referred to as the "Celtic New Year," separating the light and dark halves of the year: since it derives from *sam* 'summer' (thus interpreted by some as "summer-end") it may be that when winter begins in the human world, summer is beginning in the Otherworld.* It is also claimed to underlie modern Hallowe'en, whose popularity in North America would stem from Irish emigration in the nineteenth century. But all of this should be approached with care: see Ronald Hutton, "The Celtic New Year and the Feast of the Dead," *Folklore* 135.1 (2024) 69–86, https://www.tandfonline.com/doi/full/10.1080/0015587X.2023.2282282#d1e347.

satire, satirist "Satire" translates *áer* (pronounced "ayr"), etymologically 'cutting' (the primary meanings of the two verbs "to satirize," *áeraid* and *rindaid*, are 'cut' and 'gouge'). In the early Irish context, this did not mean imitative parody for entertainment. It was a mocking but direct attack or a coercive demand, expressed in poetry, with the power of a magic spell. In the sagas, the target of satire might break out in multicolored facial blisters (representing the destruction of their "face" or public honor) and might die. If the satire was unjustified, it might also turn on the poet* who uttered it—not instead of but in addition to the original target. As a matter of early Irish law, a king who was the target of satire could lose his honor-price,* i.e., his legal rights and legal status as a king. For an example of the first satire supposedly made in Ireland, from "The (Second) Battle of Mag Tuired," see *The Broadview Anthology of British Literature* vol. 1, 3e, 31–33. Otherwise, Roisin MacLaughlin, *Early Irish Satire* (DIAS, 2008) is a comprehensive resource on the subject. See *Coire Sois*, 95–100, on the similarity to saints' curses.

A satirist (*cáinte*, pronounced "KONCH-yuh") who was not a properly qualified poet, or a woman with the ability to satirize, like Leborcham in "The Exile of the Sons of Uisliu," was regarded with a mixture of contempt and fear. ("Fitness of Names," II, 137, explains the word *cáinte* as being from Latin *canis*, 'dog': "For a satirist, while 'barking,' has the head of a dog.") Cú Chulainn faces several satirists, and apparently by the rules of fair play* he has to outwit them verbally as a prelude to any violence. They ask him for his weapons, threatening to satirize him for being ungenerous. This gives him an opening to generously "give" them his weapons in a way they don't expect.

Related to satire were positive and negative forms of haranguing or inciting someone to greater efforts: *laíded* (pronounced "LEE-thuth," with voiced *th*) involved heaping on praise, and *gressacht* (pronounced "GRESS-ockt") involved "tough love"-style insults. One didn't need to be a poet* to engage in those. The druids of Emain say that Súaltaim is subjecting Conchobor to *gressacht* when he warns the Ulstermen about the invasion, and Cú Chulainn asks Lóeg to use both types of incitement on him when he fights Fer Diad. See Proinias Mac Cana, "*Laíded, gressacht* 'formalized incitement,'" *Ériu* 43 (1992) 69–92.

shinty-stick Otherwise known as a hurley or *camán*, this is similar to a field hockey stick, used to play a game now known as hurling (when played by men), camogie (when played by women), or shinty (in Scotland).

sister's son The Irish for this was traditionally *nia* (*eDIL* s.v. *2 nia*), but could also be *mac sethar* or *gormac*; *gormac* was also used of a dutiful or filial son, or one adopted with the expectation that he would support his parents in their old age. The relationship of a "sister's son" to his mother's people is a special one in early Irish culture: see *Coire Sois*, 65–94, esp. 72–78 on the terminology for it. As the son of Conchobor's sister, Cú Chulainn has this relationship to the people of Ulster as a whole.

sleeping-compartment The *imdae*, often translated "couch," is a kind of partitioned sleeping-compartment that includes a bed, and might be rendered "sleeping-compartment," "cubicle," or "bed" depending on context. See Mallory, *In Search of the Irish Dreamtime*, 152–53.

sunwise To the right; clockwise. The Irish is *deisil* ("DJESH-il"). This was an auspicious direction, to show goodwill or bring good fortune. To turn to the left was an insult and/or a challenge to battle.

surety The early Irish legal system was heavily dependent on contracts which, since there was no police force (see *GEIL*, 22–23) and it wasn't always easy to go to court, had to be enforced or guaranteed by sureties. There were several types. A "paying surety" (*ráth*) was like a modern cosigner on a loan, and would pay for something if the contracting party fell through. An "enforcing surety" (*naidm*) could physically force someone to deliver on a promise. A "hostage surety" (*aitire*) was held hostage until the contract obligations were completed, and could be killed or enslaved if they weren't. See *GEIL*, 167–73. "Surety" is also used to translate *commairge* when it refers not to protection* itself but to someone who legally provides it. The major example is in "The Exile of the Sons of Uisliu," when the sons of Uisliu are brought back to Ulster under the formal legal protection of Fergus and others.

suspension-beam(s) There is a detailed discussion of the Ulster Cycle chariot in Mallory, *In Search of the Irish Dreamtime*, 211–21 (compare Karl, "Iron Age chariots and medieval texts"). The pair of *fert* are the suspension-beams that branch out from the chariot-pole and hold up the back of the chariot. The *fertas*, which Cú Chulainn smashes with his slingstone on Conall's chariot (p. 192), seems to be the axle.

swear When starred, this identifies a formulaic oath: *toingu a toinges mo thúath* ("I swear what my people swear," i.e., "I swear by what my people swear by"), *toingu do dia toinges mo thúath* ("I swear by the god my people swear by"), *toingu do dia* ("I swear to god," translated here with a lower-case *g* since the characters are supposed to be pagan), and so on. This is so typical that the *Táin* literally quotes some characters as saying *tongu et reliqua* ("I swear, and the rest of it" / "I swear, etc."), although one assumes they're supposed to have said it in full. The formula seems to have a pagan origin and to correspond to similar formulas in Welsh and Gaulish, but this is debated: see, e.g., Ruairí Ó hUiginn, "*Tongu do dia toinges mo thúath* and related expressions," in *Sages, Saints and Storytellers: Celtic Studies in Honour of Professor James Carney*, ed. Donnchadh Ó Corráin, Liam Breatnach, and Kim McCone (Maynooth: An Sagart, 1989) 332–41; John T.

Koch, "Further to *tongu do dia toinges mo thuath*, &c.," *Études Celtiques* 29 (1992) 249–61; Kevin Murray, "A reading from *Scéla Mośauluim*," *ZCP* 53.1 (2003) 198–201.

That's easy A rhetorical question with the answer "[it is] not difficult" (*ní hansa*, pronounced "nee HAN-suh") is a standard way to begin discussion of a topic in early Irish. It shows up all the time in law-texts and other didactic material. I adopt "That's easy" as the functional equivalent in English.

Túatha Dé Danann Pronounced "TOO-ah-tha DAY DAN-un." The "Peoples of the Goddess Danu," i.e., the pagan gods of Ireland, who agreed to share it with the Gaels by retiring to the Otherworld* or hollow hills. A comprehensive resource on the Túatha Dé Danann is Mark Williams, *Ireland's Immortals* (Princeton University Press, 2016). Their involvement with humans is most recently considered in Joanne Findon, *Bound and Free: Voices of Mortal and Otherworld Women in Medieval Irish Literature* (Turnhout: Brepols, 2024).

uncle When starred, this translates *popa* ("POB"-uh), which *eDIL* characterizes as "a respectful form of address to an elder or superior, but occas[ionally] familiarly to an inferior," when Cú Chulainn is talking to his elders, like Conchobor, Fergus, or Culann. In this sense, *eDIL* glosses it as "lit[erally] a father, hence 'master,' 'sir'." "Uncle" has enough currency in world cultures as an honorific for unrelated elders that it felt like the best fit, besides which Conchobor is in fact Cú Chulainn's uncle. (For Cathbad only, I translate "grandpa.") Speaking to a friend, a foster-brother,* or the charioteer Lóeg, the translation is "my dear.*"

white-bronze This is *findruine* ("FINN-rin-uh"), a silvery alloy valued more than bronze and less than gold.

List of Important and Recurring Characters

Pronunciations assume difficulty with non-English sounds including /x/ (see pp. 369–73). "Voiced *th*" is the *th* sound in *then*, not *thin.*

Aífe, daughter of Airdgemm
"EE-fuh"
Sister and rival of Scáthach in "The Wooing of Emer," mother of Cú Chulainn's son Connla

Ailbe
"AL-vuh"
Mac Dá Thó's special dog, protector of Leinster

Ailill mac Máta (son of Máta)
"AL-ill mock MAW-ta"
King of Connacht, married to Maeve; brother of Finn, King of Leinster, and Cairbre Nia Fer

Ainnle mac Uislenn (son of Uisliu)
"AN-leh mock ISH-lenn"
Brother of Noísiu

Amairgen mac Eccit Salaig (son of 'Filthy' Ecet)
"AV-ir-gen," with a hard *g* (so like "AV-ir-gun")
Ulster poet* (for how he becomes chief poet of Ulster, see *The Celtic Poets*, 35–37); foster-father* of Cú Chulainn; married to Finnchóem; father of Conall Cernach; throws stones in the *Táin*

Ardán mac Uislenn (son of Uisliu)
"AR-dawn mock ISH-lenn"
Brother of Noísiu

Badb, the
"BATH-uv," with voiced *th* (Modern Irish pronunciation is more like "bive")
Aspect of the war-goddess; the war-goddess as carrion crow or raven

Blaí Briugu (the Guesthouse*-Keeper)
"BLEE"
Foster-father* of Cú Chulainn

Bricriu mac Carbada, known as 'Nemthenga' ("Poisontongue")
"BRICK-roo mock KAR-vuh-thuh," with voiced *th* / "NEV-theng-a"
Ulster troublemaker; member of the exiles. William Sayers explores this character in "Bricriu nemthenga ('poison-tongue'): onomastics and social function in early Irish literature," *Mediaevistik* 30 (2017) 87–102

Cairbre Nia Fer
"KAR-bruh NEE-a FER"
King of Tara, usually called a son of the Leinster king Ross Rúad, which would make him a brother of King Ailill of Connacht. But on his epithet Nia Fer, see *Coire Sois*, 77–78: "The probability is that Cairbre was deemed to have a supernatural father, and to have belonged to the human race through his mother. Hence the name "Cairbre, Sister's Son to Man (lit. 'of men')"

Calatín (or Gaile Dána in Recension I)
"KAL-uh-deen" / "GAL-yeh DON-uh"
Opponent killed by Cú Chulainn on the *Táin* (p. 250), father of Cú Chulainn's magically empowered enemies in "The Death of Cú Chulainn"

Cathbad mac Rossa
"KATH-vuth," second *th* voiced (parallels "bath smooth")
Ulster druid,* father of Conchobor, grandfather of Cú Chulainn

Celtchar mac Uthechair (son of Uthechar)
"KELT-har mock UTH-uh-hir"
Ulster hero, featured in "Mac Dá Thó's Pig" and "The Death of Celtchar" (see p. 75)

Cet mac Mágach (son of Mágu)
"KED mock MAW-gock"
Connacht hero, uncle and rival of Conall Cernach, featured in "Mac Dá Thó's Pig" and "The Death of Conchobor"

Cethern mac Fintain (son of Fintan)
"KETH-urn mock FIN-din"
Ulster hero, diagnosed by Fíngin in the *Táin*

Clothru, daughter of Eochaid Feidlech
"KLOTH-roo"
Sister of Maeve, mother of Lugaid Ríab nDerg and possible mother of Furbaide

Conaire Mór ("the Great")
"KON-ur-ruh"
King of Tara in "The Destruction of Da Derga's Hostel"

Conall Cernach ("the Victorious")
mac Amairgin (son of Amairgen)
"KON-ull KYER-nock"
#2 Ulster hero, foster-brother* of Cú Chulainn; member of the exiles. Cernach is conventionally translated "the Victorious" (*2 cernach* in *eDIL*) but can also mean "angular," perhaps related to the indications that Conall has a bent or crooked neck (*eDIL*, s.v. *1 cernach*, suggests "having an excrescence?"; see pp. 130 and 332–33 above). "Fitness of Names" (II, 141–43) gives both the crooked neck and the warrior skill as possible explanations, plus Latin *cerno* 'I see,' crediting Conall with being able to see as well at night as during the day. It provides a birth-tale for Conall, according to which Finnchóem had trouble conceiving, was instructed by druids* to bathe in a well, and (like Cú Chulainn's mother) swallowed a worm that made her pregnant. The druids revealed that the child would be a "dutiful" sister's son* to the Connachta by dutifully killing half of them, and his uncle Cet stepped on the baby's neck and broke it, hence Conall's crooked neck: his name would reference Cet's betrayal

Conchobor mac Nessa (son of Nes)
"KON-kuh-vur mock NESS-a" (modernized as Conovar or Conor)
King of Ulster, son of Cathbad or Fachtna Fáthach, maternal uncle of Cú Chulainn. His name means "Dog-Desiring [One]," which dovetails (coincidentally, or by design?) with Cú Chulainn's identity as a "dog"

Connla
"KON-luh"
Son of Cú Chulainn by Aífe, highly precocious but bound by *geisi** not to share his name with any single individual, or refuse to fight any single individual

Cormac Conn Loinges ("Leader of the Exiles")
"KOR-muck KON LOING-us"
Son of Conchobor, and his successor; member of the exiles

Crunnchu/Cruinniuc
"KRUNN-hu"/"KRINN-yuck"
Ulster landowner married to Macha in "The Ulstermen's Paralysis"

Cú Chulainn ("Culann's Dog/The Hound of Culann"), born **Sétanta**
"KOO HULL-in" / "SHAY-dan-duh"
#1 Ulster hero. The name Sétanta seems to be based on *sét* 'path' (hence "pathfinder," or one who sets out on a journey?)

Cú Roí mac Dáiri
"KOO ROY (or REE) mock DOY-rih"
West Munster king and hero who tests Cú Chulainn in "Bricriu's Feast" (pp. 132–33) and is later killed by him; father of Lugaid mac Con Roí. His royal seat was at Temair Lúachra, site of the battle in "The Intoxication of the Ulstermen" (pp. 131–32)

Cuillius
"KWIL-yus"
Ailill's charioteer, who steals Fergus's sword

Culann
"KULL-an"
Ulster smith, owner of the dog Cú Chulainn is named for

Cúscraid Menn Machae ("the Stammerer of Macha")
"KOOS-kruth MEN MACK-eh"
Son of Conchobor, and his successor in "The Battle of Airtech"; featured in "Mac Dá Thó's Pig"

Dáire mac Fiachna
"DOY-ruh/DAH-ruh mock FEE-ock-nuh"
Ulster lord, owner of the Brown Bull

Dechtine
"DECK-tin-uh"
Sister (and charioteer) of Conchobor, wife of Súaltaim, mother of Cú Chulainn

Deirdre (Old Irish form: Deirdriu)
"DER-dra" or "DEER-druh" ("DIRR-droo")
Beautiful woman of fateful prophecy, in "The Exile of the Sons of Uisliu"; see p. 137 on the meaning of her name

Derbforgaill
"DER-ver-gil"
Daughter of the King of the Isles; shot in bird-form by Cú Chulainn; married to Lugaid Ríab nDerg

Donn Cúailnge
"DONN KOOL-nyuh/KOO-ling-yuh"
The Brown Bull of Cúailnge, belonging to Dáire mac Fiachna of Ulster; once a supernatural pig-keeper

Dub Sainglenn ("the Black of Saingliu")
"DUV SANG-lenn"
Cú Chulainn's second-favorite horse

Dubthach mac Lugdach (son of Lugaid)
"DUV-thock mock LUG-dock"
Ulster warrior and member of the exiles; has the epithet *Dóeltenga* ("DOYL-chenga") 'Beetletongue' and *Dóel Ulad* ("DOYL ULL-uth," with voiced *th*) 'Beetle of Ulster,' in reference to his vicious temper and mockery that mirrors Bricriu's. The beetle is technically a chafer (*OED*: "a flying beetle, the adult and larva of which can be very destructive to foliage and plant roots respectively"), but "Roachtongue" might give a similar effect in English. As "Fitness of Names" (II, 144) puts it, "Just as everyone thinks the chafer venomous and foul, so Dubthach was venomous in speech and sharp-worded towards everyone"

Eithne, daughter of Eochaid Feidlech
"ETH-nuh"
Sister of Maeve, possible mother of Furbaide

Emer
"EV-ur"
Daughter of Forgall, wife of Cú Chulainn. There is a modern name Emer that is pronounced "EEM-ur," in contrast to the evolution of the name in Irish, Eimhear. Her name might mean "granite" (*eDIL*, s.v. *1 eimer*); otherwise it's not transparent

Eochaid Dála
"UCK-uth (or UCK-ee) DAW-luh," with voiced *th*
Consort of Maeve and king of Connacht, in "Maeve's Series of Husbands"

Eochaid Feidlech ("Faithful" or "Long Sigh")
"UCK-uth (or UCK-ee) FETH-leck," with voiced *th*
King of Tara before Cairbre Nia Fer; father of Maeve and her sisters

Eochaid Sálbuide ("Yellow-Heel")
"UCK-uth (or UCK-ee) SAWL-vwith-uh," voiced *th*
Past king of Ulster, father of Ness

Éogan mac Durthacht
"OH-han mock DUR-thockt" (modernized as Owen)
Ulster hero and king of Fernmag (now Farney, County Monaghan); former rival and later henchman of Conchobor; killer of the sons of Uisliu; one-eyed according to "Mac Dá Thó's Pig"

Erc mac Cairpri (son of Cairbre)
"URK mock KER-brih"
Son of Cairbre Nia Fer and Fedelm Noíchride; darling of the Ulstermen in the *Táin*; out for vengeance in Cú Chulainn's death-tale

Etarcomol
"ED-ar-kov-ul"
Obnoxious Connacht warrior whose life Cú Chulainn tries to spare

Fachtna Fáthach ("the Wise")
"FAKT-na FAWTH-ock"
Past king of Ulster, one candidate for father of Conchobor

Fedelm
"FETH-elm," with voiced *th* (as in "feather")
Connacht poet* who prophesies ruin for Maeve's army

Fedelm 'Noíchride/Noíchrothach' ("Pureheart/Nineform")
"FETH-elm NEE-hrith-uh/NEE-hroth-ock"
Daughter of Conchobor; wife of Cairbre Nia Fer and mother of Erc mac Cairpri (but "Bricriu's Feast" makes her the wife of Lóegaire Búadach). "Fitness of Names" (II, 143) explains that her beauty was constantly renewed, and "nine forms used to come upon her every time she was seen," or else her pure-heartedness reflected her capacity for kin-love*

Fer Báeth

"fer BOYTH"

Foster-brother* of Cú Chulainn, fellow student of Scáthach. Literally, "silly/stupid/reckless man." The adjective is also a legal term "applied to one not fully responsible either through non[-]age or mental deficiency" (*eDIL*, s.v. *báeth*). It is tempting to render this name as Dumbass, Jackass, or Badass—or a combination of all three

Fer Diad mac Damáin (son of Damán)

"fer DIATH mock DAV-oin," voiced *th* (modernized as Ferdia, stressed on the first syllable)

Connacht hero, foster-brother* of Cú Chulainn, fellow student of Scáthach. His name means "Man of a Pair," i.e., Cú Chulainn's other half (although "Fitness of Names," II, 135, explained it as "belonging to two lands, i.e., he was born at the border of two territories")

Fergus mac Roích (son of Róech)

"FUR-gus mock ROYH"

Ulster hero and former king; foster-father* of Cú Chulainn; member of the exiles and lover of Maeve. His name means "Manly (*fer-*) Vigor (*-gus*), son of Great Horse." But "Fitness of Names" (II, 149) identifies Róich or Róch as his supernaturally-connected mother

Fíacha mac Fir Fhebe (son of Fer Febe)

"FEE-uck-uh mock FIR EV-uh"

Ulster hero and son-in-law of Conchobor, member of the exiles. But "Fitness of Names" (II, 149) explains his name as "Son of the Husband of Feb," and reasons that Feb was a daughter of Conchobor; her husband was Conall Cernach; and so Fíacha is Conall's son

Fíal

"FEE-al"

Emer's sister, in "The Wooing of Emer"

Fíngin

"FEENG-in"

Conchobor's personal physician and expert diagnostician, e.g., of Cethern

Finn mac Rossa Rúaid (son of Ross Rúad)

"FINN mock ROSS-a ROO-ith," with voiced *th*

King of Leinster; brother of Ailill of Connacht and Cairbre Nia Fer

Finnabair

"FINN-uh-vwir"

Daughter of Ailill and Maeve, used as a lure for allies on the *Táin*. Her name means "White Ghost" or "Pale Spirit," cognate with Welsh Gwenhwyfar, which underlies Guinevere and Jennifer

Finnbennach ("White-Horned")

"FINN-VENN-ock"

The great bull of Connacht, belonging to Ailill; once a supernatural pig-keeper

Finnchóem

"FINN-hoyv"

Sister of Conchobor and/or of Cet mac Mágach (both could be possible if she were Cathbad's daughter by a different mother, as claimed at https://www.dib.ie/biography/conall-cernach-a1910), wife of Amairgen, mother of Conall Cernach, foster-mother* of Cú Chulainn

Flidais

"FLITH-ush," with voiced *th*

Fergus's wife, mentioned in various texts (pp. 66, 155, 326) but not the *Táin*

Follamain

"FOLL-uh-vwin"

Son of Conchobor, head of the boy-troop of Emain Macha

Forgall Manach ("the Wily")
"FOR-gull MAN-ock"
Father of Emer; Cú Chulainn's antagonist in "The Wooing of Emer"

Fráech mac Idaith (son of Idath)
"FROYK mock ITH-ith"
Connacht hero with Otherworld* parentage, featured in "The Cattle-Raid of Fráech"; drowned by Cú Chulainn in the *Táin*

Furbaide, known as Fer Benn ("the Horned Man")
"FUR-vwith-uh"
Son of Conchobor by Maeve's sister; cut from the womb after Lugaid Red-Stripes or Maeve killed his mother, and renamed Furbaide ("Cutout"?) based on *furbad* 'excision' (otherwise, his name was Diarmait, "DEER-mid," as on pp. 70 and possibly 247). "Fitness of Names" (II, 143) adds that there were "two silver peaks and a gold peak [coming] out of his helmet"

Láiríne mac Nóis
"LAW-ree-nyuh mock NOYSH"
Obnoxious brother of Lugaid mac Nóis

Leborcham
"LEV-ur-hum"
Female satirist* in Ulster, confidante of Deirdre, daughter of an enslaved couple in Conchobor's household. Her name means "long and crooked": "The Siege of Howth" adds that her legs were back-to-front, and that she would travel around Ireland in a single day and report the day's news to Conchobor

Líath Macha ("the Gray of Macha")
"LEE-uth MACK-uh"
Cú Chulainn's favorite horse; see p. 306 for where he came from

Lóeg mac Riangabra (son of Riangabair)
"LOYH (or LOW-eg) mock REE-an-gav-ruh"
Cú Chulainn's charioteer

Lóegaire Búadach ("the Triumphant") mac Connaid
"LOY-uh-ruh BOO-uth-ock" (or even "LOY-ruh"; the modern outcome is Laoghaire, "Leary")
Ulster hero, sometimes explicitly #3 after Cú Chulainn and Conall Cernach

Lug mac Eithlenn or **mac Ethnenn** (son of Eithliu or Ethniu)
"LUHG" with a softened *g* (Modern Irish pronunciation: "LOO") "mock ETH-lenn/ETH-nenn"
Cú Chulainn's supernatural father, one of the Túatha Dé Danann,* featured in "The (Second) Battle of Mag Tuired." Eithliu/Ethniu was his mother and belonged to the Fomóiri.* His father was Cian, so he is also sometimes mac Céin (son of Cian), pronounced "mock KAYN." He corresponds to the Continental Celtic god Lugos/Lugus, reflected in the names of Leiden (Netherlands) and Lyon (France)

Lugaid mac Con Roí (son of Cú Roí)
"LUG-ith (with voiced *th*) mock KON REE"
Son of Cú Roí mac Dáiri, out for vengeance against Cú Chulainn

Lugaid mac Nóis
"LUG-ith (with voiced *th*) mock NOYSH"
Munster king, foster-brother* of Cú Chulainn

Lugaid Ríab nDerg ("Red-Stripes")
"LUG-ith (with voiced *th*) REE-uv NERG"
Son of Clothru and her triplet brothers; foster-son* of Cú Chulainn

Mac Dá Thó
"mock DAW THOE"
Leinster king and guesthouse*-keeper, owner of the dog Ailbe; brother of Mes Gegrai. His name means "Son of Two Mutes": according to "The Siege of Howth," he and his brother were "two sons of Two Mutes, i.e., their mother and father were deaf and dumb"

Mac Roth
"MOCK ROTH"
Connacht herald; his name has been understood by some as "Son of Wheel" (see *eDIL*, s.v. *roth*), but then we would have expected a possessive case (Mac Ruith or Mac Rotha)

Macha
"MACK-uh" (or "MAH-ha")
Goddess who curses the Ulstermen with paralysis; horse associations

Macha Mongrúad (the "Red-Maned")
"MACK-uh (or MAH-ha) MONG-roo-uth," with voiced *th*
Other possible namesake of Emain Macha, in "The Wooing of Emer"

Máenén
"MOY-nane" / "MY-nane"
Connacht jester

Maeve (Medb) of Crúachu, daughter of Eochaid Feidlech
"MAYV" (Old Irish pronunciation "METH-uv," with voiced *th*)
Queen of Connacht, married to Ailill. Her name could mean "Intoxicating One," in which case the *med-* element would be the same as the English word *mead* (alcohol made from fermented honey). On that basis, some people have tried to link her with the female personification of Sovereignty who appears in some of the sagas and gives a drink to the future king. For merely one example, see the cross-cultural study by Matthias Egeler, "Some thoughts on 'goddess Medb' and her typological context," *ZCP* 59 (2012) 67–96, https://ub01.uni-tuebingen.de/xmlui/bitstream/handle/10900/115801/Egeler_048.pdf. Nevertheless, in the Ulster Cycle tales she seems entirely human

Maine (x7)
"MAN-yuh"
Seven sons of Ailill and Maeve, given a name change according to "Maeve's Series of Husbands"

Menn mac Sálchada ("Glory, son of War-Heel")
"MEN mock SAWL-ha-thuh," with voiced *th*
Ulster hero with an embarrassing patronymic, featured in "Mac Dá Thó's Pig" with an encore in the *Táin*

Mes Gegrai
"MESS GEG-ri"
King of Leinster, killed by Conall Cernach and his brains used to make the ball that wounds Conchobor; brother of Mac Dá Thó. His name apparently means "Fosterling of Gegrae"

Monodar mac Conrach Cais (son of Conra Cas), renamed Mac Cécht
"MON-uth-ar," with voiced *th* / "mock KEHCKT"
Killer of his brother Tinne at Conchobor's behest, in "Maeve's Series of Husbands"; champion of Conaire Mór in "The Destruction of Da Derga's Hostel"

Morann mac Maín
"MOR-an"
Judge who determines Cú Chulainn's fosterage* arrangements; credited with "The Testament of Morann" (see *The Celtic Heroic Age*, 188–93); Christian believer before Saint Patrick

Morrígan, the ("Phantom Queen")
"MOR-ree-han" (but popularly "MOR-i-gan")
Aspect of the war-goddess. The mor- element is the same as -mare in English nightmare, but her name is sometimes reinterpreted as Mórrígan, "Great Queen." The subject of many neo-pagan and popular treatments, most recently *The Morrigan* by Kim Curran (Michael Joseph/Penguin, 2025)

Mugain, daughter of Eochaid Feidlech
"MUH-hin"
Queen of Ulster, married to Conchobor; sister of Maeve; has the epithet "Prickly-Fuzz" ("having gorse-like body hair")

Muinremor mac Gerrcinn ("Thickneck son of Shorthead")
"MWIN-rev-ur mock GYURG-in"
Ulster hero, featured in "Mac Dá Thó's Pig"; throws stones in the *Táin*. While his name implies that he is brawny and bull-necked, as stated in one version of "Fitness of Names" (I, 190), another (II, 148) claims that he was speared in the neck by Cet (along the lines of the injuries Cet brings up in "Mac Dá Thó's Pig") and his neck was swollen as a result

Nad Crantail
"NATH KRAN-dil"
Connacht *fían*-warrior,* killed in single combat by Cú Chulainn

Nechta Scéne
"NECK-ta SHKAY-nuh"
Mother of the three warriors Cú Chulainn kills on his first foray in a chariot. Her sons are Fóill (FOIL), 'Sly'; Fannall (FAN-al), 'Swallow'; and Túachell (TOO-uh-kel), 'Cunning'

Nemain
"NEV-win"
Aspect of the war-goddess

Ness, daughter of Eochaid Sálbuide
Mother of Conchobor (and possibly of Cormac Conn Loinges), known as Assa ("Easy") in her youth and renamed "Not-Easy" per Conchobor's birth-tale

Níab
"NEE-uv" or "NEEV" (like the modern name Niamh, Neve)
Wife of Conall Cernach, according to "The Death of Cú Chulainn" ("Bricriu's Feast" says that Conall's wife is called Lendabair)

Noísiu mac Uislenn (son of Uisliu)
"NEE-shyoo mock ISH-lenn"
Ulster warrior, brother of Ainnle and Ardán, lover of Deirdre

Óengus, the Mac Óc ("Young Son")
"OING-us" the "MOCK OHG"
Son of the Dagdae of the Túatha Dé Danann,* featured in "The Dream of Óengus"

Óengus mac Láime Gabuid (son of "Hand-of-Danger")
"OING-us mock LAI-vuh GAV-with"
Ulster hero with an embarrassing patronymic, featured in "Mac Dá Thó's Pig" with an encore in the *Táin*

Órlám
"OAR-lawv"
Son of Ailill and Maeve, killed by Cú Chulainn; leader of Connacht forces in "The Raid of Dartad's Cattle"
(see pp. 155–56)

Redg
"RETH-ug," with voiced *th*
Satirist* who challenges Cú Chulainn in the *Táin*

Rochad mac Fathemain
"RO-huth mock FATH-ev-in"
Ulster warrior who has a budding romance with Finnabair

Ross Rúad ("the Red-haired")
"ROSS ROO-uth," with voiced *th*
Past Leinster king, father of Cairbre Nia Fer, Finn, and Ailill

Scáthach ("the Shadowy One"), daughter of Airdgemm
"SKOTH-ock"
Cú Chulainn's martial arts teacher in Scotland/the Alps

Sencha mac Ailella (son of Ailill)
"SHEN-ha"
Ulster 'elder statesman' and peacemaker (his name could mean "he who sees what is old" or "old seer"); foster-father* of Cú Chulainn; no relation to King Ailill of Connacht

Senchán Torpéist

"SHEN-hawn TOR-baysht"

Chief poet* of Ireland who initiates the search for the *Táin*; see *The Celtic Poets*, 38–42, for an explanation of his name as "Mr. Tradition," "to whom the monster came" (cf. "Fitness of Names," II, 146)

Súaltaim

"SOO-al-duv"

Cú Chulainn's human father, husband of Dechtine

Taman

"TAV-an"

Connacht jester, killed by Cú Chulainn after donning Ailill's crown

Tinne mac Conrach Cais (son of Conra Cas)

"TIN-uh," with voiced *th*

Consort of Maeve and king of Connacht, in "Maeve's Series of Husbands"

Úathach

"OO-uh-thock"

Daughter of Scáthach and lover of Cú Chulainn. See p. 114 on the meaning of her name

Early Irish Spelling and Pronunciation

The Ulster Cycle tales are a riot of names of people and places, not all of which are obvious to translate. You don't need to pronounce Irish words and names correctly to enjoy the story, and there are anglicized workarounds for some of the major characters, but it helps to have some understanding of how the early Irish spelling system works.

These comments on pronunciation deliberately avoid International Phonetic Alphabet (IPA) symbols.[1] My suggested pronunciations have been field-tested with my students in New Jersey and, while not perfect, should be good enough to help North Americans avoid embarrassment.

Stress and "accent" marks, vowels

Irish words are stressed on the first syllable. The marks on vowels that look like French acute accents or Spanish stress accents (*á, é,* etc.) are notionally length-marks, although they do incidentally change the quality of most vowels. Irish *sin* is pronounced like English *shin*, and *sín* like *sheen*. Short vowels in unstressed syllables often have a neutral pronunciation ("schwa," /ə/ in the International Phonetic Alphabet) that leads to a variety of spellings: the king of Ulster's name shows up as *Conchobor*, *Conchobar*, *Conchubur*, etc.

Word-final *e* is always pronounced and usually adds a syllable; unlike in English, it never communicates anything about the pronunciation of a previous vowel. The name *Maine* is pronounced "MAN-yuh," not like the state of Maine.

"Broad" and "slender" consonants

Irish consonants have two versions, "broad" (velarized—further back toward the soft palate) and "slender" (palatalized—further forward toward the hard palate and behind the teeth), although the difference can be subtle enough with some of them: the most noticeable

1 If you do know IPA, then besides textbooks like the ones by de Vries and Stifter under "Further Reading" above, Dennis King has a useful guide to Old Irish pronunciation at https://www3.smo.uhi.ac.uk/sengoidelc/donncha/labhairt.html.

difference is probably with *s*, which is like English *s* when broad and *sh* when slender. The difference is shown in writing by the vowels that surround the consonant (or the vowel that follows it, if it's at the beginning of a word, or the vowel that comes before it, if it's at the end of a word): *a, o,* and *u* indicate broad quality, *e* and *i* indicate slender quality. (Actually, in Old Irish, *e* indicates slender quality on the consonant before it, but not necessarily on the one after: Old Irish *Temair* becomes Modern Irish *Teamhair*, for example, as Modern Irish is more insistent on making sure there is the same type of vowel on both sides of a consonant.)

Mutations and spelling

A consonant is a sound we make by cutting off or restricting the flow of air that comes out of our lungs; a vowel shapes the flow of air without restricting it. When a consonant comes after a vowel, the vowel can, over time, make the consonant "soften" by increasing the flow of air. For example, in the English word *water*, we rarely say a hard *t*: it comes out more like "wadder" (which technically involves more of a tap or flap of the tongue against the roof of your mouth than a full-blown *d* sound). The French outcome of the Latin word *liber* 'book' is *livre*, with the *b* softened to a *v*. Irish does the same thing with consonants in the middle of words: the Old Irish word for 'book,' also from Latin *liber*, is *lebor*, pronounced "LEV-ur," and in Modern Irish that change in the *b* is shown by writing *h* after it: the word is written *leabhar* and pronounced "LYOW-ur." In Modern Irish, then, *h* after any consonant shows that it undergoes the same kind of change, the technical name for which is "lenition" (or, in Irish, *séimhiú*, "SHAY-voo"). In Old Irish, that change might be shown by writing *h*, or by putting a dot over the affected consonant, or it might not be shown, and you just have to know that it happens.

To make things even more complicated, when Old Irish was first written using the Latin alphabet, it was written to be read the way British Latin was pronounced at the time. So some ways of "softening" consonants that are implicit in the spelling system are British rather than Irish. The Irish lenition of a *t* is to *th*, but a *t* in the middle of an Old Irish word is pronounced like a *d*. This explains why, even though the Irish didn't have the inherited Indo-European *p* sound (at first they replaced it completely when they borrowed Latin words like *purpureus*, getting *corcur* 'purple'), it shows up in spellings like *Cairpre*, where it's pronounced like a *b*—if it were written *b*, that might suggest it should be pronounced *v*, although the spelling *Cairbre* occurs too.

The softening mutation (lenition) first happens organically, but over time it becomes systematic ("grammaticalized"). For example, it affects consonants at the beginning of words after the definite article whenever the article *used to* end in a vowel, even if it no longer does: the feminine singular *in ben* 'the woman' is pronounced "in VEN" (in Modern Irish it would be written *an bhean*).

Another mutation is called nasalization for Old Irish, *urú* or eclipsis for Modern Irish. It affects consonants after words that end (or used to end) in a nasal. In Modern Irish this is expressed by writing the new pronunciation of the consonant in front of the old one: *gc, bp, dt, mb, nd, ng,* and *bhf.* That doesn't mean to try pronouncing both the consonants you see: *gc* is pronounced as *g*, *bhf* as *bh*, and so on. It just makes it clear what the underlying consonant is, which helps if you want to look up the word in a dictionary. In Old Irish this mutation is often shown in writing, but not always.

Putting all that together, we get something like this for the pronunciation of Old Irish consonants:

b Word-initial: English *b,* unless something is making it lenite to *v* (which might be written *bh*). Middle or end of a word: *v*, unless written double.

bh English *v.* (Modern Irish distinguishes a broad version, *w*, and a slender one, *v*.)

c Word-initial: English hard *c*, like *k*, unless something is making it nasalize to *g* (lenition would be shown as *ch*); before *e* or *i*, think of it as *ky-*. Middle or end of word: hard *g*, unless written double.

ch Never like the *ch* in English *chuck* (*Conchobor* should NOT sound like "punch a boar"). Before or after *a, o, u*, pronounce it like the *ch* in Scottish *loch* or the composer *Bach* (IPA /x/), which, assuming difficulty with this sound, might make sense to pronounce as *ck* or *h* depending on context (so *Macha* would be "MACK-ah"). Before or after *e* or *i*, pronounce *ch* like German *ich*, not unlike *hy-* in English *hyuck, hyuck, hyuck.*

d Word-initial: English *d*, unless something is making it lenite (then see *dh*), or something is making it nasalize to *n*, which, if written, looks like *nd.* Middle or end of word: voiced *th*, as in *then they bothered the others.* ("Voiced" means you can feel your vocal cords vibrate. Compare *th* below.)

dh Before or after *a, o, u*, like English hard *g*, but more raspy. Before or after *e* or *i*, like English *y* in *yes.* A word like *síde* starts off as "SHEATHE-uh" but, via something like "SHEE-yuh," ends up in Modern Irish as *sídhe*, pronounced "SHEE."

f Same as English, unless something is making it lenite, then not pronounced, or something is making it nasalize to *v.*

fh Not pronounced (at all). *Áth Dá Fherta* is "awth dah erd-uh."

g Word-initial: English hard *g*, unless something is making it lenite (then see *gh*), or something is making it nasalize to *ng.* Middle or end of word: see *gh.*

gh Before or after *a, o, u*, like English hard *g*, but more raspy. Before or after *e* or *i*, like English *y* in *yes*: *Lóegaire* is "LOY-uh-ruh"; *slige* is "SHLI-yuh."

h Word-initial: same as English. Otherwise it is probably after a consonant to show lenition.

l Basically the same as English. You can get the broad/slender distinction by contrasting the *l*-sounds in English *all* and *million.*

m Word-initial: English *m*, unless something is making it lenite to *v* (which might be written *mh*). Middle or end of word: *v*, unless written double. Sometimes a lenited *m* comes out more like *vw*, as in *Emain*, "EV-win."

mh English *v.* (Modern Irish distinguishes a broad version, *w*, and a slender one, *v.*)

n Same as English.

nd English *n.*

ng Like the *ng* in *ring.*

p Word-initial: English *p*, unless something is making it nasalize to *b* (lenition would be shown as *ph*). Middle or end of word: *b.*

ph English *f.*

r Basically the same as English. The "slender" version, most clearly shown by *-ir*, gets a trill.

s Before or after *a, o, u*, same as English. Before or after *e* or *i*, English *sh.*

sh Like English *h*, NOT like English *sh.*

t Word-initial: same as English, unless something is making it nasalize to *d* (lenition would be shown as *th*); before *e* or *i*, think of it as *ty-*. Middle or end of word: *d*, unless written double.

th Unvoiced English *th*, as in *through thick and thin.*

Cases

In standardized Modern English, pronouns take different forms, called "cases," in different grammatical circumstances:

I (subject case)	***saw***	*him, her,* and *them* (object case).
He, she, and they (subject case)	***saw***	*me* (object case).

In Old English—the language of *Beowulf*—all nouns used to change like this. In fact, the possessive *'s* in Modern English comes from an old case ending. The Old English word for "king," for example, was *cyning*, and the possessive form, "king's," was *cyninges*. So "the king's men" was *þæs cyninges menn.*

Like Old English, early Irish is "highly inflected," meaning that nouns take multiple cases. Besides the subject case, called the "nominative," which is how words are listed in the dictionary, the other case that is important for reading early Irish in translation is the possessive case, otherwise known as the "genitive." All nouns had a possessive form, but of course these have been translated into English in this book. The major exception is personal names.

Early Irish people had a first name but no last name. Instead of a last name, they were almost always identified in terms of a parent—usually the father, but sometimes the mother[1]—or an ancestor. Genealogy was very important to them.

Men's names use the word *mac*, meaning "son," or *ó* (also spelled *ua*), meaning "grandson" or "descendant." Women's names use *ingen*, meaning "daughter."[2] The word *mac*, *ó*, or *ingen* is directly followed by the possessive case of the parent's, grandparent's, or ancestor's name—there's no preposition "of."

For example, a king named Cormac had a father named Art and a grandfather named Conn. He would be known as Cormac mac Airt ("a son of Art's") or Cormac Ó Cuinn ("a grandson of Conn's").

Airt and *Cuinn* are the possessive case forms of the names *Art* and *Conn*. In Old Irish, there were fourteen different patterns ("declensions") for forming cases, so the possessive forms of names might seem unpredictable. Here are some of the common patterns.

---

1 The part of a name that identifies the father is a "patronymic." The part of a name that identifies the mother is a "matronymic." Various modern languages have these. Many English last names, like many Modern Irish last names, started off as patronymics. At this point, we wouldn't expect a Michael Jackson to literally have a father named Jack, or a Dwayne Johnson to have a father named John—but that would be a fair assumption in, say, Icelandic. Conchobor mac Nessa is a good example of an early Irish character with a matronymic.

2 *ingen, meaning "daughter"* *Ingen*, the feminine counterpart of *mac*, evolves into *Nic* in Modern Irish. The feminine counterpart of *Ó* is *Ní*. Unlike *Mac* and *Ó*, *Nic* and *Ní* both cause lenition of the name that follows, so Modern Irish last names based on the ancestral name Conn include Mac Cuinn and Ó Cuinn, Nic Chuinn and Ní Chuinn. You can expect that a modern Irish person with *Nic* or *Ní* in their name is a woman. But people with *Mac* and *Ó* names, like modern English names that end in *-son*, could perhaps be any gender.

Palatalization ("slenderizing") of the final consonant, usually shown by putting an extra *i* in front of it:

Name	Possessive form
Art	Airt
Celtchar	Celtchair
Conall	Conaill
Conchobor	Conchobuir
Conn	Cuinn
Cormac	Cormaic
Fráech	Fraích
Niall	Néill

Changing the final vowel to an *i*:

Name	Possessive form
Conaire	Conairi
Lóegaire	Lóegairi
Nera	Nerai

Putting an extra vowel on the end:

Name	Possessive form
Ailill	Ailella
Emer	Emire
Fergus	Fergusa
Lug	Loga
Medb	Medba / Meidbe
Nes	Nessa
Óengus	Óenguso
Riangabair	Riangabra
Scáthach	Scáthaige

Putting an extra consonant on the end:

Name	Possessive form
Bricriu	Bricrenn
Deirdriu	Deirdrenn

Eochaid	Echdach
Lugaid	Lugdach
Núadu	Núadat
Uisliu	Uislenn

An entire group or lineage might identify as somebody's descendants. The plural of *mac* is *meic*, and the plural of *ó* is *uí*. So the dynasty known as the Uí Néill were the "descendants of Niall" (King Niall Noígiallach, "Niall of the Nine Hostages").

The possessive shows up all the time in placenames and titles of stories.

Very often in the *Táin*, someone is killed near a geographical feature that is named after them. In that case, a word like *áth*, "ford, river-crossing," or *cnoc*, "hill," is paired with the possessive form of a name.

A title usually starts with a word for the kind of story it is—*compert*, "conception and birth"; *cath*, "battle"; *tochmarc*, "wooing"; *aided*, "(unfortunate or violent) death"—followed by the possessive form of whose birth or death it is, who's being wooed, or which battle.

Just like in English—where "Maeve's bull" is always a specific one, otherwise we'd need to say "one of Maeve's bulls"—a word paired with a possessive is considered definite in Irish. And sort of like in English—we wouldn't say "the Maeve's bull" to mean "the bull that belongs to Maeve"—Irish doesn't use the definite article for a word that's paired with a possessive. English lets us say "the bull of Maeve," but Irish doesn't. So *Áth Fraích* translates to "The Ford of Fráech," *Tochmarc Emire* is "The Wooing of Emer," and so on. *Táin bó Cúailnge* is "The Cattle-Raid of Cúailnge," or, more literally, "The Driving of the Cows of Cúailnge." Calling it "the *Táin bó Cúailnge*" with the article is kind of like saying "the *The Lord of the Rings*."

The name *Cú Chulainn*, which means "Culann's Dog" or, more poetically, "the Hound of Culann," involves the possessive form of the name *Culann*, which is *Culainn* (the *Ch-* on *Chulainn* is an effect of *Cú*). The possessive form of *Cú Chulainn* itself is *Con Culainn*, so the title of Cú Chulainn's birth-tale is *Compert Con Culainn*, and "Cú Chulainn's son" would be *mac Con Culainn*.

Acknowledgments

Besides the intellectual debts acknowledged throughout this book, I'm tremendously grateful to Don LePan, publisher of Broadview Press, for the opportunity to work with Broadview and for the invitation to take on this project, and to Max Uphaus for his unending patience and editorial guidance.

Thank you to all the professors who responded to market research inquiries from Broadview, especially Andrew Scheil at the University of Minnesota, who suggested the title.

Thank you to the family of Desmond Kinney for permission to use his magnificent mosaic mural as the cover image.

An anonymous reviewer was extraordinarily generous with comments.

Great thanks to Paul Gosling for the maps. It's wonderful to see the work of Gene Haley, whom I knew when I was a grad student, so ably continued.

I valued the encouragement of Don Lents, Sharon Paice MacLeod, Catherine McKenna, Paul Muldoon, K. Sarah-Jane Murray, Joseph Falaky Nagy, Thomas O'Donnell, Emerson Richards, Carolyn Roark, and Rebekah Stackhouse.

Thanks to my students at Fairleigh Dickinson University—especially my medieval class in Spring 2023: Kaitlyn Armonaitis, Kathleen Conlon, Shannon DiCristina, Jeankarlew Mora, and Amy Swain—for their comments after reading excerpts.

Thanks to the participants at the 2024 meeting of the Celtic Studies Association of North America for their feedback on excerpts and problems. Special thanks to Fiona Rain Murphy for the undergraduate perspective.

I was introduced to early Irish language and literature at University College Dublin by the extraordinary team of Patricia Kelly, Próinséas Ní Chatháin, Edel Bhreathnach, Doreen Carty, Gerald Manning, and Aifric Mac Aodha, and went from them to the wise and exacting guidance of Tomás Ó Cathasaigh at Harvard, one of the world's great experts, who for many years taught courses on the *Táin* and on The Hero of Irish Myth and Saga. There I also learned from Patrick Ford, Barbara Hillers, and Catherine McKenna.

While I hope to be a credit to my teachers, they bear no responsibility for any of my choices here.

I am regretfully sure that all kinds of errors, omissions, and imperfections have survived my best efforts to eradicate them. And as scholarship and art go on, no doubt these will be revealed, along with new and exciting insights into the early literature. With ongoing thanks to everyone who has been, is, and will become involved with this publication and that larger work, I hope my translation will have helped the *Táin* and the Ulster Cycle tales, in their ancient power and seeming strangeness, to go on speaking in ever-new ways to old and new audiences.

Finally, I am grateful to my wife Stacie Lents for valuable conversations, suggestions, and perspective over the years spent working on this book.

About the Publisher

The word "broadview" expresses a good deal of the philosophy behind our company. Our focus is very much on the humanities and social sciences—especially literature, writing, and philosophy—but within these fields we are open to a broad range of academic approaches and political viewpoints. We strive in particular to produce high-quality, pedagogically useful books for higher education classrooms—anthologies, editions, sourcebooks, surveys of particular academic fields and sub-fields, and also course texts for subjects such as composition, business communication, and critical thinking. We welcome the perspectives of authors from marginalized and underrepresented groups, and we have a strong commitment to the environment. We publish English-language works and translations from many parts of the world, and our books are available world-wide; we also publish a select list of titles with a specifically Canadian emphasis.

broadview press

This book is made of paper from well-managed FSC® - certified forests, recycled materials, and other controlled sources.